Blacl

Rachael Holyhead

First published in 2024 by Blossom Spring Publishing
Black Hollow Copyright © 2024 Rachael Holyhead
ISBN 978-1-0687019-4-8
E: admin@blossomspringpublishing.com
W: www.blossomspringpublishing.com

In memory of my Uncle David,
who always knew I could do it

Prologue

1977

The girl falls to her knees, her head bowed as though in prayer. She could easily be a shadow, or one of the weeping angels that mourn on the hill beside her. Until she moves. She jabs at the ground, the spoon in her fist completely unsuited to the task. Wiping her face, she smears dirt across her temple, into her pale hair. As the air thickens with the smell of earth, the darker girl at her shoulder watches through black-framed spectacles. Satisfied the hole is deep enough, she squats beside her companion and pulls a package across the grass towards them.

Within the folds of a handkerchief is a dead crow, its beak jewelled with blood, its feathers crushed and twisted. The blonde girl binds the bird in its makeshift shroud, then places it into the grave. Brushing soil from her hands, she begins to speak, her voice low and solemn.

'Ashes to ashes. Dust to dust. May this bird go to heaven, like all of us.'

The dark-haired girl scans the slopes where the gravestones lean, her eyes coming to rest on her friend. She is fascinated by her, the mysterious language she uses, strange words like mass and blasphemy and consecrated ground. This feels wrong, yet she is thrilled by it. Excited, even though she knows they are trespassing. Another word she has learned from her.

As if her fears have conjured him, a figure appears from the corner of the church, his cassock billowing in the wind. She throws the last clods of earth into the grave. When she looks again, the figure has gone.

1

1

Anna

The rectangle of light provides just enough illumination as she slots her key into the lock. She pauses in the hallway. Silence, except for the familiar sound, almost imperceptible, which tells Anna her father is still up.

Slipping her coat off, she peers into the living room. Lit by the glow of the fire, he is sitting at the card table, as he does every evening, a cigarette burning in the ashtray. He looks at her, his hand suspended in mid-air, a scarlet-backed card between his fingers.

'Enjoyed yourself?'

'Very much. We're reading *Lady Chatterley's Lover.*'

Her father snorts, a smoker's rattle in his chest. 'Penny dreadful,' he mutters, as he snaps a card down. Anna has heard the phrase countless times before. She tells herself it's a private joke between them but she knows he is deadly serious.

Upstairs, she stands at the window. It has started to rain and the streetlights cast an amber glow across the pavement. As she buttons her pyjamas, she looks at the teeming bookshelves, her few possessions. Not much to show for a life and yet she loves this room. It is her haven and her sanctuary. Her hiding place.

She lies in the darkness, listening to the rain. After a while, she lights a candle and takes the book from her handbag. The feel of its spine, its weight in her palm is a comfort, a kind of company, but it isn't enough. She reaches again for the bag and pulls out a silver hipflask, swallowing from it deeply. Later, when the rain has stopped and the flask is dry, she puts the book aside and blows out the candle, knowing there is no chance of sleep.

2

Kate

Detective Sergeant Katharine Fox lights a cigarette and blows smoke into the cool morning air. Her eyes scan the trees as they drip and sway at the foot of her garden. She sees something dark, spinning. A sycamore key spirals down to join the carpet covering the lawn. The rain kept her awake in the night, although she doesn't sleep well at the best of times. Inhaling deeply, she checks her phone again. Just the thought of the station fills her with a shaming dread. Every drag on her cigarette buys a few more seconds. What they knock from her actual lifespan is anybody's guess.

The phone rings in her hand and she clamps the cigarette between her lips.

'Kate. Do you know the Trick Shop on the high street?' There is no preamble with her boss Newton.

'I think so, yes, sir.'

'We've got a suspicious death. Meet me at the Miners in fifteen minutes.'

Any response she might have been about to give is lost as the line goes dead. She tosses the stub of her cigarette and heads for her car.

The morning rush hour has started but she should make it in plenty of time. Putting her foot down, she feels a stab of guilt that someone's untimely death has given her a temporary reprieve. She considers what she knows about the Trick Shop, which isn't much, considering she drives past it every day.

When Kate first arrived here three months ago, she read up on the history of Black Hollow. A haul of Roman coins was discovered near the pit, so there's little doubt how ancient the place is. The town had grown prosperous, iron being mined here first and later, coal. For over a century, the colliery dominated the skyline, employing most of its men. All that's left are the remains of the shaft head gear, preserved by the local council, a bleak monument to the past. She sees it now, an abandoned gallows on the hillside, as she threads her way through endless rows of blackened terraces. Originally occupied by miners and their families, they now house a mix of inhabitants, many of whom she has had the pleasure or misfortune to meet in her job.

The road bends sharply past the war memorial and onto the main high street. Through the steamed-up windscreen, she can just make out the half-derelict shops and pubs that were once the town's lifeblood. The blur of orange catches her eye, pumpkins leering from a window. A carton blows across the pavement, *'Red Lion'* carved across the stone above a neon Balti sign. There were ten pubs when the pit was booming, now only two remain.

Checking her mirror, she slows down at the Trick Shop. Two marked cars are parked outside, a PC pushing back a growing horde of bystanders. She drives past and turns into the Miners Arms' car park.

The roof of Newton's black Audi is plastered with leaves. She locks her car and gets into his, noting the immaculate interior compared to the crumb-strewn footwells of her own.

DI James Newton looks dressed for the occasion. He is wearing a grey suit beneath a dark overcoat, the remembrance poppy in his buttonhole a splash of bright red. His shirt brings out the blue of his eyes, his pale skin a stark contrast to his black hair, which is cropped short and slightly greying at the temples. Kate thinks he has an Irish look about him but his accent is hard to pinpoint. He is over six feet tall and has his seat pushed back to accommodate his legs. She takes in his polished shoes, the blade-sharp crease of his trousers and the smudge of blood on his hand, just above his wedding ring.

There is always a stillness about him, a directness to his gaze. Not for the first time, she feels self-conscious in his presence as she waits for him to speak.

'It's a strange one,' he says eventually. 'Do you know the family?'

'I don't think so, no and I've never set foot in the place.' Kate grew up in Sheffield about six miles away, moving here on her promotion to CID. She's had little time for browsing the shops.

'Me neither until today.' He shakes his head. 'There was no point closing the road, the weapon's still stuck in his gullet. Stabbed in the neck with some sort of ornamental dagger.'

'Jesus!' Kate's hand flies to her own throat. 'Do we have an ID then?'

'Yes, the owner, Charles Collins.' Newton peers at the notebook balanced on the dashboard. 'Confirmed by the daughter, Anna. No sign of forced entry and she claims to have heard nothing.'

'Claims to? Don't you believe her?'

'I don't know. She was covered in blood when we got here, obviously in shock. His bed wasn't slept in, so the assumption is she found him when she came down this morning.' Kate notes the third person. Newton never assumes anything.

'The doctor's been,' he continues. 'Gave her something to calm her down. Forensics are still in there and Family Liaison. I couldn't get much sense out of her. I'm hoping you might.'

'What, now?' The words are out before she can stop them.

'Yes, now. It's best to get in quick before they get their story straight.' He looks straight at her, giving Kate the feeling he's talking about something else entirely. She looks away, nodding in agreement.

'She might respond better to a woman. Oh and you'd better arrange accommodation — she can't stay here. I'll see you back at the station. Duffy will go with you.' He starts the car.

Kate's stomach drops as she sees a figure striding towards them, the lapels of an old biker jacket flapping at his sides. She gets out as he draws level, stopping with his back to Newton's bonnet. He grins, bent teeth glinting as he runs his tongue across his lips. As Newton pulls away, Duffy mouths one solitary word.

'Foxy.'

With a sickening chuckle he walks on.

Kate reaches for her cigarettes, her heart like a drum in her ribcage.

3

Newton

Detective Inspector James Newton closes the door and locks it behind him. The first thing that always hits him these days is how quiet the house is. Nothing except the hum of the heating and the drip of the kitchen tap. Loosening his tie, he makes for the stereo, relief washing over him as Van Morrison drowns out the silence.

Walking past the bottle on the worktop, he makes a mug of tea and warms his hands on it. His eyes fall on the empty dog bowl he kicked into a corner this morning. An image comes to him, Louise serving food, Georgie waving a spoon from his highchair and Lottie waiting patiently for any scraps that might drop from the table. He shoves the thought away, forcing himself to focus on the day's events.

Newton has been on the force for 25 years. In his family all the men wore uniforms. His grandfather served in Dunkirk and India and his father had followed in his footsteps. His earliest memories are of the army bases in Germany. Dad spent a lot of time on exercises but there was always a sense he was doing something of national importance. Their mother instilled in Newton and his sister a deep sense of pride in what they were all a part of.

Then came the final posting. They moved to a barracks on Salisbury Plain but Dad had not come with them. He remembers how quickly things changed then, how much he missed him. Sitting at the top of the stairs, they would listen to their mother's rantings, the regular slam of the phone and the sound of her weeping. They never saw their father again. They were told the bare minimum but pieced things together as children do. Dad had been posted to Belfast, his mother's hometown and she had refused to join him.

Newton will never forget the day they heard he was dead. The brisk knock, the soldiers, cap in hand on the doorstep. His mother's scream. Years later, they discovered the truth. Dad had been blown to smithereens by a car bomb in Castlereagh. There wouldn't have been much left of him to bury.

He thinks of the woman he saw today. She'd been sitting on the floor when he got there, drenched in her father's blood. A low keening was coming from her, like the sound of a wounded animal, and he had looked at the sea of red, knowing he had to cross it. Prising her hands away, she trailed gore across his sleeve. The body was stone cold, rigor mortis already set in and a knife sticking out of his throat. The shop was almost in darkness, the morning hardly penetrating the shadows. He had switched on the lights then wished that he hadn't, the crimson arc sprayed across the cabinets still imprinted on his retina. It had stunk like a slaughterhouse, the air thick with the stench of blood but the thing that struck him most was the expression on the dead man's face. It was a look of utter surprise, his mouth an O of shock, the blade glinting obscenely from the flesh beneath his tongue.

He'd managed to sponge his sleeve clean when the pathologist took over. Newton hopes they can make him look presentable for the daughter's sake. At least then she'll have the chance of a more palatable farewell than the one she had this morning.

His instinct tells him she isn't her father's murderer. He's been wrong before but that level of distress would be hard to fake. He will look up the statistics on patricide later.

He moves and stiffens, his hand flying to his back. Opening a drawer, he pulls out a strip of painkillers, swilling them down as he looks through the window. His running days might be over but he can still go for a walk, even without a dog.

Throwing the remains of his tea down the sink, he heads upstairs to change.

4

Kate

It is well after dark by the time Kate gets home and she is far too tired to cook. Pulling out a plate, she piles it with salad and some droopy looking spinach leaves. At the back of the fridge, she finds a chicken breast and the remains of a carrot she grated yesterday. She might smoke thirty a day but she tries to eat well and can't think on an empty stomach. Flopping onto the sofa, she takes a bite of celery and closes her eyes.

Kate's gran used to say she has a photographic memory and it's true, when she replays an event in her head, she is often surprised by the clarity, the detail of everyday objects and conversations she hadn't noticed at the time. It can be both a blessing and a curse.

Pushing the plate aside, she goes over to the window, pressing her nose against the glass. She is about to turn away when the cat flap rattles. Butting her shins with a mew, Luther fixes her with his unblinking, emerald stare.

Shredding the rest of her chicken into his bowl, she returns to her place on the sofa. No doubt he'll join her once he's had his supper. She would never admit this to anyone but his warm little body is the only comfort she gets these days.

Firing up her laptop, she begins the sifting process, fixing her mind on what she has seen through the course of the day. It's something she has done since childhood. As a detective, she is honing the ability, sharpening her memory like a tool.

One of Kate's greatest sorrows is that her gran didn't live to see her transition out of uniform. The other is that neither of her parents witnessed any of her career.

Her father died when she was five years old. One minute sprinting down the football field, the next he was dead at the side of the pitch. It was instant, Gran assured her when she was old enough to understand, the faulty heart valve a condition Kate thankfully hasn't inherited. In her memory, he is little more than an impression, too far back to grasp but she has a vague recollection of how safe she felt in his presence.

Twelve months later, her mum had joined him in City Road Cemetery. The lump in her breast had gone unnoticed, so stricken had she been with grief. As a child, Kate often wondered why her six-year-old self hadn't been enough to make her mother want to hang around.

Luther jumps up, settling himself on the cushions. Ruffling between his ears, Kate flips open her notebook. Photographic memory or not, her notes are meticulous, facts stored away to analyse later, hieroglyphic scribbles that to anyone else would mean nothing.

Closing her eyes, she sees Duffy's twisted smile. Like a gargoyle on the village church, he has a sidelong way of smirking, as though at some secret joke to which only he knows the punchline. His dislike for her had been immediate. She'd made a good impression on her first case, maybe that had narked him. Or it could be just plain old misogyny, which still exists on the force, despite what the pamphlets say. Kate considers herself thick-skinned and Duffy's attitude has never bothered her. Until now, that is.

She wonders about his setup, she's pretty sure he isn't married. He probably still lives with his mother. She's done a bit of digging, she is a detective after all, but he's not on Facebook or any of the other social media platforms. The thought gives her an idea and she taps a name into the search bar. Reams of Anna Collinses come up, but not the one she met this morning.

Closing her eyes again, she is back outside the building. Duffy holds back the flap concealing the door.

'Ladies first,' he says, and in her mind he bows theatrically. The shutters are down, a sign overhead creaking like something from a Dickens novel. She drops her cigarette and ducks under the tape. The shop is packed with forensics and strategically placed screens. No chance of a glimpse of the body but she lingers for a second, watching. The room is lit like a stage and her eyes are drawn to the cabinets, where an arc of blood is sprayed like paint on canvas.

Duffy is still smirking and Kate could happily smack him. He gestures for her to go upstairs ahead but even in her mid-length coat, she doesn't want him ogling her backside. She isn't about to ogle his.

Gripping the banister behind him, she notes the old-fashioned newel post. She braces herself for some smart-arse comment but he says nothing, which is somehow more unsettling. Not until they reach the halfway point. Then he turns, arms spread across the staircase and leers down at her.

'Proper little vixen, aren't we?'

'Shut it, Duffy.' They can't be more than five feet away from the grieving daughter above.

As they reach the top, Julie Darrow, the Family Liaison Officer, appears with two steaming mugs. Kate can see the room with crystal clarity. The walls are a clutter of bookshelves, dark curtains and tasselled pelmets. Again, the word old-fashioned comes to mind. *Very* old-fashioned. Crystal decanters gleam on a sideboard and a grandfather clock ticks. And is that a real fire? The poker and tongs in the hearth suggest that it is. She wouldn't fancy lugging coal up those stairs.

Her gaze moves to the mantelpiece, where two brass candlesticks stand either side of a framed photograph. As she steps towards it, a figure rears up from a chair, her face streaked with tears.

Anna Collins is tall, with dark hair pulled back at the nape of her neck. Kate can see no grey but guesses her age around forty. Her skin is smooth as porcelain and behind her dark-framed glasses, her eyes are unmistakably intelligent. She looks like a librarian but an attractive one and Kate finds herself wondering why she still lives at home with her father.

She makes their introductions, platitudes she learnt in training. They sound insincere but she really means them. Duffy skirts the table, nearly spilling the drinks and Kate takes out her notebook for something to do with her hands. Other than that, it isn't necessary. She will remember every word.

'Was it just the two of you living here?' Anna nods.

'And when did you last see your father alive?' She winces inwardly but it's a question that needs to be asked. Anna clears her throat before responding.

'It must've been about nine o'clock last night.' Her voice is little more than a whisper but Kate recognises the local accent, a curious cross between Sheffield and North Derbyshire. She has modulated her own speech over the years, careful not to drop her aitches and steering well clear of the harsh dialect that once came naturally.

'I'm sorry to ask, but can you think of anyone who might wish him harm?' This sounds stupid even to Kate. As though Anna might stand up and point out the killer, saving them all the trouble. Instead she just shakes her head.

'I know it's been a shock but these first few hours are critical.' Strictly speaking, the first hour after a murder is most crucial but that's long gone now. Anna drops her head and seems to crumple into the chair. Kate gives her a moment to compose herself.

'Is there anyone we can call to come and stay with you?'

Anna stares into her lap, eyes narrowed behind her glasses, as though seeing something unbearable. She pulls at a sodden handkerchief, her head shaking from side to side. Julie gives Kate a knowing look as she retreats to the kitchen to put the kettle back on.

Anna's features have settled into a pallid mask. It's then Kate remembers she has been sedated.

'You won't be able to sleep here tonight. Is there someone you can stay with?'

'I'm not leaving.' The blank stare Anna turns on her suggests that she means it.

'I'm afraid you have to. This is a crime scene.'

'Not up here, it isn't.' Her voice is suddenly strident, as though she has roused herself. 'My father was killed in the shop.'

With a glare at Duffy, who hasn't uttered a word since his comment on the stairs, Kate excuses herself and goes in search of Newton. There is no sign of him, either in the shop or outside. Walking round to the pub, she sees the media have already begun their siege. A Yorkshire TV van is parked beneath the trees where Newton's car had been.

Pulling out her phone she taps in his number, aware she is running to her boss at the first hurdle.

'Christ, Kate. She can't stay there!' The line falls silent and she waits, hoping he is at least giving it some thought.

'No, she'll have to go elsewhere for now. If there's no family or anyone, you'll have to sort a B&B. I'm sure you'll come up with something.'

The line goes dead and she runs back inside, still clutching her notebook. She has no idea what she's going to say but one look at Anna makes her mind up.

'We'll make the necessary arrangements for you to stay.' She hasn't the heart to try and reason with her. She can't even tell if Anna hears her, so vacant is her expression. The sedative must have fully kicked in and Kate has a terrible mental image of dragging her out comatose. Either that or kicking and screaming. *Surely Anna is right, the shop is technically the crime scene.* Still she continues to deliberate, pacing the rug and gnawing her pencil.

'Thanks for your input,' she growls at Duffy. He turns from his position at the window, his face deadpan.

'Look at her, she's catatonic. Any case, Newton left you in charge.' He stalks off into the kitchen, Julie emerging seconds later.

'You'll be OK to stay, won't you?' murmurs Kate. 'She's not fit to be left on her own.'

Julie nods and with that agreed she feels a little better but is already formulating the argument she will present to Newton. Forensics have already swept the upstairs but before they leave, she'll ensure all access points to the shop are secured. They'd better include Charlie Collins's bedroom, that being the room most likely to yield important evidence. As if reading her thoughts, Duffy comes out of the kitchen ripping yellow tape from a roll.

At last, he contributes something.

She turns back to Anna, whose head has fallen forward. She looks so bereft, Kate feels she must say something more.

'I know how hard this is for you.'

Anna looks up, her eyes fathomless pools.

'Do you?'

And as she toys with her spinach, Kate has to admit that she doesn't. Losing her parents so young, she was shielded, the details sanitised before being presented to her. Even described plainly, they were nowhere near as brutal as these.

Her thoughts return to that mausoleum of a room. It was like time stood still there, long before Anna was born. Gilt frames and so many books, it's a wonder the shelves weren't bowed. She pictures father and daughter reading in companionable silence, the fire crackling in the grate. If not for the laptop discarded on a chair, the room could easily be Victorian. On her way out, she had stopped by the picture on the mantelpiece.

'What a lovely photo. Is this your mother?'

Anna hadn't responded but there was no mistaking the likeness. Her hair was swept up into a beehive, a teardrop pearl in her ear. She was young, the plumpness of youth in her lips. A clear intelligence shone from the kohl-lined eyes looking boldly into the camera.

None of this is in her notes, her thoughts forming a backdrop as she taps away at the keyboard. She is careful to include her reasoning for letting Anna stay put. It had felt like the right decision but she doubts Newton will see it that way.

She slams her laptop shut, sending Luther scuttling from the sofa, the cat flap rattling in his wake. Why, when she always tries to do the decent thing, does she so regularly cock things up?

Finishing her supper, she drops her plate into the sink. A murder is certainly a distraction — she has hardly given her own problems a moment's thought.

Pushing things back into her work bag, she yawns as she looks at the clock. It's too late now to ring Newton and a text would be cowardly. She will have to face the music tomorrow.

A tapping sound comes from the French doors. Despite the cat flap, Luther likes to be admitted by whichever route he demands. He raps his paws against the glass in an impatient tattoo. Opening the door, he brushes past her calves as she lights a final cigarette. She thinks of Anna and shivers, not just from the cold. Flicking the stub, she is about to shut the doors, when something catches her eye. A pinprick of light hovers, then moves off between the trees.

She listens for a moment but there is nothing to hear, except the distant hum of traffic on the main road. Satisfied it must have been a dog walker, she closes the doors and double locks them.

Her sleep is broken by a dream but not her usual one. A woman lies beside her, dark hair spread across the pillow, her skin slick with sweat. Kate awakes in a twist of bedsheets, flooded with shame. As the dream recedes, she rationalises it must have been triggered by one of the pictures in the Collinses' flat. The Queen of Spades, she thinks it was. She will take a closer look in the morning.

5

Anna

Anna has no idea how long she has been sitting here at the card table. It has a flip top, so it can be folded away but they never put it away. It is a permanent fixture in the room.

She had polished the table as soon as the police had gone. A shroud of fingerprint dust had covered its surface and she couldn't rest while the powder settled in the grooves and whorls.

She rubs her finger along the inlaid patterns. Walnut, mahogany, teak. She has known the types of wood since before she can remember. There is a sliver of blood beneath her nail. She must have showered but has no recollection of doing so. The whole day is a blur, except when she closes her eyes. Then she sees with terrible clarity.

Thoughts assault her mind, memories thrown at her. As a child, she played at this table, counting buttons and coins. Hangman, noughts and crosses, snap and old maid. Whatever the game, he would beat her. *You won't learn if I let you win.*

Her father taught her to write at this table. Like everything else about him, his writing was meticulous. From an early age, she learned that if a job is worth doing, it is worth doing well. She had thought him a difficult parent but with an adult's eyes, she could see his never-ending patience and whatever they were doing, the bar was always set high. She was brought up to believe herself capable of anything if she worked hard enough.

Tracing the knots in the wood, she thinks of all this

table has witnessed — the tantrums and the lectures, the teenage rows. Then later when her heart had broken into pieces.

She thinks of the last time they sat here. They had played bezique, which was one of Father's favourites and ideal as it calls for two players. They were old hands at it, like automatons and as they played, their conversations would be endless. Did Wilkie Collins fill his spare time with bezique, or some other parlour game? Did he play with his wife or his mistress? Were his wits dulled by the laudanum to which he was addicted? Had Charles I amused himself whilst captive in the Tower? One last hand before the executioner's knock.

And then it hits her like a wave. She will never speak to him again. Not here or anywhere else, for all eternity. It comes like a physical blow, bending her double over the table, her tears washing the surface she has just so painstakingly polished.

She must have made her way upstairs at some point. She wakes in her room, pale morning light filtering through the curtains. For a moment she has forgotten, then reality floods in. She sees the empty bottle by the bed.

Everything looks just the same. The books on the shelves, the pictures on the walls. But they are not the same. Nothing will ever be the same again.

6

1977

The girls are pushing an old Silver Cross pram, bumping it along between the trees. They come to a stop in the shade, fists of baby pears and apples budding in the branches above them. The blonde girl leans over and pulls back the covers. Nestled in the folds, six tiny kittens lie blinking, as though disturbed from sleep. Four are almost identical, their fur an uneven patchwork of tan and blackish brown. One is pure white with huge blue eyes and a pink, mouselike nose. The last one nuzzling the pillow, is jet black all over. Their faces turn towards the light, paws kneading the blankets.

'White cats are deaf, you know,' pronounces Marie, in that knowing way she has. *It's Marry,* she likes to remind her. It's how the Catholics say it. She is tall for her age, her hair cut short like a boy's, her jeans pulled in at the waist by a fawn snake belt. As she picks up the black kitten, its legs become entangled in the covers. Anna watches the light dapple her forearms as she pulls it free.

'I'm going to keep this one,' says Marie. 'I shall call him Oscar, after Oscar Wilde.' She spins round to face her, the cat held tight against her chest. 'You choose one, Anna. They know we're mothers.'

Squinting into the pram, Anna is uncertain. The white one looks strange and fragile, so she scoops up one of the others and holds it in a mirror image of her friend.

'I think we should take them back now.'

'They're fine,' says Marie, stroking the kitten's seal-like coat. Suddenly, her face lights up. 'I know! Let's go to Father Vincent's. I bet the door isn't locked.'

Without further discussion, the cats are placed back beneath the covers and they head off across the fields towards the rectory.

At the door with its fanlike window, Anna puts the brake on the pram. She pulls the hood as far forward as it will go.

'They'll be alright, won't they?'

'Of course they will. Look, they're going back to sleep.'

The door isn't locked and they tiptoe in, as a hoover bangs against the skirting boards above. Smothering their giggles, they head for the room they always go to. Father Vincent's study.

Visits to the rectory make Anna feel uncomfortable. This is her friend's world, not hers, and whether the priest is aware of their presence or not, Anna knows she is a trespasser. She doesn't belong here. They enter the study and close the door soundlessly behind them.

The most interesting thing about this room is that they aren't supposed to be here. It is quite unremarkable really, rows of musty books and a cross on the wall. A crucifix, that's the word. A metal Jesus stretched across the wood.

A shaft of light sweeps the floor and a branch taps softly at the window. There is always a funny smell in here, which Marie has told her is incense. She strides towards the desk and Anna follows, peering over her shoulder.

Something of interest for once. Father Vincent has left his leather-bound notebook open on the blotter. At the top of the page, scrawled in black ink are the words THOUGHTS FOR SUNDAY. Underneath is written:

*There are cowards and unbelievers amongst us. The
vile and the murderous. Those who practise magical arts.
Liars. Cheats. The immoral. Hear me and hear me well.
All will be forbidden God's glory, cast in the fiery lake.
To suffer perpetual agony. A second, never ending death!*

The girls collapse against each other, their laughter out
of place in the monkish room. Suddenly, there is a loud
crash. A paperweight has fallen to the floor, the glass
shattering into tiny pieces. They bolt from the room,
charging down the hallway and back through the front
door. Anna knocks the brake off the pram and they run as
fast as they can back across the fields.

Anna throws herself down under a tree, bursting into
fresh giggles. 'Oh, that was absolutely brilliant! Do you
think anyone saw us?'

But her friend isn't listening. She is leaning into the
pram, pulling frantically at the covers.

'What is it?' says Anna, 'What's wrong?'

'It's Oscar,' replies Marie, her face drained of colour.
'He's gone.'

7

Kate

I need to stop smoking, thinks Kate as she puffs her way up the hill, but she loves this time of year, the colours of the trees, the leaves collecting on car bonnets. An unmarked car is parked outside the shop. The window winds down as she draws level.

'Been here all night, boss's orders,' says the driver through a mouthful of breadcake. Kate's stomach jolts as the smell of greasy bacon wafts towards her. There was no mention of an all-night vigil in Newton's text this morning. She does her best to appear unruffled.

'Any sign of life?' she asks, aiming her cigarette into the gutter.

'Curtains have just opened. Up late, from the time the lights were on.'

No shit, Sherlock, thinks Kate looking up at the shop. She is struck by its symmetry, the perfectly painted sash windows, a pair of dormers jutting from the roof. The shadow of a cloud crosses the glass but there is nothing more to see. She knows she should wait for Newton, but it's freezing out here and she really doesn't know what to expect from him. Fighting the urge to light up again, she thrusts her hands in her pockets and heads towards the wrought iron gate at the side of the building.

Unlike the creaking shop sign, it swings silently inwards onto a small courtyard of dark paving stones. The area was swept and searched yesterday but leaves are already gathering again in the corners and by the bins. Some of the stones are patterned with what look like hearts and three leaved clovers. Then she spots the angles of a diamond and it dawns on her. She's looking at the playing card suits, evenly spaced across the yard. The Collins family are certainly passionate about their trade.

Her previous murder case had taken place near a school and they'd set up an incident room in the gym. Looking at the layout of this place, there's no chance of doing the same here and with the busy street out front, it's just as well the station isn't far away. She cups her hands against the window but jumps at a cough from behind.

'Bit impatient, aren't we?' She shrinks under Newton's stare.

'Sorry sir, I was just...'

He walks towards her stone faced, halting her attempt at explanation. 'Have you knocked?'

'Not yet.' She wants his approval — she realises how much she wants it and dreads what he's going to say next.

This is her second murder case, the first beginning the day after she arrived. Fresh out of uniform, Newton had called it her baptism of fire. The victim was a woman not much older than herself, beaten to death by her boyfriend. Seeing such violence first-hand had shocked Kate, not least because the woman was heavily pregnant. It had served as a warning, to be prepared for anything. She earned a lot of praise on that case, so why does she feel so inept right now, like a complete novice? As Newton raises his hand to knock, she straightens her back and tells herself she has every right to be here.

The door opens instantly, as though Anna has been waiting right behind it. She stands on the threshold, her hair unkempt, eyes swollen — every inch the grieving daughter. Her red quilted dressing gown reminds Kate of the blood she saw yesterday. Without a word, Anna steps back, opening the door wide to let them in.

They pass the crudely barricaded doors, crime scene tape twisted thickly around the handles. Upstairs in the kitchen, Julie is making tea. Newton asks if they slept, but Anna doesn't respond, walking straight past them up a second flight of stairs.

'How is she?' Newton asks, keeping his voice low.

'As well as can be expected,' says Julie, rubbing the back of her neck. 'I'll jump in the shower now you're here, if that's OK?'

'Of course,' says Newton. 'And thanks again, Julie.'

That's probably another dig at me, thinks Kate, as she pours the tea, remembering Newton doesn't take sugar. Surely, she can get that right.

'Surprised it's not a cup and saucer,' he whispers conspiratorially, and she realises he is trying to put her at ease, which makes her feel even more useless.

They stand either side of the table, awkwardly sipping their tea as they listen to the indistinct sounds above. A brick fireplace fills one wall, a stack of logs beside it. Iron hooks stud the ceiling, various kitchen implements hanging from them. Kate can easily picture a cook stirring pans at the range, the timeworn surface of the table filled with unplucked fowl. Yet she struggles to imagine Anna spending much time here. She knows she should say something but is conscious of being overheard and doesn't want to make things any worse than they already are.

The creak of the stairs breaks the silence as Anna reappears. She is dressed head to toe in black now, her hair pulled back in its clip. Kate clears her throat but it's Anna who speaks first.

'I want to see my father.'

Kate looks at Newton, her mind suddenly blank.

'I'm afraid that won't be possible. Not today, anyway.'

'Why not?' She glares at them both as she sits at the table.

'These things take time, Anna. We need to find out as much as we can. That's why we've come to talk to you again.'

Newton sits down opposite her, his voice still hushed. 'Anna, there's going to be quite a bit of media interest. We'll do what we can but you need to be prepared.'

'I'm fully aware of that,' says Anna, smoothing her skirt.

Kate opens her mouth but still nothing comes out.

With a brief glance in her direction, Newton continues. 'Can we ask you a few more questions?'

'You can ask whatever you like but I'm not discussing anything until I've seen him.' There is a cold finality to her words and she stares down at her hands where they lay rigid in her lap, as still as the death which seems to hang in the air around them.

8

Newton

'Well, that was a complete waste of time, wasn't it?' Newton storms off, the gate clanging shut behind him.

'She is behaving quite oddly but she's in shock,' calls Kate, struggling to keep pace.

'I'm not talking about her! Get in the car.'

Inside he sees how pale she is, her face drained of blood. He tries to choose his next words carefully.

'Would you care to explain what the hell you were thinking, letting a potential suspect stay overnight at a crime scene?'

Kate looks genuinely surprised at this. 'She's not a potential suspect!'

'Of course she bloody is! And your recklessness could have put Julie in danger as well.'

That really hits home, as intended.

'Well?'

'Sir, I acted with the best intentions. I carried out a full risk assessment but she was extremely distraught and coupled with the strong sedative, which was administered before my arrival, I wasn't comfortable moving her. Her safety was my priority.'

Newton clenches his teeth. 'You know the procedure at a crime scene. The FLO could have accompanied her to a bed and breakfast if you had concerns.'

'How would that have been any safer if Anna's a suspect?' She glares at him. 'She was like a zombie, sir. In no fit state to go anywhere.'

'You could have compromised crucial evidence.' It's typical of Kate to have an answer for everything. In truth,

Newton is satisfied that forensics had done all that was currently needed on the upper floors. To her credit, Kate had ensured the primary crime scene wasn't compromised at all. Even so, there are strict guidelines, and he would be failing in his duty as Senior Investigating Officer if he didn't ensure she is aware of them.

'What's going on, Kate?'

She looks puzzled. 'What do you mean?'

'You know exactly what I mean. Whatever's going on in your private life.'

'There's nothing going on in my private life.'

'Look, it's none of my business but you were next to useless in there and your decision making isn't what it should be. And that *is* my business. You're normally so good with people, I would've thought this was your forte, dealing with women in —' He stops himself, unsure how he planned to finish this statement.

'What do you mean by that?' A flush of anger sweeps her neck. Newton knows he is handling this badly.

'I didn't mean anything. In this day and age…'

'I can explain.'

'There's no need and I don't want you to.'

Silence follows. Newton stares through the windscreen, aware of Kate's agitation and the warm scent of her, overlaid as it always is with tobacco. She'll be dying for a cigarette.

'I know you've been avoiding the station.' He turns in his seat to face her. 'You're a police officer first and foremost. Whatever's happening, you need to front it out and get on with it.'

'Something's been said, hasn't it?'

'It's just banter, Kate. Nobody's interested.' Another

30

silence follows.

'Is that all then?' She is staring forward, her knuckles white on the door handle.

Newton sighs. 'For now, yes but I'm relying on you not to do anything else to undermine the public's faith in us. Do I make myself clear?'

'Yes, sir.'

'OK. Start the door-to-doors. I'll see you back at the station.'

She almost leaps from the car, slamming the door behind her. Pushing back the seat, he stretches his legs as he watches through the rear-view mirror. He was right, she lights up straight away. Sometimes he wishes he smoked. Then he might not be so tempted by the other stuff.

9

Kate

Kate strides up the hill, clutching her coat tightly against the rising wind. She lights a cigarette, certain she can feel Newton's eyes boring into her. Rounding the corner, she leans on a wall, her face burning with shame. The thought of him hearing Duffy's version of events is beyond embarrassing. It isn't the kiss and it isn't even the drunkenness. It's the person she chose to show herself up with and if she isn't careful, this business with Anna and the crime scene could make matters a whole lot worse. What if Superintendent Vardy gets to hear about either incident? Her eyes fill at the prospect. Newton is overreacting, surely — and not one mention of that bastard Duffy's lack of input yesterday.

Her thoughts are interrupted by a noise close to the ground. Beyond the wall, she sees an old woman squatting in the gravel, her apron swelling in the breeze. Dark eyes dart towards her, then quickly away as she tugs at a dandelion clock.

'Bloody weeds,' says the woman, wrenching at the stalks, silver tufts floating up between them. Again Kate hears that accent, so different from her own. The eyes fix back on her, like dim shards of coal beneath whiskery brows.

Kate pinches her cigarette and puts the dog end in her pocket. 'Are you alright down there?'

The old woman ignores her as she shakes soil from the roots. Then she stands up, hardly reaching Kate's shoulder.

'I take it you're the police?'

'That's right.'

'Thought as much. Saw you this morning at the *Trick Shop*.'

Was there an edge to the way she said that, a slight curl of the lip? Kate finds herself straightening to her full height. 'Would now be a convenient time to speak to you?'

'Good a time as any, I suppose.' The woman heads towards the house and Kate follows, lifting her coat clear of the brambles. Broken plant pots litter the path, leaves rotting in the shale. As she reaches the doorstep, the woman drops the severed stems, seeds dispersing on the wind.

She looks over her shoulder, as though challenging Kate to question her. 'I try to keep on top of things but it's not the same without my Alvin. Would you like a cup of tea?'

'Yes please, Mrs…'

'Wood. Margaret Wood. I'll put the kettle on.'

A rusty horseshoe is nailed above the door. Kate steps beneath it as her host disappears down the hallway. Turning into a low-beamed living room, the first thing she sees is a hard-backed chair beside the window. A ball of wool and knitting needles are placed on the seat, the nets pulled back from the frame.

She sits on the sofa and looks around her. In what was once an open hearth, the bars of an electric fire glow red. The stone above must be ten inches thick, the year 1771 carved crudely into it.

To the left of the hearth is an ancient television set, beside it a wooden sideboard, brass handles gleaming in the firelight. A perfect semi-circle of photographs sits on top, a vase dead centre at the back. The carpet is streaked in whorls where a vacuum cleaner has meticulously swept back and forth in a regimented pattern. Mrs Wood might struggle with the garden, but her house is kept in fastidious order.

'How long have you lived here?' she calls, sliding her notebook from her bag.

'Forty-four years in December,' comes a voice from the kitchen. 'Do you take sugar?'

'No thanks,' shouts Kate, hoping Mrs Wood can hear her over the boiling kettle.

She comes in with a heavy looking tray, a knitted cosy on the pot. However old she is, there is nothing decrepit about her. Placing the tray on a table, she slips a liver-spotted hand into her apron pocket and stands there for a moment, as though about to speak. Evidently thinking better of it, she pours the tea, then settles herself against the cushions of an armchair. Kate makes a silent wager it's not her usual spot.

Sipping her tea, the scalding liquid burns the roof of her mouth. She replaces the cup with a splutter and picks up her notepad.

'Alvin was your husband, was he?'

'He was. Been gone nigh on twenty-five years now.'

'Sorry to hear that. I'm used to seeing coal fires round here, did he work at the pit?'

'Don't need any reminders of that place, thank you. And any case, electric's cleaner.'

She hasn't answered the question and Kate looks up at her. The lace of an underskirt pokes from beneath her pinny and her legs are wider at the ankle than the knee. *Dropsy, Gran would call it.*

'You're aware something's happened at the Trick Shop, then?'

'Hard to miss it, really. Could see it weren't t'lass in t'body bag. Had to be him.'

Her tone is matter of fact, as though death doesn't bother her at all. Kate is well accustomed to this outlook in the elderly. From where she is sitting, the low sun shines through the woman's dyed hair, giving it the appearance of an orange halo. Her first impressions are always strong, an imprint she can reference quite reliably. Mrs Wood must be at least eighty and her face reminds Kate of a wizened apple. If she needs to recall it, she will think of shrivelled fruit and it will be there as clear as a photograph.

'Yes, it's Mr Collins who's passed away. Do you know the family well?'

The old woman slurps her tea. 'I have lived a stone's throw away from them for over forty years.'

'So, what can you tell me about them?'

'I'm not one for gossip.'

'I'm not asking you to gossip. Just the bare facts would be helpful. Were you on friendly terms?'

Mrs Wood squares her shoulders, her chin jutting out above her cup. Kate realises in that moment that what she sees in her face is satisfaction.

'Can't say I was, no.'

Kate scribbles in her notebook, as she thinks of a suitable response. 'I'm surprised to hear that, living next-door for so long. Any particular reason?'

The old woman presses her thin lips together.

'No particular reason. They thought they were a cut above, that's all. Too good for the likes of us. Daughter's the same. Went off to university, came back with her tail between her legs.'

'Oh, really? And why was that?'

'I told you, I don't gossip.'

'OK. Going back to Mr Collins then.'

The old woman mutters something under her breath.

'I didn't quite catch that.'

'I said Pat used to do the tarot.'

That's not what it had sounded like to Kate.

'Tarot?'

'Cards for telling fortunes.' She looks at her as though she is utterly stupid. 'Mumbo jumbo if you ask me but she was popular in her time.'

'I see,' says Kate, her pen scudding across the page. 'And Pat would be Mr Collins's wife, would she?'

The old woman's glare is unflinching. 'That's right. Died a couple of years back. Heart attack took her in the end.' She takes another gulp of tea, the wrinkled flesh at her throat quivering as she swallows, her eyes never leaving Kate's face. 'What's he died of then?'

'I'm afraid I can't discuss that. We're just making local enquiries at this stage. Can I ask, have you noticed anything unusual over the last couple of days?' She glances towards the chair by the window.

Mrs Wood shakes her head. 'I haven't seen a thing. I would say nowt ever happens round here but plainly it has.' Placing her cup down, she rises from her chair. 'Sorry I can't help further.'

Her hand is on the door before Kate can close her notebook. Hauling herself up, she slips a card from her pocket and places it on the ledge above the fire.

'Well, thanks for the tea and if you do think of anything, please give us a call.'

Back on the street, Kate pulls her collar up against the wind, which is building now to a fury, leaves whipping past, branches flailing. The sun has dropped behind the rooftops, plunging the buildings opposite into shadow. She looks at the dark doors and dimly lit windows, the bricks barely visible in the fading light. Casting her mind back to her training, she knows she must have some sort of system, not just start knocking at random. Lighting the dog end from her pocket, she mulls over the strange interview that just happened. *I'm not one for gossip.*

I bet you're not, thinks Kate. It will be all round the village by teatime.

A letterbox rattles across the road and she walks towards it. It's as good a place to start as any.

10

Anna

Anna turns the key, rattling home two heavy bolts and a chain. Then she runs for the toilet, yanking the flush as vomit spews out of her, spraying the seat and the wall. She hopes to God the rushing water drowns out the noise.

Wiping her glasses and the seat, she sags against the door. The police had been easy to get rid of but she is painfully aware there is still one of them in close proximity.

Back in the kitchen, she paces the floor, keeping her eyes averted from the taped-up doors. She is barricaded in, forbidden entry to the rooms of her own home. Why are they asking all these questions? She knows why of course, they're only doing their job but she can't think straight and her head is splitting, which is less to do with grief than the amount she had to drink last night. She breathes into her hand, wondering if the police could smell it.

Julie is still in the shower, she can hear the water surging down the overflow. *There will be no shampoo left at this rate. Or coffee.* Taking two painkillers from a drawer, she swallows them dry, something she is quite used to. She walks purposefully into the living room and takes her mother's picture from the mantelpiece. Cradling the frame, she strokes the glass, her mother's eyes looking back at her. It's been two years now but Anna still thinks of her every single day. Inwardly, she corrects herself. There are times now when she doesn't think about her, whole guilty hours when she doesn't cross her mind at all. Rocking back and forth, the motion

38

calms her.

She has stored her grief away, taking it out from time to time like a family heirloom, then returning it to its dark hiding place. Now it has come slamming back at her in all its rawness. She feels confused, not knowing who the grief is for, her parents fused in death and both beyond her now.

Gripping the picture, she closes her eyes and tries not to think about her father lying on a cold slab, stacked like a kipper in a smokehouse. She won't allow herself to dwell on what they have done to him. More cutting. She has no desire to see him, she just said that to shut them up. Seeing her mother was enough, the paper shroud and that awful, clinical smell. Her eyes were already sinking into her skull and she remembers the howling sadness of knowing they would never open, never see the sun or look at her again. She had made the mistake of touching her, her fingers recoiling from the rock-solid flesh. Frozen through like a joint of meat, it was then she had realised how absolute death is. There is no coming back from it. Just an empty shell left behind like a discarded overcoat. Her mother's spirit, her essence was gone.

She looks at her father's chair, the imprint of him still there on the cushion. In a moment he'll come up for his glasses. He'd forget his head if it wasn't screwed on. Tears threaten to spill but she swipes them away. Since it has been just the two of them, they had reached a mutual understanding. She has felt, if not happy, then at least a kind of peace.

She throws the picture aside and sobs into her hands but the thought of Julie in the bathroom stops her. She needs to get out. If she doesn't, she'll start drinking and it's far too early. She can drink when she likes now but there will be time enough for that later. It's the only way she can see herself ever sleeping again.

She puts the photo back in its place and tiptoes up to her room. The shower is still on. Julie must be suffering after her night on the sofa. She changes into jeans and boots, shoving her skirt in a drawer. Pulling a coat from the wardrobe, she shrugs it on as she creeps back downstairs. Sliding the bolts off as quietly as possible, she steps into the courtyard.

Once outside she breathes with relief, then realises how cold it is. Pulling a hat from one of the pockets, she jams it over her ears and just stands there. The news will be all around town by now but she isn't ready to face people. Burying her chin in her coat, she turns into the street.

Through a gap in the shutters, she sees the shop is still swarming with police. She passes the unmarked car that's been there all night. They don't even notice her. She fixes her eyes on the pavement and keeps walking.

11

1977

Today is *Passion Sunday*, if what Marie tells her is true. Whatever the case, it means half-term and Anna is looking forward to two whole weeks off school. They are on the swings at the playground, the chains quietly creaking as they move back and forth in the breeze. Across the potholed asphalt, Alan Bamford is scaling the space rocket climbing frame, to the narrowest point at the top. A weighty lad, if he ventures much further, he will surely get stuck but he continues to squeeze himself upwards, egged on by the small crowd forming below.

Between the slide and the hopscotch squares, two girls are playing cat's cradle, their fingers a blur of blue wool. Three older girls in long white socks occupy the roundabout. They sit with their backs to the bars, blowing plumes of smoke from their Silk Cut, trying to look disinterested in what the boys are doing.

If only they had the place to themselves, thinks Anna. Then they'd be pushing each other, legs whizzing through the air, or spinning on the roundabout until they were dizzy. But not today. Not with all the others here.

She was right, Alan is stuck, one chubby arm flailing at the top of the climbing frame. The girls on the roundabout snigger as the others shout instructions. Then they start clapping and chanting.

'Jack Sprat could eat no fat, but Alan Bamford could!'

Anna leans back on the swing, wondering at their cruelty but happy to watch the drama unfold.

She met Marie here, almost a year ago. It was the hottest summer on record, every day as dry as the last.

The roads had bubbled like lava, the crops withered and died and the air was filled with the constant smell of burning from the moors. They'd gone so long without rain, the reservoirs were nearly empty and all anyone seemed to talk about was the looming possibility of standpipes, whatever they were.

One good thing to come of the drought had been an abundance of ladybirds. Anna had thought so anyway. She loved the little beasts and would wander for miles, collecting them in a matchbox. She didn't keep them long, just time enough to compare the colours and count the spots. Then she would let them go on a leaf or a gatepost, watching the cases crack open, the tiny gauzy wings carrying them away.

She'd been sitting there on the roundabout, two deep red ladybirds just about to emerge from the box. *Don't go far*, her parents told her. *And don't talk to strangers*. The playground was deserted, the swings abandoned on their chains. It had seemed the ideal place to set them free.

'You shouldn't capture ladybirds. It's cruel.'

Anna had been startled. She hadn't heard anyone approach. Looking up into those deep blue eyes she hadn't known what to say. That was how it was at first. Tongue tied, a little shy, she was happy just to listen.

'Have you got any money?' Marie demanded. Sitting down beside her, she had pushed her foot against the ground, so they began to spin.

Anna had counted the coins in her pocket and declared she had nineteen pence.

The next thing she knew, they were heading for the village, the ladybirds forgotten on the roundabout. Buying a nine and a ten-pence mix, she had given the bag with the extra sweet to her new friend. Marie had taken the white chocolate mice and one by one bitten their heads off.

Collecting bugs is a distant memory, a childish pastime. Anna buttons up her cardigan. Dusk is creeping across the fields, turning the playground cool. Alan has managed to free himself and is climbing down the rocket, red-faced. Marie seems lost in thought and Anna wonders what she's thinking about. Probably the kitten. As though conscious of being watched, she looks up, her expression changing suddenly.

'Come on,' says Marie, jumping off the swing, and Anna needs no persuasion. She prefers it when it's just the two of them.

'Totally boring!' shouts Marie as they run off laughing. One of the things she loves about her is she can laugh even when she feels sad. Only Anna knows this and she holds the secret knowledge tight within her. They pass a cherry tree on the corner, petals like snow on the pavement.

'Do you want to come to mine?' asks Marie, scooping up a handful of blossom.

Anna looks up at the darkening sky. 'Maybe I should go straight home.'

'Just come for a bit then.'

Two miners in orange overalls are coming towards them, nets slung across their shoulders filled with clean clothes and snap. Anna knows this from eavesdropping, they are regulars at the shop. She also knows they take an alarm clock down the pit, find a hidey hole and set it for the end of their shift.

Anna has been to Marie's house once before. Another warm day, they'd been to Ochre Dyke, stripping to their pants to paddle. The fields had shimmered with heat haze

43

and they were nearly dying of thirst, guzzling lemonade in Marie's kitchen till the bubbles came down their noses. Anna had never seen a house like it, not that she's seen that many, not in real life anyway. The walls were covered with holy pictures and there were statues everywhere but it was the cats that had shocked her most of all. They were everywhere. Stretched across worktops and chairs, basking in sunspots by the windows. Cats of all colours and sizes, preening and fighting or curled up fast asleep. Her mother would have had a fit if she'd seen them.

Stepping over the furry bundles, she had followed Marie upstairs. She had a continental quilt in turquoise satin and beads hanging from the headboard. A statue of Saint Theresa stood by the side of the bed, the first in a long line of glorified souls Anna would come to know. Running back downstairs, the cats had scattered and they'd thrown themselves in a heap on the floor. She stayed there for ages, gazing at a picture of Jesus and had never felt so happy. And that wasn't a picture, it was an icon. He held a ruby red heart in his hands.

And then Marie's mum had swept in. She was wearing a flowing kaftan, in a deep dark sea blue. On catching sight of Anna, she had stopped and stood still in the doorway. For a moment, the air seemed to crackle as she stroked the strange cat in her arms. Then she smiled and draped herself amongst the cushions on the sofa.

They had listened to records all afternoon. Marie seemed quite the expert, placing them on the turntable with the utmost care. Some were scratched and kept jumping and she would give the needle a flick. Her mum sang like a bird, the cat fast asleep across her midriff. Anna had hummed along, gradually losing some of her shyness.

She had lost all track of time until her father appeared at the window. She could tell at once he was furious but the strangest thing happened next. Marie's mum had gone to the door, Anna hardly daring to follow. She had crept into the hallway and there they were on the doorstep, heads bent close as though they knew each other. She must have been mistaken. Her father blazed with rage as he marched her to the car.

'Don't you dare let me find you here again!' He had spat the words out and they had driven home in silence. Why was he so angry and how had he known where she was? Anna had no idea and something told her not to ask. She pushes these thoughts away as Marie opens the gate. This time she will keep her eyes firmly on the clock.

'Mu-um!' Marie shouts as they enter the hallway. 'Is there anything to e-eat?' The Blessed Virgin stares at Anna from a plastic frame by the door. Her cloak floats in ripples, her eyes like chips of ice. She turns away just as Marie emerges from the kitchen. In her hand is a large bar of chocolate and just the sight of the purple foil makes Anna's mouth water. Putting a finger to her lips, Marie pushes open the living room door. The curtains are drawn, the only light coming from the flicker of the television.

'Shh!' comes a hiss from the shadows. She can just make out Marie's mum among the cushions and the Siamese cat that seems permanently fixed to her knee. 'You're just in time to watch this if you promise to be quiet.'

Anna tiptoes in. Apart from the ten o'clock news and the cricket in summer, her parents rarely have the TV on.

'Does your dad know you're here?'

'Yes,' says Marie, in a stage whisper before Anna has time to think. And then she sees the man her friend keeps telling her about and knows with absolute certainty she must be silent.

Jesus stares from the screen, his eyes the bluest blue she has ever seen. From beneath his crown of thorns, blood runs in streaks. His mother Mary weeps at the foot of the cross and the rain begins to pour.

'And you can put that away,' says Marie's mum, pointing at the bar of chocolate. 'It isn't Easter until next week.'

12

Newton

The mortuary is in the oldest part of the Northern General Hospital, at the back of the building. Hidden away from the living, thinks Newton. One of his secret passions is history, so he knows this wing is Victorian and once formed part of the workhouse. A regular visitor to the pain clinic in the modern front of the building, this dark underbelly gives a very different perspective. As he climbs the steps, he takes no pleasure in the gothic edifice above him. Instead, he thinks of the misery it must have witnessed over the years, not to mention the number of corpses that have crossed its threshold.

By rights, it should be Kate here, not him. Post-mortems form part of basic training but Newton believes she still needs more exposure to the tough end of the job. Not that he thinks her wet behind the ears. Far from it. But the way she's been behaving lately, he hadn't felt comfortable sending her.

By his reckoning, it should all be finished by now. A simple matter of obtaining a report from the pathologist. He's looking forward to a chat with his pal Bernard Oates, a wily old Scot with over thirty years' experience and the perception to have detected Newton's squeamishness at the dissecting table early on. He also has the discretion never to have made an issue of it.

The stink hits the back of his throat immediately. No amount of antiseptic can hide it. He gulps as a trolley is pushed screeching past, a sheet crumpled across it. Before he makes it to the desk, a stocky, white-coated individual he doesn't recognise bustles through a swing door towards him.

'Ahh, DS Fox,' says the man, hand outstretched. 'Glad you got the message re the time change. Just about to start if you'd like to follow.' Before Newton can take his hand, the pathologist makes a shooing movement, as though keen for him to get a move on.

'I'm DI Newton, the Senior Investigating Officer. I wasn't aware of a delay.'

'Ahh, right. Bernard took ill so I've stepped into the breach, as they say. Gareth Hastings, Home Office. I was here on other business. Glad to see I'm not the only one mucking in.'

Outmanoeuvred and unable to think of an adequate reason to escape, Newton hears the door close behind him. Pulling on a clothing protector, he has just enough time to switch the volume up on his phone. Please God let it ring so he can excuse himself.

Every instinct tells him to get out of there but he takes a deep breath and faces the table. Hastings is stepping into a pair of plastic clogs. He ties an apron over his lab coat and slurps from a mug of tea. Newton envies his composure, his clinical detachment. There is no one else in the room except the two of them and the body. An old-fashioned Dictaphone lies on a tray beside scalpels, knives and a pair of pliers. Taking a final swig, Hastings switches on the recorder and whips the sheet away with a flourish. Summoning his nerve, Newton looks down for the second time that day on the remains of Charlie Collins. The face is angular, waxy now with the hue of death, the shoulders broad. It struck him at the murder scene, that even in death it is hard to envisage this man being easily overpowered. Harder still to imagine those spade-like hands fingering the delicate cards that were his livelihood. In his prime he would have been imposing. He notes the mouth has slackened from its previous O before pulling his eyes away, fixing his gaze instead on the cardboard tag on the toe.

Hastings is circling the table, already more interested in the corpse than in him.

'As you know, Detective Inspector, the external examination is just as key as what the insides tell us. It can't be rushed.' His eyes never leave the body as he walks deliberately on. 'Every scratch, every bruise and broken fingernail tells us something.'

He picks up an instrument, tapping it against his gloved fingertips. 'So, here we have Mr Charles Collins, a seventy-year-old male. My first observation is that he looks in pretty decent nick for his age and considering the number of cigarettes he must have smoked in his lifetime.' He scrapes beneath one of the fingernails, the beds of which are blue.

'Scrupulously clean, our Mr Collins, but there are slight nicotine stains to the right index and middle fingers.' Hastings turns slightly, looking towards the head. 'Nicotine staining to the moustache as well. He's righthanded but there's nothing of note beneath the nails. He must have washed his hands thoroughly shortly before death.' From his expression it is clear he is thoroughly enjoying himself. 'What was he wearing when he died? Let me guess. Pyjamas? A dressing-gown?'

Newton nods.

'Exactly,' says Hastings, smiling to himself. 'Don't worry Detective Inspector. I'm not psychic, I read the notes. So, our friend was ready for bed when he met his maker. Nothing to indicate a struggle. He didn't scratch or hit out at his attacker. Just the usual keratin deposits under the nails and no grazes on the knuckles. No defence wounds of any kind.'

Newton breathes in slowly, then on the outbreath manages to speak. 'Can you tell the approximate time of death?'

Hastings prods the upper thigh, kneading the flesh like dough.

'Rigor already dissipating in the larger muscles. I'd say twelve to fourteen hours or so. Impossible to be more specific than that.'

He continues slowly around the body, stopping at the head. 'The bruising here is interesting.' Taking a ruler from his pocket, he measures the gash in Collins's throat. 'I've seen the weapon of course and this contusion matches the hilt but the initial impact can't have been that forceful.'

'Forceful enough to kill him,' manages Newton, trying not to look at the gaping hole Hastings is poking.

'Alas, you might think so,' says the pathologist, fingers knuckle deep. 'A weapon left in situ can work in one of two ways, as you undoubtedly know. It can perpetuate suffering but on the other hand it may prolong life for a while. Ordinarily, it would go some way to stemming blood loss but this wound goes in and then across. Here beneath the tongue, the supra hyoid is severed. It's your job to hypothesise but I'd suggest he fell on the weapon, forcing the blade sideways, where it then sliced through the common carotid and jugular veins.' Newton hears a slopping noise as he pulls his fingers out and stalks off around the table. 'Death would have been certain either way. He would have either bled out or choked but it seems to me the job was done as he fell on his own petard.' He looks pleased at this, eyeing

Newton gamely. 'And by the way, it's not self-inflicted, in case you're wondering. The angle's all wrong. Man's inhumanity to man, eh? Or woman for that matter. No slashing or hacking, just the one controlled jab, like an uppercut.' Hastings thrusts his arm as if to demonstrate, a look of glee on his face. Seeing his enthusiasm isn't shared, he quickly lowers it and turns back to the body, his expression sobering. Silently, he starts swabbing and taking samples, carefully placing them into tiny plastic bags, the process seeming interminably laboured.

Newton is willing him to get on with it, but his eyes are drawn to a mark on the corpse's chest, just above the left nipple.

'Is that a birthmark?' he asks, not wishing to get too close.

'It's a tattoo and nicely done.' Hastings is busy selecting a knife and doesn't look up. 'A heart entwined with some other symbol I can't make out. I took some close-ups before you got here. You're welcome to look at them afterwards.'

Whatever floats your boat, thinks Newton. It looks like the Ace of Spades from here, which would make a kind of sense. He wishes he could think straight and take all this in. These tools belong in a builder's yard, not something to be wielded against human flesh. He holds himself rigid, sweat running down his temples, into his collar.

'Shall we see what he had for his supper?'

Newton's breakfast tips in his stomach as light glints off the blade. Hastings holds the knife aloft, then cuts Charlie Collins down the middle.

Even after years of experience, the opening up of the body never fails in its impact. Newton gulps for air as the saw whines and the smell of burning bone floods his nostrils. The cracking apart of the ribcage is a physical affront, a violation. Again, he fights the urge to look away. The room tilts, a wave of nausea hitting him as Hastings folds the flaps of skin out like the covers of a book. By the time he slops the organs into the scales, he has to resist the need to steady himself on the side of the examining table, hoping the pathologist is too engrossed to notice. He tries to focus on all the things this man has been. A cherished child, a lover, a father. Now reduced to nothing more than meat on a butcher's slab.

Dimly aware of the words *'smoker's lungs'*, the cause of death is plainly obvious. In his mind's eye, Newton sees the dagger where it jutted from the jaw, as if thrust from below. He just about registers Hastings's final, enlightened conclusion that the murderer was probably shorter than Collins and righthanded.

He has been in the room a full hour when the call finally comes. It's the station with a routine enquiry, and he has never been so grateful to hear from them. He lurches from the room, narrowly avoiding spilling the contents of his stomach across Hastings's clogs.

13

Kate

The wind has dropped but the relative calm of the afternoon does not reflect Kate's mood as she pulls into the station car park. Her feet are killing and she has nearly run out of cigarettes. Twitching nets and dodgy silences, those who came to the door had precious little to say, or were on their way to work, or some other pressing engagement. *What's wrong with these people? Surely Margaret Wood can't be the only one to have something to say about what's happened.*

As she mounts the steps, her stomach starts to knot. This is the moment of reckoning. *Stop being so melodramatic*, she tells herself. Like Newton said, she just needs to front it out, simple as that.

When Kate first transferred here, she had been disappointed. She isn't sure what she'd expected, something reminiscent of *Heartbeat* perhaps, certainly not this concrete monstrosity. Touching her pass to the wall, she steps through the automatic doors and is met with the smell of bleach that always pervades the building. She tucks her head down and makes eye contact with no-one. Opening the door to the incident room, she presses through the desks, holding her breath and wishing the ground would swallow her up. Everyone is watching, the murmurs filling the room are all about her, she is sure of it.

Stop it, Kate! She throws her bag onto the desk, sets her shoulders back and exhales.

Newton is reading his notes, a look of intense concentration shrouding his features. He is even paler than usual and his tie isn't straight, his shirt damp beneath the armpits. Duffy is standing by the window with a cup of coffee. He raises an eyebrow and grins. Kate glares at him as she takes her coat off.

Newton glances up as though only just noticing her presence. He nods and squares some papers off against his desk. No further reprimand for now then, unless he's waiting to get her on her own. He stands up and the room falls silent

'So, you all know why we're here.' As he looks around the group you could hear a pin drop. 'We're here to catch the killer of this man.' He points to the photo of Charlie Collins, who stares down from an otherwise empty whiteboard.

'What do we know about him? Anyone want to kick us off?'

Duffy clears his throat, itching as always to be first. 'Born in Chesterfield, sir. 21st of October 1940. Just had his 70th birthday.'

'Great work, Duffy. Is that it?' Newton can be a hard taskmaster.

Kate sees Duffy's jaw clench as he consults his notebook. 'I checked the database. No criminal record and no outstanding debts. Lived at the property since 1968 and drove a Honda Jazz. The vehicle is currently being processed.'

Newton writes these meagre facts on the whiteboard, then turns his eyes back to the room. 'And what do we know about the family?'

'Just the one child,' continues Duffy. 'Anna Laura Collins. Born third of January 1968. Read English at Liverpool Uni.'

So the old woman was right, thinks Kate but Newton

seems unimpressed.

'What school did she go to?'

'Erm.' Duffy fumbles with his notebook but it's clear his investigative prowess hasn't taken him that far.

'Find out,' barks Newton.

Kate hesitates, gauging whether Duffy has any more to add. When he remains silent, she picks up the narrative.

'I believe his wife Patricia died a couple of years ago. I understand the cause of death was a heart attack.'

'Do we have a copy of the death certificate?'

'No sir. I'll get one.'

'And get her maiden name. There's got to be relatives somewhere.' Newton glares at them, his eyes almost feverish. 'I want to know everything about these people. Were they popular or not, any disputes with the neighbours?' He jabs the air with his pen at every point made. Kate absorbs his intensity, the passion she saw on their last murder case. She finds it contagious.

'The shop passed to Charlie on his father's death,' says Duffy. 'Some of the older residents remember his dad, Stanley Collins. Used to run a card school back in the day. Gambling and the likes. All above board nowadays, from what I can gather.' As he looks smugly around the room, Kate wonders if Margaret Wood is aware of these details and if so, why she hadn't mentioned them.

'Follow that up,' says Newton, scrawling on the board. 'We need to know if Collins Junior carried that on. If he did, it could give us a motive.'

Duffy nods keenly. 'Been going through his mobile sir. Nothing of interest *as yet*.' He draws out the last two words for dramatic effect. 'It's pay as you go. Typical for his age group. I'm waiting to hear back from Cellnet.' He glances up, as though awaiting a response but there isn't one. 'We found ledgers going back decades plus an address book in his bedside table. I'll be working my way through that lot plus the bank statements. At first glance, looks like business is booming.' He closes his notebook, clearly pleased with himself.

'I dropped in at the Post Office,' says Kate. 'Spoke to the woman who runs it. They do their banking there daily so no cash should be left on the premises, which corroborates what Miss Collins told you, sir. Most of their business is online these days, which probably explains why they're doing so well. Bank statements should give us a more accurate picture. Large deposits, regular payments, that sort of thing.'

'Precisely Kate, check everything. Business, personal, the daughter's accounts included.'

Duffy glowers at Kate over his coffee cup.

'We need to fetch the computer in,' continues Newton.

'Got the laptop, sir.'

'Good. And has anyone checked CCTV?'

'Out of order,' comes a voice from the back of the office. Amy Khan is the team's data analyst. Kate thinks her a bit of a geek, a sort of female version of Q from James Bond, but she admires the way her brain works. There's nothing Amy loves more than technology and gadgets and as far as Kate is concerned, she can keep them. Turning in her seat, she sees Amy's eyes are filled with disappointment at the failed cameras. A birdlike woman, no more than four feet ten, she would never have got on the force before the height restrictions were lifted. The rest of the team appear completely engrossed in the discussion. Bob Sharp — by name, not nature — is leaning against a desk, probably wondering how he will fit all this into a spreadsheet. His stomach strains against his shirt. Maybe they ought to bring in weight restrictions. Next to him sits Debbie Barstow, her perfectly made-up face tilted in rapt concentration. Not one of them is looking in Kate's direction.

'We've still got traffic cams to check sir,' says Amy. 'Plus the ones from other shops in the vicinity. Let's hope they're in better working order.'

Newton nods and pulls his laptop towards them. 'I checked out the web page this morning. Have a look at this.'

Still clearly peeved, Duffy puts his coffee down but doesn't budge from the window. Kate and the others group around the boss's desk.

The website is impressive with fancy borders and text, like an expensive menu. Newton moves the mouse and up pops the shop's interior. Kate sees the cabinets that were spattered with blood yesterday.

'They stock a variety of stuff but their speciality is playing cards.' He clicks on another box. 'The stock is worth a fortune. Take this for instance.' A deck of cards appears, fanned on black velvet showing the backs as well as the faces, twisting vines of gold on a deep red background.

'I thought this was foil but it's gold leaf. Look at the price.' Kate sees the tag is over two hundred pounds.

'And that's not all,' he clicks again. 'They also sell tarot cards.' Kate's heart jumps as the screen fills with images. The fool, the hanged man. An odd feeling creeps up the back of her neck, like cold fingers. She doesn't believe in such claptrap but she's known people who do.

'One of the women I spoke to said his wife read tarot.'

Duffy snorts into his coffee.

'Really?' Newton ignores him and switches off the laptop. 'You might want to ask about that then and bear in mind if they trade online, they'll have all sorts of different customers. She says nothing was nicked but get an inventory once forensics have finished.' Looking up from her notes, Kate sees him wince as he gets off the desk. His back must be playing up again. Maybe that's why he's so pale.

'And that leads me nicely to these.' Newton pulls a brown envelope from a drawer. Taking out a stack of photos, he places them on the desk one by one. The team draw closer and Kate is struck by their expressions. No matter how often they see this stuff it still gets to them. The first few shots show the victim from different angles, the jewelled hilt of a dagger protruding from his throat. The last two show the weapon after removal, the blade cleaned of blood.

Duffy whistles. 'That's a piece of kit," he says, and Newton nods in agreement.

'It certainly is. Victorian, I think, although I'm getting that confirmed. Ivory handle, no prints, of course, and that heart in the hilt is a garnet.'

'The card theme maybe?' says Kate, thinking of the stones in the courtyard.

'Could be, yes. It's not the type of thing you'd expect to find lying around. Ivory is worth a fortune but it's very difficult to sell. I'd like to know why it wasn't in the safe or a display case at the very least.'

Conscious she is doing a lot of talking, Kate thinks of something else. 'Would the killer have been covered in blood?'

'Hard to say. There was significant spray but the

weapon being left in situ could have staunched the bleeding. We'll know more when we get the full PM report.'

Duffy is chewing the rim of his cup and Kate can tell he's racking his brain for something else to say. Right on cue, he puts the cup down and walks over to the desk.

'What did you make of the living accommodation? All that *Mother* and *Father* stuff?'

'I didn't know what to make of it.' Newton's tone is neutral.

'I thought it was rather charming,' says Kate, still studying the photographs. 'In an old-fashioned kind of way.'

'Weird, more like,' says Duffy.

'Weird or not, as soon as forensics have done, we need to get back in there, pull the place apart if we have to.' Newton strides to the window and holds one of the photos up to the light. 'Before we go any further, I want to ask you all to consider something.' His eyes move from Kate to the others then back to Kate again. She is relieved when he looks away. 'What stands out about this murder?'

Amy sucks her pen. Bob shuffles his feet. Debbie's spider lashes flit towards the ceiling.

'What do you mean, sir?' asks Duffy, unable to stand the suspense any longer.

'I mean what I say. Does anything strike you?'

'It was controlled,' says Kate, the words out as soon as she thinks them. 'Just the one stab and no defence wounds visible. It wasn't a frenzied attack.'

'Exactly,' says Newton. "So I'll ask you to bear this in mind.' He sweeps the pictures into a pile and replaces them in the envelope.

'Would his death have been quick, sir?'

'I don't know, Kate. Let's hope so. Now, I need someone to check out the book club.'

'Book club?' blurts Duffy, his expression now a mixture of confusion and barely suppressed rage.

'Yes, apparently the daughter attended one last night. We need to interview whoever else was there.'

Kate can easily imagine Anna Collins at a book club. She could hold it in the flat with that collection. She waits, giving the others chance to volunteer.

'I'll do it,' she says, when the silence stretches. Duffy's face is like thunder.

'Have we had an update from Julie?' Kate knows this is aimed at her.

'No, sir.'

'Get one,' says Newton, without looking up. 'Right, it goes without saying but I'll say it anyway. All non-essential leave is cancelled. I've made a preliminary statement to the press but we need more. A lot more. I want everyone in this town questioning, anything unusual recorded. We need to know who the night owls are, who was taking their dog for its last piss, any shift workers coming home. They can't all have been in bed, not sleeping anyway.' He slams his drawer shut and locks it. Picking up his laptop, he slides his coat from the back of his chair. Kate has never seen him so keen to get away and wonders what his wife has planned for him this evening. He looks suddenly tired, as though his previous energy has burnt itself out.

The room fills with chatter and the scrape of chairs but Kate takes her time. She doesn't want to bump into Duffy and makes a trip to the ladies to be certain. Back outside the station, she breathes a sigh of relief. Newton seems to have said his piece but she isn't naïve enough to relax just yet. Today might have passed with little incident but she needs to be wary, at least where Duffy is concerned.

There is one thing she hadn't mentioned, she isn't sure why. The smell of booze coming off Anna was almost palpable. Lighting her last cigarette, she makes her way through the drifts of leaves to her car. She'll call for another twenty on her way home.

14

Newton

Newton has been in the shower for over forty-five minutes. Crouched beneath the scalding torrent, he has scoured his skin so roughly he burns as though he's been flayed. Soapsuds spill from his shoulders, running down his body in rivers but he feels no cleaner and in his mind's eye, the water pooling at his feet is stained red. Switching off the shower, he grabs blindly for a towel, passing the steamed-up mirror with no wish to wipe it clear and see his reflection.

Throwing on some clothes, he pads downstairs and sits rubbing his hair dry. Louise would often come into a room and find him quietly reading. *Aren't you going to put the telly on?* she would say. At least now he can please himself. He's never been one for watching TV for the sake of it — happier with a book or listening to music. Now he has no desire to do either.

The pain in his back suddenly flares. It is never not there but the incessant dull ache now blooms into a deeper, gnawing throb. He needs a distraction. Pulling things out of the fridge, he starts to make cheese on toast, trying to convince himself it's cooking, better than a ready meal for one. As he grates the cheddar he thinks of the whiskey, where he hid it behind the kettle this morning.

Chewing at the window, he stares into the darkness. The wind has dropped but the rain is still falling in huge drops against the glass. Not for the first time, he marvels how modern life keeps us so separate from the elements. Unlike the winters of his childhood, the orange glow of a paraffin stove warming the memory, huddled with his sister by the steaming clothes horse. He should give her a call but knows that he won't.

His body is beginning to thrum like a tautened wire. Pushing the plate aside, he goes back upstairs and curls beneath the duvet in foetal position. He wishes he had a pound for every hour he's spent like this. Like the pilot light on a paraffin stove, the pain never fully goes out. Kneading the flesh of his buttocks, he digs his fingers in but the muscles burn like molten shrapnel is embedded in them. Lying flat on his fists, he presses down and attempts to slow his breathing. He has been trying to train his mind, to find the thread and follow it, retreating from the pain to somewhere deep inside himself. Very rarely it is possible. Mostly, the best he can do is just wait for it to pass.

Bunching up the sheets, he thinks of his mother. What would she make of all this? He knows the answer to that, can almost hear her voice in the silence. *Now what have you done, Jimmy?* She would blame him, of course. Always her default reaction.

She might have a point. How can he, of all people, lecture Kate? There was no need whatsoever for him to attend the post-mortem. He should have told that stuffed lab coat where to get off. So, why hadn't he? Was it punishment, some kind of self-flagellation? For what? He knows exactly what. For his failure. Failure to keep his marriage together and failure to overcome his issues. Issues only Louise knows anything about.

He reaches for her pillow but her scent has long since washed away. His need for her comes in waves. Like a craving, visceral and ingrained, he longs for her. In the early days she would lie here with him. She would hold him and comfort him and for a while it would all go away. Such ambition she'd had for the two of them. Studying together at the table with the whole world at their feet. Newton's *Blackstone's Police Manual* propped against a milk bottle, Louise poring over her pharmacy books, looking at him with something close to adoration. What he would give for a glimpse of that now.

He had injured his back playing rugby. He doesn't even like rugby but had somehow been persuaded to join the station team. Louise had been all for it, it would do him good to get fit. He got fit alright, for the knacker's yard. He had slipped three discs and never been the same since.

It had been the worst experience of his adult life. Newton has no time for shirkers. He hadn't had a day off sick in his entire career but being shot at point blank range or repeatedly stabbed with a red hot poker couldn't have been any worse. It was off the scale. Total, bone crunching pain. He could barely stand or even think straight for the screaming in his body and there was no way in hell he would let anyone see him in that state.

It would right itself in a couple of weeks, he was sure of it. It soon became clear that wasn't going to happen. When he heard the words *degenerative spinal disease,* he thought there'd been a terrible mistake but the private doctor said the same, if a little more graphically. *It's like you've fallen out of a tree and hit every branch on the way down.* He'd paid five hundred quid to hear that. There seemed to be a consensus, though. The rugby tackle had been a catalyst — in time, it would have happened anyway. It was like a death knell to Newton. His discs had worn away, the bones of his spine heaped on top of each other like a tumbledown drystone wall.

In those first few months he tried everything. Osteopaths, chiropractors, traction, acupuncture, cupping. Good money thrown after bad. Nobody would operate, far too risky. The only thing that gave him any respite at all was medication.

He remembers what Louise went through bringing Georgie into the world. Men would never know such agonies. Newton had agreed with her at the time. He can't stand people who exaggerate but he can honestly say there are times when he feels like he's been hit by a lorry, ploughed through a wall, steel slamming into him, through him. There is nothing clean about this pain. It is the brutal, bloody pain of mangled body parts and severed limbs. Vicious. Searing. Cruel.

Long before the pain clinic, Newton had decided it was black. *You need to visualise it James, imagine the colour and texture.*

Bollocks to that. All he wanted was to knock himself out until it went away.

But it never went away. He met a man at the clinic whose suffering had become so unbearable, he had tried to cut his leg off with a chainsaw. The man, who was perfectly sane, had been sectioned, but Newton understood his desperation. Regularly, mostly in the dead of night, he could gladly drive a stake into his own flesh just to break the relentlessness; would bargain with the devil for an hour's respite.

Balls to this, thinks Newton, throwing back the duvet. The pain is going nowhere, the only thing in his whole life he has ever felt truly threatened by. Threatened but never beaten and he tackles it in the only way he knows. As an adversary. Like some murdering bastard out to screw him over. He takes some pills from a drawer and swills them down in the bathroom.

His usual weekend pursuits became completely out of the question. No more scaling the Pennines or running across the moors, he had to strengthen his core. Over the last year this has been his focus and now for the most part, he can hold himself together. He hasn't touched the hard stuff in months, mainly because in this job, he can't afford to be anything but fully in control. Ironic really, that Louise should leave now when he has the upper hand but in those early days, that had seemed impossible.

It had been a moment of madness. A freezing cold day, she had just returned to work after having Georgie. She'd been right of course, the pharmacy had gone to pot without her. One of the Peak District branches had run out of stock and she'd taken it upon herself to drive over with supplies. Her car had broken down on Snake Pass. She'd called the AA, but the stuff was urgently needed. It's a memory Newton wishes he could forget.

It was almost dark when he pulled up behind her. The breakdown truck was there, lights blazing, her bonnet up.

'Head gasket. I'll have to tow it,' the mechanic declared mournfully as Louise stamped her feet by the roadside. Newton told her to get in his car but she refused, insisting she was needed back at the shop. He had watched impotently as she climbed into the truck. She never listened to him, so there had been no point trying to argue. Was that the real reason he hadn't pressed her, didn't insist she come with him? He doesn't dwell on that. The next thing he remembers are the little white boxes lit up by the beam of his torch as he transferred them from Louise's boot to his own. The pain had been particularly vicious around that time. He hadn't planned what happened, no matter what she believed. It was a split-second decision, to push the bottle of morphine under the spare wheel. They wouldn't miss one, would they?

They hadn't.

The relief as the morphine washed through him literally brought him to tears but Newton is all too aware of the pitfalls of drugs. He had rationed himself to no more than a swig when he could stand the pain no longer. Louise had found the bottle, a week later. The most galling thing was it was still half full when she poured it down the sink in front of him.

She had called him a thief and an addict. Not what a police inspector wants to hear from his wife. He had covered Georgie's ears, even knowing he was far too young to understand.

If he's honest, their problems started long before that. For seventeen years they'd waited for a baby. At one point Louise had become obsessed. Sex wouldn't even be considered unless her temperature was right or the ovulation chart consulted but at least they were in it together, a kind of joint venture. Eventually, after numerous failed attempts at IVF, they had resigned themselves to childlessness. Or at least Newton had. He had thought their lives complete, with their respective careers, two holidays a year and Lottie. And then just as Louise turned forty, when he thought she'd stopped thinking about babies, she announced she was pregnant. It was everything they'd ever wanted, wasn't it? It was everything Louise had wanted and once she'd got it, it seemed she was no longer interested in him.

Would she comfort him tonight if she was here? He doubts it. Her indifference, the roll of her eyes had become all too familiar. She'd suggested counselling, for him of course, not as a couple. There was only so much a wife could cope with. One issue maybe but two? And that one foolish act had been the final nail in the coffin. Or so she said. Newton knows she was fed up of him well before that happened.

In the end, all she wanted was to hurt him. Ridiculing and deriding his choice of job. Laughing at his phobia. If the pain hadn't unmanned him, she did her best to.

'A policeman scared of dead bodies! You're a joke, James. A crippled drug addict!'

He has never told a soul about any of this. He can't stand the thought of their pity. Newton knows he's a joke — nobody else needs to. He has managed to hide his horror of blood for long enough, he can do the same with the pain. He's not an invalid and he never will be. As far as anyone's concerned, he pulled his back at rugby and made a full recovery.

Somehow, the whiskey bottle has found its way out from behind the kettle and is standing there on the table, in all its amber glory.

15

1977

Anna is miles away, lost in the thick blue atlas spread open across her knees. The crusts of a potted meat sandwich lie curling beside her and a half-eaten apple has rolled into the corner of the cushions. On the rug by the fire, Jack whimpers in his sleep. From time to time his ears twitch and Anna's eyes flick towards him then back to the page, her finger tracing the rippling hills, the snaking rivers and seas. How she wishes she could visit these places. Maybe someday she will.

Pushing the atlas aside, she gets up and goes over to the window. Her father went out after breakfast, leaving his pride and joy behind, which is strange because he rarely walks anywhere, especially in this weather. She looks down at the Vauxhall Victor, the paintwork dotted with rain, the headlamps glinting like eyes in the watery sun.

She had spent the morning *making herself useful*, holding the ladder whilst Mother dusted, polishing the counter and shelves. She had started opening deliveries but had clumsily dropped a box. Cards had scattered across the floor and she was told to *make herself scarce*. She knows why Mother wants her out of the way, she must be expecting a customer. Her customers are quite separate from her father's customers. They have a very different reason for coming here. They might browse around the shop, make a show of feigning interest but what they really come for is a *reading*.

Mother has always had her own special customers. Every one of them is a woman and as far as Anna can tell, every one of them is stupid. Well of course they are. Since she was barely big enough to hold them in her hands, Anna has lived and breathed the cards but who in their right mind would think these oblongs of compressed paper could foretell the future? Mother's customers do and so they come, usually after closing, often a little embarrassed but always with that same look of wanting in their eyes. Mrs Brown comes most and her question is always the same. *When will I have a baby?* Never, as far as Anna can see, but Mother doesn't like to upset people. It's the same with Mrs Thorpe. Her husband isn't coming back, not after all this time but Mother's words are like mist, curling around the women like Father's cigarette smoke. She is good at it. She practises. *It's not a gift but a curse.*

Cards aren't the only thing Mother reads. The women are offered refreshment and if they choose tea, the cup is secreted away to be examined after they've gone. Mother pores over the dregs but Anna never sees the signs she insists are there. They do this on the quiet, tipping the cups down the sink if Father appears. Tarot is allowed because they pay for it but he draws the line at tea leaves. Gypsy work, he calls it.

Tarot is Anna's favourite. She has learned the secret symbols, devised her own way of remembering things. It's easy really. Swords are strong men like soldiers and the police, coins are anyone with money. Cups are like a chalice in a church, men like Father Vincent.

Anna listens to every word of her mother's readings. She knows the most powerful forces, the ones you must really beware and the ones that are just a kind of background, the padding out of the story her customers expect. That way they feel they've had their money's worth.

Whether you believe in it or not, there are certain cards you never want to see. The man with ten swords in his back, or the tower being struck by lightning. These cards never bode well but Anna looks forward to their appearance. She loves to see the customers' faces, the tales her mother weaves to stop them panicking.

At least, this used to be the case. More often these days, she is banished to her room or sent on some errand or other. Anna isn't stupid. She knows it's because she is getting older. They don't want her listening to their private business. It doesn't stop her, though. From the staircase she can still hear every word.

Picking up the apple, she nibbles carefully around the browning flesh. She'll get into trouble if she leaves finger marks on any of the books. Wiping her hands down her jeans, she settles into the cushions and pulls a slim volume towards her. She loves being with Marie but reading is her passion. She likes to look up the things she tells her, partly to see if they are true. She's been reading about Oscar Wilde and can't think why she'd name her cat after him. She didn't understand half the things it said about him and will have to ask her what they mean. Reading the chapter again, she snaps the book closed and takes it back to the shelf it came from. Then she tiptoes to the landing, avoiding the floorboards that creak. Mother says eavesdroppers never hear anything good about themselves. That may be true but they hear plenty of interesting things about other people.

'What are you doing up there, girl?' Anna jumps at the sound of her voice, like a foghorn echoing up the stairwell. Sometimes she'd swear her mother has X-ray vision.

Jack stirs and stretches but she shoos him back and shuts the door firmly behind her. Downstairs she sees she was not mistaken, they do have a customer.

'I thought I heard you loitering,' says Mother, her lip almost curling into a smile. 'It looks like the sun's coming out and Mrs Wood has come to see me. Why don't you get some fresh air?'

The lady in the knitted cardigan is a regular.

'Can I take my scooter?'

'I don't see why not but remember what I told you. Keep away from Never Fear and that Ryan girl while you're at it.'

Anna nods politely to Mrs Wood as she heads through the back door. Her scooter is where she left it, propped against the back wall. She would much prefer a Chopper but the scooter is faster than a bike when you're going downhill. She thinks of Mother's parting words, she always calls Marie *the Ryan girl*. Her parents don't approve of her. Anna has no idea why, but their attempts to thwart the friendship haven't succeeded. She remembers the time before Marie, how lonely she had been. The girls at her school are dull in comparison and they can be cruel. Their taunts of Bamber Gascoigne and boffin are less frequent now but still she feels marked as different. Something she never feels when she is with Marie.

Using the sleeve of her jumper, she wipes the rain from the scooter's rubber handles. The route is all downhill and soon she is hurtling into the cul-de-sac with the most ridiculous name she has ever seen or heard. Marie lives on Park Drive — her father's brand of cigarettes.

Dragging her toe along the pavement, she comes to a

stop and wheels her scooter up the path. Leaning it against the fence, she half hopes it might get stolen. She makes her way up the side of the house, pausing at the corner. Between the sheets on the washing line she sees Marie sitting on the lawn, the mother cat and her litter grouped around her.

'Boo!' Yells Anna, jumping out at her. Taken by surprise, Marie drops a kitten into her lap. It tumbles off to join its siblings, who are nuzzling their mother.

Anna flops down on the grass and watches them for a while.

'Still no sign of Oscar then?'

'It's only been a couple of days.' Marie scratches her temple, hiding her face.

'Is your Mum in?'

'No, she's just gone out.'

Anna is a little disappointed. She likes Marie's mum. She is pretty and kind and lets them do things her mother would never let them do.

They sit tormenting the kittens with a ball of wool. Anna wonders if the mother cat misses her baby. She can tell Marie does and decides that now is not a good time to raise the subject of Oscar Wilde.

The mother soon tires of the game and slinks off indoors, the kittens trailing after her.

'What shall we do now?' asks Anna, but Marie appears not to hear her.

'I'm not going back indoors,' she says, surprised by her own words. She usually lets Marie make all the decisions.

'Come on then!' grins her friend, pulling her to her feet. 'I've got an idea!'

'Oh God, not another one,' groans Anna, brushing

grass off her jeans but secretly she feels a prick of excitement.

They pass her scooter on their way down the path. It seems more childish than ever and Anna is glad to leave it there. She knows exactly where they're going but doesn't say a word as they make their way towards the busiest part of the village. On the steps of the Lion, the landlady is picking up bottles. She has a hairnet on and rollers, so tight you can see her scalp. Her husband goes to the greyhound track, laying bets for all the miners. Father is dead against this but Anna gives her a smile. The pavements are emptying, people trying to reach cover before the rain returns.

They dash across the road, between cars and buses. As they reach the war memorial, Anna's guess is confirmed. They are going to the church. The Catholic church of course. When she's on her own, Anna sometimes goes to St Peter and Paul's to read the headstones. If she's with Marie, it's always this church they come to. Our Lady of Lourdes.

They run the last few steps as the heavens open. Rain bounces off the path, pouring from the gutters. They stand in the porch for a moment, watching the ground turn dark and wet.

'Just in time,' gasps Marie, the small gold cross she always wears rising and falling at her throat. She cracks the door slowly open, just enough to see. 'Empty,' she whispers, and Anna follows her inside.

Marie stops at a small, stone font set into the wall by the doorway. Dipping her fingers in, she makes the sign of the cross on her forehead.

Their secret visits to the rectory never sit right with Anna but she has no sense of unease here. She knows it is wrong to trespass but the church is open to everyone. Why else would the door be left unlocked? Anyone can come in but only Catholics can join in the fun. She came to midnight mass once with Marie and her mum and watched the congregation take Communion. Anna had thought it was magical, with all the candles lit and Father Vincent whirling his box of smoke around.

Their footsteps echo, the rain pelting the windows like gunfire. Anna breathes in the cool, dusty smell as they make their way across the back row of pews. Stained-glass windows rise either side of the nave, pictures of Jesus hanging between them. The Way of Sorrows, Marie calls it. She always lingers there but Anna prefers not to look at them.

She enters a pew, pulling out the embroidered cushion she knows is stashed beneath the seat. Kneeling in mock supplication, she begins to recite the Lord's Prayer.

Marie turns, the crucified Jesus staring over her shoulder.

'What are you doing?' she sniggers. 'It's not funny.'

'Obviously it is,' replies Anna, stifling her own guffaw. She likes it here. The high, vaulted ceiling, the statues and the candles. Especially the candles. She walks down the nave, placing her feet as quietly as possible on the marble floor. Climbing the steps, she circles the altar. A white cloth is draped across it, covered in symbols. Fishes, doves, hearts, they remind her of her father's playing cards. She strokes one of the candles, her fingers lingering at its base.

'Anna!' Marie's stage whisper interrupts her reverie. She scuttles back down the steps, as her friend drops down before the altar. Making the sign of the cross, she bows her head before taking a seat near the front.

Anna is about to join her when she hears a sound behind them. Darting into the pew, she grabs Marie by the arm.

'Did you hear that?'

'What? I didn't hear anything.'

'Listen.'

The girls sit in absolute stillness. The rain has stopped and all they can hear is the steady rhythm of their breath.

'Most likely a mouse,' says Marie. 'Haven't you heard of church mice?'

'It wasn't a mouse. It was coming from over there.' Anna points to the dark wooden box set in the wall on the opposite side of the church.

'The confessional?' Marie stiffens, her eyes immediately flying in the same direction.

The sound of a chair being scraped across the floor pierces the silence.

'Now do you believe me?' Anna hisses but there is no question this time. Marie heard it too and plunges to her hands and knees.

Panicked by her friend's reaction, Anna huddles down by her side. Burrowing like animals, they press themselves as far beneath the pews as possible.

A man's voice rings out through the cold air above them. Anna ducks her head, squeezing herself into the shadows. Then a woman's soft, hushed tones come across the nave, low and trembling as though she has been crying. Unmistakably the voice of Marie's mum.

'Thank you so much, Father. I don't know what I'd do without you.'

'Remember what I said.'

'Of course I will.'

Anna holds her breath, her eyes never leaving Marie's

face. They hear two sets of footsteps, the creak of the door, then the church falls back into silence.

16

Anna

The parish church of St Peter and Paul is shrouded in a fine mist, its solid square tower all that's visible as Anna approaches. She is glad she changed into her boots as the grass is saturated and the ground quite muddy. Passing the priest's well, she imagines, as she always does, water being drawn there in times gone by and the gypsies she has read of who used to camp here. There are few markers this side of the church but Anna is mindful of all the souls buried beneath her, as she steps across the earth.

She always comes this way, walking through the graves in chronological order. The path climbs gradually between the ancient stones, some no more than tumbled slabs, half buried and covered in lichen. A few steps further on and the grass begins to fill. Ornate crosses push through the earth, towering pillars and angels, all choked in ivy and so weathered with time, the lettering is almost unreadable. The trees hang heavily above her and she breathes in the sharp, resinous tang of soil and wet leaves. As she walks beneath a horse chestnut, she looks up at the russet branches and is glad she wore a hat as a huge drop of rain hits her nose. She already feels calmer, as though she is among friends. All the names are familiar here and she has taken the time to decipher even the most worn epitaphs. She stops at one of her favourites, the inscription remarkably clear despite its age.

Here lies Matthew Staniforth, Schoolmaster of the Parish

Left this earthly life, 7 February 1848 aged 25 years
Also his wife Jane, 11 November 1847 in her twenty-first year
Resting in Eternal Slumber

Underneath, in smaller letters is the name of their son Isaac, who died first on the day he was born, *Reunited* carved at the base of the stone. Anna often lingers here, picturing the little tableau. Scholarly, handsome Matthew, crossing the fields to school, a pile of books wedged beneath his arm. She wonders what happened to him that he followed his family so swiftly into the grave.

As the church clock strikes the hour, she spots a group of youths loitering under the trees. They look too old for conkers and in any case, the pastime seems to have all but died out. They don't appear to be doing any harm but she keeps an eye on them as she bears left at a fork in the path. Here, the graves are more uniform in size, packed in regimented rows. Anna can estimate the date from the colours and style, the white marble a sharp contrast to the passing fashion for black, giving way to muted greys and greens, even plum as the newest section of the cemetery comes into view.

Anna still feels a sense of unreality as she approaches her mother's grave. It's as though she has moved out and now lives here in the graveyard, a ridiculous thought, she knows. When it was freshly dug, she couldn't bear the sight of it, the earth sinking inexorably down, crushing her mother beneath it. She had lain awake at night, picturing her out here all alone, her mouth and nostrils filling with soil. Secretly, she had wanted to dig her up and bring her home, keep her safe and warm, even though she knew her mother could no longer feel the cold, or anything for that matter. Burying a loved one in the dark wet earth still seems to Anna the cruellest thing imaginable.

It is strange what grief does to you in those first raw weeks. Anna has an open mind but she believes the soul departs soon after death. She is certain of it. For her there is no comfort in coming to the grave. Her mother isn't here or anywhere in any earthly sense but still she comes, partly to please her father but also to honour a promise. Her mother had insisted there must always be flowers on her grave. With a jolt, she realises her arms are empty but today's visit has a different purpose. Again she knows it's absurd but she feels a strong sense that she is bringing news of her father's passing. In an abstract way she wonders if Mother's spirit is already aware, that wherever she is and in whatever form, she knows. May have even borne witness to what happened.

As the grave comes into view, she sees the blur of white flowers. Her first thought is that Father must have been here in the last days of his life but as she gets closer her footsteps slow. Wrapped in tissue and positioned carefully against the headstone is a spray of creamy lilies. Anna hates lilies, the cloying scent bred to cover the reek of rotting flesh. She almost gags, knowing her father didn't bring them. The stamens are bright against the petals, the tissue perfectly dry. They must have been placed here quite recently. How strange, no-one else comes here. They have no living relatives, and her mother had no friends. Lilies would never be her father's choice and he would always put them in water, so they would last.

The ground is scattered with cones and dead leaves. Anna is barely used to seeing her mother's name here and now her father's will join it. The neat grass will be torn up again, the peaceful soil disturbed.

When her mother died, she had held herself together for her father's sake. She had to stay strong and keep the business going. Outpourings of grief, tears God forbid, would not be tolerated.

Suddenly the panic is back, rising in her chest and out through her mouth, a cry so raw and guttural it sends the birds squawking from the trees. She puts a hand to her face and steadies herself against the headstone. Deep breaths. In through the nose, out through the mouth. She repeats this, as she has learned to do, until her heart rate gradually slows. Then she straightens her hat and walks back the way she came.

17

Kate

Kate drives the short distance to her home, a small modern semi in what she likes to think of as the fashionable foothills of Black Hollow. She isn't a snob by any means but it's a long way from the council estate she grew up on. The new roads spread like tentacles across what's left of the fields. A few trees have survived, the only sign the land was once covered in ancient woodland and presumably an orchard. The old fruit trees and the sycamore Kate fell in love with on first viewing the property helped her put aside her previously held views on urban sprawl.

It might be Friday night but there is no sense of weekend with a murder investigation underway. Kate is as keen to catch the killer as Newton evidently is. She switches on the TV but has missed the local news. That's probably not a bad thing. In her view, the media is responsible for just about everything that is wrong with the world. Although to be fair, it was watching TV news reports that made her want to become a detective in the first place. That and *Secret Seven* books. Highly unlikely as it is, she hopes the coverage has been tasteful, for Anna's sake at least.

Running a bath, she sinks beneath the scented bubbles, intending to stay there until the water cools, then snuggle up with Luther in her dressing gown. She tries to forget the case but as she soaps her body, the events of last weekend fill her mind instead. She thinks back across the months to her first meeting with Helen.

Kate hadn't known a soul when she first arrived here

and the locals were so close-knit, she'd felt lonely and isolated. She had made the most of the time, channelling her energies into her new job and home but the endless evenings and weekends had started to get her down, making her question her decision to move here in the first place. So, when Helen approached her at the coffee machine, she accepted her invitation straight away. She'd seen her around the station. It was impossible not to. Easily the best dressed woman in the building, she stalked the corridors like a catwalk model. Tipping shampoo into her palm, Kate rubs it roughly into her hair. They'd gone to the Miners Arms and she'd discovered Helen was the superintendent's secretary. Like Kate, she was a relative newcomer and hadn't met socially with anyone else from the station. She'd felt pleased, flattered even, at being singled out for friendship by this well-heeled, successful woman.

And well-heeled she certainly was. Everything about her screamed designer label. Her sports car was a little flash for Kate's taste but Helen was much more down to earth than she first appeared. Her suggestion they go hiking came as a complete surprise but Kate found her new friend more than happy to swap her Jimmy Choos for boots, her Hermes tote for a backpack. She knew all the best rambles; she'd grown up in the area, although she never said exactly where and Kate had never asked.

Smoking was something else they bonded over. Taking it in turns to drive, they would walk across the moors, stopping for a cig on an outcrop of rock, or a patch of heather. Words have always been superfluous to Kate in the face of such beauty and Helen seemed to get this, happy to soak up the view in companionable silence. It had seemed idyllic.

Rinsing her hair, she casts her mind back to the day they climbed Mam Tor. This is where her photographic memory gives no comfort. As they reached the summit, Helen took her hand, her face flushed with exertion. They'd watched the gliders float on the thermals then drift to the fields below. Like children they giggled, as the sheep dashed for cover, like cotton wool balls at the bottom.

Now she sees them, huddled together in the wind, cupping their hands around her lighter. *How could she have been so naïve?* It had been a shared vice, like smoking behind the bike sheds but she should have known it was more, should have sensed it.

As summer drew to a close, it became too cold for hiking and Helen suggested another night out. As she tops the bath up, Kate recalls the dress she bought for the occasion, the trouble she'd taken choosing it. How suddenly out of her depth she had felt. In their walking boots they were equals but Helen in her finery, she hadn't a hope of competing with that. She baulks at the memory, her bed piled high with discarded clothes as she tried on every item in her wardrobe but when the night arrived, her outfit hadn't mattered at all.

She remembers Helen's though. It had clung like a second skin, a metallic, shimmering sheath. On the bus into Sheffield, she'd seen their reflections and her nerves began to fade. She was back on home turf and as they grew steadily drunker, her confidence grew.

Her memory clouds at this point. She hates that she can't remember. She knows she drank wine because that's what Helen had. Her first big mistake. She has a hazy recollection of teetering arm in arm. Her stiletto had caught in a crack in the pavement, sending them sprawling. That would have been a sensible time to call it a night but the next thing she remembers they were in a club. Kate detests getting drunk precisely because she prides herself so much on her memory. The aftermath taunts her, only letting her recall the bits she would rather forget.

Drink transformed Helen, a metamorphosis took place. Kate sees her now with photographic clarity, head thrown back, dress straps flapping from her shoulders. Downing shots, slamming her glass on the bar, demanding more. Kate was swept along, she had felt euphoric, all her inhibitions sloughed off. Like being unshackled.

Helen must have dragged her onto the dancefloor because Kate never dances, not unless she is wasted. Lying back in the water, she sees her dress rippling in the lights. She moved with a liquid looseness, with her eyes half closed, seductively Kate sees now, in retrospect. Taking her hands she had whirled her around, the room spinning out of focus and she had fallen into her arms in a laughing, dizzy embrace. They swayed together and the music must have slowed. The next thing she knew, Helen was kissing her full on the mouth. It hadn't registered at first and she had closed her eyes to make the room stop spinning. The first thing she saw when she opened them was Duffy.

Kate pulls the plug out, sick of thinking about it. She has tried explaining things to Newton but he clearly doesn't want to know. Fine. As for Duffy, it's none of his god damned business. Pricks like him are enough to put you off blokes for life.

Wrapping herself in a towel, she walks through to the bedroom. Luther is stretched across the duvet, watching her. She flops down beside him on the pillows.

85

Kate had half imagined someone joining her here at some indistinct point in the future. Maybe even the faintest outline of a cot in the spare room, a baby border on the walls. She keeps these thoughts to herself. The chances of either happening to her seem to diminish with each passing year.

This room, or rather its aspect, was one of the main reasons she bought the place. It forms the corner, with windows facing in two directions. At night, the sky is like a jewellery box, the daytime views equally beautiful. She loves the ancient landscape, the dark peaks in the distance, the drystone walls that criss-cross the hills. From the other window, the fields stretch as far as Chesterfield, the land tightly packed with streets and pylons and roads.

She had loved the room's simplicity, the white walls and linen curtains, the watercolours purchased when her new life lay before her. Now it seems plain, the pictures bland and unimaginative. She has spent too much time here on her own.

As she combs her hair, she thinks of Anna. They are both alone now but that's where the similarity ends. Her pictures were bold and vivid, her furnishings, if nothing else, striking. Catching sight of her reflection, she stops mid-stroke. Her hair snakes the hollow of her collarbone in dark, wet ribbons and she realises with a start she has lost weight. Suddenly the prospect of a night in with Luther and the television has lost its appeal. She looks at her watch and decides it isn't too late to call Anna. She might even be grateful for some company.

18

Newton

According to local legend, there's been a Miners Arms on this spot since the reign of King Richard the Third. Newton is inclined to believe it. He knows iron has been mined in the area for hundreds if not thousands of years. He'd stumbled across an old smelting shop on one of his walks with Lottie. Sickles had hung from the walls, scythes swaying precariously. Little more than curiosities these days but Newton had found the place fascinating, the old man working the furnace like his forefathers, centuries before him.

He looks up at the current pub as he strides across the car park. Solid Derbyshire stone hewn from the hillside, the low doors and mullioned windows must be seventeenth century at the latest. An iron ring is set in the wall and Newton likes to picture horses tethered there, their riders worse for wear after a night of roistering. All the downstairs rooms have open fires and he's pleased to see smoke drifting from the chimneys.

Putting distance between himself and that bottle of whiskey had been an urgent necessity. The pain has dulled to its usual white noise but the thought of Lottie makes him even more needful of a pint. You'd think taking his son would be enough for her but Louise's voice echoes in his head as he ducks beneath the lintel. *You're never home, James. It's not fair leaving a dog on its own all day.* She had spat the words out as she left him, Lottie's chain rattling in her hand.

He nods at the men at the bar, exchanging the universal greeting in these parts.

'Eyup.'

'Eyup.'

Nearest to him is a farmer of indeterminate age, known hereabouts as Knocker. Newton has never asked what he did to earn such a nickname. With his haystack hair and motheaten coat, it's easy to imagine straw escaping from his seams and a family of sparrows in his pocket, (or a ferret even) but Newton isn't fooled by his tatty demeanour. Knocker doesn't miss a trick and his tongue is prone to loosening in exchange for a pint or three. Pubs can be enlightening places.

In pride of place on the bar is a miner's lamp, its brass gleaming like gold. Staring at his glass beyond it stands Chuck, an ex-pit deputy of similar indeterminate age. His hands are tattooed with swallows, one of the green-grey birds split open by a flower-shaped scar. A pit prop collapsed on him, the splintered end slicing his fist like butter. He had been dug out but never set foot down the pit again. Newton has never conversed with him. He was left mute by the accident. All this he's learnt from Knocker, who more than makes up for his companion's silence, especially when well oiled. Both men have the rosy colour of the habitual drinker. It amuses Newton they never stand together, always separated by the old pit lamp.

Dave the landlord appears at the pumps. 'Usual?'

Newton nods, feeling in his pocket for change. He looks around but the taproom is otherwise empty.

'It's quiet,' he says, counting out coins in his palm.

'We were busy earlier,' says Dave, as he always does.

Newton is in no mood for chit chat, so he takes his pint and goes to sit by the fire. The coal is nicely ablaze but the ancient table wobbles. Throwing a beermat on the lino, he pushes it in place with his foot. Satisfied with the adjustment, he sits down and takes a long swig of his Guinness, wiping the froth from his lip.

This place can't have changed much since Richard the Third was here. They only sold beer until the 70s, having no license for spirits. Hard to believe anywhere could be so backward but he takes Knocker at his word. Glancing up, he sees cobwebs hanging in swathes from the beams above him. *Dave needs to sack his cleaner*, thinks Newton, then spots the skull in the window and groans. That crazy time of year is almost upon them, when the streets are full of little shits in masks and setting fire to things becomes suddenly acceptable. It's the last thing he needs. Taking another swig, he stares into the depths of his glass.

The walls have the mellow tint of nicotine, despite it being years since the ban but it's not unpleasant in the firelight and his mind begins to wander. He thinks of his pal Steve, who recently transferred to Manchester. He'd craved more excitement and he'll certainly get it there. Newton has led an itinerant life, used to leaving friends behind. Content with his own company, he shuts his eyes, willing the Guinness and the warmth to work their magic. His constant companion is fixed to his spine, his nose still filled with abattoir and foetid fag smoke from the Collins's flat. He wonders if Kate could smell it or whether she's immune.

He deliberately kept certain aspects of the post-mortem to himself. He doesn't want to send his team in the wrong direction. In any case, as Hastings remarked, it isn't the pathologist's job to speculate. Nevertheless, Newton wishes he'd been able to ask more questions. He puts down his pint, trailing his finger across the table.

The wood is well polished but the lustre doesn't hide the scars, a patchwork of crude initials and cigarette burns. He wonders how many others have sat here before him, drinking themselves into oblivion.

If there's one thing Newton can't stand, it's self-pity. He downs his pint and strides back to the bar.

'Stick another one in there, Dave,' he says, 'And an Irish.'

The landlord pulls his pint, eyeing him over the glass as he measures the whiskey but he says nothing as Newton counts out the change.

As he sits back down, the door swings open, the draught momentarily flattening the flames in the grate. A tall blonde appears, her long black coat brushing knee-length high-heeled boots. It is quite an entrance. Newton catches her eye and instinctively nods but she looks away. Walking straight to the bar, she stands level with the miner's lamp. Even with their backs turned, Newton knows Chuck and Knocker's eyes will have swivelled towards her.

It reminds him of the first time he came in here. He wasn't exactly welcomed with open arms. Conversation had hushed to a murmur and all eyes had fixed on him. They close rank around here when it comes to outsiders. Especially coppers.

The woman orders a large red wine, then disappears to the other side of the bar. Newton wonders who she is. Even in these enlightened times, it takes a certain type of woman to come in a pub like this on her own. He knocks back his whiskey, savouring the heat on his tongue.

He'd hoped for a bit of life in here, some music or a match on the telly. He might get a frame of snooker later, but he isn't really in the mood. He considers picking

Knocker's brains but dismisses that idea too. He takes another swig of his pint.

Pulling out his phone, he finds Louise's number. It rings and rings but she doesn't pick up and seems to have switched off her voicemail. What if he needs her in an emergency? Like now for instance. He scrolls again, picks up his glass and goes outside.

Louise's mother answers straight away. 'Is she there, Jean?'

'If you mean Louise, no.'

'Of course I mean Louise. Where is she?'

'She's gone out.'

'Is Georgie with you?'

'He is, yes.'

'Where's she gone?'

'I don't know James and even if I did, I wouldn't tell you. She doesn't want to talk to you, not until you calm down.'

'Calm down?' Newton would laugh if it wasn't so tragic. 'Did you just tell me to calm down?'

'Have you been drinking?'

'No, I haven't. Look, can I come round and see Georgie? I won't stay long.'

'No. You have been drinking, I can always tell. Anyway, he's in bed.'

'He's staying the night, then? Where is she? Who's she gone out with?'

'It's none of your business. Look, she needs a break from all this stress. If you want my advice, you'll leave her alone, give her some time to herself. I've got to go now James. Bye.'

The line goes dead and Newton wants to punch something. His mother-in-law often has this effect on him but even by her standards this is bang out of order. He boils with rage. Of course it's his business where Louise is, she's his wife for Christ's sake and if she has gone out, who the hell is looking after Lottie?

He's almost tempted to drive over there, to the house Louise is renting rather than live with him but he is on his second pint, not to mention the whiskey and it's not worth the risk of being pulled over by one of his own. In any case, what would be the point? He might get a glimpse through a window but the dog would only get excited or more likely confused.

He downs the rest of his Guinness and makes his way back inside.

'Same again, Dave,' he says, slamming the glass down. Between the pumps at the other side of the bar, he sees the shadow of the mystery woman flicker against the wall.

The landlord takes his glass. 'Another Irish?'

Newton nods. 'Make it a double.'

19

Kate

Kate slops some Sheba into Luther's bowl and shrugs back into her coat. As she pulls the door closed, something catches her eye. The slightest glimmer of light between the trees.

'Who's there?' she calls, not expecting a response. The fields at the bottom of her garden are a popular dogwalkers' spot. Ever the detective, she peers into the darkness. It had looked like the tip of a cigarette, and she should know. She listens but whoever was there has gone. Locking the door, she buttons her coat and walks past her car in the driveway.

Kate breathes in the crisp, cold air. The pit might be long gone but the town is full of retired miners, all claiming their allowance. The smell of coal fills the air, overlaid with the whiff of fireworks, now bonfire night is close. With less artificial light than Sheffield, the heavens are revealed in all their glory. Orion gleams overhead and she can easily pick out the plough. The whole sky appears scattered with diamonds, and even half covered with cloud, the moon lights her way.

There is a point to this trip. With any luck she'll discover something useful and rescue what little reputation she has left but she needs to tread carefully. The visit isn't official. Looking down the street, she wonders which way the killer came. The reporters seem to have gone AWOL and there's no sign of the unmarked car. Taking one last drag, she passes beneath the shop sign, through the gate and into the courtyard. As on their previous visit, Anna is framed in the doorway before she has chance to knock. Following her up the stairs, she notes again the taped-up doors, how stark they look in the dark.

'Forgive me if I leave the lights off. I've got a bit of a headache.' They have reached the living room and Kate stops short at the threshold. The mantelpiece is ablaze with candles, the picture of Anna's mother reflecting light off its frame. A fire burns in the hearth, the scent of wood filling the air. No free coal allowance here, then.

'It's cedar you can smell,' says Anna, as though reading her mind. 'I thought it might clear my head. Please, sit down.'

'You should have said if you don't feel well. It's nothing that can't wait till morning.'

'It's fine.' Anna gestures to the wingback chairs by the fire. 'Let me take your coat.'

Unbuttoning her jacket, Kate is beginning to wonder if this was a good idea or not but the room is pleasantly warm and there is a window open, the curtains stirring in the breeze.

It occurs to her that one of these chairs would normally be occupied by Anna's father. A battered book is spread across one, so she chooses the other, noting the title with approval. *Wuthering Heights* is one of her favourites.

'I hope I haven't disturbed you.'

'Of course not. Is this an official visit?'

'Not really. I just wanted to check you're OK.'

Anna picks up the book and settles into the chair. She looks different tonight, calm and self-possessed, tranquil even. Her hair is up in a bun and her mourning outfit has been replaced with jeans and a dark T-shirt. She looks out of place here, far too modern but a whole lot better than this morning. Grief is a strange thing, Kate has seen its many guises. One minute the bereaved can be hysterical, the next a quiet serenity comes over them, a shock-absorbing numbness. She is just about to ask where Julie Darrow is when Anna stops her.

'I told your colleagues they could go. I don't need babysitting.'

'Yes, they left a message at the station, that's why I thought I'd look in.' The white lie won't hurt but she expected Julie to be here. She shouldn't have left her post no matter how strong the craving for her own bed. Maybe Newton had agreed to it.

'I've told you, I'm fine,' says Anna, marking her place in the book. *Reading in this light won't help her headache*, thinks Kate but she can see how the windswept moors would be a comfort.

'Would you like a drink? I'm having one.' Anna gets up and goes over to the sideboard. The candles don't reach that side of the room but Kate hears the chink of glass and the glug of liquid.

'Whisky or vodka? Or I've got some beers in the fridge?'

'I shouldn't really.'

'Oh, a small one won't hurt.'

'Whisky then. Thank you.'

Anna emerges from the shadows and hands her a glass. Kate feels the bite of scotch on her tongue. She prefers Irish.

'The water of life,' says Anna, as she sits back down. The phrase seems out of place in the circumstances.

'It's an extraordinary room. You obviously love reading.'

'We do.' Kate notes the instinctive use of the plural.

'Although, I prefer books to people.' She stops for a moment, then rushes on. 'We all love to read but my father was never happier than when he was playing cards.' Her voice trails off, as though she has lost the thread of her thoughts. Kate finds it's often best to say the bare minimum and waits until Anna continues.

'He was born in the wrong century,' she finally resumes. 'He cultivated a kind of Victorian gentleman persona. Wilkie Collins was his hero. He'd have you believe we're related — but we aren't. You've probably never heard of him.'

The Woman in White is another of Kate's favourites, but she makes no comment.

'Hence the open fire, the décor. He even wore a pocket watch. I guess the acorn doesn't fall far from the tree. You'd doubtless call us eccentric but it's all I've ever known.'

She gazes into the fire, as a log crackles and shifts and the candles wink on the mantelpiece.

'Playing cards was an extension of that, I suppose. They were his real passion. As far as my father was concerned, there was nothing finer than the smell of a freshly opened deck.'

'Did he do tricks?' asks Kate, thinking suddenly of the shop's name.

'No, that was my grandfather's doing. He was quite the card sharp, or so I'm told. I never met him. He'd have hidden pockets sewn into his clothes, little tucks in the sleeves for stashing things. A stooge on hand, chairs with hollow legs. Not my father's style at all.' This is quite a different account to the one Duffy reported, thinks Kate, as she stops for another sip but she doesn't interrupt her flow. 'Mother used to say my father was bewitched. It used to drive her mad but he never tired of them. He was probably a little bit obsessed.' She points over Kate's shoulder. 'As you'll see from his art collection.'

Kate turns towards the pictures she saw earlier, the firelight dancing off their glass.

'May I take a closer look?'

'Of course.' To her astonishment, Anna leans over and passes her a candlestick. Feeling like a character from a Brontë novel, she stands in the pool of light thrown against the wall. At the top is a medieval queen, her cloak shimmering with jewels. Next is a pair of art deco prints, stark white faces and blocks of black hair, the image reversed beneath in the style of a playing card. Kate makes her way along, her attention caught by another queen, this time unmistakably tarot and she remembers what the old woman told her. In place of a crown, she has horns and a crescent moon at her feet. A high priestess, not a queen. She steps forward and is faced with the woman from her dream. Her hair flows like spilt ink beneath the glass, covering her nakedness. The picture is erotic, sexual. Kate coughs, suddenly conscious of how long she has been staring and turns back to replace the candle on the mantelpiece.

'They're beautiful,' she says. 'And quite valuable, I would imagine.'

'Some of them might be, I don't know.' Anna's tone suggests she doesn't care but Kate isn't sure if it's genuine. 'He was more interested in their beauty than their value.' She takes another sip and Kate raises her glass but only touches her lips to the liquid.

'The most valuable things are kept in a safe, I presume.'

Anna nods, a habit Kate is growing used to.

'But the safe was undisturbed?'

'I'm sure you know the answer to that question, Sergeant Fox.' She looks over her glasses, making Kate feel like a child being reprimanded at school. 'The safe wasn't disturbed and only my father and I know the combination. It would have been impossible to get into.'

'And the cabinets, they weren't disturbed either?'

'That's right. We are insured if you're wondering but it appears theft was not the motive.' She takes another mouthful.

'Just to be certain, we'd like you to carry out an inventory. Julie or I could help.'

Anna swirls the drink around her glass but makes no response. Kate wonders how much she normally puts away, she'll be legless at this rate. Little wonder she didn't hear the murder.

'Are you sure there's nobody we can call to come and stay with you? A friend or someone?'

'I've told you. I'm fine on my own.'

Kate isn't sure what to make of this insistence on being alone. She decides on a change of tack.

'You must have an interesting clientele. I don't think I've ever come across a shop like yours.'

'I think we're quite unique, certainly in this country. There are similar places by the coast but they're more commercial. Tacky.' *So, she's a snob as well,* thinks Kate.

'I was looking at your website earlier. Did you design it?'

'Technology was anathema to my father but we needed to bring the business up to date. We'd had some lean years but things really took off once we went online. It opened a whole new world to us. Quite literally. We have lots of overseas customers now. Enthusiasts from all over Europe and America. My father had many connections. He could get hold of anything.'

Kate stores this information away. It strikes her Anna speaks of the business with pride but there is little warmth in her comments. She decides tact will get her nowhere.

'Can I ask about the weapon?'

Anna leans forward, as though finally she has asked a question worthy of her interest.

'The dagger that was used. Does it not have a sheath and why wasn't it in the safe? It must be worth a fortune.'

Anna sits back with the faintest glimmer of a smile but her face quickly resumes its blankness. 'No it doesn't have a sheath and I would hardly call it a dagger. We use it as a letter opener. You're right, it probably is worth a fortune but it's always left lying around.'

'Where is it usually kept?'

'Anywhere and everywhere. We use it for opening boxes.'

Kate isn't convinced but sees no point pressing her for now.

'And what about tarot?'

'Yes, we sell tarot cards. We've had all sorts of salesmen here, trying to persuade us to stock their tat but we prefer tradition and quality. They were my father's watchwords and his father's before him.'

This little speech is said mechanically, as if by rote. How many times must she have heard it, growing up in a strange place like this.

'And do you read tarot?'

'Me? No, I don't.' Anna looks appalled by the idea.

'It's just I would have thought tarot are quite different

to playing cards and I wondered…'

'Are they so very different?' Anna rises from her chair and picks up the poker, rattling it around in the fireplace. A log bursts into flames, lighting up her face and bouncing off her glasses.

'It was very much diversion not divination for my father. I've told you, he loved all kinds of cards although he drew the line at Top Trumps.' She smiles again at this, then turns and drains her glass. 'Fancy another?'

'No thanks.' Kate hears the clink of glass again but can barely see Anna. She wonders if she ever puts the lights on.

'Your mother read tarot though, didn't she?'

'She did, yes.'

'And she passed away a couple of years ago, I'm told.'

'That's right.' Anna makes her way back across the room, her glass full to the brim.

'Can I ask what she died of?'

'A heart attack but that isn't what killed her.'

'I'm sorry?'

'She had COPD for years. A heavy smoker, like my father.'

'I see. It must be difficult for you. Two years is no time at all to lose both your parents.'

Anna stares into the depths of her glass. She has a habit of not responding to questions she doesn't want to answer. Kate tries another.

'On the night your father died, you'd been out, is that right?'

'Again, you know it is. I've been through this with your boss.' She sounds more tired than annoyed.

'And it was a book club you'd been to?'

'A reading group, at the library.' She tilts her head to

one side. 'Can you hear that?'

So intent has she been on her questioning, the insistent blare of sirens hasn't registered with Kate. Anna dashes to the open window.

'Can you see anything?'

'It's coming from the houses.' Anna pushes the window wide and leans out. 'It's an ambulance.'

'Whereabouts is it?' Kate tries to see but Anna is blocking her view.

'I'm not sure,' says Anna, 'It's one of the old miners' cottages. I can't be certain but I think it's Mrs Wood's.'

Kate's heart jumps at the name. 'Let me see,' she says as Anna steps aside.

Craning her neck, she sees the blue flashing lights but the angle makes it impossible to make out much more.

'I really should be going now anyway. I'll walk that way and check everything is all right. May I have my coat please?'

Anna disappears into the gloom, returning with two jackets. 'I'll come with you.'

'There's no need for us both to trail out.' Even in the semi-dark, it's clear Anna is more than a little worse for wear. Kate heads for the stairs before she can argue. 'Thank you so much for tonight. I'll be in touch.'

'But I wanted to ask —' Anna is halfway down the stairs, clearly surprised at the rapid departure.

'I'll get back to you tomorrow. I promise.'

Kate steps out into the cold, closing the gate behind her. Just a few short steps beyond the soft light of the street lies a deep, fathomless black. She checks her watch and is surprised to see she has passed a full hour without a cigarette. Lighting one, she makes her way cautiously along the pavement. The temperature has dropped and the slabs glitter with frost.

She draws level with the ambulance, its siren now silenced. It is parked against the wall she leaned against this morning, just before she met Margaret Wood.

20

1977

Anna pummels the door, pushing the bell until her finger is numb. She listens intently but all she can hear are the birds and the sound of a bus on the main road. Giving the wood another hammering, she opens the letterbox but all she can see are the black bristles of a draught excluder, clamped like rotten teeth on the other side. Walking to the front of the house, she tries to look through the windows but they're far too high and the nets are too thick to make out anything. She goes back to the door and bangs again, this time with the side of her fist, her knuckles are so raw.

Picking up a jar from the path, she wonders where on earth they can be. She kicks a stone along the pavement, picturing them at the church, whispering something in Latin. She knows they go to mass but can't remember the times. As she makes her way into the village, she skips to keep the stone from the gutter, then lets it drop down a grate.

She gazes through the shop windows. The butcher in his blood-smeared coat leans between links of sausages. Next-door is a pyramid of apples, every other one wrapped in tissue paper. She would love to pull one out and send the whole pile crashing. Maybe she'll suggest it to Marie when she finds her.

She has no intention of going home yet and heads towards the churchyard. Her class came to do brass rubbings here, just before the end of term. Anna hadn't told anyone she knew the names on nearly every headstone.

The contents of the jar are turning brown. Some of the petals are from grass verges and hedgerows but most were pulled from under people's privets. The plan had been to make perfume but Anna has no idea how to do it and there is no point without Marie. Licking her stinging knuckles, she thinks of all the people buried beneath her, what their lives must have been like. She is about to turn back when from the corner of her eye, she sees a figure flit between the stones.

'Marie!' she shouts, almost dropping the jar. Running across the grass, she heads for where she had seen her. At the end of a row is a large, pillared monument, its columns a tangle of weeds. She is certain it was this one but suddenly feels wary, standing here among the graves.

'Got you!' Anna jumps as Marie springs out. 'I've been following you for ages! Didn't you see me?'

'No, I didn't,' replies Anna, unsure whether to believe her. 'Where have you been?'

'I haven't been anywhere. What's that you've got? Let's have a smell.'

Anna knows she is avoiding her question but she untwists the lid and holds the jar out.

'Ughh! That stinks!' shrieks Marie and they both start giggling. 'Shh! This is consecrated ground!' Marie grabs the jar and places it behind an angel. 'Let's leave it there to ferment in holy sacrilege. What shall we do?'

'I don't know, you decide.'

'We could go to Never Fear.'

A stab of unease flickers in Anna's belly. 'Oh, I don't fancy going there.'

'You said *I* could decide! Come on, it's only right!'

They walk back through the village, the shops even busier now. As the houses thin out, they stop to pat the horses in the field. They carry on down the hill, along by the wire fence and over a stile. Wheat sways in every direction, in green-gold rows. They once walked all the way into the middle, it took them ages to get out. They stick to the path now, which is peppered with rabbit droppings. As they walk, Marie pulls at the nodding stalks.

'We could make some bread,' she grins, shoving it into her pockets.

'It's not ripe,' says Anna, not knowing if this is true. 'Besides, you shouldn't touch it. The farmer won't like it.'

'He might shoot us!' says Marie and they both snigger.

The hedgerow is thick with mother-die. Anna knows you mustn't pick this plant and never ever take it home. Birds fly in and out with twigs in their beaks and in amongst the branches are plump, dark blackberries. Marie tugs one off and bites into it, making her lips go red. Anna knows they will be sour but she does the same.

'I can't wait to dip my feet in the water,' she says, wiping her hands down her top.

'Me too!' says Marie, through a mouth full of purple mush.

Running the rest of the way, they throw themselves onto the banking. Breathless and sweaty, they pull off their shoes and race to get their feet in first.

Never Fear is an ancient millpond. Stunted trees surround it and tall, brown grasses. The water is green, flies and midges hovering on its surface. The girls plunge their feet in, gasping at the cold. The water ripples then calms again, smooth as a mirror.

'We'll call it a draw,' says Marie and Anna splashes

her, making her squeal with delight. She wants to bottle this moment, like the petals in the jar. Soaking wet and with their feet still submerged, they stretch across the sun-baked earth. The mill is hidden from here but Anna knows it is there in the trees. She has seen it in her father's books with the huge wheel churning. Propping herself on an elbow, she sees a kingfisher dart past and a moorhen floats between the reeds. Her clothes soon begin to dry in the heat, the weeds brushing her legs. Marie's head droops and she falls asleep, snoring with her mouth wide open. Careful not to disturb her, Anna slides her feet from the water and walks along the edge. Picking up a stone, she skims it across the pond, wondering why this place is always so deserted.

A dark mist of flies blurs the water's edge and something solid catches her eye. Something black, bobbing. As she draws nearer, the buzzing intensifies and a sickening unease gnaws her stomach. She picks up a stick, looking back to see if Marie is still asleep but she can't tell from here. Swatting at the flies she pokes the crawling blackness, gasping as the stick hits something soft. Prodding, she wiggles it back and forth against the object's surface. As it moves, she sees the gleam of wet fur. Stifling a scream, she drops the stick and almost falls headfirst into the pond. Scrambling backwards, she lands on her bottom. She must not let Marie see this. She gets to her feet but it's too late, she has woken up and is coming towards her.

'No!' the scream pours out of her and Anna realises she is crying. 'Don't look!'

She tries to push her away, flattened ears of wheat tumbling from her pockets but Marie wants to see and heaves her aside. Stumbling to the water's edge, she sinks to her knees.

Anna can hardly bear to look as she grabs a piece of string and starts to wind it around her fingers. Slowly, horribly, the dripping body of Oscar pulls clear of the water. At first, she thinks there are weeds clinging to him but then she sees the tangled threads are his innards. A great chunk of his guts is missing, half his belly torn away.

As though blind to the horror, Marie probes his fur, batting at the flies as she tries to get some purchase on the string around his neck.

With every tug the limp body jerks and dances, giving the illusion he is still alive. At last the knot comes free and Marie throws the string into the pond. It floats for a second then sinks.

Taking off her cardigan, she gathers up the slippery parts and folds Oscar into it, cradling him like a baby. Anna thinks how brave she is, how fearless, always knowing what to do. Fumbling with her sandals, she sees her hands are shaking, unlike Marie's which were steady as a rock even as she freed the mangled kitten from its noose.

She wraps him up tightly, just like they did with the crow and Anna knows she will want to bury him. They don't speak, walking through the fields like a funeral procession. Even the birds have stopped singing.

21

Kate

With a strong sense of déjà vu, Kate grinds her cigarette beneath her heel and makes her way up the overgrown garden. Light spills from the open door, urgent voices coming from within.

She calls from the step, 'Hello!'

A woman in her twenties appears. She is clearly upset and from the size of her stomach, about eight months pregnant.

Kate holds out her warrant card and steps inside. 'DS Fox, North Derbyshire Police. I was passing and saw the ambulance.'

The woman steps aside and Kate peers into the living room. Two paramedics are knelt on the carpet. Between them lies the lifeless body of Margaret Wood.

One of the medics removes the blue plastic pads of a defibrillator from her chest. He stands and looks past Kate into the hallway.

'I'm sorry, miss. Nothing we could do. I think she's been gone for a while.'

Already, the lips have shrunk into a rictus grin but the eyes are still half open. With a practised sweep of the hand, the paramedic closes them. An IV line sticks out of her arm and a streak of blood has stained the carpet. The buttons of her dress are ripped open, the shrivelled breasts exposed.

She turns to the woman weeping behind her.

'Did you call the ambulance?'

'Yes.'

'And you are?'

She takes a deep breath inward, tries to gather herself. 'Alice Ashby. I'm her great niece.'

'Well, I'm very sorry for your loss. You should probably sit down. Shall we go into the kitchen?'

Alice nods and heads down the hallway.

Kate turns back to the medics, who are zipping Mrs Wood into a body bag. Only this morning, she had sat here discussing death with her.

'What was it, do you think?'

'Heart attack would be my guess,' says one of them, as they hoist the bag onto a trolley, 'Might need a PM with it being at home but at this age…' He shrugs and leaves the sentence unfinished.

'OK. I'll look after Miss Ashby.' As she makes her way towards the kitchen, Newton's words pop into Kate's head. *I would have thought this was your forte, dealing with stressed out women.* She thanks God she didn't drink more than a sip of that scotch. Pushing open the door, she sees Alice at the sink.

'Let me do that,' she says, grabbing the tea pot. The kitchen takes her right back to childhood. To the smell of baking, the constant activity of knitting and sewing. Hands that were always busy, the kettle permanently on. An earthenware bowl stands on the worktop just like one of Gran's and a shopping list is stuck to the freezer, a 'Skegness' magnet holding it in place. She lights the gas and pulls a chair out.

'Sit down, you've had a shock.' A thought occurs to her. 'You should have let the paramedics check you out. They're probably still here.'

'I'm all right.' Alice lowers herself onto a chair, her legs splayed either side of her bump. Kate quickly pours the tea and brings it to the table.

'You don't take sugar, do you?'

Alice shakes her head and grabs one of the mugs. She slurps noisily, tears still running down her cheeks.

Kate wonders how best to handle this. Should she mention her visit this morning, or should she stick to what has happened tonight? Pulling a packet of Kleenex from her pocket, she pushes it across the table.

'How many weeks are you?'

'Thanks. Thirty-five.'

'A few weeks to go yet then.' She pauses as Alice blows her nose. 'Were you close?'

'Yes. She's my Grandad's sister. She's been knitting for the baby. They're a bit old fashioned but I never have the heart to say so. She didn't have kids of her own.'

Kate remains silent as Alice sips her tea. There is no wedding ring on her finger. Instead a tattoo of a serpent snakes from her sleeve across her hand. There is a definite family resemblance around the eyes to Mrs Wood.

'Has she been ill?' she ventures.

'No, she's never ill. That's what I don't understand.' Frown marks appear between her brows. 'I spoke to her at teatime. She's been convinced all along it's a girl and was doing one final thing, a christening gown like the one she made for me and my mum. She said it was a bit complicated but she'd managed to dig out the pattern. She sounded fine.'

'And what happened when you got here?'

'Well, she said come round anytime but I was busy with my little boy, Joe.' She pauses, wiping her eyes, as though thinking carefully. 'Then I put him to bed and was waiting for my partner Aidan to get home from work, so it was later than planned when I got here. I expected the latch to be down, but it wasn't. I thought that was strange, as it was after dark and then I found her.' Another tear trickles down her cheek.

'Would you mind showing me where?' asks Kate.

Her expression becoming puzzled now, Alice pushes up from the table and leads the way. Kate had already noticed the fire wasn't lit and the curtains were drawn. The room is cold but otherwise the same as this morning, the chair by the window, the semi-circle of photographs. All unchanged except for the knitting on the floor and the bloodstain on the carpet.

'Where was she when you came in?'

'She was here.' Alice points to the armchair Mrs Wood had sat in earlier. 'She was slumped with her head down and the knitting on her knee. Look, why all this interest? It must have been a heart attack or something, she was eighty-five.' She glares at Kate, her eyes so like her great aunt's.

'I'm just piecing things together in case there's an inquest, with her dying at home,' she bends and picks up the needlework. The stitches are spread across both needles, in the middle of a row. Kate used to knit, her grandmother taught her, so she appreciates the work that's gone into it, the intricacy of the pattern.

'She was clearly an expert needlewoman,' she says, gathering up the yarn. 'And it was on her knee you say?'

'Yes. I threw it off to see if she was breathing and I thought she might be, so I phoned for an ambulance.'

Kate walks over to the hard-backed chair by the window. There on the sill, almost hidden beneath the folds of the curtain, is what she expected she might find but hoped she wouldn't. A cable needle, short and double pointed, the kind used for twisting stitches. Pushing it back, she parts the curtains briefly as though looking out, then walks back to where Alice is standing.

'I'm sure you did everything you could.'

22

1977

Anna wipes sweat from her forehead as she plucks another daisy, carefully splitting the fragile stalk with her fingernail, threading it onto the rest. Jack lies sphinx-like beside her, ears pricked forward, scanning the land for rabbits. The fields are riddled with them here and just the slightest sniff and he'll be off.

She looks across at Marie, who is lying flat on her back staring up at the sky.

'You still haven't told me what Father Vincent said.'

Marie turns over with a sigh. 'He said Oscar is like the lost lamb but I'm not to be sad because the shepherd has found him. He's with Jesus now.' Pulling up a handful of grass, she runs the seed heads through her fingers.

'He's an angel,' she continues. 'A dark angel.' Suddenly, she turns to Anna, a half- smile playing on her lips.

'Do you know how many buttons there are on a priest's cassock?'

Anna isn't surprised at this rapid change of direction. They are on familiar territory and to ensure she keeps up, she has been reading her father's copy of The Layman's Catholic Treasure.

'Thirty-three,' she says, unable to hide her pride.

'Brilliant!' says Marie, clearly impressed. 'But I bet you don't know why.'

'I do. It's one for every year of Jesus's life.'

'Wow Anna! You have been swotting!' They both know she looks things up. It's part of the game they play.

'And what about the other buttons?'

'What other buttons?' Anna must have missed that bit.

'Father Vincent showed me. He's got five on each sleeve, for the wounds He suffered on the cross.' Marie's face becomes sombre, as it always does when she talks about Jesus. Anna wishes she had a pound for every time she mentions either him or Father Vincent. 'And He is always written with a capital. I'm sure you've seen that in your books.' Squinting into the sun, Marie gets up, brushing grass from her socks. 'Come on, I'm sick of this godforsaken place!' She is off before Anna can get to her feet, dropping the daisies behind her.

'Where are we going?'

'The forest!' Marie shouts this like a battle cry as they hurtle past the herd of cows munching by the hedgerow, Jack arcing around them, his tail flying like a banner. The grass is cropped short here and studded with cowpats and droppings. Stepping carefully, they come to a wooden bridge and Anna quickens her pace to get to the other side.

Marie's belief in the power of prayer had convinced her Oscar would be found. When they had reached Ochre Dyke, Anna imagined his little body drifting in the weeds or wedged in the stones at the water's edge. She looks straight ahead now, afraid if she looks down, she will see him floating by, even though she knows this is impossible. They buried him half a mile away.

At the far side of the bridge, a flight of worn steps is set into the bank. Anna climbs behind Marie, her breath becoming ragged. Jack leaps past, keen to reach the summit first. He looks down from the top with his tongue lolling out, then bounds away.

As they reach the top of the hill, the trees come into view. Marie calls it the forest but its real name is

Hangman's Wood. The first time she had heard this, Anna was secretly worried. The same as she was about Never Fear. She can't quite believe real places have such names but it adds to the excitement. They sound scary but they aren't.

Jack runs off into the trees and she hears him crashing through the undergrowth. It is cooler as they enter the woods, their arms stained green by the shadows. A frayed rope hangs from a branch and she pictures a man swinging there, his feet dangling above the ground. She tells herself it's just a Tarzan swing as they sidestep carefully around it.

The floor spreads before them in a carpet of bluebells. They wade through the cold heads, covering their legs in cuckoo spit but Anna loves the wildness here, how far away she feels from the village. The trees press in, the track narrowing so they have to walk Indian file, her skin itching from the midges and nettles.

After a while, the path splays out and she tears up a dock leaf, rubbing it roughly against her. A canopy of silver birch soars above them and she tilts her head to see the pearly trunks stretching up to the light. A shattered oak leans towards them, struck by lightning by the looks of it and completely hollowed out. An ideal place for a fox to make its den, or perhaps a badger. Pulling burrs from her cardigan, she peers inside but it's empty apart from a few blown leaves.

Marie picks up a stick and begins swiping at the vegetation, beating a path for them.

'This way,' she says, veering off between the trees.

Anna follows, Jack stuck close to her side. Apart from his panting, the only sounds are the ticking insects and the squelch of their feet in the mud.

'We never usually come this way.'

Marie doesn't answer but has slowed down and continues to swipe at the brambles.

'Are we lost?'

'No!' Marie turns, walking backwards for a moment. 'Stop panicking!'

Anna continues to follow, her eyes on Marie's shoulder blades. She doesn't like this part of the woods. The trees look primeval and the air is rank, as though something has died here. She is about to insist they turn back when Marie stops so abruptly, she almost collides with her. Half hidden in the twisting branches, are the crumbling remains of a house.

'I told you we hadn't been this way before!'

'Wait!' says Marie. 'We need to be careful.'

Anna grabs Jack's collar as they edge forward, Marie holding the stick out in front of her. There is no roof, just an angle formed by the two remaining walls. Halfway up is a glassless window, tendrils of ivy and weeds spilling from the frame like old curtains. The edge of the wall looks like teeth where the bricks have broken and collapsed.

Marie works her way along, using the stick to test the ground. The earth slopes away from them, so that when they reach the other side, another level is revealed below.

Someone has been here recently. The weeds are trampled but any paint the door once had is gone, the wood warped and pitted. There is a hole where the handle must have been but the hinges are still in place. Jack barks as Anna pushes it open, darting across the threshold. She leans in, a dank, peaty scent filling her nostrils. As her eyes adjust to the gloom, she sees him sniffing the floor, light banding his fur through the rafters.

'Who do you think used to live here?'

'I don't know and I don't care,' says Marie, for once standing back. 'I'm not going in. I'll stay here and keep watch.' She holds the stick slantways across her chest, as though ready to defend them.

Stepping inside, Anna stares at the fragments of wallpaper clinging to the walls. A pattern of birds and branches is just visible, like a pale imitation of the woods, speckled and streaked with damp. A length of rusty pipework skirts the floor, which is dry as though someone has swept it. Looking up, she sees a polythene sheet has been tucked between the beams to make the place waterproof.

Jack disappears round a corner and she follows, eyes squeezed shut in dread of what she might see. Opening them, she sees a foldaway bed, covers as neat as any bedroom. Feeling the wet of Jack's nose in her palm, she takes in the dark blue blanket, the white pillow. At one side of the bed is a camping stove, at the other an upturned orange-box, and now she stops, her hand rigid on Jack's collar. On top of the box is an ashtray, the letters stark against the base. *Park Drive.* Suddenly her heart is banging, her breath tight in her chest. She turns and runs from the room.

23

Kate

It's well after ten by the time Kate has walked Alice back to her flat. A thickset man, presumably her boyfriend, was looking out of the window. She wonders what she will tell him about her aunt's death.

They found two sets of keys in Mrs Wood's kitchen and she has kept hold of one, 'just in case'. Alice is clearly intelligent and Kate was relieved she didn't ask what 'just in case' might mean. She'd noticed the line of her questioning and she couldn't afford to give any further cause for alarm, not until she is sure. Which is why she must act fast. She can't have the family suspecting foul play if there isn't any.

The moon is covered with cloud and Kate places her feet almost blindly between the broken plant pots. Stepping inside, the house is pitch black and silent. She pulls a torch from her pocket, following its beam to the chair Mrs Wood apparently died in. Pushing the knitting aside, she sinks to her knees and slides her hands around the back and sides of the cushion, feeling for anything that might have dropped beneath. There is nothing. No crumbs, no fluff, no lost coins. Probably to be expected in such a tidy house. Her eyes fall onto the drawers down the centre of the sideboard. Reaching again into her pocket, she pulls out a pair of latex gloves. With the torch between her teeth, she slips them on and opens the top drawer. A collection of pens lies to one side, a writing pad and cheque book aligned symmetrically beside them. Shoved to the back is a pack of dog-eared playing cards. Kate wonders who the old woman played with or maybe she passed the time with patience when she wasn't spying at the window. She closes the drawer and tries the middle one. Here she finds a photo album and a long, tapestried sheath with a press stud fastening. As expected, it contains knitting needles, her gran owned something similar. The last drawer reveals what she is looking for, Mrs Wood's knitting patterns. She carefully picks up the top one. It has been folded in half at some point and is creased and yellowed with age. In the corner is printed *3 pence*, below a faded picture of a christening gown, covered all over with intricate lace and cables.

Replacing the pattern, she lets the torch drop from her mouth and takes out her phone. No matter how late it is, this can't wait.

The phone rings but he doesn't pick up. *Come on* thinks Kate, *Answer the bloody thing.* She imagines Newton curled up with his wife, watching some sophisticated rom-com. She hasn't met his wife but assumes she'll be attractive. She's about to give up when the ringing stops and Newton's voice, sounding muffled, hollers down the line, 'Who is it? What do you want?'

'Sir. I'm sorry to disturb you but there's something I need you to see.' He doesn't reply, so she continues. 'There's been another death and I'm afraid it's one of the residents I spoke to this morning. Can you meet me at number nine, High Street? It's next-door to the Trick Shop?'

She hears the trickle of water, then the line goes dead.

'Oh, cheers!' she says out loud to the empty room. 'Thanks a frigging bunch!'

With a final sweep of the torch, she locks the door behind her, pocketing the keys. She will return them to Alice at some point but for now she intends to keep them.

A noise from the street startles her and she turns, at once alert.

'Hello?' Peering into the darkness, she steps forward. There it is again, from the other side of the wall. A shuffling then a thud and a muttered curse.

This is all I need! A bloody drunk! She checks her bag but knows she hasn't any cuffs on her and at five foot one, is ill prepared to tackle a pissed-up wino. She stands listening but whoever is there has gone quiet. Perhaps they've fallen asleep, or worse, unconscious. Either way, she's had enough tonight and really needs her bed. She strides down the path, braces herself, then swings around the wall, stopping dead at the sight before her.

For a second, she thinks she is seeing things. Stretched across the pavement, legs splayed, flies wide open is Newton.

'Sir!' Running forward, she crouches beside him. A gust of booze hits her as he turns his face.

A low rumbling comes from his throat and she realises he is laughing, the rollicking, carefree laughter of the drunk. He throws his head back, banging it on the pavement and stops abruptly.

'Come on sir, let's get you up.' Her hands on his shoulders, Kate is relieved when he starts to sit up, not least because in this position his boxer shorts are no longer visible through his zip.

The glare of the streetlight above them is unforgiving. Aside from the gaping flies, Newton's hair stands in tufts and there is a wet patch down his trousers but the bang to the head must have sobered him slightly. Lifting his hand to inspect for damage, he looks surprised, as though only just registering her presence.

'Is that… you, Kate?' His words are slurred, his face

creased with confusion. Kate steps back, utterly shocked. Newton may be old school but in the short time she has known him, she has grown to admire and respect him and she trusts him implicitly. In that instant she makes a decision. Whatever has happened, whatever the cause, she must get him off the street and ensure no-one else sees him like this.

She hasn't a hope of getting him upright without his cooperation but has dealt with enough drunks in her time to be confident she can move him. Bending at the knees, she shoves her arms under his oxters and slowly pulls him towards her.

'Come on,' she says again, this time firmly, locking her eyes onto his. He seems to understand her intention, even in this addled state. On the second pull, he follows her momentum and rises from the pavement.

The sound of voices comes up the street and it suddenly occurs to Kate where he must have been. The Miners Arms. It's almost closing time and people will be starting to leave, she needs to move quickly. Newton hiccups and sways, sending them staggering sideways. She puts an arm around him and grasps a fistful of shirt. Using the wall to support them, she pulls him the few steps back into Mrs Wood's garden. His feet crunch the gravel, clattering into the pots. Swearing, Kate grabs him and steers him towards the house.

The voices are coming closer, a man and a woman arguing. Newton lurches forward, landing awkwardly on the step.

As the couple draw level, Kate ducks her head and prays they're too distracted to care what's going on here. In the darkness they might not even notice. But then what, thinks Kate, looking down at her boss. He isn't even capable of walking straight and is far too unsteady for her to safely guide him anywhere.

Standing over him, she grabs his collar and turns his face up towards her. Pressing her finger to her lips, she wills him to stay quiet as the couple walk by.

'I'm sick of it, Kev!' shouts the woman, the man's response unintelligible. Seconds pass, Kate's heart hammering in her ears. The voices drift across the bottom of the path, then fade up the street with their footsteps.

There is just enough light to see Newton's expression. He looks like a child sitting there on the doorstep. Fully aware of the irregularity, Kate can think of no alternative. Pulling out the key, she leans over him and unlocks the door.

For the fourth time today, Kate finds herself inside the home of the recently departed Margaret Wood. This time she switches the light on. They can't risk stumbling around in the dark with Newton in this tangle. As if reading her thoughts, he rolls back across the threshold, colliding with the wall then somehow gets to his knees. From his furtive movements she guesses he's trying to fasten his trousers.

Hauling him up, she sees he hasn't succeeded. She pushes him through the living room door, where he lands on the sofa. He slumps against the cushions, his eyes immediately falling closed. Caffeine, that's what he needs and plenty of water.

Still clutching the torch, she makes her way down the hall to the kitchen. As she turns on the tap, the sheer madness of what she is doing hits her. She believes this house is a crime scene, a crime of the utmost seriousness. Murder, for God's sake. Which probably took place in the last few hours, if her suspicions are correct. So why is she, a detective sergeant, holed up here in the dead of night, with her drunken superior officer? She puts the kettle on and leans against the worktop, trying to marshal her thoughts. The consequences, the repercussions of such irresponsible behaviour do not bear thinking about but what choice did she have, given the circumstances? Ought she have left him there in the street, for all the world to see? Damage limitation, that's what this is. She just hopes Newton will see that when he comes to his senses.

She has already touched enough surfaces to see no reason to worry about fingerprints. All the same, she slips the latex gloves back on and works by torchlight. The mugs she and Alice used are still in the sink. Leaving them there, she takes fresh ones from the cupboard and makes two black coffees. She could murder a cigarette but puffing smoke from the doorstep is probably not a great idea. With the torch again lodged between her teeth, she picks up the coffees and returns to the living room. The door has swung closed, so she pushes it open with the tip of her boot. Newton is where she left him, propped slantways on the sofa. His head lolls, a string of drool hanging from his chin.

How the hell is she going to handle this? As a uniformed officer in Sheffield, drunks were meat and drink to her. Friday nights were the worst, especially after pay day. Most were harmless enough, singing and dancing in the street, embracing strangers as they made their way merrily home. Others rolled about in the gutter, shitting in shop doorways, having sex against the bins. Brawling and falling, sometimes seriously injuring not only themselves but others. She thought she'd seen it all.

She takes a mouthful of coffee as she looks down at

Newton. His hands cover his crotch but she can smell the piss from here, along with the stink of whiskey. Her eyes trail over his unlaced shoes, coming to rest on his face. His lashes are dark against his skin, his jaw smudged with stubble. She takes in the deep grooves around his mouth, the cleft in his chin.

Placing the mug down, she takes a deep breath. 'Sir! Newton!' She shakes his shoulders, at first gently, then more roughly, jolting his head back and forth. There is still no response, so she slaps his cheeks, once, twice. He comes to at that, with a torrent of gibberish. Squinting, he lifts his hand to shield his eyes from the overhead light, then quickly closes them. Kate is familiar with the drunk's reluctance, the shame. She gives him a moment, then with a light touch on his shoulder, her voice softer now, she says his name again and he opens his eyes. Sitting up, he reaches for the mug, his movements slow and deliberate, his head hung over the steam.

'Drink it sir. It'll sober you up.' He gulps deeply, gasping as the scalding liquid makes its impact. Replacing the mug carefully on the table, as though with an extreme effort of will, he raises his head and looks at her. His eyes veer left, then right, then back to her.

'Where are we?' His voice is steadier than Kate expected. She is relieved to hear the familiar authority in it. She takes another sip of her coffee, playing for time. She has no idea what to say.

'Where are we?' She jumps, the words a booming demand, her mug overturning on her sleeve and the arm of the chair.

Newton's hand flies to his temple. 'I'm sorry,' he mutters, as Kate mops at the spillage with a tissue from her pocket. He stands up, swaying only slightly.

'I'll ask you again Kate. Where the hell are we?'

24

Newton

All he wants to do is crash out and sleep but there isn't a cat in hell's chance of that. Through half closed eyes, he sees her kick the door open, with a torch between her teeth. The smell of coffee makes him nauseous, but he doesn't react, remaining still on the sofa.

He needs time to think but his mind is like soup. Did he really have that much to drink? He can usually handle it. The whiskey he necked can't have helped and then with a jolt he remembers. God knows how many pills he'd taken. He groans inwardly.

Eyes still closed, he breathes deeply as though oxygen alone might sober him. He'd been about to go home and then those lads came in and challenged him to a frame of snooker. Best of three had turned into best of five. Before he knew it, he could hardly see the balls. Kate's face looms, looking down on him in the gutter and he shrinks with shame. The image is cut off as she is shaking him. Then she slaps him hard, twice across the side of his head.

He can't pretend to be asleep after that and sits up, not wanting to face her but knowing he must. He can't believe what she's just done but is in no position to complain.

The room is spinning but he's certain he has never set foot in this place before. He bends his head over the steaming mug and is about to take a sip when he sees the stain down the front of his trousers. Oh God, he remembers. He was having a pee when she called. He takes two gulps of coffee, more than he intends. It burns but the shock seems to galvanise him. He needs to retrieve this situation but right now he hasn't a clue how.

He asks her where they are. When she doesn't reply, he repeats the question, this time so loud she spills her drink. His head hurts. As Kate cleans up the spill he gets to his feet, willing himself to take charge. Focusing on the mantelpiece, he keeps his head still until the room rights itself. He has been drunk many times before and passed for sober.

'I'll ask you again, where are we?'

Kate replaces the sodden tissue in her pocket and looks at him.

'We are at the home of a possible witness, who may also have become our latest murder victim. Sir, your flies are undone.'

Newton twists away, catching his foot against the coffee table. He stumbles but manages to right himself and with his back towards her, pulls his zip up.

'I'll fetch some water,' says Kate. Relieved she has left the room, Newton falls back onto the sofa. He hangs his head from shame and the pain in his temples. He hears a tap being run in the kitchen and drawers being opened. Within seconds she is back.

'Here, take these. Drink it all.' She shoves two paracetamols into one hand, a pint of water in the other. Newton gulps them down, quickly draining the glass.

'Take as long as you need.'

She must have me down as a complete idiot, thinks Newton, clamping his eyes back shut. Can she be trusted to keep this to herself, or will it be all round the station? That can't be allowed to happen. He opens his eyes and arranges his features into what he hopes is a semblance of authority.

'What did you say before about a witness and a murder?'

Kate bites her lip. He can tell she wants a cigarette.

'I tried to call you.' Yes, he knows she did, making him piss down his trousers. He nods for her to continue.

'I came here this morning, on my house-to-house enquiries.' She retrieves her bag from the floor and takes out a notebook. Flicking through the pages, he can tell she isn't reading whatever is written there. 'I spoke to the occupant, an elderly lady, Mrs Margaret Wood. She knew the Collins family and had seen our vehicles.' As she pauses Newton notes how bright her eyes are, her cheeks flushed. 'The thing is, Mrs Wood died this evening. That's what I wanted to tell you.'

The room shifts behind her. Newton ignores it.

'You said she was old?'

'Yes.'

'Spit it out Kate, we haven't got all night.'

'Sorry, I know sir. Well, the thing is, she'd been knitting when they found her, quite a complicated pattern. My gran used to knit, so I know she'd probably need a pattern in front of her but she would *definitely* need a cable needle. She had neither.'

Newton's head is pounding. There appears to be a lag between her words and his brain's attempts to make sense of them. But the caffeine has cleared his mind considerably and the uncomfortable realisation is dawning that whatever is going on here, Kate has saved him from a great deal of embarrassment. He needs to keep her on side.

'You're going to have to explain what any of this has to do with us,' he says, keeping his voice low and calm.

Kate stands up and indicates the armchair by the fire.

'She was found here, with the knitting in her lap.' Her arms are outstretched, as though imploring Newton to understand. 'She was right in the middle of a row of cables,' she swallows. 'They're a kind of twisted pattern and it's impossible to do them without a third needle. A *cable* needle.' Baffled, Newton watches as she crosses to the window. She slips a latex glove on and slides her hand under the curtain.

'I found this here.' Kate holds aloft a double pointed steel pin, about four inches long. 'I've checked in case another one might have dropped down the cushions but there's nothing sir and there's no way she could have done that row without one.' She looks at him intently. 'Are you sober enough to understand me?'

'Understand *what?*' Again, his voice comes out louder than he intends. Kate flinches and suddenly he has to get out of the room. He staggers through to the kitchen, filling a glass at the sink. Drinking thirstily, he fills it again and again, until he is gasping, his shirt soaked though. Then he turns the tap on full and sticks his head beneath it, tilting his face from side to side so the freezing jet hits his temples. Once his head feels numb enough, he turns off the tap, water dripping from his nose onto the mugs in the sink.

A bright flare of pain stabs him in the spine. Gritting his teeth, he grabs a tea towel, rocking his hips gently as he rubs his hair dry. Walking back into the living room he finds Kate by the sideboard, a photo frame in her still gloved hand.

'Do you feel better for that?' She says, replacing the picture. Newton is only now beginning to process what she has been telling him, her words finally penetrating his consciousness. Sitting down, he drapes the towel over the wet patch on his trousers and clears his throat.

'Thank you, for what you've done tonight.'

'I didn't know what to do for the best, sir.'

'I can appreciate that. I've made quite a fool of myself.'

'Not really. It's nothing we haven't all done, and it could have turned out a lot worse.'

Newton isn't sure he agrees with this. His head and his back throb in unison.

'You mustn't think me ungrateful.'

Indebted, more like.

'But we shouldn't be in this house, Kate, and if what you're saying is true, we're going to have to think very carefully about what we do next.'

He can see from her face she knows exactly what he's getting at.

'This actually couldn't be much worse, Kate.'

'I couldn't just leave you there in the street.'

'Maybe it's what I deserved,' says Newton, but he doesn't mean it. He cannot lose his job, of that he is certain. He looks down at the tea towel, appalled at the thought of how Louise would react if she found out about this. Not to mention his boss, Vardy.

'Start from the beginning and tell me what you were doing here in the first place.'

Kate recounts the events of the evening, starting with her visit to Anna Collins and ending up here, noting as he listens, her gift of recall, how precise her memory is. He knows the account will be perfectly accurate.

'Well, I'm glad you seem to have won Anna over but I can't pretend to have a clue about knitting. It seems an enormous leap to suspect murder based solely on the position of a needle.'

'I know, sir.' Kate has made more coffee and Newton takes a large gulp, determined to further excise the alcohol from his body.

'So, what are you suggesting and how can it be linked to what happened to Collins?'

'I'm not sure but I think it must be. When I was here this morning, there was something she wasn't telling me. She had her chair by the window, a proper old snoop. Maybe she saw something, I don't know.' She grips her mug as though warming her hands on it. The temperature in the room has dropped significantly.

'Her niece told me she'd done the design before, so she wouldn't necessarily have needed the pattern all the time. But she couldn't have done that row without a cable needle. It would be impossible, sir. I think the knitting was placed in her hands afterwards.'

'Could she have sat down to do her knitting and forgotten she'd left the needle on the windowsill?'

'I suppose so,' replies Kate, her expression suddenly despondent.

'I'm not convinced, Kate. The fact is, whether it happened or not, there's no way we can have this house swept for evidence now. Our DNA and fibres will be everywhere.'

'I know, sir.'

'And your valiant attempts with the gloves have been pointless.'

'I just thought prints would be the most incriminating thing we could leave. I wasn't really thinking.'

'Well, we need to think now.' Newton is doing his best to avoid this sounding like a reprimand. He wills himself to stay calm. 'We're going to have to let this go, Kate.'

His words drop into the silence and she stares at him, her eyes unfathomable. That isn't true, he knows exactly what he sees there. Contempt. Disgust. He doesn't blame her. What kind of man is he? One that is willing to cover up a possible murder, purely and simply to save his own skin.

25

Anna

Sunlight filters through her eyelids but Anna makes no effort to get out of bed. It's not like anyone will know. Her head feels like it's been hit with a blunt machete. She buries her face in the pillow. She hates hangovers. The wasted days and the guilt. Yet this one she can surely forgive herself. The same as yesterday and the day before.

She'd taken a drink up to bed with her, intending no more than a nightcap. She had known which house the ambulance was at, feeling only a passing curiosity as she fell asleep. If you could call it sleep. The nightcap had led to a bottle and with every successive glass she had welcomed oblivion.

She dozes for a while and is woken by a sound outside. Still half asleep, she goes to the window. A police car is parked by the kerb, its blue and yellow chequerboard doors obscene against the leaves in the road.

How dare they come in a squad car? Is she under surveillance? Is she a suspect? They have taken away all but one pair of her shoes. The thought shocks her and she sits down heavily on the bed.

She ought to enquire about the ambulance, at least look as though she cares. Picking up her phone, she sees three missed calls and voicemails from a number she doesn't recognise. She presses a key and listens.

'You've missed two appointments, Anna, so if you don't make the next, we'll have to remove you from our services. You've been doing well, we don't want to do

that, so I hope we'll see you on Monday.'

Deleting the message, she tosses the phone aside. Within seconds, the shrill of the landline rings through the ceiling below. Will they give her no peace? The news will be everywhere by now. Whoever it is, they're persistent but the ringing stops eventually.

Looking at the clock she sees half the day is gone. She steps onto the landing, throwing off her nightshirt as she goes. She can walk around naked if she wants to. In the shower, she smiles at what her parents would say.

By the time she is dressed, her headache is fading and Anna feels strangely restless. What was she thinking, lying in bed when there are so many things to be done? She should make a list, get organised. She grabs at the idea, desperate to keep her mind occupied.

Going in search of paper and a pen, she stops at the living room door. Last night's candles have guttered into cold puddles of wax, dripping into the hearth like stalactites. Fetching a dustpan, she clears it all away, tipping the mess into the grate, then brushing it into the bin. She finds the task soothing and is conscious of her mother watching her from the mantelpiece as she works. *Make sure you do it properly, Anna. Get into the corners, that's right.*

Once the ashes are swept, she lays fresh wood and stands back, catching her breath. It might be soothing but it's hard work. Maybe now she can make enquiries about having a gas fire fitted.

At this mutinous thought, she makes herself a cup of strong black coffee and sits down at the card table. It feels appropriate somehow to do it here. Taking the lid off her pen, she turns to a fresh page and thinks. Her father would want an obituary, she is sure of that. She makes a note to ring the local paper on Monday. They won't be open today.

But how can she write an obituary? People will be queueing up to read it. *Murdered in his own home.* Her body stiffens at the thought of his death certificate. Nothing as mundane as a heart attack or a stroke for her father.

She throws the pen down and pushes the notepad aside. There must be something practical she can do. She could start on his clothes, choose something for him to be buried in. The thought depresses her. She pictures herself flicking through hangers and rails, the contents of all his drawers strewn across the floor. It seems such an intrusion, unthinkable that seventy years of a life's remains must be picked over and discarded at her whim.

It had fallen to her of course, to sort through her mother's possessions. Clothes she hadn't worn since the 1970s, shoes that hadn't seen the light in decades. Anna's first attempts had been half-hearted. She hadn't been ready to accept her mother had no further need of them.

The hardest things to part with were the clothes she wore at the end, the dressing-gowns and nighties she spent her final months in. Her father couldn't stand to see them and so Anna had steeled herself for his sake. He had no idea most only travelled across the landing, to be folded away amongst her own. In her mind's eye, she sees herself holding her mother's coat to her face, inhaling the faint trace of her perfume. The coat still hangs in her wardrobe.

Suddenly, a horrific thought occurs to her. Who will sort through her things when she is gone? She gets up abruptly from the table, throwing her coffee away and taking the stairs two at a time.

She is stopped in her tracks by a thunderous knocking at the door. Who the hell is it now? If it's reporters or those moronic police again, God help them. She feels her anger build with every step but when she opens the door, she struggles to recognise the man standing there.

'DS Duffy,' he says, flashing his ID. 'We met the other day.'

Ah yes, the one who almost tipped over the coffee table.

'I was wondering if I could have another look around, now forensics have finished.'

Anna has no idea if this is routine. Is this the norm in a murder investigation? She considers how refusing might look. Would they obtain a search warrant? She'd probably be wise to comply.

'Yes, of course. Come on in.'

Once upstairs, she sees him more clearly. He really is an unpleasant looking individual.

'Actually,' he says, sucking his teeth as though deep in thought. 'I should really start in the shop, if you don't mind.'

Thank goodness, thinks Anna, but he immediately changes his mind again.

'On second thoughts no. My colleague will be joining me shortly. I'll wait for him.'

'DS Fox was here last night.'

His eyebrows shoot up at this. 'Oh, was she?'

'Yes.' She has no idea why she said it. Nerves probably. She mustn't give any more away to this idiot.

'OK if I make a start?'

'What exactly are you looking for?'

'That's the million-dollar question, love.'

Unable to bear another second in his presence, she

walks away into the kitchen and stands listening behind the door. Within seconds, she hears another knock and clumping feet on the stairs. The door slams shut, the walls almost shaking as they clatter back up. Now there are two men's voices. She puts the kettle on to drown them out but she can still hear them. They are discussing the 3.30 at Haydock.

She opens the kitchen door with such ferocity, she is surprised to see the handle still attached but they don't even notice her. Still chatting, they disappear into her father's bedroom.

Her eyes drift across to her own room and suddenly, she remembers the empty wine bottles. She's been stashing them under her bed and God knows how many there are.

Panic grips her, the familiar strap tightening across her sternum. Is it too late to retrieve them? She looks down at the rise and fall of her chest, the folds of her baggy sweatshirt. It isn't baggy enough to conceal a stash of empties. Should she get a binbag, a pillowcase or something? She realises immediately this is a stupid idea. They're hardly likely to turn a blind eye to her leaving with a sack over her shoulder. Fear builds in her chest, her field of vision narrowing. She has to get out of there.

Casting around for her boots, her fingers fumble with the laces, as she wills her breathing to slow.

'Going for a walk!' she shouts, her voice little more than a croak but the policemen are too engrossed in whatever they're doing to hear her. Grabbing a coat, she almost trips and falls down the stairs. Through the gate, she sees a reporter skulking across the road. He takes out a large umbrella, distracted as he struggles to put it up. She runs in the opposite direction, rain mixing with her tears.

26

Kate

A thin drizzle shrouds the high street as Kate approaches the Trick Shop. A panda car is parked by the kerb, its occupants so lost in conversation, she doubts they see her. Across the road a reporter lurks, his eyes turned up to the windows. She stands on the corner, partly to finish her cigarette and partly to compose herself.

She has spent the morning going through the shop's landline records. She has found no obvious patterns, no clusters of calls except to and from Anna and her father's mobiles. She was only stalling for time. Kate has no idea what kind of reception she'll get from Anna but after last night's events, it's Newton she's more concerned with.

The shutters are still down, so she walks round to the courtyard. As she turns the corner, a wagon rumbles past, grimy coal sacks heaped beneath a black tarpaulin. *The town that time forgot*, thinks Kate as she knocks on the door. There is no response so she knocks again, much louder. This time it nearly swings off its hinges and Duffy leers out at her. She flinches at the sight of him.

'Oh, here she is, Dick van Dyke! Thought you weren't bothering.' He makes a show of checking his wristwatch.

Kate pushes past him and runs upstairs, leaving him at the bottom. To her surprise, she finds the living room empty. She hears Duffy's breath behind her.

'You've just missed your girlfriend.'

'Piss off, Duffy.' She looks straight past him, to the second flight of stairs.

'No sign of the boss yet?'

'Nope.' He walks into the kitchen, pulls out a drawer

and tips the contents onto the floor. It's only knives and forks but she knows he won't give even the family's most precious possessions any more respect.

'Have forensics definitely finished?'

'Yeah, they wrapped up yesterday. Me and Sharpy's made a start. He's gone to the bookies.' Duffy pulls out another drawer. *It's a miracle any case gets solved*, thinks Kate, as she takes in the back of his greasy head, the ridiculous jacket. She bets he's never been on a motorbike in his life. He opens a cupboard at random, then another. Leaning back against the worktop, he grins at her. 'She told me about your little get together. You don't hang about, do you?'

Kate really isn't in the mood for this. 'Why don't you just shut it, Duffy? Where is she anyway?'

'Gone for a walk, she said.'

His face cries out for a fist in it. 'I don't blame her.' Climbing the stairs to Anna's bedroom, she slams the door, grateful for the distance between them, for the moment anyway.

The room is set into the eaves of the roof and like the ones below, can't have changed much in the last century or so. The whole place is like a time capsule. The sloping walls are off-white, like her own, but that's where the similarity ends. Anna sleeps in a single bed and instead of the usual duvet, the satin edge of a blanket lies folded over a candlewick bedspread. It reminds Kate of her childhood room except she never owned a picture like the one she is looking at now. The Brontë sisters stare down at her as though demanding to know what she is doing here, their faces ghostly against the dark background. She has seen the reproduction before, complete with creases where the original was folded. She read somewhere their brother Branwell painted himself out, the blurred pillar between them all that's left of him.

The bedside table is marked with rings, the scars of a night-time drinker. A faded photo of a dog is almost hidden behind a pile of books, beside them, a box of matches and a tall church candle. On the opposite wall between the wardrobe and a chest of drawers is another image Kate is familiar with. Daphne du Maurier regards her from a thick, gilt frame. The picture is timelessly beautiful, taken when the writer was young. Her hair is cut in a chin length bob, a strand of pearls adding to the luminescence of the print. She finds herself unnerved by both the pictures, stashed away in here like museum pieces.

The floorboards creak as she walks over to the window. She thinks of Anna standing here as a girl, a teenager, a woman. Her presence hangs heavily in here. Pulling on her gloves, she looks down into the street. Could someone walk along the pavement and enter the shop without waking her? Almost certainly they could, especially bearing in mind the amount of drink she's seen her put away.

Turning her attention to the bookshelves, she catches her breath at the titles. The top row is full of Beatrix Potters. Without needing to disturb them, she knows every plate inside. Tiny blue-jacketed rabbits and mitten-clad kittens and mice. They were her nursery favourites.

Further down, she sees more long-forgotten memories. *Little Women, Black Beauty, Lorna Doone* and surely everything Enid Blyton ever wrote. Kate sinks to her knees, her head tilted as she drinks them in. *Mrs Frisby and the Rats of Nimh* — oh, she loved that book! She is transported back in time, her ten-year-old self worried sick about the fate of those poor rodents. Spilling from the shelves below are encyclopaedias, atlases and yet more adolescent treasures. *Emil and the Detectives, Nancy Drew, Charlotte's Web*. She gets to her feet and finds she is smiling.

Strange though, to keep all your childhood books but then she remembers when her gran died, she found her room much the same as she had left it. The difference being, she never dreamt of owning this kind of collection. It's more like a private library than a personal bookshelf.

The second case contains her grown-up novels and again, Kate sees some of her own favourites. *The Moonstone*, the copy of *Wuthering Heights* she had seen downstairs. She pulls out *The Far Pavilions*, instantly back on the beach in Corfu where she read it. It seems Anna wasn't joking when she said she prefers books to people. There is a sound next door and she realises she hasn't given Duffy a thought since she stepped in here, which reminds her she is here for a purpose. Opening a drawer, she is surprised to see piles of lacy underwear. She hates this side of the job, the voyeuristic rooting around in other people's private places. Which is why it's important not to get too personally involved. It doesn't do to be supping by the fireside with a person one minute and searching their knicker drawer the next.

Slipping her hand back in, she carefully sifts beneath the neatly folded pants and bras. She searches the wardrobe, conscious she does all this in a fraction of the time spent at the bookcases. Anna's tidiness puts Kate to shame, everything organised methodically but she is surprised to find the skirt and tights she was wearing yesterday shoved haphazardly in with scarves and gloves.

She turns back to the bed. It looks childlike, totally

unsuitable for a grown woman. Running her hands under the mattress, she feels all the way round then removes the pillows, revealing nothing but a crumpled handkerchief. Getting back onto her knees she pushes the trailing blanket aside and peers underneath. Three dark green bottles lie side by side. No surprises there, although three is excessive by anyone's standards. Behind them is a shoebox, pushed against the skirting board. She reaches towards it with a finger, coaxing it out without touching the sides. It is covered in dust and evidently hasn't been opened for a while. Using the same method, she pushes the lid off, careful not to disturb the surface.

Inside is a pile of letters, the envelopes yellowed, the biro faded to a murky brown. She takes in the postmarks, all of them addressed in the same looping hand. Pulling out the first, she sees the date. Seventeen years ago. The page is creased, as though it has been read many times and is signed with a flourishing D. Beneath the letters is a worn, leather pouch. She opens the flap and looks inside. A skein of baby hair lies on top, tied with a white ribbon, beneath it an oblong block wrapped in silk. Instinctively, she knows it is a deck of tarot cards. Uncovering them, she gasps at their beauty. As she fans them in her hand, she remembers reading somewhere, that tarot should never be handled by anyone but their owner. She quickly re-wraps them and replaces them in the pouch, sliding in the baby hair after it. She is about to put everything back when she spots a photograph face down on the bottom of the box. Flipping it over, she sees a youthful, smiling Anna, a dark-haired man by her side. So she hasn't spent her entire life locked away with only her books and her bottles for company. She feels a strange relief for her.

Leaving the remaining letters unopened, she puts them

back in the order she found them. If the investigation warrants it, they may prove useful but for now there is no need to pry further into Anna's business. She pushes the box back against the wall, exactly where she found it.

As she gets up, she sees a wastepaper basket, half hidden in the folds of the curtains. She almost missed it, so engrossed had she been in the books. Going through people's bins has to be one of the lowest points of policing but she picks it up and looks inside. The bottom is covered in fine, grey ash, similar to cigarette ash but with a different smell. As she shakes the basket, a sliver of paper pokes up, burnt at the edges. Taking a pair of tweezers from her pocket, she pulls it out. Smoothing it out on the windowsill, she sees it is a fragment of a typed letter. The paper is thick and of good quality, which is probably why it hasn't burnt entirely. There are too few letters to mean anything but just inside the blackened edge is a pound sign written in ink. A receipt of some sort then. Her gran used to keep them but why would Anna burn it and why would she burn it now? Slipping a plastic evidence bag from the same pocket, she drops it in and closes the seal. She replaces the basket in the curtain folds, just as the door bursts open. Duffy stands there and she is relieved to see Bob Sharp hovering at his shoulder.

'Thought you'd got in bed to wait for her.'

Kate doesn't respond, pushing past him onto the landing. 'Alright Bob, didn't hear you come in.' She gives him one of her widest smiles as she passes and heads back downstairs.

'Been here a while,' says Sharpy, as he joins her in the living room. 'Find anything interesting?'

'Not really. More books than the Bodleian but that's about it.'

Kate can relax now Sharpy is here and is able to take the room in properly. The pictures look different in daylight and she sees the Queen of Spades again and Anna's mother. Beside it on the mantelpiece is a pamphlet with a cardboard cover.

'Have a look at that,' says Sharpy.

Opening it, Kate sees the certificate style of an old life insurance policy.

'Wow. This should make her comfortable.'

'Not half. I thought you might like to see this as well.' He holds out a sheet of paper, edged in black. Anna's mother's death certificate

'You were right about the heart attack, so the boss'll be pleased. You know what he's like.'

'Still no sign of him?' asks Kate.

'No and he's not answering his phone.' Sharpy walks off to the kitchen, leaving Kate alone with Duffy.

'Your girlfriend must be walking the Three Peaks,' he mutters from his perch on the windowsill, his voice just low enough not to be overheard. 'Gave you plenty of time to sniff her knickers though, didn't it?'

Kate looks straight through him. She pictures the window suddenly falling open, sending him plunging through the air, splattering on the pavement. It's a satisfying image, and she beams at him. With her middle finger in the air, she pulls out a cigarette and heads for the stairs.

27

Anna

The early evening sun slants through the window. Anna sits and watches the dust motes dance in the air.

They had left things much as they found them but still, she can't pretend they haven't been here. She had watched them from across the street, unable to see what they were doing which somehow made it worse. This must be how it feels to be burgled. Or raped. Well, whatever they were looking for, they won't find it.

Once she had calmed down, she knew that even if she had retrieved the bottles, it would have been pointless. The recycling is full of them. She can just imagine that ugly prick with his head in the bins, like the vermin that he is.

She would have known Kate had been here even if she hadn't seen her. The smell of her cigarettes lingers but Anna doesn't mind. It's close enough to her father's scent to be almost comforting.

The panic is still there in her chest. Going to the freezer, she pulls a bottle of vodka from beneath a pork joint. She'd forgotten it was there until she'd wracked her brains for where else she had stuff stashed. As her father never cooked, it was an ideal hiding place. Searching the cupboards for a glass, she finds a porcelain cup. She pours herself an inch, shuddering as it burns a freezing streak down her throat. Then she pours another.

Kicking off her boots, she heads upstairs, sipping as she goes. The cup is one of Father's favourites, so thin and delicate the sunlight shines through it. He'd spontaneously combust if he could see her drinking vodka from it. Placing it on the bedside table, it almost skids to the other side and she rights it just in time, stifling a tipsy giggle. She drags the bottles from under the bed and is about to get up when she sees the box shoved against the skirting. Pulling it out, she sees it is covered in dust, with only her own finger marks fresh on the surface. She sits back on her heels. The smell of cigarettes is stronger in here, which means either Kate isn't as thorough as she seems, or that she's exceptionally careful. Anna knows which option her money's on. She just hopes she was in here alone.

She knocks back another slug of vodka. With each swallow she will care even less. Sitting on the edge of her bed, she blows the dust away and opens the lid.

One by one she opens the letters. In her half numb state, they barely register but she knows exactly what they say, she memorised them years ago. She doesn't cry, which is progress, tracing the strokes and curves as they sweep across the page. Some things she got rid of, the burning a kind of catharsis. She should have burned them all but she couldn't. She touches the baby hair, the faded ribbon. She'd had no idea how sentimental her mother was, until she was dead and buried.

She takes out the soft Morocco wallet. It always feels warm, even now, as though she put it aside moments earlier. She always hoped, right to the end, that Anna would one day embrace the gift she was convinced she possessed.

She slides out the cards, light catching the silver stars on the backs. The edges are worn, the characters all so achingly familiar. Long before she could read, these pictures peopled her mind. Perched on a cushion at the table, her tiny, dimpled fingers clutching the oblongs of magic, creating her own worlds. Clashing swords and mighty castles, kings and queens in dark enchanted towers.

Her mother always said she had a wayward imagination. She puts the letters back and pushes the box aside. With practised hands, she shuffles the cards and spreads them across the candlewick in a smooth, wide arc.

28

1977

Anna is lying on the sofa pretending to read. Instead of following the words, she traces the cracks on the ceiling, along the pelmet's edge. One of them looks like the coastline of Ireland and that damp patch could easily be Lough Neagh. She pulls her cardigan around her. The fire has gone out but Jack is still sprawled in front of it. Her mother went up early, complaining of another headache. Anna hadn't heard them quarrel but she's pretty sure her father's dark mood has something to do with it.

She watches him over the top of her book as he prowls from room to room. Dealing another game of patience, he sticks a cigarette to his lip. Chain smoking, Mother calls it, lighting one from the butt of another. He blows a noxious plume and as each card is flung down, his knuckles strike the table.

'Find yourself a book,' he had commanded earlier. 'You don't read as much as you used to.'

She had known what he meant by that of course. Another veiled dig. Taking one from the shelf, she had feigned complete absorption, while straining to hear them in the kitchen. She had chosen *Tess of the D'Urbervilles*. Her father forbade her to read it until she is fourteen years old but he is far too preoccupied to notice. Still she keeps her fingers spread across the cover. She turns a page but it is impossible to concentrate. Judging by the way he is slamming the cards down, maybe now would be a good time to go to bed.

He squints at her through the cloud of smoke which swirls like a white miasma.

'Go to your room, Anna, and take that blasted dog with you.'

At the sound of his voice, Jack jumps up, wagging his tail in anticipation.

'Too late for a walk now, boy,' says Anna ruffling his fur.

'Keep him out of the way and don't come back down. I've got friends coming.' He lights another cigarette and carries on with his game.

Being sent to her room is used as a punishment but Anna is invariably glad to escape. With the book under her arm she climbs the stairs, Jack's claws tapping behind her. She stops at her parents' bedroom door but there is nothing to hear but silence.

Drawing her curtains, she pats the bed for Jack to jump up. Once settled, nothing will shift him, short of rattling his lead. She lies down with the book but her eyes just skim the pages. After a while, she wonders if her father lied to get rid of her but as her eyes grow heavy, she hears a sharp knock downstairs and the slam of the door.

Knowing her father will be busy taking coats and pouring drinks, Anna steals onto the landing and down to the bottom of the staircase. Her heartbeat thumps as she settles herself to listen. A thick curtain is all that separates her from her father and his guests.

'That's grand, Charlie,' says one of them. She cringes as she hears him smack his lips. 'Definitely hits the spot.'

The single malt will be out but it won't be Father's best. She recognises the voices and knows tonight's gathering is made up of men from the village. One of them is a farmer, she forgets his name. Always prattling on about cows and the weather. The noisy drinker is

Shelley Barker's dad. Johnnie, she thinks his name is. He works down the pit, as does the third man, Alvin Wood.

When she judges they will all be fully absorbed in themselves, Anna pulls the curtain back by no more than a hair's breadth. With four men now smoking, the miasma has thickened and hovers like smog around the table. Stifling a cough, she watches Father shuffle and square the pack. His hands are bigger than any of the men at the table, his fingers blunt at the edges.

'What are we starting with tonight then, gents?'

Mr Wood taps the ashtray with his cigarette. 'You know me. Creature of habit, Charlie.'

'Aye, keep it simple,' says the farmer. 'None of your fancy stuff.'

Quick as a croupier, her father deals clockwise but to Anna's shock, she sees he is using the marked deck. Why would he do that? He only marked them to show her how, she never thought for one minute he would use them. Nobody will see the pinpricks, like the raised bumps of Braille, especially not in this light through the coiling smoke. Anna only noticed because she recognises the design on the back of the cards. She sees the flash of blue and green as the men begin placing notes in a pile at the centre of the table.

Her father smiles as they scrutinise their hands. Or in his case *sleight of hand*. Something he prides himself in. *Cardistry* he calls it, a word she knows he's made up. *Not a mindless game of chance, like dice or roulette and a damn sight more skilful than chess*. When she was younger, his words bewildered Anna. Now she is beginning to understand exactly what they mean.

'Missus gone to bed early?' asks the farmer, one eyebrow cocked. Her father smirks but doesn't answer.

151

As always, he keeps things even at the start. More drinks are poured, more drivel spoken. He has lit the fire and gets up to throw more coal on. The notes become more colourful. Brown and purple are added to the heap. Sometimes she sees a red one but not with this group. The pile grows and falls, then grows again.

Anna watches her father control the game. His aim is always to win of course but what he really enjoys is to see them sweat and squirm. He likes to prove how clever he is, *pit his wits* against them.

'I'm out,' says the farmer, throwing his hand in.

'Me an' all,' says Mr Barker, shaking his head. 'Too steep for me.'

The room is deadly quiet. Anna holds her breath.

'I'll raise you, Alvin,' says her father.

'Can't go any higher, Charlie. I know my limit.'

'Sky's the limit, that's what I say.'

Her father narrows his eyes, then places his cards face down as he lights another cigarette.

'How long have we known each other?' he says, shaking out the match. 'Twenty-five? Thirty years?'

The farmer pushes his chair back. 'I'm calling it a night. Some of us 'ave to be up in a few hours.'

'Same 'ere,' says Mr Barker, rising unsteadily from his chair.

'Typical,' mutters her father, taking a swig from his glass.

'What's that supposed to mean?'

'Ignore him, Johnnie,' calls the farmer, already halfway to the door. A gust of cold air blows through the room as he pulls it open. Mr Barker, clearly worse for wear, gets tangled in his coat sleeves as he stumbles towards the threshold.

'Are you coming, Alvin?' the farmer calls to Mr Wood, who is still seated at the table.

'He's going to chance his arm,' says Anna's father. 'Aren't you?'

'I'm asking Alvin,' says the farmer.

Mr Wood lights another cigarette but says nothing. Smoke eddies around in the draft from the doorway.

'Don't do anything stupid,' says the farmer, as he helps Mr Barker with his coat. He casts them a final look, then slams the door with such a bang, Anna almost jumps out of her skin. She looks behind her. Surely Mother can't be sleeping through this, but her door remains closed.

'Just the two of us then,' says Father, picking up his cards. Mr Wood is studying his hand with great care. A skilful player, Anna has watched him before but tonight is different. Tonight, he is up against a rigged deck.

'The trouble with some people is they have no imagination,' says her father, draining his glass. Anna can tell when he has had too much to drink. He speaks more slowly, the words running into each other.

Mr Wood appears deep in thought but still he remains silent. Her father gets up, leaving his cards unattended. He refills his glass, then returns to the table.

'Have you made your mind up then, or what?' He speaks as though it couldn't matter less to him. Lighting yet another cigarette, he leans back in his chair. Beads of sweat stand out on Mr Wood's brow, the throb of a vein in his temple visible even from this distance.

'I'll put my car on it,' he blurts, the words coming out in a gush. Anna gasps, covering her mouth with her hand too late but they don't hear her. Her father laughs, *he actually laughs*. With both hands now covering her face,

153

Anna wills Mr Wood not to do it.

'Are you sure, Alvin?' The throaty, smoker's chuckle turns into a cough, as it often does with her father. He takes a long drink, his eyes never leaving his opponent's face.

'You must have one hell of a hand there.'

This makes it worse. Her father knows exactly what hand he has. He is toying with him.

'I'm sure,' says Mr Wood, sounding anything but. Anna considers throwing herself out from behind the curtain. She could easily make an excuse. Jack needs to go out or a nightmare has woken her but she remains frozen, her heart banging against her ribcage.

Alvin Wood throws his cards on the table, sending a pungent cloud up from the overflowing ashtray. 'Straight flush,' he says, picking up his drink and downing it in one.

Her father frowns as though uncertain. He is playing for time, eking it out, Anna knows he is. With the cards in his left hand, he raises the other and with one finger strokes his moustache, first one side, then the other.

'Remind me Alvin, what car is it you drive?'

Anna can't bear to see anymore. She stands up and climbs the stairs, placing her feet where the boards don't creak. Father has won, except he hasn't won, not really.

Jack hasn't moved from where she left him. Suddenly feeling cold, she gets under the covers and huddles beside him. Downstairs, she hears raised voices, the sound of breaking glass.

The door slams with such force this time a picture falls on the landing, the smash of more broken glass.

Outside, Mr Wood's footsteps take him the few yards home. She holds Jack tightly, waiting until she hears her father climb the stairs to bed.

29

Anna

Anna often wonders what Daniel would make of her drink problem. It's not as though he hadn't known about it, hadn't been present at its birth. But it would be just like him to think she's fine now. It would never occur to him there might be long-term consequences.

Lighting a fire, she waits for darkness to fall. With the sun well over the yardarm, she can drink without conscience. Even an old lush like her must have some standards. Pouring herself a generous measure, she heads upstairs to bed.

Wafting a match, she draws in the scent as she lights a candle. The weight of the blankets is a comfort and she settles herself with a book propped against her knees. Books have always been Anna's refuge. So much more than paper and ink, to her they are a door to somewhere else. Somewhere better. As a girl, she would read by torchlight when everyone else was asleep. There were never enough hours in the day. *Literature can be so illuminating*, her father used to say and for Anna, books have always been like a light amidst the darkness. Somewhere along the line, the candles replaced the torch. They became part of the ritual, setting the scene for the most cherished time of her day, when she can cut herself off from reality and lose herself between the pages.

Except tonight she is unable to concentrate, which isn't surprising really. The vodka has dulled her senses but not enough to stop her thinking of DS Fox and her cronies rooting around in here. It had dawned on her today, the shocking realisation that she is totally alone.

There will be no figure of authority, no one monitoring her comings and goings from here on in. The police will move on and then there will be no one above her in the pecking order. So why did she run and hide, today? Conditioning, she supposes. *Subordination.* But tonight, she had flung those bottles in the bin with such force, revelling in the sound of them shattering and didn't care who heard. All her life, everything she has done, every decision made has had the caveat *What will my parents think?* Now, for the first time ever, she answers to no one.

Her father always said she was a loner. He was right about that, she has never been one for mixing but she has known friendship and there are times when she misses it. Kids larking about, couples glimpsed through a window. Sharing cigarettes outside the pub, running for their taxi in pairs. They are fleeting thoughts, nothing more. Of course, it's a cliche but books really are all she needs. And it is a need, she knows that. To be able to spend at least part of the day completely alone to read is as necessary to Anna as food and water are to others.

After gaining a first in English Literature, it seemed natural she would go into publishing. It was the ideal job and her parents were immensely proud of her, glad all that reading had paid off.

She had loved university life, relishing her newfound independence, the freedom it gave her to completely immerse herself. At last there were no interruptions, no awkward customers or deliveries to unpack or displays to arrange in the shop. She had revelled in the booklined seminars, spellbound as she listened for the first time in her life to someone other than her father talk about literature, fascinated to discover there were others who shared her passion.

Of course, she had met new people but the friendships were only ever skin deep. Not really friendships at all, just like-minded strangers who happened to be on the same course as her. She had formed no real attachments, preferring instead to spend her free time wandering the libraries, her appetite for reading becoming ever more unquenchable with so many books at her disposal. The power contained within those pages, the endless knowledge just waiting to be discovered, filled her with an excitement so intense, nothing in the real world compared.

She remembers her father at her graduation ceremony. Shaking hands with everyone, lapping it up. He had been in his element rubbing shoulders with the intelligentsia. Anna knows he would have loved the chance to attend university himself, but his life had been mapped out for him. He was always destined for the shop.

One of his pet names for her was the Bookworm. She hated it. It was an ugly word and conjured visions of wriggling little creatures, burrowing through white pulp. It made her want to bury herself even deeper within the pages.

So it came as a complete surprise when Daniel noticed her. He had come to fit a new door and put shelves up in her office. Joiner was a term he never used, or, God forbid, chippy. He was a carpenter and just the idea of him working with his hands was like poetry to Anna. His was a timeless occupation, like stonemason, potter or smith, from bygone days when men toiled in the fields and sweated at the anvil.

Her first job after graduation had been as a proof-reader with an educational publisher in Leeds but her real love was fiction. When asked to consult on a du Maurier literary festival, she jumped at the chance. It opened the door to her dream job. She had been at Chatto and Small for only a matter of weeks when he arrived.

Anna had sensed him watching her and she in turn watched him. She couldn't help herself. Her eyes were drawn to his hands as they gripped the plane, smoothing the timber. She glimpsed his skin beneath his shirt as he stretched over the wood. Embarrassed, she looked away but she was far too distracted. Then he looked right at her, his hair falling over his eyes and they had smiled at each other. He always said it was love at first sight for him. His first lie.

Anna once read somewhere that over 60 percent of us can't go more than ten minutes without lying. Little white lies and embellishments, half-truths to make ourselves sound better. Daniel took it to another level entirely. He could have made an Olympic sport of it.

Her parents hadn't liked him from the start. He's a *chancer* said her father, her mother's judgement no less promising. *Svengali* was the word she used. A *fascination*. They loved to pigeonhole people like that and of course, the cards foretold it all.

But the idea of being pursued, of being courted was like an awakening to Anna. He was Heathcliff to her Cathy, her very own Romeo. She knew full well it was corny but it was all she'd ever known, except this time instead of merely existing, she was finally playing a part. And there was something edgy about him. Something dangerous. She would never admit this to anyone but even so many years distant, just the thought of him still has the power to take her breath away.

The only book he had ever read was *Stig of the Dump*. It was a standard joke of his and he was proud of it. His

159

reading might have been lacking but he wasn't stupid. Far from it. He was very clever, cunning even and always perfectly credible.

What a fool she had been. How gullible. She picks up the glass and takes a large mouthful, the book still closed against her knees.

She found out he was married after five and a half months. She suspected long before this but he was always ready with a lie. No matter the evidence she presented him with, he would always talk her round. In time, she came to realise there was no situation, however damning, that he could not explain away with ease, never showing the slightest hint of conscience. And the more outlandish the lie, the better, he liked to sail close to the wind. As though he was testing how good he was, how far she was willing to go. Yet none of it stopped her from loving him. She would have walked though fire for him and followed him to the ends of the earth. Melodramatic as that may sound, it doesn't make it any less true.

And so within a few short months she went from virgin to mistress. Virgin to whore. Sucked into a role she was not prepared for. Hurt beyond her comprehension, she had sunk like a stone. As he promised to leave his wife, she sank further. He swore on his daughter's life they would have their happy ending, she just had to give him time. Then more time and then more. The panic attacks had started and she had begun to drink.

She gulps down the rest of the vodka. Even now, she refuses to think about what followed.

Should she go and top her glass up? *Just a wee dram, a wee snifter?* She suppresses a giggle. *No, the bastard isn't worth it.* And if she's tittering at that, she's had enough.

He used to tell her she was making it up, make her think she was crazy. *It's not a lie until you get found out.* Did he *actually, really* say that? So many untruths, she could have held her own hand in front of her face and not been sure it was her own.

She kept a diary for a time but it read like the ravings of a madwoman. *Compulsive liar, habitual liar, consummate, pathological liar. Conman, confidence trickster, psycho, swindler, cheat.* Liar running through him like a stick of Blackpool rock. It messes with your head being lied to on that kind of scale.

She'd had a nervous breakdown, although her parents would have none of that talk. They couldn't understand she had wanted to die. Walking down the railway tracks, urging herself to jump. She had lost her job at Chatto and Small and with it her flat and everything she had worked so hard to achieve.

She came close to calling him today. Just to hear his voice. She hadn't, of course, she wouldn't but she wonders if he's seen it on the news. It doesn't matter, he won't get in touch and she should be glad of that. Worse than heroin addiction, he was a cancer she had cut out, with no sense whatsoever of the damage he so casually inflicted. It all seems alien now, like looking down the wrong end of a telescope. She finds it hard to believe she was ever capable of such feelings in the first place.

Draining her glass, she drops the book and blows out the candle. She doesn't blame him entirely. A solitary child became a lonely woman and secretly, she cherishes the time they had. Sometimes, when she allows herself, she imagines he is lying here beside her. She remembers every inch of him, the feel and the taste of him. The wounds might heal but they still throb, to remind her she didn't imagine him. No matter what they said, no matter what he did, she knows in her heart that he loved her. She prays sleep will come before she loses the nightly battle and goes in search of another bottle. A tear rolls down her cheek into the pillowcase.

30

Kate

Kate is standing by the window on the top floor of the station. From here she has a bird's eye view of the car park and Helen's BMW is nowhere to be seen.

Scanning the rows, she sees her own car slightly adrift of the markings and makes a mental note to park more carefully. She can match every car to its owner, from Newton's gleaming Volvo, perfectly positioned in its designated bay, to the caretaker's old rust bucket, tucked in sideways by the bins.

A gust of wind spins leaves into the air and a spume of rain against the glass. She is about to turn away when Newton emerges beneath her, his phone clasped to his ear. He appears to be in a hurry, striding quickly across the tarmac. He gets in his car and speeds off in the direction of town.

Frowning, she leaves her vantage point and heads down the corridor to the vending machine. The one up here is always well stocked, probably because there are only a handful of occupied offices on this floor, one of them belonging to Superintendent Vardy. Kate studies the various chocolate bars and crisps. She isn't remotely hungry but it will provide an alibi should anyone question yet another trip to the top floor.

Helen's office is next to the super's. Retrieving her Mars bar, she pauses briefly outside the two adjacent doors. Both rooms are currently unoccupied, the only sound the incessant buzz of the vending machine. She heads back down the stairs to the main office. Returning to her desk, she unlocks her computer and stares indifferently at the screen.

It has been a busy morning. Kate hadn't realised how common the name Collins is. The electoral rolls have come up with eighty-two households of that name in North East Derbyshire alone. Working her way back from Patricia Collins's death certificate, she discovered her maiden name was Smith. At that point, she had almost thrown her PC through the window.

She had then paid a visit to Black Hollow Library and Community Centre. Closed at weekends, today had been her first chance to visit. A notice was displayed in the foyer, between *Knit and Natter* and *Yoga-rhythms: Reading Group, 8pm Wednesdays. All Welcome.* A jaunty picture of what Kate presumed was meant to be a bookworm wriggled across the bottom of the poster, along with a name and contact number. As luck would have it, Sally Clark was on her way that very minute, to prepare for this week's meeting. She agreed to speak to Kate on her arrival.

If Anna looked like a librarian, Sally Clark blew her out of the water. Peering through owlish spectacles, she wore a crisp, high–necked blouse, drab skirt and flat, sensible shoes. To complete the ensemble, she hauled a hessian bag with her, full of books. Their conversation had been lacklustre to say the least. Yes, Sally had heard about the murder, wasn't it terrible? No, she couldn't tell her much about Anna, other than she is very well read and keeps herself to herself. She had given her the names of the other group members but baulked at providing their phone numbers. *Data protection and all that.*

Across the office, Duffy burps and scratches himself. Kate isn't sure what he's supposed to be doing but she'd seen a betting shop logo splashed across his screen when she passed.

At least he's not bothering me, thinks Kate, as she reads through her notes again. She'd had high hopes about the book club and knows Newton will share her disappointment. She pushes her mouse away and flicks at the Mars bar. Why is she still bothered what he thinks?

Keeping focused hadn't been an issue at the library but back here she finds it impossible. Numerous trips to the vending machine, loitering in the corridor has confirmed what she suspected. The superintendent's secretary has phoned in sick.

Kate isn't prone to paranoia but the only conclusion she can draw is that Helen is avoiding her. Leaning back in her chair, she looks around the room. Amy is chewing her pen, dark head bent in concentration. Sharpy is at the next desk, narrowed eyes fixed on his screen and beside him Debbie Barstow stares, as though hypnotised, through the window. Nobody is interested in what may or may not have happened between two plastered women on a night out. Nobody that is, except Duffy.

She had tried to call Helen last night, relieved when she didn't answer. What could she possibly say? She had wanted to reassure her, that's all, that there were no hard feelings.

Of course, it's possible she is genuinely poorly. The thought of coming into the station had made Kate sick with nerves and it's unlikely Helen will have benefitted from a pep talk like the one she received from Newton.

Bloody Newton. Where the hell was he all weekend? He should have been here steering the team but instead was conspicuous by his absence. Going AWOL just isn't Newton, especially in the middle of a murder case. It must be linked to what happened Friday night. *Come to think of it, he was acting strange before that, unkempt by his standards and far too eager to get away*. She knows he's got a bad back but it gnaws at her how inconsistent his behaviour has been. In the brief time she's known him, she has seen a basic decency she believed they both shared. She had thought him a man of integrity. Clearly, she knows nothing at all.

At least he turned up this morning. Kate was sure he would pull her to one side, to get their stories straight if nothing else but he had done nothing of the kind. He was already ensconced in the super's office by the time she arrived. *A strategy meeting, whatever that means*. Kate wonders who took the minutes. They had passed on the corridor at lunchtime. She had looked at him, certain he would speak but he had given her no more than a perfunctory nod, quickening his footsteps to demonstrate how busy he was.

Something else has been bothering her. What on earth is she supposed to say if Alice Ashby gets in touch? No post-mortem has been requested and there is nothing so far to link her aunt's death to their investigations but Kate has made her own discreet enquiries. The hospital confirmed her cause of death has been recorded as myocardial infarction. She had a history of ischaemic heart disease. A fait accompli.

She needs to discuss it all with Newton. Does he blame her for contaminating the crime scene, or even take her seriously about it being a crime scene in the first place? So many unanswered questions. He won't have made his own enquiries, to do so would arouse suspicion. Even broaching the subject would be to admit it had taken place.

More than anything, she is disappointed. So badly had

she wanted to match his standards, to find he doesn't match up to them himself is quite a shock. Even now, she still looks for explanations, makes excuses for him. *Maybe he's embarrassed, and so he should be*, thinks Kate, her anger building. *Is this what CID is all about? Covering up for colleagues? Covering up murder?*

Shoving her notes aside, something catches her eye that wasn't there before. Glancing down she looks again, her guts lurching. The whole office seems to shift then straighten as she takes hold of the corner and slowly pulls out a glossy magazine. *Bumper to Bumper*, reads the title. *Girl on Girl Action.* Two blondes are splayed across the cover, stark naked except for their strategically positioned police helmets.

She scrapes back her chair as Duffy bursts into raucous laughter. Making eye contact with no one, she strides out of the building, slamming the door shut behind her.

The wind almost knocks the breath from her as she turns her back to light a cigarette. How the hell had she kept her hands from the bastard's scrawny neck? Rage courses through her as she draws smoke into her lungs. She wills herself to calm down as she looks back at the station, leaves and litter scudding past. Behind those windows all manner of filth amasses. *The most backstabbing, bent, morally devoid scumbags ever to grace society. And then there are the criminals.*

The cold cuts through her and it has started to rain again. She walks back towards the building, Mrs Wood's keys jangling, cold and metallic in her pocket.

31

Newton

The 999 call comes through at 4 pm. A little boy has gone missing, the mother frantic. As a priority case, the recording is forwarded from the force control room and Newton is listening to it at 4.09 pm. Making a note of the address, he leaves the station immediately, calling the family liaison officer on his way.

The missing boy is only two years old, about the same age as Georgie. His mother left him in the garden for no more than a few minutes while she went inside to make lunch. Leaving a child of that age outside unsupervised sounds careless to Newton at best, especially in this weather. He looks up at the darkening sky.

The wind almost whips the car door off as he gets in. Putting his foot down, he tries to imagine what it must feel like to lose a child. He doesn't need to imagine, he knows exactly how it feels.

A child went missing once before in the town, not long after he arrived. She had been found, physically unharmed, but Newton always felt he let her down, that he hadn't found her soon enough. It's something he has never been able to forget.

Pulling his mind back, he concentrates on the road. The boy has probably wandered off and will come back home when he is hungry. Or one of the grandparents picked him up and didn't think to tell the mother. He hopes to God he is right. In almost every case there is an innocent explanation. As he parks outside the house, he tries not to think of the thirteen registered sex offenders currently living in and around Black Hollow.

Less than half an hour later, he's dashing through the rain back to his car, relieved to be out of there. Julie Darrow has again proved herself invaluable and he has left the mother in her capable hands. Mandy Freeman kept repeating she only left him for a matter of minutes. They'd been collecting leaves in a toy wheelbarrow, chasing them around in the wind. Little Archie was enjoying himself so much, she saw no harm in popping inside to make sandwiches. When she returned, there was the upturned wheelbarrow on the lawn but no sign of Archie. *It was just five minutes*, she kept saying, a look of abject pain in her eyes along with something else he sees a lot of. Guilt.

'This is all I bloody need,' mutters Newton. The murder investigation is barely started, not to mention Friday night. That certainly wasn't his finest hour, and he has a nagging feeling he hasn't heard the last of it. He grips the steering wheel and tries to think. Crimes are like bloody buses round here. He reminds himself this isn't necessarily a crime, not yet anyway. There is still every chance the lad just followed a cat or something.

Coming to a decision, he phones the station and asks for Duffy.

Minutes later and not entirely sure what the hell he is doing, he starts the car, switching on the headlights as a curtain of rain sweeps the windscreen. The sky is a clotted, roiling black, the wind unrelenting. Wherever the boy is, he is likely to be swept away in these conditions.

The mother hadn't liked it when he'd asked if he could look upstairs. *Just to check, Mrs Freeman. You know what kids are like*. He had frozen at the door of Archie's bedroom, the frieze of spaceships so like the décor in Georgie's room. Looking under the bed, inside the

169

wardrobe and behind the curtains, he had checked every room, even the airing cupboards. He had pulled down the loft ladder as quietly as he could, but it was clear from the way he had to shoulder the hatch, no one had been up there in a while. It's safe to say Archie isn't playing hide and seek. Before going back downstairs, he had pulled a T-shirt from the linen basket in his bedroom. It would have his scent on it.

By the time he gets back, Duffy should have carried out his instructions, which were simple enough. Get the ball rolling with a search and contact the local radio and TV stations. Mandy Freeman has given a good enough description and the boy shouldn't be too difficult to spot.

As he pulls into the flow of traffic, he is all too aware that this time last week it would have been Kate he asked for at the station. She is the best on the team by far, more capable than the lot of them. In every respect. Without question.

So why the bloody hell did he ask for Duffy? He puts his foot down and follows the cats' eyes through the storm.

32

Kate

Kate knows something has happened as soon as she re-enters the station. Raised voices fill the corridors and people burst through doors, blind panic etched on their faces.

Pushing through the melee back into the incident room, she sees Duffy and the others bent over an Ordnance Survey map on his desk. The mood has changed completely.

'Good of you to join us,' he sneers, pointing with a pen. 'Major incident here. A child's gone missing.'

'Where's the boss?' she asks, glancing at her desk. The magazine appears to have gone. Leaning over, she pulls the map towards her.

'On his way,' replies Duffy, tugging it back to the centre. As if on cue, the door flies open and they all turn towards Newton. The next few minutes pass in a blur as he fills them in with his usual calm authority. Kate looks through the window. It is almost dark and the thought of a toddler out there on his own doesn't bear thinking about.

'What about the boy's father, sir?' she asks.

'I'm going to ring him now before we go public.' Newton follows her gaze as though willing the darkness away. 'Right, you all know what you're doing, so get on with it.' He throws a harrowed look over his shoulder as he slams the door behind him. Kate doesn't envy him his position, her anger seeming suddenly redundant. She glares at Duffy, the hilarity of just a few minutes ago completely forgotten. Despite the gravity of the situation, he looks like the cat that got the cream.

33

Newton

Newton's back is hammering. A searing, mortal pain from the backs of his knees to the depths of his armpits. Louise used to say it got worse when he was stressed but he doesn't believe that. It has nothing to do with damp or cold either. He takes a couple of painkillers from the glove compartment and swills them down with the bottle of water he keeps in the car purely for this purpose. It is tepid and tastes of plastic. And why is he already thinking about Louise in the past tense, as though she's dead?

The car sways and beyond the headlights, the trees tip sideways. He peers into the darkness, swerving round broken branches. The search had been more like a battle, volunteers staggering with exhaustion, half blinded by the wind. Communication had been almost impossible, voices snatched away and the constant dread hanging over them of what they might find. They found nothing. Newton knows he must keep positive but he is a realist. The temperature on the dashboard says four degrees. The chances of a lone two-year-old being OK in these conditions are next to zero. The best they can hope now is that some sad bastard has snatched him and pray it's someone who means the child no physical harm.

These are the jobs Newton hates. There is nothing bleaker than having to tell a parent their child has been hurt or worse. But as much as he hates it, he's glad to be in a position to do something about it. He wouldn't broadcast this but he sees it as his personal responsibility to find the child and save him.

He's done all he can for tonight. It's up to the copter

and the dogs for now. He hadn't wanted to leave but he'll be no use to anyone if he doesn't get some sleep. Yawning, he arches his back as he turns onto his estate. He feels like he's been trampled by a horse, the pain radiating from his bones to the surface of his skin. He refuses to think about it, wrenching his mind back to the case.

The conversation he'd had with the father had been surreal. He lives in Scotland for God's sake, just outside Aberdeen. Something to do with oil rigs, Mandy Freeman said. She had spat the words out. They will check this information, of course, but how could the bloke live so far away, happy to see his son no more than once or twice a year? Newton can't get his head round this. It's been only a matter of days since he last saw Georgie and it feels like forever.

If nothing happens overnight, they will have to do a TV appeal. As he pulls onto the drive, he rehearses the lines in his head. Vardy also wants to give the press an update on the murder but Newton is in no rush to beam their lack of progress across the nation. At this rate, he could end up with a double slot on the 6 o'clock news.

The rain is still streaming down the pavements, the gutters overflowing. Half blown up the steps, he shuts the door with relief but the temperature inside is little more than Baltic. Kicking off his boots and wet trousers, he switches on the heating, his breath clouding in front of him.

They'd had pizzas at the station, so he is spared the decision of what to eat. Making a cup of tea and a hot water bottle, he takes them into the living room.

Placing the bottle at the base of his spine, he sits back carefully. The slightest touch when it's this bad is unbearable. He is well used to adrenaline but these days it runs through him in one continuous hum. Being permanently wired on a cocktail of caffeine, drugs, booze and pain is exhausting, the constant struggle to stop it bleeding into every part of his life. If he's honest he knows that ship has well and truly sailed. He sits for a while in silence, as the heat penetrates his bones. The base of his back is scarred from boiling water bottles but the burning seems to trick the mind away from the pain, a ruse he learned at the clinic. As the bottle cools, he finishes his tea. Then he picks up a cushion and gets down on the floor.

The boy's father will be on the road by now, probably at the halfway mark. He could do it in six hours, maybe less if he puts his foot down. What he plans to do when he arrives, Newton has no idea. Every hour that passes could change what everyone will do. He has made his mind up to dislike the man but can understand his need to be here.

Rolling into the sphinx position, he ticks off the list in his head. Were the outbuildings near the boy's home checked thoroughly enough? He knows they were. Had they covered as much ground as possible in the circumstances? Yes, they had. Every security camera in the town has now been checked and all the local hospitals alerted. He thinks of the mother. What kind of hellish night is she spending, the father as well, for that matter? He tries to keep the image of the missing boy separate to the one he carries of Georgie but it is proving difficult.

He pushes up into the cobra, breathing deeply. Kate was brilliant tonight. Organised, calm and clear thinking. All the qualities needed in a crisis and not even a hint of bad feeling towards Duffy, whose performance had been adequate, no more. Who the hell made him a DS? Newton shakes his head. He will milk the situation for all it's worth, his pathetic ego pre-set to score points from every situation.

Tonight has told him more about Kate than it has about Duffy. She's a bloody good detective. A good person. She puts him to shame.

The pain is like a living thing; pulsing, merciless. He tries to visualise the texture, see its surface, its core. He sees it, huge and jagged, like a purple veined boulder he carts around with him. No help whatsoever.

Pushing into the cat, he realises what he must look like with his bare arse in the air. Not a soul knows he does this, apart from Louise. In his mind, yoga is the last thing a police officer would do.

His thoughts drift back to Kate. If he allows what's happened to spoil their working relationship, he is a fool. She is unquestionably his best detective, the one with most potential. She had only been trying to help him. If she has any faults, that's it. Forever trying to do the right thing and there isn't always room for that in CID. He gets to his feet, the word *shame* still resonating in his mind as he makes his way into the kitchen.

Picking up the whiskey bottle, he holds it to the light, shocked to see how little there is left. It might be the last Christmas gift Louise ever buys him. Single malt as well. He pours it down the sink.

Swallowing a couple more tablets, he gets undressed in the dark. That way he doesn't have to look at the empty half of the bed. He is still listening to the wind when he finally falls asleep.

34

1977

'Put the closed sign on, love. Let's have a few minutes.'

Anna looks up from her dusting, her mother's meaning clear. The cards are never far away but more and more these days they look at them together, poring over the pictures, dealing the different spreads. Anna senses a shift and knows the reason. It is time. Time for her mother to pass on her knowledge.

She flips the sign and puts her cloth under the counter. Mother takes out the leather pouch. It is always warm from being in her pocket. Anna wipes her hands down her jeans, as a kind of quiet solemnity falls upon them, a bit like when Marie talks about Jesus or Father Vincent.

'Hold them for a moment.'

Anna does as she is told.

'That's right, give them a shuffle.'

Anna slides the cards over each other, watching them cascade between her fingers, the surfaces smooth and glossy.

'Now put them down and cut them.'

She puts the cards on the counter, squaring the sides as she's been shown. A thrill of excitement runs through her as she grips the straight edges, the judgement requiring concentration as she lifts away the top half of the pack.

'You know what to do.'

Anna's hand hovers for just a second, then she slides three from the top, placing them in front of her. She turns the first face up.

Mother frowns and Anna sees a slow redness creep across her cheeks. Is there a problem with the card? It looks like Angel Gabriel, a man with golden hair and great arched wings on his back. He stands by a pool of water, a chalice in either hand, pouring liquid from one to the other. Temperance it says at the bottom of the card. Not a word Anna is familiar with.

'What does it mean, Mother?'

'It can mean all sorts of things.'

'Is it bad?'

'Whatever gave you that idea? Turn the next one.'

'But you haven't told me what this one means.'

'Just turn the next one for now.'

Her excitement somewhat dampened, Anna flips the middle card. Water again and this time a girl with long, flowing hair, a star shining at her shoulder. She has one foot on land, the toes of the other brushing the surface of a pool.

'This is a card of hope,' says Mother quickly, her cheeks still red as though slapped. 'It brings strength through hard work and learning. Finding truth from within. Now turn the last one.'

Anna is about to demand a better explanation then decides against it. She will look up the meanings herself, in the book pushed where they think she can't see it, on the top shelf upstairs.

Suddenly, the shop bell jangles, a cold gust of air blowing through the door. Mrs Wood stands there, a knitted hat pulled low over her ears, a scarf like a noose around her neck.

Mother gathers up the cards and shoves them hurriedly into the pouch. 'We're closed, Maggie. Can't you see the sign?'

'Oh, begging your pardon. Half day, is it?'

'Stocktaking, seeing as it's quiet. Anna, go and peel

some potatoes.'

Anna glares at Mrs Wood. She has a habit of turning up uninvited.

'Anna! Stop daydreaming and do as you're told!'

Upstairs, Anna stomps on every creaking floorboard as she crosses to the kitchen. Jack looks up from his usual spot as she turns back, this time stepping much more carefully. At the top of the stairs she sits down, straining her ears to hear the conversation below.

'I've told you. I'm not doing it.'

'You do it for everyone else. Is my money not good enough?'

'It's not about the money and I don't do it for everyone. It's just a select few.'

'Oh a select few, is it? Teaching the girl though, aren't you?'

'Keep your voice down, Maggie.'

'So come on then, what's the big secret?' Anna hears Mrs Wood's footsteps as she crosses the shop.

'There is no secret and I'm tired of this. I won't tell you again. The cards decide.'

'The cards decide! What's that supposed to mean?'

Mother doesn't respond and Mrs Wood's footsteps continue then stop abruptly.

'You make me sick, do you know that?'

'I think you should leave.'

'Oh, you think I should leave, do you? Listen to Mrs High and Mighty. It's alright for you in your nice little shop. You don't sit here worrying if your husband's coming home in a box every time he goes down the pit, do you? Oh no. Other worries you must have though.' Mrs Wood pauses and Anna holds her breath. 'You do know what he gets up to, don't you? Apart from making

179

my husband's life a misery. You must have seen it in your precious cards.' Her voice has taken on a spitting malevolence. Anna can't see her face but she can picture it.

'Get out,' says Mother.

'Don't worry, I'm going. You named this place right. He'll have you turning tricks before long.'

The bell clangs as the door slams and Anna rushes to the window. Mrs Wood's woolly hat bobs along the street towards the precinct, where she is swallowed up by the Saturday afternoon crowds. All the shops are busy except theirs.

At that moment, Father's car pulls up. Stepping behind the curtain, she watches him adjust his tie and smooth his hair in the mirror. He gets out, locks the car and disappears below.

Anna dashes back to the stairs, straining her ears again but this time, all she hears is Father opening boxes and Mother making tea.

35

Anna

Anna is woken by the sound of birdsong. Her mouth is dry, her head fuzzy but she has known a lot worse. Throwing back the covers, she gets up and walks onto the landing. The house is silent, except for the familiar creak of the floorboards. She goes to the bathroom for a drink of water, then opens the door opposite her own. It already feels different. With her father's passing, the room has moved into yet another phase.

The sparseness strikes her as it always does on the rare occasions she comes in here. Their wedding photo used to stand on the drawers, the couple young and hopeful as they started married life together. After her mother's death, her father put the photograph away. Now all that stands there is a portable television and a saucer where he keeps his change. *Kept his change*, she corrects herself.

From the window, she sees the police car still standing guard outside. A woman she doesn't recognise is leaning in, talking to the occupants. *Probably a reporter*, thinks Anna. She feels no anger now, just a sad acceptance.

The trees across the road are almost skeletal, a few scorched leaves clinging to the branches. Then she sees a roof tile in the middle of the road. Not hers, she hopes, especially now the building's maintenance is her sole responsibility.

She used to love this time of year, the colours and the smells, the early frosts. Daniel's birthday at the start of the month, along with her father's. How does the saying go? *There is a time and a season for everything. A time to be born and a time to die*. The dates will always be there, permanent markers in time but for her, autumn will now be forever tainted.

Her thoughts are interrupted by a knock at the back door. *Not the police again, surely.* Hurrying downstairs, she yanks it open.

For no more than a heartbeat, she is confused. It isn't the police, it's the woman she just saw leaning into the car and she would know her face anywhere.

Anna's knees almost buckle and she grips the doorframe for support. She knows it is her immediately, the tilt of her nose, the way her hair curls over her ears.

Across the gulf of thirty years, she stares into her eyes. Absent for so long yet so familiar.

'Hello, Anna.' Her voice hasn't changed, although the accent is slightly different. Marie's sombre expression tells Anna she knows what has happened. She could even be dressed for mourning. Her black coat almost reaches her ankles. There can be no other explanation for her being here. Her next words confirm it.

'I saw it on the news and I had to come.'

Realising she is staring, Anna lets go of the door frame and stands up straight.

'Marie. This is a surprise. You'd better come in.'

Up in the flat, things feel even more surreal. *What the hell is she doing here?* The kitchen is so untidy, pots in the sink, a dirty knife on the worktop. She tries to take in the apparition before her. Whatever Marie has been doing since their paths last crossed, she looks well on it. Anna is painfully aware of what a wreck she must look in comparison.

'I'm so sorry — me turning up out of the blue is probably the last thing you need.'

'No, not at all. It's just unexpected, after all this time.'

182

'I know. I tried ringing you. I didn't know if you'd want me to come.'

Anna stays silent, lost for words.

Marie pulls out a chair. 'Sit down. I've clearly shocked you.'

Anna remains standing. For some reason it feels important not to let her take control. The two women stare at each other, taking in the changes three decades have wrought. Marie's hair is still blonde. Not the warm honey gold Anna remembers but bleached the colour of straw. There are creases around her mouth and those vivid blue eyes she hasn't seen since childhood are now surrounded with lines as fine as spiderwebs. Her hands haven't changed, still the same slender fingers unadorned with rings. She finds her eyes drawn there, looking for the marks like her own but her sleeves reach well below her knuckles.

First to look away, she picks up the knife and places it into the sink. 'Where are my manners? I'll make us a drink.'

With her back turned, she fills the kettle, allowing herself time to think. For years, she dreamt of this moment. Now it is here she feels cheated, taken unawares with no chance to prepare.

For a split second, she considers escaping to her room to get changed and run a comb through her hair. Dismissing the idea just as quickly, she faces her reflection in the window. She isn't ten years old anymore.

'Come through. I'll light a fire.' Fixing a smile, she leads the way, hoping Marie doesn't notice the teacups rattling on the tray.

It occurs to Anna that Marie has never been up here before. As she bends at the hearth, she recalls her parents' disapproval, their snobbery. What would they think if they could see her here now?

By the time the fire is lit, Marie has removed her coat and is already seated. She hasn't lost her confidence. It seems strange to see her in Father's chair, almost as though she has been biding her time, waiting for them to be gone and now she sits there, large as life, bold as brass at their fireside.

She leans forward, the collar of her shirt falling slightly open. Anna sees the gold crucifix at her throat. She is certain it is the same one she wore as a child.

'I'm so sorry it's taken something like this to bring me back.'

Anna searches for the right words. She almost says her parents will be disappointed to have missed her.

'And I was sorry to hear you'd lost your mum as well,' continues Marie, her voice low and sympathetic. 'I had no idea.'

Why would she have any idea? She hasn't been anywhere near the place for over thirty years.

'Is there anything I can do to help?'

Anna finally finds her voice. 'There's nothing anyone can do.' That seems to sum up the situation. Since her father's death, she has never been in such demand. For three decades, this so-called friend has never shown the slightest interest in her existence. *So why now?*

Marie is still speaking, her eyes roaming around the room, as though she's sizing the place up. What was it her parents called her? Brazen, that was it. She remembers having to look the word up.

'Wow, all these books! No wonder you were so well informed.'

Anna follows her gaze to the shelves but a suitable

response feels beyond her. She is finding it difficult to process this, to believe it is really happening.

'Well, anyway,' continues Marie. 'I'm glad you didn't forget me.'

The words drag Anna out of her reverie. *Forget her? Is she joking?*

'I knew straight away, of course. There's only ever been one Trick Shop.' She pushes her hair behind her ear, a gesture Anna recalls but there is something very different about her. She feels torn between wanting to know what Marie has been doing with her life and a fear of revealing how little she has done with her own.

She is suddenly pierced by a memory and shuts her eyes to blink it away. Anna's world had shrunk when Marie left her. Withered back between the pages, to the nothing she'd had before. No farewell or explanations, she'd been forced to hide her distress with no-one to comfort her. Her parents had been glad to see the back of her. Just like they had with Daniel.

Her head feels as though it is about to explode. She is behaving like a fool. This woman is no more than a stranger. She might have meant something all those years ago, but they are nothing to each other now.

'It was kind of you to call. I'll be putting an announcement in the Derbyshire Times with the funeral details once I know them.' She is amazed how calm her voice sounds.

'Yes, of course, I would like to be there. Pay my respects.'

Anna stands up, noticing neither of them have touched their tea.

'I have a lot to do, as you can imagine, but thanks for coming.'

Only now does Marie pick up her cup, clearly intent on prolonging the visit. What more can she possibly have to say? She sips painfully slowly, then cradles the cup in her lap.

'I lost my mum too,' she says, and even as Anna is thinking she hasn't room for anyone else's grief, she finds herself responding.

'Oh. I'm so sorry,' and she really is. Drawn back to her chair, she is surprised how much this saddens her. 'How long ago?'

'Quite recent. It came as quite a shock.'

Even when fully expected, death takes you unawares. Anna knows this but says nothing. She has no words of comfort after all.

Marie puts her cup down and rises from the chair. 'I'm glad I came. It's good to see you again.' She smiles as she pulls her coat around her shoulders. Anna's gaze is drawn to the ripple of the silk lining.

Ushering her back down to the hallway, she hardly registers her parting words, cutting her off midsentence as she closes the door. Maybe that was a little rude of her. She shoves the bolts on and half runs, half stumbles back up the stairs. Pouring what's left of the vodka into a mug, she slumps down heavily at the table.

There isn't much so she holds it reverently on her tongue, letting it slip down slowly. By the fourth sip, she feels calmer and her mind begins to roam. Letting out a breath, she drifts back in time. Marie's mother floats past, a cat draped across her, settling itself into the azure folds. Two girls sprawl on their backs at her feet and on the wall above them, a blood red light shines from the arms of Jesus.

Marie had been obsessed with the stuff. Only now

with the benefit of hindsight does it strike her how weird it all was. She namedropped saints like other people talk about their cousins. Saint Bernadette, Saint Peter, Saint Mary Mother of God. Tripping off her tongue like a catechism, a mantra, her secret Catholic code. I am the Resurrection and the Life. Holy Communion. Sacred Heart. Blessed Virgin. Anna had loved it, rolling the words around her tongue, listening to the sounds and the cadence. She had soaked them all up, hoarded them lovingly, adding them to her ever growing collection.

It went much deeper than words for Marie. Anna knows it did. She thinks of the ceremonies, the burials. Has she outgrown it all, put her fixations behind her? The crucifix around her neck and the timing of her visit suggest she hasn't grown out of it at all.

She knocks back the rest of the vodka.

36

Kate

Kate has always loved the sound of the wind. Her gran's house was in the hilly north of Sheffield and when it blew there, you knew about it. As a child tucked up in bed, the sound of the wind gusting round the chimneypots and moaning in the eaves would send her to sleep like a lullaby.

Last night it had the opposite effect. Newton had sent her home at 1 am. Arguing had been pointless. He needed at least one of them on standby, plus she'd been on shift for nearly 16 hours already. So had Duffy but he had been nowhere in sight. She had fallen asleep at the table, dreaming briefly, the sound of Archie's name being called jolting her awake. She spent most of the night at the window, looking out into the dark. Luther had sat beside her, intrigued by the nocturnal vigil but quite content to keep her company. The trees had thrashed and flailed so violently she thought they might snap, the rain pelting the glass like bullets. She kept her phone in her hand, putting it down only to light a cigarette. It remained silent and she had felt utterly helpless.

At 6 am she goes in the shower and is at the station by half past. The incident room is busy already, the tension palpable. Bleary-eyed and overwrought, Kate can't be sure whether they are finishing the night shift or just starting the day. She wonders briefly which of them were in on Duffy's prank.

Charlie Collins stares down from the whiteboard, bearing no resemblance to the blood-soaked corpse he would become. Newton had said it was a recent picture.

As always when looking at a photo, Kate wonders who took it. Despite the shock of white hair, he looks well for seventy. She takes in the impeccable moustache, the piercing blue eyes. It's a Nordic face, Kate could easily imagine him in a Viking helmet. In his prime, he could well have been terrifying.

It occurs to her she has been concentrating too much on Anna, when her focus should be the man himself. What was it she had said about her father? *Cards were his passion.* There must have been more to him than that. Whatever the case, Anna had been at great pains to stress his family's conjuring exploits rather than anything linked to gambling, even referring to his *Victorian gentleman persona.* Kate can see nothing of Anna in his features. She wonders what his state of mind had been in the days leading up to his death and whether he knew about his daughter's drink problem.

And where does Margaret Wood fit into all this, if indeed she does? If she was murdered, as Kate suspects, *could Anna be in danger too?*

Her thoughts are interrupted by a cough behind her, and she turns to see Newton has arrived. He looks like everyone else. Exhausted.

'Morning, sir. Any news?'

He shakes his head as he turns on his PC. 'No. The search resumes at first light.'

She is about to ask what he wants her to do today. The missing child has thrown everything into the air but Newton answers her unspoken question before she has the chance.

'I want you to speak to Anna Collins again.' So that's why he had wanted her to be fresh this morning. Surely, finding the boy must be their priority.

'We can't afford to lose momentum, just because this has happened. You seem to be getting on well with her.' Newton seems distracted, rummaging around in his drawer. 'I'm probably going to need the FLO to stay with the boy's mother, unless...' His voice trails off and he slams the drawer shut, his eyes veering towards the window.

'Depending on the next few hours, we're going to have to do an appeal. Hardly great publicity, is it? A murderer on the loose and a child missing. The super's going mad.' He turns to face her, and Kate sees he looks utterly worn out.

'Hasn't the search come up with anything? Not even the copter?'

Newton shakes his head again. 'Nothing. The dogs were hampered by the weather. We're going to have to widen the search, bring in Mountain Rescue.'

The use of dogs hadn't occurred to Kate at first. Weren't they trained to find bodies, not living children? Newton looks as though he could do with reassurance.

'It's not necessarily bad news if the thermal imaging hasn't picked anything up.'

He straightens at this, as though remembering he is supposed to be in charge.

'I know. Let's hope he's safely housed somewhere. He can't have gone far on his own steam.' His voice has regained some authority but Kate suddenly remembers Newton's own son is about the same age as Archie.

'You might want to warn Miss Collins, Up North want to interview her. See if you think she'd be up to it. She'll be knocked off the headlines if we don't get a breakthrough soon.' Newton's fingers are now flying across the keyboard, his eyes fixed firmly on the screen.

Kate knows when she is dismissed. Looking at the time, she sees it is just after seven, far too early to call on Anna yet. She walks towards the coffee machine, then decides she needs food.

Half an hour later, she is sat in her car in the precinct, trying unsuccessfully to warm her hands on a cardboard cup of coffee. She isn't sure what it says about her that she has just polished off a bacon sandwich and a doughnut while, to quote Newton, *there's a murderer on the loose and a child missing.* So much for healthy eating. She wonders if Newton had any breakfast. Probably not, by the look of him. *You seem to be getting on well with her.* What was that supposed to mean? He's probably right, she had felt she was making headway, until things were prematurely cut short. Her eyes are drawn to the windows of Alice's flat above the chemist's. There can't be much space up there with a toddler and another on the way. She is relieved to see the curtains are closed.

The murder investigation can't just stop because a child has gone missing. Even so, Kate can't help feeling Newton is giving her a wide berth. She gets out of the car and walks up the steps of the war memorial, pulling up her collar against the ever-present drizzle. Lighting a cigarette, she takes a deep drag, her eyes narrowing through the smoke. A mangey looking mutt trots up, cocks its leg and disappears. It makes her think of the sniffer dogs. From here she can see the moors, the dark peaks shadowed by cloud. She hopes to God the little lad isn't out there.

Across the precinct, the old red phone box stands on what was once the village green. The shops here still have a quaint feel about them, ancient bricks and timbers still visible beyond the modern signs. Most of the shutters are down but a few early risers are going about their business, seemingly unaffected by the dramas unfolding around them. Maybe that's unfair of her. The local turnout for the search had been good, in spite of the weather.

It is now a little after eight. Kate checks her car is locked and sets off up the road. Anna's bedroom is at the front, so she should be able to tell if she is up. As she draws closer, she sees a group of reporters milling around on the pavement and swears under her breath. It's true, nothing sells like murder.

Crossing the road, she sees Cagney and Lacey still parked up, this time in an unmarked car. The window winds down.

'I hope you've got permission for this.'

Cagney smiles. 'Her ladyship's orders and it's all above board.'

'So I heard. Is she up?'

'Dunno. Curtains are open.'

'This lot haven't been hassling her, have they?'

'Only from afar.'

'OK, cheers.' Kate walks towards the group, making eye contact with none of them. Journalist is too strong a word for any of these individuals although she can't help wondering if they've had more success than she has with the locals. Her blood boils as they flow as one into the road. With any luck, they'll get mown down by a passing lorry. There can't be many things lower than hanging around on the doorsteps of the recently bereaved.

A flashbulb hits her like a blow to the chest. She has no idea why but even out of uniform, people invariably guess she is a police officer. Another flash temporarily blinds her and a giant, fluffy microphone is thrust into her face, the previous low-level utterings now a din of questions.

'Anything to say?'

'Should the public be worried?

'Is it true a child's missing…?'

'Are you her lesbian lover?'

Her head snaps back and she realises too late they have captured her expression. Did she hear correctly? Yes, it was clear enough. Feeling her cheeks aflame, she turns her face away and pushes through the last of them. She almost falls through the gate, hatred coursing through her and for the first time in relation to the press, she feels fear. *They really are a pack of animals*. She drops the latch and turns her back on them. As on her previous visit, the door is already open and Anna waiting on the threshold.

'I don't know how you cope with that rabble on a regular basis.' Kate is wrong footed already. This isn't how she envisaged the meeting would start. Her heart banging as she follows her up the stairs, she feels like a drowned rat.

'I'm just making a drink. Would you like one?'

Kate could do with a brandy but is relieved to see Anna reach for the kettle this time and not the decanter. She agrees to another coffee. Being high as a kite by lunchtime is an occupational hazard. As they enter the living room, she sees the fire is lit, books and papers scattered everywhere.

'Oh, don't worry about these,' says Anna, clearing a seat. 'I thought I'd make a start…' her voice trails off as she sits down. Taking the chair opposite, they resume their positions of Friday night. Support has been on hand 24/7, should Anna have needed it but Kate knows she has refused this. Two days is a long time for the family of a murder victim to be alone and the indignity of having her home searched must have added insult to injury. She thinks of the empty bottles, the way Anna was drinking. How callous she must seem, ransacking the place at the weekend but only coming to speak to her now.

'The neighbours have been hovering like vultures. They'll cross the road to avoid me but break their necks to gossip. I don't know who's worse, them or the press. I was tempted to throw a bucket of water over the lot of them. Or worse.' Anna grins mischievously. Trading repartee at a time like this takes some doing, if indeed it was a joke. She seems to be coping well but Kate is all too aware how good people are at putting on an act.

'We can get them shifted if they're bothering you.' Nothing would give her greater pleasure.

'It's fine. I just pretend they're not there.' A log shifts in the fireplace — fragrant wood again. Not coal being hauled up the stairs but still hard work. The fire spits, flaring momentarily green. Kate knows nothing about it but guesses there must be moss or lichen on the logs for them to hiss like that. Or maybe they haven't been dried properly. She wonders if Anna gathers and cuts the wood herself. She pictures her with an axe.

'How have you been?'

'I've been thinking about the night it happened. If only I'd heard something.'

Maybe it's as well you didn't, thinks Kate. They could have had two corpses on their hands.

'The panda car annoyed me,' Anna continues. 'Not exactly subtle.'

'I'm sorry about that. It's been rectified.'

'So I see. I don't need my father's murder

advertising.' Anna blinks rapidly.

'As I said, I'm sorry. The car is there for your protection and unfortunately, your father's murder is now in the public domain.' *Public domain?* She's beginning to sound like a police training manual.

'Do I need protecting?'

'There's no reason to think so,' says Kate, this time choosing her words more carefully. 'The last thing we want is for you to be worried. The car is purely precautionary, to give you peace of mind.'

Anna's eyebrows raise visibly above her glasses at this. 'So, how is the investigation progressing?'

'It's still early days. Do you mind if I ask you a few more questions?'

'Fire away,' says Anna, as though she couldn't care less.

'OK. So, forgive me if any of this seems insensitive, that's never our intention. We're just trying to piece things together, get a picture of your father's life.' Kate takes her time retrieving her notebook from her bag. 'I'm sorry we weren't able to speak over the weekend about seeing your father.' The least she can do is apologise.

'I've had second thoughts about that now.'

This change of heart comes as no surprise to Kate. She has seen it many times in the bereaved. An overwhelming desire to be with their loved one, just one last time, an understandable reluctance to let them go. In Kate's experience, this can change over a period of days and is just as likely to change back again before the funeral, as the person left behind tries to come to terms with their loss.

'Let us know if you change your mind.' She coughs, clears her throat. 'So, can I ask, were you aware of any worries your father might have had? Had he fallen out with anyone recently?'

'Did anyone want him dead, you mean?'

Kate almost smiles as she takes a sip of her drink.

'In answer to your first question, I wasn't aware my father had any worries.' The firelight is dancing on Anna's glasses again, making it impossible for Kate to see her eyes. 'The shop is doing well, as you've no doubt discovered. I'm certain he can't have annoyed anyone enough to justify murder.' She pauses to sip her coffee. 'It still doesn't seem real.'

'So, you don't have any idea at all who could have done this?'

'Of course not. Don't you think I would have told you if I did?'

It's a fair point. Kate scribbles on her notepad and lets the silence stretch between them. Not for the first time, she wishes she could draw on personal experience of the parent child relationship. She'd had Gran of course and knows unequivocally that if she'd had any worries, Kate would have been the last person in the world she would have burdened with them.

'I don't know how you'd feel about this Anna, but I understand Up North would like to speak to you. Have they been in touch?' It occurs to her they may well be among the crowd outside.

'Up North? No, I haven't heard from anyone and I've avoided the news all weekend…' Her voice trails off again and she turns towards the fire, seemingly absorbed by the flames.

'That's probably just as well. You won't have seen that a little boy has gone missing then?' Kate only says this to fill the silence but Anna sits bolt upright, her interest clearly piqued.

'What little boy? I haven't seen anything.'

'He went missing yesterday.' Kate is glad to have her attention back. 'A local boy, only two years old.'

'Oh, how awful!' Anna moves to the edge of her seat, a look of genuine concern on her face. 'Local, you say? What's his name? I might know them.'

'Freeman is his mother's name. The little boy is called Archie.'

Anna frowns as though deep in thought. 'No, I don't think I know them. Even so, it's terrible.' She looks more bothered about this than her father's murder. Displacement thinks Kate, something else they covered on the bereavement course.

'His mother must be going out of her mind,' continues Anna, her face etched with worry. 'Has there been a search?'

'Of course there has.' Kate finds she is using her most placatory tone. 'There was a thorough search, throughout the night. The helicopter was out, too, and dogs.' She regrets the words as soon as they are out. Even to her, the thought of dogs tracking a little boy's scent is distressing. Anna jumps from her chair and rushes to the window, as if she expects to see the search going on in the street. Her expression changes from concern to contempt.

'Just look at them. How dare they hang around doing nothing, while that poor little boy is out there all on his own?' She turns towards Kate, her hands spread in disbelief.

'Well, you might be able to just sit there while a child freezes to death, but I certainly can't.'

'I don't think this is wise, Anna.' Kate stands up to remonstrate with her. 'I can see you're upset but it isn't sensible.'

Anna has found a pair of boots and bends to tie the laces. 'It's absolutely sensible!' she yells, coming to stand in front of Kate, so close she can smell the wine on her breath. With a deep sigh, Anna leans on a chair as if for support, then turns again to meet Kate's eyes.

'Humour me, please. I've been sitting here like a caged hen! Normally, it doesn't bother me but I'm just stuck here.' She sweeps her arm at the papers strewn around the room. 'I need to keep busy.'

'I get what you're saying,' says Kate. 'But there are trained professionals out there. They know what they're doing.'

'I'm sure they do.' Anna is damping down the fire, her voice high as she thrusts the poker into the ashes. 'I've lived here all my life. I know where all the best hiding places are.'

Kate very much doubts the child is hiding. 'OK, but I'm coming with you.' A walk might calm her down and encourage her to talk more openly but first they must run the gauntlet of reporters outside.

'Just ignore them, OK?' she says as they make their way downstairs. It occurs to Kate that her attempts to grill Anna have once again been thwarted.

37

Newton

Newton slams his phone down so hard he thinks the screen has smashed. He has called Louise every morning since she left him and today was no exception. He misses the routine they had. It's been two weeks now and a pattern has already formed in its place. He asks how she is and receives a one-word response. He asks after Georgie and gets pretty much the same. On the days he sees his son, (he refuses to use the term 'access'), they arrange pick up and dropping off times. Nothing more. There is no small talk but at least she usually answers.

After sleeping off the worst, he had driven to the house Louise is renting. Despite the state he was in, he recalled Jean saying she'd gone out the night before. Parking a few doors down, he had sat there and seethed. It was a nice, compact semi. Dormer windows, newly painted drainpipes but you don't just walk out of one house into another. It takes organisation, forethought. Exactly how long did she have this planned?

It was a pitiful stakeout. His head had been splitting and it was only by sheer force of will he hadn't spewed his guts up in Louise's new street. Seeing another car nose to nose with hers, he was ready to batter whoever it belonged to. When her hairdresser Natalie emerged, Newton had slunk home to bed.

He walks over to the filing cabinet at the far end of the office. Most stuff goes straight onto the computer these days but you can't beat a proper filing system, in Newton's opinion. *What would happen in the event of a power cut or a fire, or if everything was erased by mistake? Stranger things have happened.*

He pulls out a lever-arch file, standing ramrod straight as he does so. He read somewhere that JFK wore a back brace. He doesn't like the sound of that but it's reassuring to know he's in good company. *Or maybe not, come to think of it.*

The file is soft and felted with age, *North Derbyshire Violent Crime Archives, 1968 to 69* stamped across its cover. The Police National Computer wasn't introduced until 74. Almost everything prior to that has been transferred online but some paper records remain, as well as newspaper cuttings and photographs. Newton spent most of his Sunday trawling through these records and feels a flicker of excitement at the rest but he'll save that pleasure for later. With no real leads, maybe the past can shed some light onto Charlie Collins's murder.

He has another file in his drawer, the contents of which were removed from Collins's bedroom. Newton never dreamt there could be such a thing as playing card porn but evidently there is. He pulls out the file and studies the contents. A dominatrix type straddles an ace of spades, naked except for elbow-length gloves and fishnet stockings. He turns to the next one. A woman lies spreadeagled across a five-pointed star, her skin completely covered in red hearts. The bloke attending to her has horns and a forked tail. *Surely, they're mixing their metaphors?* It's all pretty tame and seedy but Newton often impounds such material to save a family's blushes. There was no need for Collins's daughter to see this. A man looking at porn isn't any kind of lead but such things can give an insight into character, how highly sexed an individual is. Added to what else they've heard about him, Newton thinks he knows the answer to that.

Replacing the file, he suppresses a yawn. Having two investigations running parallel is a challenge to say the least. He gets up and walks over to the window. Where on earth can the boy be? They had searched the entire town, every garage and greenhouse, every last coal bunker and shed. The net had been spread across the whole of the surrounding area. Hundreds of people had joined them, scouring the woodland, searching the streams, right up to the old pit, Never Fear and beyond. Olive Stratton of Black Hollow's historical society had delighted in telling him how the old mill got its name. Something to do with a child drowning there and haunting it ever since. It really wasn't what he wanted to hear.

Newton has a niggling feeling the boy isn't far away, almost as though he is hiding in plain sight. He could even be somewhere they have already looked.

He should be out this morning, on a drugs outreach programme at the local comprehensive school. *Paramount we work in tandem, hand in hand*, Vardy had blustered, chest puffed out as it always is when he gets on his soapbox. *Building bridges not walls* is another of his favourites, along with *heart of the community* and *deeds not words*.

Despite the naff lingo, Newton agrees it is an excellent idea. Educating kids on the evils of drugs, drink, any addictive substance has to be worthwhile, he of all people knows that. *Prevention is better than the cure*, as Vardy loves to say. Newton has finally found his painkillers wedged at the back of the drawer and is counting the hours until his next dose. Vardy hasn't a bloody clue what he's talking about.

The school will have to wait and so will Charlie

Collins. The missing boy takes precedence, as long as there's still a chance he can be returned to his mother alive. Newton blinks rapidly, his eyes stinging from lack of sleep. The car park is in shadow, the sky just turning from black to pearlescent grey. Archie is out there somewhere and it's his job to find him. *The town's safety is not your responsibility*, Louise would often say to him. He would beg to differ.

The search resumes at first light and he intends to be there. He hadn't needed Vardy to point out that the press will be all over this. If the boy isn't found today the town will be invaded. He is about to pick up his phone when Duffy's name appears on the screen.

'Sir.'

Newton doesn't like the hesitancy in that one solitary word. 'I was just on my way over. What's up?'

'Sir, we came back to the house before the search resumes.'

'And?'

'The thing is sir, it was still dark but we had another look round the garden while we were waiting for the mother to answer the door.'

'Get to the point Duffy.'

'Well sir, it looked pretty secure, but I was shining my torch round and I spotted a hole in the privet. Big enough for a small child to get through.'

Newton takes a moment to process this information. The team had searched the garden. Other than a cursory glance, he hadn't taken much notice of the hedge but he is supposed to be in charge. As someone who prides himself on being a trained observer, it shouldn't have been missed it.

'Better late than never, Duffy. At least we know he

could have got out on his own. Did you tell the mother?'

'No. I think she feels bad enough as it is.'

'OK. I'm on my way.'

'Alright sir.'

Newton hangs up. He could tell from Duffy's tone he was surprised to get off so lightly. He needs to get a grip. Slipping the packet from his drawer, he takes two more pills out. Then one extra for luck. It's going to be another long day.

38

Kate

The baying mob appear wrongfooted as Kate pushes past them, unsure whether to stay or follow. She growls at them, doing her best to block out their comments as she pulls Anna behind her. Questions of her own race around her head as the pair make their way up the high street.

How much do you normally drink, Anna?

Is that the last relationship you had? Seventeen years ago?

There was no break-in and nothing stolen. Did your father know his killer?

'Where are we going?' she asks, telling herself she is storing them up for later.

'Hopefully to find the little boy.' Anna smiles as she breathes in great lungsful of air. She seems relieved to be outside despite the icy temperature and there is something purposeful about her stride. She looks almost as though she is enjoying herself.

Walking past her car in the precinct, Kate can't help another glance towards Alice's windows. The curtains are still tightly drawn. It is only a little after nine but much busier than an hour earlier, the pavements crowded with shoppers, traffic coiled around the war memorial. They stop to let a bus pull out and Kate covers her face to avoid the choking fumes.

Now the shutters are up, a neon medicine bottle is revealed in the chemist's window, the shelves of the bakery next door jam-packed with ghoulish treats. Acid hued cakes spill from a witch's cauldron, the shelf piled high with ghost-shaped gingerbreads. Today is

Halloween and Kate wonders if the parents of Black Hollow will allow their children out trick or treating with both a murderer and a child snatcher at large.

With little sense of where they are heading, she follows Anna down a cobbled alley she didn't even know existed. The noise of the precinct fades behind them as they emerge into open fields. The contrasts of this place still surprise Kate. One minute in the midst of a busy street, the next, you can turn and find yourself in breathtaking countryside. Although it isn't particularly breathtaking today. The rain has eased but the sky is leaden, darker still over the hills. She makes a mental note to do more exploring when she has the time. With all her trips into the Peak District, she may have missed the beauty right under her nose.

The path is a quagmire and Kate steps around deep puddles as the mud sucks at her boots.

'Where *are* we going?' she asks again, as she scans the murky landscape. In one direction, the hills are just visible, a bruised purplish mass blocking the horizon. In the other, a mist drifts, visibility reduced to just a few metres.

'Just along here is Ochre Dyke,' replies Anna, pointing in front of her. 'It's fast flowing when there's heavy rainfall. He could have fallen in or got trapped down the banks.'

It sounds as though she speaks from experience. Sneaking a sideways glance at her, Kate sees her eyes are bright and their breaths plume in front of them, coalescing and merging in the fog.

She has tried to imagine what it must have been like for Anna, finding her father that morning. Would he still have been warm or was he long dead by the time she discovered him? Was there even a chance he could have been saved? She ought to ask Newton, he was first on the scene. She would have liked to attend the post-mortem. Like is the wrong word but the ones she's been to previously fascinated her. There are other questions she was too afraid to ask. Could the wound have been self-inflicted? Surely not. She looks again at her companion, almost marching by her side.

'I'm sure the search parties have been out here, you know.' Kate's feet are already feeling heavier with every step.

'They don't know it like I do,' says Anna, shaking her head. 'There are so many dips and hollows, it would be easy to miss him.'

'I have it on good authority that lots of locals joined the search. People who know the area as well as you do.'

Kate knows her words are futile. They trudge along in silence and it strikes her they could easily be friends, out for a walk together. Just like it was with Helen — and look how that turned out. How the hell has this happened? She's pretty sure this is not what Newton had in mind.

'Did you say you've always lived here?' she asks, keen their impromptu expedition isn't a complete waste of time.

Anna doesn't answer straight away, placing her feet carefully between puddles and holes. 'Almost always,' she finally replies, her eyes narrowed behind her glasses as she scans the fog. For what, Kate has no idea, there is absolutely nothing to see. But as she frames another question, the outline of a crude bridge appears through the furling mist. As they draw closer, Kate sees it is little more than a plank with wooden rails either side.

'You wait here,' instructs Anna. 'There's no point both of us getting soaked.'

'Where are you going?' asks Kate, surprised at this sudden turn of events.

'To check the banks. They're quite steep in places but I know every inch. I won't be long.' And with that, she is enveloped by the fog which is denser here by the water.

Taking out her cigarettes, Kate steps onto the bridge. Once she is sure they are strong enough, she rests her weight against the rails and lights up. Cursing, she leans over the edge, blowing smoke into the whirling depths. The water's surface is invisible but she can hear it surging over rocks. The level must be high after last night's rainfall. She gets a sense of its width from the dark masses either side, which she assumes to be trees and bushes. A small child falling in here would be lucky to get out.

Now she has stopped walking, she is feeling the cold again. Her jeans are wet through and the tips of her fingers are frozen. Finishing her cigarette, she flicks it over the rail, watching guiltily as its glowing tip disappears. Hardly the countryside code but no-one is likely to see her. The way she feels right now, she doesn't care. Hands deep in her pockets, she kicks mud off her boots and begins to walk up and down, to keep her circulation going. She pictures her surroundings on a summer's day, the stream sparkling, the grass ablaze with gorse, the drone of bees instead of fog. She can't even tell if she's been here before with nothing to see except the curling tendrils crawling across the bridge, the murky void beneath her.

Turning for the third time she realises she has no idea which direction Anna went in. More to the point, she doesn't know her way back. She stands still, trying to get her bearings but at all four points of the compass, the view is the same. Becoming increasingly annoyed with herself, she lights another cigarette, shaking her head at her own stupidity. *What a complete idiot, to end up stuck on a rickety bridge, out in the middle of nowhere.* She pushes against the rail. It's sturdier than it looks. The rest is true though. The unearthly wall of fog could be quite scary if the circumstances weren't so utterly ridiculous.

She wonders how the real search is progressing. *Are they out there now on the moors?* Duffy was so up himself last night but it wouldn't bother her if he saves the boy single-handedly so long as he is found safe and well. She takes out her phone again. Still no signal. All she can do is wait. Surely Anna won't leave her here and even if she does, the fog will eventually clear and then she can make her way back.

Maybe it's best she doesn't tell Newton about this. Wasting police time is an offence not normally committed by CID. But then again…

She is about to light another cigarette when a disembodied voice floats towards her and a shape starts to form. Anna comes into view, waving her arms in greeting. Kate can tell from her lack of urgency she has found nothing.

Joining her on the bridge, she leans against it, wiping her glasses on her jeans. 'I've been all the way down to the ford, then back up the other side.' She stops to catch her breath, clearly disappointed. 'It's really muddy, so I think I'd be able to tell if someone had fallen in. I could see where the search party's been. Lots of tracks but quite blurred with all the rain.'

What is she, some sort of female Bear Grylls? thinks

Kate, a far cry now from the librarian persona.

They set off back along the footpath, which is in the opposite direction Kate thought it was. 'At least we tried.'

'We haven't finished yet,' replies Anna. She is caked in mud, her fingers encrusted with dirt.

'We should be getting back,' says Kate, looking at the time on her phone. Could she inveigle her way back into Anna's home? Maybe then she can conduct something more akin to a proper interview. But clearly Anna has other ideas.

'There are some old woods up here. Very overgrown in places. A child could easily get lost in them.' She points ahead to where the fog is lifting, to a dark smudge on the horizon.

'I'm sure the search parties have covered this whole area, Anna.' Kate is tired of repeating herself and her patience is wearing thin. Water has seeped into her boots, her toes squelching. Today should be written off as a lost cause.

As though sensing her reluctance, Anna stops dead in her tracks. She turns her back on the woods and looks down the valley towards town.

'You're probably right. I can always come back later if there's still no news.'

Kate is too busy picturing the hot bath she intends to run herself as soon as she gets home to consider whether this is a good idea or not. It seems Anna will do whatever she pleases anyway.

39

1977

'Me and your mother have decided. We don't want you knocking about with that Ryan girl anymore.'

Anna looks up from her book, placing her finger on the page to keep her place.

'She's a bad influence.'

'No she isn't!' This isn't strictly true and Father won't stand for insolence.

'Don't answer back!' He glares at her from the card table. 'From now on you come straight home from school. I won't have you hanging round street corners with the likes of her!'

Anna swallows down any further retort. Her father in this mood is not to be crossed. She has known from the start her parents disapprove of Marie but she has never understood why. Then she thinks of the things they have done, the secrets they share.

Father stalks out, leaving her alone in the room. The very thought of going back to how things were before doesn't bear thinking about. Pushing the book aside, she buries her face in the sofa, trying to muffle her sobs. The cushion smells of Jack and she brushes away the dog hairs.

Father comes back in and pours a drink from the decanter. It must be bad if he's drinking this early in the day. A clatter from the kitchen tells Anna her mother is keeping out of the way.

'I won't stop seeing her!' The words are out before she can stop them and she cowers in anticipation of his reaction. Once or twice his hands have flown at her, faster than cards from a deck but it's his words she really shrinks from and his stare alone can lacerate. He takes a sip of the dark liquid, glowering into its depths. Anna holds her breath.

Without warning, he hurls the glass into the fire. It shatters, sending blue flames shooting up the chimney. 'Read your book and keep your stupid little mouth shut!' he roars, spittle flying from his lips, his face purple with rage. Anna ducks past him and runs from the room. She keeps running, through the back door into the courtyard. Jack is dozing by the dustbin. Seeing her, he gets up and follows her into the street.

She puts her trembling arms around him, squeezing her eyes shut. His smell and the warmth of his fur calm her. He lets her rest her face against him until her tears subside.

She looks back at the shop, expecting one of her parents to burst out, but the gate and the door remain closed. With no idea where she is headed, Anna sets off walking, Jack padding beside her. What on earth could have brought about such anger, such rage? Anna has seen her father lose his temper before but the look on his face was one of pure, burning hatred.

She stops in the shadow of a patch of scrub, so overgrown it takes up half the pavement. Father complained only this morning, that the council need to get it cut. *Before it blocks out the sun*, he had grumbled but Anna is glad of its shade because from here she can stand unobserved and see right into the window next-door.

She looks through the leaves and there she is as usual, with her knitting on her knee, thinking no-one can see her. The nets are parted slightly, the chair to one side but

Anna can see her, she always does, watching as people pass by, spying on them. Mrs Wood who cleans at the rectory and comes to see her mother. *Could the old witch have said something? Is she the one responsible for trying to take away her only friend?*

Anna turns things over in her mind. After a while, the damp poke of Jack's nose reminds her of his presence. Ruffling his fur, she turns away from the houses and crosses the road. She won't stop seeing Marie, she won't! Her father can go to the Devil. *He can burn in hell.*

40

Kate

'Where did you say the boy lives?' asks Anna, as they trudge down the hill.

'Ditch Street.' Actually, she hadn't. 'Why?'

'I just wondered. There's somewhere else I'd like to look.'

Jesus, thinks Kate.

'Just one more stop, before I can even think about going home.'

'Anna, I really don't think this is a good idea.' It has started to rain again and Kate knows she needs to exert some authority. Something she should have done hours ago. 'I can understand your need to keep busy but I can't be seen wandering around town with you. I've got important work to do.'

'What could be more important than finding Archie?' The look on Anna's face is one of pure indignation.

'You need to take it easy,' says Kate wearily. So much for authority. 'I'm sure the search will still be ongoing. Once you've had a rest you can go and join them.' She pulls out her phone but there is still no signal.

'I can't go back yet, it doesn't feel right,' replies Anna, as they reach the alleyway they came down.

'Where exactly do you want to look?' asks Kate, as they emerge into the precinct. 'We're hardly likely to find him in the middle of town.'

'There's an old well in the graveyard,' says Anna, apparently oblivious to her sarcasm.

The pavements are packed with excited children, some already dressed in scary costumes. A group of chattering girls streams past, their bin bag capes flapping in the breeze, prematurely giddy on E numbers. Kate resolves not to answer the door this evening, that's if she manages to get home by nightfall.

It's the first she's heard of an old well. Surely, health and safety mean it will be secured and no child could be in danger of falling into it. She says as much to Anna.

'I'm sure you're right. It's just a feeling I've got.' They pass beneath an ancient lychgate onto a cobbled path. The rain is like a fine mist and Kate brushes her dripping fringe from her eyes. What a complete wild goose chase this is. She should have insisted they left things to the professionals, instead of allowing herself to be so easily persuaded.

As they reach the church, Kate thinks of Duffy as the gargoyles leer down at them. Rainwater trickles from their gaping mouths so they're forced to leave the path to avoid a further soaking. The grass is flat in places, the earth gouged and churned with the marks of heavy footfall. The search has obviously been here already. Of course they have, thinks Kate. She will humour Anna only as far as the well. Then she must put her foot down.

They pass the newest graves, the headstones smooth, their inscriptions easily legible. Most are well-kept and cared for but the storm has clearly wreaked havoc. A teddy bear has been blown into the hedge and upturned urns and vases litter the ground. One of the graves is freshly dug, the imprint of a shovel still visible in the soil. As they continue, the stones become more weathered and less upright. *There can be few places drearier than a graveyard in the rain*, reflects Kate, as they weave their way between the listing monuments.

'I come here quite often,' says Anna, pointing. 'My

mother's grave is over there but I used to play here as a child.'

Kate is unsure how to respond and ponders the few facts she knows about her companion. She is without a single friend, preferring to spend her time reading books and drinking. She now adds loitering in graveyards to her list of known hobbies.

The ground slopes away and the stones have all but petered out here. Kate almost slips and Anna puts a hand out to steady her. She clearly has a bone-deep connection with the place, no pun intended. Her next words confirm this.

'There are hundreds of burials beneath us here, all unmarked. They probably had wooden crosses originally. Suicides were laid to rest here and the unbaptised.' Glancing across at Kate, her expression is quite animated. 'There's been a church here since Norman times and I think the well is even older. It's known as the priest's well. Gypsies used to draw their water from it.'

'Really,' replies Kate, aware it isn't much of a response. Maybe on a fine day and in different circumstances, she could share Anna's enthusiasm. As it is, her patience has now worn through.

'Here we are,' says Anna, as Kate hugs her elbows against the cold. All she can see are dripping yews ahead of them but Anna has sunk to her knees. As she parts the soddened grass, a ring of stones is revealed, about twelve inches across and flat to the ground. The rain has darkened the stones, so they are the same colour as the earth. If Anna hadn't been with her, she would have walked straight past it.

Squatting down, Kate sees a smooth disc like a manhole cover. It looks quite new, certainly not the original and although slightly dented it appears sturdy enough. She is about to turn away, sick of this fool's errand, when Anna reaches out and pushes one side of the cover. It tilts, leaving a six-inch gap and a glimpse of the sheer drop beneath. She pulls her hand back as though scalded and the disc falls back into place. Looking at her across the ring of stones, Kate slowly pushes the cover again. As it moves, she grasps the edges.

'Oh my God,' she utters as it comes away in her hands. It feels like aluminium or some other lightweight metal and isn't heavy at all. She lifts it clear and tosses it aside. Two decaying brackets are now visible, either side of the opening. These look old enough to be the originals. Shaking her head in disbelief, Kate rubs her finger along one of them, the gunmetal grey of iron exposed beneath the rust.

'These brackets have been sawn through deliberately. It's a death trap.'

Kate sees the fear in Anna's eyes, no sign now of the enthusiasm that gripped her moments earlier.

On all fours and getting more saturated by the second, Kate leans over the lip of the well. The cylindrical walls are a patchwork of glistening bricks, grey mushrooms blooming obscenely where the water runs in rivulets. The smell is rank, a fungal mixture of rotting earth and stagnant air. *These walls can't have seen the light of day in decades*, thinks Kate but then she notices some of the mushrooms have had their heads knocked off.

An awful feeling starts to churn her stomach. 'How deep is this thing?'

'I don't know.' Anna's voice is no more than a whisper as she cranes her neck to see. Kate pulls her torch out, aiming the beam vertically. She bends as far forward as she dares but the narrow angle means only the brickwork is visible.

Getting to her feet, she retrieves a coin from her pocket. She has seen it done in films and feels slightly ridiculous as she drops it into the darkness. Straining her ears, she listens for the definitive plop but it doesn't come.

She is about to ask another question when a noise comes from beneath them. Both women stop dead, neither moving a muscle.

'Did you hear that?' whispers Anna.

'Yes, and I'm pretty sure it wasn't my coin hitting the bottom.' Kate throws herself back onto her stomach, her face on a level with the edge of the well.

'Hello!' she calls into the abyss. Her voice echoes back at them. The only other sound is the patter of the rain.

'He couldn't be down there, could he?' asks Anna, sounding terrified.

'I don't know, but something is.' Shuffling further forward, Kate stretches her arm as far as it will go. She shimmies across the grass, using her elbows to pull herself along. Aiming the torch again, she sweeps it in a wide arc but still there is nothing to see but the curving wall.

'Be careful,' whispers Anna. She moves out of the way as Kate slides to the opposite side from where she started, guiding the beam more slowly. This time it picks out two vertical lines of rusted nails starting just beneath the rim, disappearing downwards.

'Looks like there was once a ladder but there's nothing left of it.' Angling the torch, Kate inches her upper body a little further over the edge. Even through her thick coat the sharp stones dig painfully into her breasts, making it difficult to breathe. She is about to pull herself back when the shaft of light catches something. With a gasp, she swings the beam backwards. Directly beneath her on a narrow ledge, is the huddled form of a child, his dirt-smeared face tilted up to her.

She almost screams and nearly drops the torch. Every instinct wants to cry out but the last thing she must do is frighten the boy any more than he must be already.

'He's here,' she murmurs, keeping her voice low and quiet. With one hand, she gestures for Anna to stay back, the torch firmly gripped in the other.

'Hello, Archie.' Her words seem completely inadequate. Kate has little experience of children but is well versed in crisis management, once talking a suicidal dentist down from a viaduct. Not something she's ever likely to forget and hardly comparable with this situation but the objective is the same, to get the subject out of harm's way and into a position of safety.

She needs to keep her head clear, assess the situation. Careful not to dazzle the boy, she directs the torch onto the ledge, casting a halo of light around him. He is still looking up at her, his eyes like saucers, his cheeks and tiny hands red raw with cold.

The ledge runs right across and beyond it she can see the unmistakable glint of water. She wouldn't like to guess its depth. *One slip and the child could topple. Then again, if he hasn't fallen in yet, there's a good chance he isn't going to.* She weighs up the options. They have no apparatus with them. She contemplates removing her coat, knotting it together with Anna's and trying to persuade the lad to be pulled out that way. She dismisses the idea immediately. He's too far down and it isn't worth the risk. The safest option is to ring for help. She pulls out her phone with her free hand. *Thank God, at last a signal.*

'We're going to get you out of there, Archie,' she calls to the child. His eyes haven't shifted from her face.

41

Newton

'So, let's get this straight, Newton. Almost the entire force, including dogs and a helicopter, not to mention half the population of Derbyshire were unable to find the lad and yet your errant sergeant and the daughter of our latest murder victim somehow managed to do so?'

With an hour to kill, Newton has gone for a walk. Not that he hasn't walked far enough over the last two days but the exercise will do him no harm. The super's words revolve around his head on a loop.

'How could this possibly happen?' Vardy had been incredulous and who could blame him?

'Well sir, the search was severely hampered due to the extreme weather conditions.' Even to his own ears this had sounded lame.

'It didn't hamper Fox and her pal though, did it?' He had boomed. 'What the hell were they doing there in the first place?'

Newton couldn't answer that. To say Kate's methods are unorthodox would be an understatement. Of course Vardy was pleased as punch the little boy had been found, they all were, but he was incandescent with rage at the manpower expended on the search. The cost had been colossal.

Newton winces as he pulls himself over a stile, cursing as he lands in the mud. It doesn't really bother him. He changed into his boots as soon as he got home and is well wrapped up against the elements. Sod's law it should brighten up now. He squints as the afternoon sun glints off the puddles. He isn't used to being out here on his own. Before they had Georgie, they used to come up here with Lottie. In summer, they'd bring a picnic, make a day of it. After Georgie arrived, there was always some excuse. They couldn't get the buggy up here. Then when he learnt to walk it was too far to come.

'Good thing at least one of your team used their initiative,' the super had concluded. 'She got a result in the end, that's the main thing. I'm prepared to turn a blind eye to her methods.'

Kate has done well, there's no doubt about it. She can walk on water as far as Vardy is concerned but things are never quite that simple.

'Under different circumstances, I'd consider a commendation. But none of this must get out, Newton, under any circumstances. Stress levels in the town are sky high and if the media hear about it, they'll have a field day. I'm relying on you to ensure they don't.'

He dreads to think what the papers will make of it, but matters closer to home concern him more. Vardy might be willing to overlook Kate's maverick tendencies, but he doesn't know the half of it. Friday night is never far from Newton's thoughts.

Hangman's Wood is now coming into view. Newton knows the history, the story that gives the place its name. The trees look different in the mellow sunshine to how they appeared last night. Flashlights bisecting the darkness, the volunteers and barking dogs had formed a deafening rabble, shattering any peace the place might have. Lashed by the storm and weighed down by wet clothes and heavy equipment, it was true they had been hampered from the start. The whole operation had been a waking nightmare.

Newton leans against a tree to catch his breath and

stretch his back. Splintered branches stick up from the ground and a huge oak is split down its middle, the exposed timber pale in the half-light. Slates and damaged fence panels had littered his route here, the overflowing drains unable to cope with the volume of rainfall.

He is about to head home when something stops him. The hairs stiffen on his neck, the unmistakable feeling of being watched. Newton stands motionless, scanning the gaps between the trees but nothing stirs. Probably a fox or a squirrel, or maybe just his tired mind playing tricks on him. Either way, he has no intention of picking his way through that lot.

The snap of a twig breaks the silence and a woman in a black beanie appears from behind the shattered oak. He blinks, surprised to see anyone out for a stroll in this storm-wrecked wilderness but she is surefooted, crisscrossing her way confidently through the fallen branches. It is only when she pulls her hat off that he realises he has seen her before.

She is dressed in tight black jeans today and a dark puffer jacket but her blonde hair, cut short like a helmet and curling over her ears is the same, if a little ruffled. She smiles but Newton can't tell if she remembers him.

'Lovely morning, after the night we had,' she says, her step slowing as she draws nearer.

'Yes, much calmer,' replies Newton. He watches as she rests her backside against the tree behind her. The pose is so natural, as though she has spent her life traversing these paths, which she may have done, for all he knows. With her androgynous hair, she could easily be a wood nymph but there is nothing boyish about the swell of her breasts as she unzips her jacket.

'Are you from this neck of the woods?' he asks,

pulling his eyes away.

'I was once, many moons ago.'

Newton is always curious about people. It's part of being a detective. 'I saw you the other evening, I think. In the Miners Arms.'

At this, her eyes dart towards him. Is it his imagination, or does she look momentarily rattled? As though discovered in something illicit. She soon recovers her composure.

'Quite possibly. It's the only decent pub left round here.' She pushes herself away from the tree and looks directly at him. Newton wonders at her age and accent. She sounds local but with a hint of something else and he guesses she could be anywhere between thirty and forty-five.

She hitches her sleeve to consult a wristwatch, then begins walking down the slope towards town. Newton feels a little put out at his abrupt dismissal but she spins round to face him.

'You might bump into me in there again if you're passing.' She pulls the beanie back over her hair, before turning and continuing down the hill.

Newton watches her retreating figure. She walks with purpose and doesn't turn to admire the view. She will have seen it all before if she grew up here. These fields and woods can't have changed much over the centuries, but something brought her up here and something has brought her back to Black Hollow. He hangs back. Only when she has climbed the stile and vanished from view does he follow in her footsteps.

She had stalked through the trees as though she owned them. A woman needs self-assurance to walk alone through dense woodland but maybe that's just the policeman in him. Then again, he's pretty sure she just asked him out and in his view that takes some balls.

The streets are piled with detritus but Newton is still smiling to himself as he steps onto the ancient cobbles of the Anglican church. It has always struck him as a strange hybrid of a place, with its square tower and gothic gargoyles. The path is half flooded, puddles along one edge rippling in the breeze. The fury has gone out of the wind but the damage it caused is clearly visible.

Duffy had led the search here. The vicar confirmed the church is kept locked except when services are taking place and was therefore inaccessible. The graveyard however is never locked. Newton had been surprised by this. He would have expected the place to be secured against drunkards or vandals, maybe even grave robbers. He had stored the information away in his database of accidental discoveries. He is willingly given precious few.

According to the vicar, the graveyard can be entered at three different points. Through the lychgate, by a side entrance to the south or through a narrow path to the north, in the oldest section of the church grounds.

The search parties had split, Newton's group concentrating on the woods and surrounding fields, others combing the dyke, Never Fear and the site of the old colliery. Duffy's lot had focused on the town centre, including both graveyards. Black Hollow combines both rural and urban terrain and detailed maps had been consulted before they set out. Apart from Olive Stratton and her grisly revelations, there had been the usual smart arses champing at the bit to show off their local knowledge. Most had been more irritating than helpful.

Newton had been aware of the well's existence but

until the boy's extraction, had never seen it for himself. When he first arrived here, he had sensed a mistrust of newcomers. In an effort to get to know people and learn something of the area, he had attended a history talk at the library. The church was Norman in origin, the gargoyles added later when the building was extended. The well was once used by gypsies, the speaker had said but had been sealed off many years ago, which is why Newton has never bothered to seek it out.

As he rounds the corner, he sees the council have arrived earlier than their appointed time, to do what should have been done in the first place. He quickens his pace, keen to speak to them before they leave. A van is parked by the hedge, tyre marks crisscrossing the grass. Two workmen crouch beside the well, a plastic bag beside them. They stand up as Newton approaches.

'Glad you're here,' says one of the men, not bothering with introductions. 'You might be interested in this.' His face grim, he reaches down and tips the contents of the bag onto the grass.

For a second, Newton isn't sure what he is looking at. A slab of iced Dundee cake or a hunk of brie? Cocaine isn't something you often see in these parts. Certainly not in this quantity.

Squatting carefully, he picks up the package. Beside it are dozens of smaller plastic bags, coloured pills like sweets nestled inside them.

'Wouldn't like to guess the value of that little lot.' The older of the two seems to be the spokesperson. 'About a kilo of Charlie there, not to mention the poppers.'

'These were down the well, were they?'

'Yeah, there's a cavity at the end of the ledge.' The workman points but Newton can see very little. Taking his torch out, he shines it into the blackness, sweeping the beam along the ledge where the child was found.

'How deep is this thing?'

'Wouldn't like to say,' says the workman.

Photographs have already been taken but the priority had been to get the boy to safety, ensure he wasn't injured and reunite him with his parents. Newton had arranged this return visit to find out why the well wasn't properly sealed. He hadn't been expecting this.

'I'll take these off your hands.' As he throws the stash back into the bag, he sees the discarded well cover propped against a toolbox. It seems the least of his worries now but he picks it up, weighing it in his hands. *Aluminium by the feel of it. Hardwearing but lightweight.* Turning back, he bends gingerly. The hinges, or what's left of them, have been sawn through, so the cover would have been easy to remove. He doubts a two-year-old could do it but if it hadn't been properly replaced, he could have squeezed or fallen past it.

He shines his torch into the well. The ledge is about a metre down and he can just make out the cavity at one end. An excellent hiding place. Newton would like to get his hands on the bastards responsible. The boy could easily have been killed.

Could the lad have already been here when the search came this way? Maybe the noise had scared him and he had retreated into the cavity out of sight. He pictures him, cowering in the darkness beside the bags of drugs. It doesn't bear thinking about. At least in the well, he would've had some protection from the elements but could the dogs really have missed both him and the stash? They'd come from search and rescue, not the drug detection unit. They had picked up his scent from his

T-shirt but the trail had soon been lost. Wet conditions can be good for tracking but if the air is cold as it had been, it can be impossible to pick anything up. Of course, Archie could have climbed or fallen in after the search party had passed. The drugs, for that matter, could have been placed there afterwards. The super had been apoplectic at the possibility of the boy being missed. Looking at the bag in his hand, Newton dreads to think how he will react to this.

If anyone's found to have been negligent, they will be held accountable. As it stands, the picture presented to the press has been carefully choreographed, focusing on the child's elated parents and the fact the boy was unharmed. In fact, after a warm bath and a mug of hot chocolate, Archie had positively glowed, smiling for the cameras and giggling at his mother's kisses. They'd managed to coax it out of him that he'd chased a leaf through the hedge but it is still a mystery to Newton how he ended up down the well.

Glancing up, he sees the workmen tugging a replacement cover from the back of the van. It takes both of them to lift and carry it across the grass. Rapping his knuckles against it, he is pleased to hear the dull, metallic ring of cast iron. 'Make sure it's sealed for good this time,' he says, but gives them a wry smile. None of this is their fault. Still, he intends to speak to the council about the use of cheap materials and lack of care for public safety.

Turning back, he sees a man in clerical robes emerge from a door in the transept. He shouts to attract his attention but the priest is walking briskly and by the time he reaches the church, there is no sign of him.

42

Anna

The rattle of the letterbox wakes Anna from a deep sleep. Stretching, she wonders who it can be but makes no attempt to leave the rumpled warmth of her blankets.

There it goes again, more insistent this time. Throwing back the covers, she pulls on her dressing gown and reaches for her glasses. She is about to open the door when it occurs to her it might be Marie again. Peering into the mirror between the coat pegs, she sees her face still flushed from sleep but the darkness under her eyes is less purplish than usual. She smooths her hair and opens the door to find Julie, the family liaison officer standing on the doorstep.

'Oh, I hope I didn't wake you? I tried to call over the weekend but there was no answer.'

'I've been trying to catch up on some sleep,' replies Anna, her waspish tone belying her feelings, which are a mixture of disappointment and relief.

'I was wondering if this might be a convenient time to do the inventory. I can come back later if not.'

'No, it's fine. Come in.' She throws the door wide. Julie is a bulky figure and it's a tight squeeze in the hallway.

'You can make a start if you want. I'll go and get dressed.' Anna hurries back up the stairs — she hasn't felt so rested in ages. After all that fresh air and excitement yesterday, she had fallen asleep without a drink for the first time in months. Remembering how Julie takes her coffee, she joins her in the shop with two steaming mugs.

Anna hasn't set foot in here since the day it happened. Even after the police and forensics had gone, she'd had no wish to venture in here and is grateful she isn't alone.

'I didn't really know where to start,' smiles Julie, sipping her drink. *FLO*, thinks Anna, surprising what you pick up when you're involved in a murder case.

'Shall we have some light in here?' Despite the weak sunshine seeping in through the shutters, the shop is full of shadows. Anna flicks on the lights and starts up the till, the screen coming to life with a host of brightly coloured boxes.

'All the stock is on here.' She taps expertly, endless columns and rows appearing, all neatly populated. 'There's a description of the merchandise this side, then the quantity and the price. We can't go wrong, really.'

It had been Anna's idea of course, to get them online. Dragging her father away from his dusty old logbooks into the twenty-first century had been quite an achievement. She is pleased to see Julie looking suitably impressed.

They decide on a strategy. Julie will read out the items and Anna will check they're still here. It seems the most sensible plan, as Anna can identify everything and has a good idea where it should be.

It could have been an arduous task. The shop is packed, shelves and cabinets lining every wall but Anna finds it strangely therapeutic. She can't remember the last time they did a stocktake and finds an unexpected pleasure in handling the different packages and boxes. From time to time, she glances towards the door, not entirely sure who she is expecting. They are still closed for business and the neighbours appear to be losing interest already.

'The Penguin Book of Tarot,' calls Julie. Anna spins the carousel, finding it with ease. Some of the stock is brand new and still in its cellophane wrappings, others faded with age, collector's items that must be handled with care. Another reason Julie is the one reading from the till.

'Some of these were never meant to be sold, you know,' Anna tells her, pulling on a pair of cotton gloves. Opening one of the cabinets, she takes out a yellowed sheaf and begins to count. 'Unless we got lucky of course. These are a German Woodcut. Eighteenth century. Have a look at the price.'

Julie looks at the screen and lets out a low whistle.

'It'd be twice that if there wasn't one missing. You rarely find a full deck of this age but my father always said they're too beautiful to hide away in a safe and I agree with him. The glass is tinted, so it protects them from further fading and we always keep the temperature cool. Humidity can make them curl.' At this, a memory comes to her. Her father's head bent, his voice almost reverent. *These cards have travelled further than you and I put together. Passed through unknown hands at unknown tables.* A shiver runs through her. Every one of these cards has a history and is as familiar as an old friend.

She begins to enjoy herself and time passes quickly. Julie seems genuinely interested in the snippets of detail she shares with her and Anna finds her presence undemanding. She could almost believe she is here to help and support. Unlike DS Fox that is. *Kate.* She might act all friendly but Anna isn't fooled.

Her gloved fingers search the dark wooden edge of the shelf behind the till. She steps back as it swings forward, revealing a square, solid looking safe sunk into the wall. Julie's mouth drops open. 'It takes everyone by surprise,' smiles Anna, tapping in the combination. 'Not that we show it to just anyone. Ah, look! I'd almost forgotten this was here.'

Leaning into the safe's interior, she lifts out a velvet box. She remembers the surface being black but now the edges are grey. Taking it across to the counter, she watches Julie's expression change again as she opens it. A row of pendants hangs from the lid, earrings and bracelets all engraved and embellished with the symbols Anna has known her whole life. Spades, diamonds, clubs and hearts. She touches a pair of cufflinks, her fingers trailing lovingly over the rings, brooches and pins.

'Playing card jewellery,' says Anna with a sigh. 'It was all the rage in the eighties but we rarely get asked for it now. Tastes change, I suppose but some of these are worth more than you'd think.' She is certain nothing is missing but they go through the motions, painstakingly ticking off every item. She isn't entirely sure why but she is determined to prove to the police that theft was not the murderer's motive. Closing the box, she turns back to the safe. 'These are the real treasures.' Taking out two small packages, she places them carefully on the counter. Pushing the jewellery box aside, she pulls a set of cards from the first. Spreading them across the counter, she is about to explain their provenance, when a waft of cigarette smoke fills the air and she is momentarily disorientated, for a split second believing her father is here in the shop.

Looking up, she sees DS Fox framed in the doorway. Of course, she should have known. The fug of tobacco follows her everywhere and now she comes to think of it, the smell is nothing like the strong, dark scent of her father's brand.

'I did knock but the back door was open.' She walks towards the counter, her expression serious. 'The last thing I want is to alarm you, Anna but you need to be more vigilant. Julie, you should know better.'

'Sorry, sarge, I should have made sure it was locked.'

'Look, we've been through this before. I refuse to live like a prisoner and I'm not in the least bit scared.' Even to her own ears, Anna sounds like a petulant child. 'Anyway, aren't your colleagues still out there and those reporters?'

'A few stragglers, yes, but you can't be too careful. I think they're more interested in Archie now.' They had agreed to keep Anna's name out of things. Better for the public to believe the boy was found during the official police search. 'What have you got there?'

'I was just showing Julie some of our rarer items. Cards haven't always had the suits we know today.'

Anna watches as the detective peers into the safe. 'Any cash in here?'

'I've told you, we don't keep cash on the premises.'

She spreads the cards so their pictures are fully visible. 'These are replicas but they're still antique and highly sought after. They're known as hunting cards. As you see, the suits are different. Shields and bells, coins and four leafed clovers. The bells are the ones used in falconry, on the birds' feet. Beautiful, aren't they?'

'What's their value?' asks Kate.

Anna points to a figure on the screen. 'That was just for insurance purposes. You couldn't put a price on them.'

'And what about these?' Kate points to the other pile

of cards. Clearing a space, Anna picks them up. As she shuffles the pack, she is keenly aware of the two pairs of eyes watching her intently.

'These are my favourite.' Her voice is almost a whisper as she handles them, trailing her finger along the edges. 'Hand painted, not printed. My father paid a lot of money for them but their monetary value is irrelevant. To me, they are priceless because they're the ones he used to show me who the kings and queens are.'

'What do you mean?' asks Kate, frowning.

Anna looks up, as if surprised by the question. 'Oh, sorry. I suppose I take it for granted.' Holding them firmly, she fans the cards in a broad arc. 'The face cards were originally based on real people. The stories have altered over the years and people believe what they want to believe. I can only go on what my father told me and what I've read. This one, for instance.' She pulls one out, placing it carefully on the counter. 'The Queen of Diamonds. She is said to represent Rachel from the bible.'

Taking Kate's raised eyebrows for interest, she selects another two, placing them beside the first. 'The Queen of Hearts is said to be a likeness of Elizabeth of York, Henry VIII's mother. She does look like her, around the eyes, but I always prefer to think of Lewis Carroll's queen and the jack as the knave, running away with the tarts.'

For a moment Anna is lost, a child in her imaginary world. She shakes herself, conscious the others are waiting for her to continue.

'I can never remember who the Queen of Clubs is supposed to be. Some warrior I think, like Boadicea or Joan of Arc. I once had a friend, who was convinced she was the Virgin Mary. The card that is, not the friend.' She smiles, then places another one down.

'The Queen of Spades. Goddess of wisdom.' Looking up, she sees Kate's face turn bright red. 'Are you alright?'

'I'm fine. It's just a bit hot in here.' She makes a show of fanning herself with her hand but there is no heating on in the shop. If anything, the temperature is even colder than usual.

'Please carry on. This is interesting.'

Her colour is returning to normal, so Anna takes another card.

'The kings are fascinating, the four great rulers of the past. The King of Spades is David from the Old Testament, with his ancient sword.'

She places the King of Diamonds on top of it.

'And here we have Charlemagne, the first Roman Emperor. Fair haired and dangerous, apparently. I never liked the look of him. Too foppish, not to be trusted.' She places another card down. 'The King of Clubs. Alexander the Great. Descended from the gods, or so he believed. And last of all my favourite, the King of Hearts.'

Anna looks at the image, then looks again. She has seen it in all its many forms and depictions, a thousand times throughout her lifetime but never as she sees it now. She will describe it for the benefit of her audience and then they must get back to the inventory.

'Why is it your favourite?' asks Kate, her expression one of absorbed concentration.

Anna's heart has begun to thud loudly in her ears.

'Oh, I've never really thought about it. He's clean shaven, so I suppose his youth must have appealed to me as a girl.' She swallows, giving herself more time to consider what to say next. She opens her mouth to speak and is relieved to hear her voice sounds as calm as it did before.

'He's sometimes called the suicide king. As you see, he appears to be stabbing himself.' Her voice trails off and she prays they aren't watching her too closely. Scooping up the cards, she begins replacing them back inside the safe, her hands shaking. A new and horrible truth is beginning to dawn on her.

Much as she loved him, after all the pain he caused, maybe being knifed in the neck was exactly what her father deserved.

43

Newton

Newton throws the newspaper down on his desk. The headlines are full of the storm's devastation, the few lines beneath Archie's picture could have been a hell of a lot worse. Even so, he knows he can expect a call from Vardy as soon as it hits his doormat.

The briefing room is almost deserted after the clamour of yesterday. The team had worked around the clock and the desks are littered with rubbish. Empty cups and sandwich packets lie scattered, as though everyone left in a hurry, which is exactly what they did as soon as they heard the boy had been found. Newton consults his watch. With Archie safe there is no time to rest. They need to refocus on the murder.

He looks over at Amy Khan, a lone figure in the corner. She can't have slept more than a couple of hours and yet here she is back at her desk, checking closed-circuit cameras. He appreciates her dedication but to him it seems a thankless task. No cars appear to have stopped on the main road on the night in question and all the dog walkers have been accounted for. Newton doesn't know why they bother with CCTV anyway. The pictures are always poor quality, especially after dark.

He pulls out the pathologist's report just as Sharpy and Debbie arrive. Nodding briefly, he shakes the sheaf of papers. He might be old-school, but he likes to print things off. Too much screen time plays havoc with his eyesight but this lot must have felled a medium sized coppice. Gareth Hastings's effusive style of writing is nearly as annoying as the man himself.

He looks up just as Kate walks in and turns the papers face down. He will read them later. The door swings back open as Duffy enters the room. At sight of him, Newton finds himself again questioning his own judgment. They will probably never know if Archie was down the well when the search passed that way. Even if he was, is it really Duffy's fault? The boy is safe, that's all that matters. The feel of him, warm and alive is still fresh in Newton's mind. He knows when to pick his battles. Or at least, when to store them. There are more pressing concerns to attend to. Especially after what else was discovered down the well, although he intends to keep that information close to his chest for now.

'So, where were we before we were so rudely interrupted?' He stands and walks over to the whiteboard, even though nothing new has been added to it for days. Duffy is already perched in his usual spot on the windowsill, as though looking for a quick escape route. Kate is still taking her coat off. He waits until she sits down at the desk in front of him. She continues to delve in her bag, making a show of looking for something. None of the team looks particularly keen to respond.

'OK, I'll start us off then, with a question. What springs to mind when you think of playing cards?' Newton has given this a lot of thought over the last few days, despite the distractions.

Kate's brow creases but it's Duffy who answers.

'They always make me think of caravans,' he says, with his customary smirk. 'Only time I ever played cards was when it rained on holiday.'

'Same here, Duffy, but that's not what I'm getting at.' Newton paces back and forth between the whiteboard and his desk. He keeps his tone conversational. 'It's probably before your lot's time. Well maybe not yours, Bob.' He nods over at Sharpy, more to check he is listening than anything else. 'I used to love old cowboy films as a kid. I'd watch them with my sister. She'd be on the chair arm pretending it was a horse. I'd be the sheriff of course. Saloons always fascinated me. Gambling, cheating, whoring and that's what got me thinking.' He looks around the group. 'I'm playing devil's advocate here but would you say in general that cards are a man's domain?'

'Not sure about that sir,' says Kate sceptically, as he hoped she would. 'My gran used to love a game of gin rummy.' She looks over at Duffy. 'Didn't you say Collins's old man ran a card school?'

'I'm glad you brought that up,' says Duffy, pulling out his phone. Newton often thinks he ought to make more effort to embrace technology but Kate still uses her pocketbook, which makes him feel slightly less prehistoric.

Duffy clears his throat, as he always does when about to embark on one of his soliloquies. 'I made full use of my position on the search.' Newton sees Kate roll her eyes. 'Gained the trust of the villagers.'

Newton casts his mind back to the motley crew assembled in wellies and cagoules in the car park. Black Hollow is more a town these days than a village but in his mind the residents are split into two distinct groups. On the one hand are the indigenous inhabitants, born and bred and often married here; these people rarely leave the place, spending their whole lives within a few miles' radius. It's a standing joke that most of them think they need a passport to go into Sheffield. Then there are the commuters, from far and wide, or just a few miles across the boundary, these upwardly mobile professionals have colonised the old miners' cottages and the new housing estate which now encircles the original village. In Newton's view, both groups are more insular than they would ever admit or even realise but he can't fault their community spirit. They had turned out in numbers despite the shocking weather.

'I saw it as a tactical opportunity,' Duffy drones on. *He's pushing his luck*, thinks Newton. 'People were off their guard, liable to say more than they might if they were being questioned in their own homes.'

That's as maybe but did you miss the boy down the well? Newton is sure the same question will be occurring to Kate, if not the rest of them, but her head is bent over her notes, her pen scrolling in circles across the page.

'Sounds like Collins was a bit of a character,' continues Duffy.

'Really? What kind of character?'

'Well, I spent quite a few hours with the locals.' *We all did*, thinks Newton. 'And I got the impression he was a bit of a ladies' man in his time. One of the older residents said he was "a bit of a one"'.

'Did they give you anything specific?'

'Not exactly sir, no.'

'Well that's just as well because we all know gossip and hearsay are inadmissible.' *In fact*, Newton thinks, *such comments could be an interesting lead but Duffy's ego needs reining in*. 'You're right, of course. Unguarded comments can be revealing. They can also be taken with a pinch of salt.' As he speaks, Newton has a flashback to the morgue, the neatly trimmed moustache and the tattoo on the corpse's chest. He picks up a marker and writes *Ladies Man* on the whiteboard, followed by a large question mark.

239

'Yes, sir but there's something else,' says Duffy. 'Turns out what I heard was right. He was a card sharp, just like his old man. Playing for money.'

Newton turns towards him and sees Duffy has Kate's full attention now.

'Anna never mentioned this.'

'She's not likely to, is she? One of the old fogeys slipped it out. Not sure they meant to. Got quite cagey when I pressed them. They could have been talking past tense but that's not the impression I got.'

'I suggest you find out, Duffy. You weren't on a pensioners' ramble. We need proper statements, evidence before this investigation runs completely aground.'

It's not often Newton raises his voice but he needs them to feel like their necks are on the line, which they are. He glares around the group. 'You've had the laptop and phone records how many days now?' No one replies.

He opens his drawer and pulls a photo from beneath the pile of papers in there. It still puts him in mind of a Dundee cake.

'This was found down the well, along with these.' He hears Kate's sharp intake of breath as he removes further photos of the pills, sorted and labelled at the lab. He sees the colour drain from Duffy's face.

'I'm not pointing fingers. They were thoroughly hidden and the boy was our priority at the time. We don't know the purity yet, or the street value but you can see for yourselves we're not talking kids' stuff. It seems the well was being used as a drop off point.' Opening another drawer, he pulls out the now familiar images of the crime scene, spreading them across the desk as though to remind them why they're all here. He lowers his voice to almost a whisper.

'If we don't start making progress, the media are going to crucify us, not to mention the locals. I don't have any evidence that all this is related, it's too soon to say for sure but in a town this size, things have a habit of overlapping.'

He slaps a picture of the murder weapon on top of the rest.

'This is still the only piece of concrete evidence we have and there wasn't a single print on it.'

Kate has stopped doodling and appears to be concentrating intently on what Newton is saying. Duffy stands motionless by the window.

'You'd think if it was used to open packages it would be covered in prints.' All eyes turn towards Amy at the back.

'Precisely. The murderer could have worn gloves but that wouldn't explain the total absence of prints. We need to find out if the knife was wiped clean at the end of the working day. If it wasn't, we know the murderer did it.'

Newton pulls out another photo. 'There were at least twenty-eight sets of boot and shoe prints on the shop floor, as well as fibres, hairs and fingerprints on every surface. I had no idea the place was so busy. More to the point, the knife might have been cleaned but the rest of the place certainly hadn't. Probably not for some time. We're working through all the samples but it is a shop, so we can expect the place to have had a steady footfall.'

'I've just been looking at the footprints from the shop sir. Most are scuffed but we should be able to get some clearer images.'

'Thanks, Amy. Get some help from this lot if you need it.'

Even to his own ears, there is no mistaking the despair

in his voice.

'Whoever did this, there's every chance they're local. At some point, it's likely they would have come into the shop as a customer.'

Duffy nods his head enthusiastically. 'Absolutely sir. I'll get back to doorstepping. Get some more statements.'

'Take this list of residents. We know how unlikely it is they'll come forward willingly. Go back and see if anybody's timeline shifts, any inconsistencies. We need to start thinking DNA. Anyone refusing, let me know. Now clear off. I don't care who does what, as long as you get some answers.' He slams his drawer shut and sits down. 'What are you waiting for? Get going. Not you, Kate, I want a word.'

He can see Duffy doesn't like this. He hates to miss out on anything. His expression sour, he picks up his jacket and follows the rest of the team. Newton waits until he hears the buzz of the vending machine in the corridor before speaking.

'We haven't had chance to catch up, with everything that's happened.'

Newton can see she is nervous and so she should be. He has thought about what he's going to say but in the end the words just tumble out.

'Christ, Kate. Since when did we start conducting interviews in the bloody graveyard?'

She blinks and swallows before responding. 'She wanted to do something useful sir. She insisted on trying to find the boy. I didn't see a problem with that. My intention was to talk as we walked, which we did.'

'Oh, a mobile interview, was it?'

'I guess so, yes. We found him, didn't we?

Newton wills himself to stay calm. 'Talk me through

what happened.'

'Well for a start, we got away from the press. They were camped on her doorstep, remember. We walked as far as the bridge at Ochre Dyke. We couldn't see much because of the fog but she knows the area like the back of her hand. She went off and searched the banks, then we headed for the woods but I'd had enough by then, so we headed back. It was then she had the idea of checking the well.'

Her account is infuriatingly reasonable, as he knew it would be. He shoves the newspaper across the desk towards her.

'Have you seen this?'

'I don't read the tabloids, sir.'

Newton shakes his head. 'I've warned you. Don't get personally involved, Kate. Until proven otherwise, Anna Collins is still a suspect.'

'I know, sir. None of it was planned. It just sort of happened.'

'Just sort of happened isn't good enough.' Newton knows he's being harsh, hypocritical even but carries on regardless. 'This is a murder investigation, Kate. From now on, everything must be strictly by the book.'

'Yes sir. Apparently, she'd seen some youths hanging around and it made her think.'

For a moment Newton stays silent, considering this. 'Well, it's a good job she did. They'll have to find somewhere else to stash their stuff now. Keep your eyes and ears open and disregard nothing.'

'Yes sir. Is that all?'

'For now, yes.'

She picks up her bag and turns to leave, then stops.

'Can I ask sir? Is Margaret Wood being cremated?'

'I have absolutely no idea, Kate.' He watches the door close behind her. She's got some nerve but their discussion and Duffy's comments have given him a couple of ideas. Pulling his jacket from the back of his chair, he waits a few minutes, then follows her out of the building.

44

Kate

Kate blows a smoke ring and taps ash against the wall. The air is turning cool, the sky dimming to a purplish grey but she would be happy to stay here until the landscape fades completely and she is surrounded by darkness. She often sits here in the small hours, watching the family of bats that nests in the sycamore. Pipistrelles, she thinks, from the size of them. She saw a fox this morning, the carcass of some small creature clamped between its jaws. Sometimes she worries for Luther but all things considered, she is sure he has a better life here than he would on a council estate.

He appears on the fence with a clatter, a black silhouette against the dusk. Jumping down, he rubs against her as he slinks into the house.

The air is more sulphurous than usual. A rocket streaks by, reminding her it's nearly bonfire night. She takes another drag as the firework tumbles in a scarlet waterfall, jumping as it explodes, a series of bangs like gunfire shaking the whole vista before her. If anyone wanted to shoot someone, this would be the week to do it.

With the peace of the evening shattered, she throws the remains of her cigarette into the shrubbery. How many fag butts are in there, she dreads to think. She tells herself they'll turn into compost eventually.

Luther is curled up on the table, the corner of her notebook poking from under his tail. Careful not to disturb him, she eases it out and turns to a fresh page. Writing things down sometimes helps get them straight in her head but so far, the exercise has proved futile.

Despite what Newton said, it is still only a matter of days since Collins's murder and yet it seems longer. Picking up an overflowing ashtray, she empties it into the bin, the intervening days playing through her mind like a newsreel.

The inventory had been a performance but Julie had not been impressed. When she first arrived here, Kate had made the mistake of thinking her a simple soul with her solid, unflappable kindness and straightforward ways, but she underestimated her. She's extremely good at getting close to people, winning their trust. If anyone can crack Anna, it's Julie, but even she appears baffled. They both noticed her reaction to the King of Hearts but what to make of it is another matter entirely. As far as Kate is concerned, all it did was make her even more conscious of just how vulnerable Anna is.

The week started well on the face of it. With Archie safe, they could focus once more on the murder. Newton had handled the press, smiling coolly as he posed for photos with the boy on his knee. He still can't look her in the eye. With every passing day, her conviction he will at some point broach the subject of what happened fades even further. He even had the nerve to bollock her and despite the public front, not a word of thanks for her part in finding the boy. Not from him, anyway.

Duffy has kept out of her way, tied up mainly with his doorstepping. Perhaps Kate's success and his failure have temporarily gagged him, or maybe he's just biding his time. Either way, it soon became clear he was completely wasting his breath. She heard that when he reminded the pensioners of what they'd said, an eery silence had fallen, a written statement proving infinitely more elusive than a few off-the-cuff remarks exchanged in the comparative anonymity of the night-time search.

Kate has found herself wondering who frequented Collins's card school. *How many had their tarot read by his wife?* It feels much more than a natural reluctance to speak ill of the dead.

Despite the apparent truce, she is keen to keep as much space between herself and Duffy as possible. She has grafted herself to Amy's side, giving the outward impression she was both absorbed and engrossed in what her colleague has been working on.

In truth, she soon was. They work well together, systematically going through everything they have so far. Amy had already scrutinised every inch of traffic footage for the night in question and with Archie's disappearance, every camera in town has now been checked. They have re-examined all the statements, including anecdotal stuff but despite the rumours and hearsay, have found nothing concrete. They still don't even have a motive for Charlie Collins's murder.

Her thoughts keep returning to Margaret Wood. All weekend, she half expected to hear from Alice but it seems she has accepted her aunt's death as natural *and why wouldn't she?* She was an old woman with a bad heart. But Alice is no fool and digging around will only arouse suspicion. There is nothing to be gained by that, for the moment.

With a sigh, she flicks back through her notes. Anna confirmed she does all the cleaning. If the state of the shop floor is anything to go by, she doesn't do a very good job. Kate was also stunned to discover they still cling to the ancient tradition of half day closing on Wednesdays. This gave Anna the whole afternoon before her father's murder and could explain the absence of fingerprints on the dagger the morning he was found.

The words swim before her eyes and she closes the cover. She had fallen down the internet rabbit hole last night, gripped by the multifarious world of playing cards. From sharing secret messages to spreading propaganda, as theatre tickets and advertisements, she spent so long flicking from site to site, her head had been splitting by bedtime.

That playing cards are such coveted items is beginning to make more sense and with the prices demanded for some of the more sought-after decks, it's easy to see why collecting them is such a popular and lucrative hobby.

The cards Anna showed them were exquisite. The delicately drawn illustrations and the colours, some even burnished with gold. Her face had come alive as she described them. Kate could see that to Anna, every one of them had a character and personality of its own.

Newton's idea that Julie should help with the inventory had been a stroke of genius. Clearly relaxed in her presence, Anna had become quite eloquent, to say the least. Maybe she had let her guard down. Does she have anything to guard? The inventory had at least confirmed one thing — nothing was missing. But they had known that already, hadn't they?

At that moment her phone rings, sending Luther scuttling off the table. Amy's name flashes on the screen.

'The very person. I was just thinking about you.' Kate smiles into the phone. She is beginning to revise her previous assessment of her colleague.

'Not disturbing anything, am I?'

'No, not at all. Just sat here going round in circles.'

'Ah, right. Well, I think I might have found something interesting.' The note of barely supressed excitement in her voice is unmistakable.

'Really?' Kate's attention is now fully piqued.

'Yes. Shall I come over?'

'I'll come to you.'

As she locks the door, she sees a flickering again between the trees. It's too low down to be fireworks and this time she is certain it is the tip of a cigarette. *Bloody dog walkers out with all these bangers going off. Are they mad?* The whole point of buying this house had been for peace and privacy. *With miles of fields to wander, what can possibly be the attraction of that particular spot?* She itches to investigate but for now it will have to wait. Kicking aside the brolly and empty coke can rolling in the footwell, she reverses off the drive a little faster than a police officer probably should. This could be the breakthrough they've been waiting for and the possibility of solving the case without Duffy is too good to miss.

45

1977

'It's a grand day for it!' says Father from the window. 'Let's hope it stays fine.'

They rarely have the television on but exceptions have been made on account of the occasion. Last night, Anna watched with a growing sense of anticipation as beacons were lit across the land. Reporters raced around the country in search of the best cake, the best poem, the best party. The nation is gripped by Jubilee fever. She sits transfixed as the Queen leaves the palace in her gilded carriage, plumed white horses and scarlet coated footmen accompanying her on her way. Suddenly, the screen goes black.

'You'll get square eyes watching that. Come on.' Mother stands by the plug socket, looking lovely. She's had curlers in and is wearing her Richard Shops dress, the same blue as the Queen's cloak. Anna's red cords and white top add to the patriotic colour scheme but she is relieved to see Father has settled for his usual tweeds. They head downstairs, Mother locking the door on a dejected looking Jack. The noise hits her as soon as she steps outside. Filled with excitement, she rushes through the gate and gapes at the sight before her.

The street is awash with red, white and blue. Bunting is strung from one side to the other, every lamp post decked with crepe paper and pictures of the Queen. The rumble of trestle tables had woken Anna at dawn. Now they are laden with jugs, buns and sandwiches. Looking round, she sees her parents have crossed the road without her. She makes her way along, admiring the jellies and cakes but her only real purpose is to find Marie.

It doesn't take long to spot her. She is wearing a new shirt, cream and blue cheesecloth, tucked into Birmingham Bags but it's her companions' outfits that stop Anna in her tracks. She'd had no idea it was fancy dress and she's pretty sure her parents hadn't either.

Marie's mum is a sight to behold. She is wearing the prettiest gown Anna has ever seen. The bodice is a froth of lace, the skirt flowing out in a sea of satin and frills. Around her neck is a string of pearls, more in her ears and across her shoulders. A silver tiara sits in her hair, a red rose pinned to her bosom. Little Bo Peep and Max Wall turn their heads and a Womble gawps from a table, his sandwich flopping in mid-air. Everyone is looking at Marie's mum except Anna. His eyes have been darkened with soot, his hair is plastered down and a horrid black beard is hooked over his ears but there is no disguising Father Vincent.

'There you are!' grins Marie. 'I've been looking for you everywhere!'

Her mum is carrying a parasol and as Anna approaches, a shadow is cast across the group. At that moment, Mrs Wood appears from nowhere, her face a moue of distaste.

'And who the dickens have you two come as, might I ask?' Her head swivels imperiously as though she is the Queen, the ends of her lipless mouth pulled down. Anna knows who they are meant to be. She had known as soon as she saw them and blurts it out before anyone else can.

'Rasputin!' she says, revelling in the word, feeling her cheeks burn as the crowd stares at her.

'That's right, Anna,' says Father Vincent, stroking his beard.

'And my mum is the Tsarina,' says Marie proudly.

Anna can feel Mrs Wood bristling beside her. 'Well, that's hardly appropriate, is it?'

'Of course it's appropriate,' says Marie's mum. 'Don't you know? The Russian royal family were close relations of the Queen.'

'I don't care what they were. A man of the church shouldn't be dressing up like that. It's not seemly.'

'It's just a bit if fun, Mrs Wood and all in a good cause.' From beneath the folds of his cassock, the priest pulls out a plastic collection tin. 'Our Lady of Lourdes benevolent fund. The church roof is sorely in need of repair.'

Anna feels Marie tugging the back of her shirt and the two of them reel away, barely containing their giggles.

'Miserable old cow!'

'I know. Your mum's dress though. It's amazing. All those pearls!'

'Yeah, she made it on the sewing machine. It's only old curtains and they're not real pearls, just beads,' says Marie. 'She wanted me to dress up. I told her, no way!'

Anna can tell she is trying to play it down but she isn't fooled. Her mother's costume is by far the best one here. In fact everyone else looks stupid, especially Father Vincent. They make their way through the tables and find a seat next to the buns. As she peels away the paper, she looks around the hordes of people, some in fancy dress, some not. Her eyes fall on her father, stood at the side of the road. She follows the line of his gaze to Father Vincent, who is moving through the crowd with his collection tin. At that moment, a hand appears and slaps the back of hers.

'Can't you wait?' Mother looms above her, so close

she can see the powder caked on her chin. 'At least have a sandwich first.'

'I'm surprised she hasn't cleared herself a table,' says Marie, once Mother is out of earshot. 'She could make a fortune reading these!' Picking up a paper cup, she crosses her eyes and sways comically, making Anna giggle.

Someone switches a radio on and time passes by in a blur of music and overindulgence. They sing to Wings and Kenny Rogers, Abba and Dr Hook, as the party gravitates towards the green. There are various games and prizes and stalls have been set up, selling pies, cans of pop and beer. A wheelbarrow race unfolds, men pushing wives, mainly, but some the other way around, depending on their size. Most of them are drunk and the race ends with people heaped in a pile. Children wander about, some in paper hats more suited to Christmas, some in tinfoil crowns, tea towels draped over them as cloaks. A boy marches past, holding a wooden spoon aloft, covered in silver paper. He bashes another boy to the ground with it and the two roll between the chair legs, wrestling.

'Look!' hisses Marie.

'What?'

'Where's he off to?'

Anna turns in the direction Marie is pointing. Father Vincent has broken away from the crowd and is heading up the high street. He walks briskly through the tables, which are now mostly empty apart from tatty streamers, discarded plates and bottles. Someone could make a packet taking back the empties.

'Let's follow him,' says Marie. 'I'm getting bored of this and all the cake's gone.'

'Where's your mum?' asks Anna. The last time she had seen her, she was sprawled on the green, her skirts hitched up to catch the sun. Now her place is empty, the grass flattened where she'd been sat.

'Dunno,' says Marie, dismissively. 'She must have gone home to watch the rest of it on telly.'

Anna's parents have already left, clearly in disagreement about something. She feels a pang she can't quite name at the thought of her mother's carefully chosen outfit. She will probably be in bed by now with another one of her headaches and she is in no hurry to get home. As she gets up from her chair, the slurred lines of *God Save the Queen* start up once more.

'Send her victorious!' shouts Marie as they head up the road in Father Vincent's wake. His flapping cassock reminding Anna of the crow they buried, or the bats that live in the orchard.

'Here,' says Marie through a mouthful of crumbs as she shoves a flattened bun towards her. Stifling a giggle, she pulls out another from the seemingly bottomless pocket of her trousers. Suddenly, her expression turns serious. 'Let's drop back a bit. He's easy to follow.'

They creep along in the shade like hired assassins. Heart pounding, Anna feels sure he will turn and see them but he ploughs forwards, as though on a mission. As the noise of the party fades behind them, it soon becomes clear where he is headed.

The girls hang back as he passes through the lychgate of St Peter and Paul's.

'What's he doing here?' whispers Anna.

'Maybe he's meeting old Pisspants.' This is their nickname for Staines, the ancient caretaker. They lean against the worm-ridden wood to catch their breaths.

'Come on,' says Marie after a few seconds. 'We don't want to lose him.'

They pass the freshly dug grave of old Molly Flinders. She had rallied the village for months with her jubilee collection, then missed it by a matter of days. Someone has stuck a Union Jack in the soil and it snaps in the breeze. Anna sees a flash of black between the headstones and the girls leave the path in unison. As the grass grows longer, she slows and drops her head to read an inscription.

'We haven't got time for that!' hisses Marie and Anna quickens her step, embarrassed. They dash on, using the stones for cover, coming to a stop behind the last, crumbling monument. The priest's dark head bobs out of sight as the ground falls away.

'He must be going to the well again,' says Marie and the pair slip down to their stomachs. Like snipers now, they pull themselves forward through the grass, Anna's elbows becoming soddened. And then they stop suddenly, their gasps choked shut in their throats. At the bottom of the slope stands Father Vincent, the well wide open at his feet.

Instinctively Anna throws herself flat to the ground but he can't see them from where he is. Neither can his companion, who has his back to them. He must have been waiting for him.

The sun catches the priest's face. He has removed the fake beard but his eyes are still blackened with coaldust. Whatever their business, they are quick about it. Father Vincent disappears through a gap in the hedge, leaving the other man on his haunches, replacing the cover of the well.

46

Anna

Anna stares at the death certificate. Edged in black, she ignores the words, focusing instead on the elegant handwriting and the fact a fountain pen was used. That way she can tell herself it is a beautiful document. Her father would be pleased with it.

She had made copies at the post office. The looks she got in there had bordered on the ridiculous. Susan Barrett for one and Olive Stratton. They break their necks to avoid her, yet Anna knows they were first out in the street when the press arrived.

Folding the certificate, she puts it away in the sideboard.

At least now she has a date and the details will be in tonight's paper. It's been impossible not to think back to her mother's funeral, how the grave had looked much more than six feet deep. The vicar's gown had blown like a bedsheet in the wind, the bible almost torn from his grip, leaves swirling as though caught up and thrown by some invisible hand. The memory always makes her think of that scene in the Wizard of Oz, where the house blows away. The book is far better, of course.

Since placing the obituary, a new anxiety plagues her. Will Marie be at the funeral? It's a rhetorical question. Of course she will. Especially as Anna was stupid enough to tell her which paper the announcement will be in. But what has really brought her here after all these years? Morbid fascination? That would certainly fit with what she remembers. Her parents always disapproved and they hadn't known the half of it

Anna prefers not to dwell on her childhood. She sits on the sofa and looks around her. The empty chair at the card table reinforces his absence, the silence in every room deafening. What could Marie possibly know about losing a father? She never had one.

Leaning back, she closes her eyes. Not all the memories are painful. Some she has secretly cherished. The two of them running through a storm, stolen sticks of rhubarb wedged beneath their armpits. Crunching the sour stalks, their T-shirts transparent with rain. Petals browning in a jar, magic potions made of leaves. Other, darker memories she isn't sure are real or imagined.

Something tells her Marie has never married and the cross she still wears suggests her religious beliefs haven't changed. She hears the echo of a girlish whisper, *wed to God in holy matrimony*. That had been one of her favourites, one of those sweeping statements she liked to make. Another memory follows. Kittens in a pram, Marie fussing over them. Whatever maternal instincts she displayed with her cats, Anna can't see her as a mother but she must have a life, a home, a living. Try as she might, Anna can't picture them and doubts there's a job in existence that would suit the girl she knew. People change, of course they do. Alan Bamford's boyhood had been made a misery but he outshone them all as an adult, running a successful accountancy firm with swanky offices in town. He is slimmer these days as well, she's even seen him jogging. So yes, people can change. The question is, has Marie?

She walks over to the mirror, squinting at her reflection. God knows what Marie must have thought of her. Her mother's eyes stare back at her, except hers are red from drink and lack of sleep , the flesh beneath them haggard.

Your father made a will, that old coffin-dodger Gibbs had said. As executor and sole beneficiary, she hardly needed him to tell her that. She knows exactly what he left her.

He'll be in the chapel of rest by now, dead for over a week. She dreads to think what state he'll be in when he finally goes into the ground. But it's different this time. For one thing, she expects there will be quite a crowd. The police will be there and the press of course. She has become quite accustomed to them and was disappointed to see not a single reporter on the pavement when she opened the curtains this morning. The whole town will no doubt turn out and she expects strangers too, people who have seen it on the news. Her chest contracts, her bowels surge.

Rushing towards the decanters, she pours so fast, the liquid slops over the side. She takes a mouthful, spilling more, ignoring the dark stain spreading around her on the carpet.

47

Newton

Our Lady of Lourdes Catholic Church is a much smaller affair than its Anglican counterpart. Newton shields his eyes from the sun as he takes in the slender spire, pointing to a heaven that for him does not exist. No ancient lychgate straddles the path, no gate at all, the entrance opening onto a cramped car park, a few concrete steps leading up to the church.

He pauses for a moment outside the porch. Huge monolithic structures rise from the grass, crosses and angels in every direction. Newton believes that what passes between a man and his god is his own business. He's with Dave Allen on that score but the paraphernalia of faith still intrigues him. He is about to take a closer look when the porch door opens with a heavy wooden creak.

His eyes are met with a sharp green gaze, peat-black brows pulled low and questioning.

'I'm afraid you've just missed Mass,' says the priest over his shoulder as he turns an iron key. 'Or was there something else I can help with?' Newton hears his mother's accent, the burr of Northern Ireland. Dressed in a long black cassock, from his short stature and build he is sure this is the man he saw leaving St Peter and Paul's.

'Jim Newton, North Derbyshire Police. I wonder if I can ask you a few questions?'

The priest scans the outstretched warrant card from beneath his heavy brows. 'Of course. Can we talk as we go? I am rather busy.' Falling into step, the two men walk along a path towards a stone building at the top of the graveyard. Newton tries to date it but the style doesn't appear to belong to any era with its steep roof and pointed gables. Pushing open an ornate gate, the priest bends to pick up a pair of secateurs from beneath a rose bush. So gardening is what keeps him so busy. Newton hopes he is more attentive towards his flock.

'Whereabouts in County Down are you from, Father Mooney?'

A quick search on Google had brought up his name but the priest's forehead creases, the open blades of the secateurs suspended in mid-air between them. 'It isn't often I'm asked that question.' He moves away and snips off the dead head of a rose. 'Do you know Kilkeel?'

'Not personally, but my mother was born not far from there. I recognise the accent.'

'Ah, I miss the Mourne Mountains but I've made this place my home.' Father Mooney smiles as he continues to clip at the bushes. His cassock brushes the path, a layer of dust and twigs clinging to the hem. *A strange get up for gardening*, thinks Newton and wonders if he ever wears trousers. *Do Catholic priests still have to be celibate?* As far as he knows they do. All that sexual frustration can never be a good thing as far as he's concerned.

'How long have you been in Black Hollow?'

'Thirty-two years, come Michaelmas. Man and boy.' He says this nonchalantly, as though three decades is no time at all.

'You must know the place well, then.'

'I do indeed.' He stops and turns to stare directly at Newton. 'What exactly is it I can help you with, Inspector?'

'I wanted to speak to you about the Collins family.'

The priest's eyes narrow, as though giving this serious thought. 'Terrible business. I was only speaking of it yesterday with Coy.'

'The Anglican vicar? I thought I saw you there. Do you often consult your opposite number?'

Mooney stares at Newton, his eyes narrowing.

'I don't consider us adversaries. In a community as tightly knit as ours, we naturally work together. In any case, Coy serves several churches, he doesn't live in Black Hollow.' Newton is well aware of this, also thanks to Google.

'Besides,' continues the priest, 'there have been more matters recently than we are accustomed to dealing with, as you know.'

'I didn't see you on the search the other night.'

'Did you not? I assure you I was there. Such a blessing the boy was found.'

'It was indeed. Tell me, were the Collins family churchgoers?'

'They weren't but I've been meaning to call on Anna.' Mooney has resumed his cutting. 'I knew her quite well as a child.'

'Oh? Why is that, if they didn't come to church?'

The priest's hand stills for a second as the clippings fall to the ground. 'It was a small village back then. Everybody knew each other. She was often to be found with a girl who attended Our Lady's. Thick as thieves they were but for the life of me, I can't remember the other girl's name.' He chuckles as he parts the foliage and snips off a perfectly formed sprig. *There'll be nothing left of it at this rate*, thinks Newton.

'Says it all, really. That it's Anna's name I remember. She was a strange child.'

'Strange? In what way?'

'Oh, maybe that's the wrong word. It wasn't her fault.'

'What do you mean?'

'Shall we sit down Inspector? I can give you a few moments.'

The priest indicates a wooden bench set into the shrubs. As they sit down, Newton gets a whiff of incense.

'Well now, let me get this right.' Mooney cups his chin in a perfectly manicured hand, his face a mask of concentration. 'I believe the mother was some sort of psychic medium. Fortune-telling and so on. The father was a disciplinarian. Not as that does a child any harm at all. Still, it can't have been easy for her, growing up in a home like that.'

Newton senses the priest is warming to his theme and says nothing.

'Of course Mrs Collins passed away. I wouldn't normally share something of this nature, you understand, but it might help you to know. Coy told me that after the burial, Anna used to go there at night and light candles. Didn't like the idea of her mother being left on her own in the dark. Of course, she soon realised it was folly and that was the end of it. Poor child.'

'And this was what, two years ago or thereabouts?'

'I believe so, yes.'

'And to the best of your knowledge, was Anna alright after that?'

Mooney fingers the secateurs in his lap, as though considering his response. 'It depends really, what you mean by alright.'

'Sorry?'

'Well, I think it's common knowledge she likes the drink. Bit of a problem with it.' The priest stands up abruptly. 'I must insist on getting on now, Inspector. You'll find your own way back?'

Newton hands him a card. 'If you do decide to speak to Anna, will you let me know how it goes?'

'I'd be happy to.'

Newton makes his way back through the churchyard, unsure what to make of the interview. After what the priest just spilled, he wonders what happened to the seal of the confessional. Perhaps it only applies to members of his own church. He knows a hell of a lot about the Collinses, considering they aren't Catholics. He clangs the gate shut behind him and makes his way back to the car.

48

Kate

Kate is hit by the smell of spices as soon as Amy opens the door. As on her previous visit, the air is filled with cooking aromas but to Kate's disappointment, it appears she has just missed supper.

'There's plenty left if you'd like some.' Her colleague nods towards a covered pan on the worktop, up to her elbows in a sink piled with pots.

'I'm not hungry, thanks.' This isn't true, but Kate can hardly contain her excitement at what Amy may have to tell her. 'Come on, put me out of my misery. What have you found?'

Amy grins as she dries her hands on a tea towel.

'OK, so look at this.' Gesturing for Kate to sit down, she pulls a laptop towards them and sits beside her at the table. 'You know we've already been through the accounts and mobile records? I was so annoyed we didn't find anything, I decided to delve a bit deeper.'

Kate takes off her jacket and drapes it over a chair. 'Don't tell me we missed something?'

'Not exactly, no, but all any of us had looked at so far were the account numbers found on the premises. Anna said that was it.'

Kate's stomach lurches. 'You're going to tell me there were more.'

'Just the one. In Charlie Collins's sole name.'

Kate puts her hand to her forehead. 'Shit! It was something I intended to check but with everything else that's happened —'

Amy shakes her head to silence her. 'We've all been

pulled out with the boy, sarge. We've hardly got started on this.'

'So what have you found?'

'Just a sec and I'll show you.' Amy's fingers fly across the keyboard, as she opens the browser.

'So, he's had this account with Northern Bank since November 2008. The reference is Online Trade but that can't be the real use as all the deposits are cash.'

The dates spin in Kate's mind, her eyes narrowing. 'His wife died in October of that year, didn't she?'

'I knew you'd pick up on that and look at the payments. We're not talking huge amounts but some days there are numerous deposits, all at different branches. Take this for instance. Four hundred pounds paid in at Chesterfield, followed by a further two fifty in Sheffield. Later the same day, he puts another three hundred in at Meadowhead.'

'Strange,' says Kate, frowning. 'I thought they did all their banking at the post office?'

'For the business account, yes, but this is separate.'

'Could he be making sales on the road and depositing cash while he's out and about?'

'That's one possibility.' Amy pulls a plastic folder towards them, a black A4 spiral notebook contained within it. 'Except Mr Collins wrote every sale in his ledgers. Has done since 1968. I asked Newton if I could borrow this. There are stacks of them in the shop, despite the sophisticated till. This one relates to that date and the only sales in it come to thirty-five quid.'

'It's a wonder they kept open on those figures. Could he have been fiddling the books?'

'Who knows? But I think there's more to it than that.'

Clicking the mouse, Amy spins the figures up the

screen. 'Things stay pretty static as you can see, similar amounts being paid in, a nice steady income.'

'As though he's paying himself a wage.'

'That could be how he saw it but then around here something changes.' She points and Kate takes in the date. 'The amounts start to rack up. Here for instance, he withdrew a *thousand* pounds in Sheffield at 2.35 pm.' She pauses, turning to Kate. 'Now bear with me here, sarge, it took me a while to see it. I compared the banking activity with his phone records.' With a click, a bill appears and she magnifies the screen. 'He got a call from this number less than an hour earlier.'

'Sorry slow down, I'm not sure I'm with you.'

'It's not obvious until you see the correlation. I'll do it this way instead.' Amy shrinks both apps, so the bank statement and the phone bill appear side by side. Then she zooms in. 'These are both the same day, August the 4th. See that number there? It rang Collins at 1.28 pm.' She flicks the cursor. 'Forty-five minutes later, he's in Sheffield withdrawing a grand.' She turns her head, to check Kate follows.

'Look at the day after, the 5th. He's back out there, depositing five thousand pounds but he splits it between three branches. A grand in Chesterfield, same again in Sheffield and the rest at Meadowhead.' Kate can hear the excitement building in her voice. 'The pattern repeats as the months progress. He gets a phone call and substantial amounts are withdrawn. The next day he's back, depositing sometimes twice as much. They must have got sick of seeing him.'

'Jesus. Talk about speculate to accumulate. A good day's work, whatever he was doing.'

'Hang fire, sarge, there's more.' Amy pulls the phone

bill back up and points at the highlighted rows. 'I put traces on these numbers.'

'That's the dialling code for Sheffield,' says Kate.

'Yes sarge, it's a phone box.'

'A phone box? Whereabouts?'

'A place called Grimesthorpe. North of the city.'

'I know where it is.' Kate scans the list, taking in the area dialling codes. 'But this one's a Dark Peak number.'

'That's a phone box in Black Hollow. He had a lot of calls from there.'

'Interesting,' says Kate, still scanning the screen. 'That one's a mobile number.'

'Pay as you go, unregistered — as is this one, and this.' Amy points at various rows, then places her hands on the table. 'The thing is, sarge, his generation are a gift. Looking through his address book, I've accounted for most of the calls to both the shop and his mobile as far back as you like. They're all suppliers, wholesalers, that kind of thing. Perfectly kosher businesses and regular contacts. They're invariably followed by a sale recorded both on the till and in the trusty ledgers.'

'So what do you think this is telling us?'

'Well sarge, there appears to be a few things going on.' She pauses and Kate sees the shadows under her eyes. She must have been at it for hours. 'Ironically, he chose the paperless option for this account, so no statements would come to the shop. Nothing for his daughter to open by accident.'

'Crafty sod!' exclaims Kate, an image of the bloodied letter opener flashing before her eyes.

'Exactly. Not such a Luddite when it suited him. He'd been squirrelling money away for years but then things changed. The calls from unregistered phones start and at the same time, the amounts he's depositing shoots up. He also starts getting calls from phone boxes. I'm not sure where they fit in. The one in Grimesthorpe and the one here in town could be unrelated. Who uses phone boxes these days?'

'People having affairs, maybe. Anyone who doesn't want to be traced. Same with the unregistered phones.'

'That's what I thought. Who knows what he could have got involved in.'

Kate's mind reels as she tries to process it all.

'I'll show you the best bit now,' says Amy.

'You mean there's more?'

Her fingers tapping the keyboard, Amy brings up a single page. Zooming in on one line, she pushes her chair back. Kate leans forward and almost yelps as she sees the figure on the screen. 'Jesus! Nine grand! What date's this?'

'Last week. Whatever he was doing, it looks like he hit the jackpot.'

'It might have cost him his life.'

'Exactly.'

Kate stares at the screen as though shell-shocked.

'This is mind blowing, Amy. I think I am hungry after all. And is that a bottle of shiraz? I think at least one of us has earned it.'

Amy gets up and pulls a corkscrew from a drawer. 'The banking reminds me of my parents. They won't do anything online, always getting those slips from the cashpoint whenever they make a withdrawal. I think Charlie Collins was trying to hide both the size of the payments and where they were coming from. It would never have occurred to him that a glance online would show everything.'

'My gran was the same but I'm thinking this could fit with the gambling rumours.' Kate picks up a pen and holds it in the absence of a cigarette. She isn't sure which aspect gives her most satisfaction, the discovery itself or the fact that Duffy isn't in on it. Either way, she intends to enjoy the moment.

49

Newton

'I can't tell you any more than that, duck. It's mainly dog walkers around that time o' night.' Knocker pronounces the word *around* as *arahnd* and Newton will never get used to being called duck, no matter how long he lives here.

'OK. Well, keep your ears open and let me know if you hear anything.' He picks up his pint and turns away from the bar. His resolve to keep out of here hasn't lasted long but this time he has taken precautions. He is here purely for research and has come in the car. He hasn't taken anything since lunchtime and whiskey chasers are definitely off the menu.

Choosing a different table to the one with the wonky leg, he takes a measured sip of his Guinness. The fire is out, the taproom dingy without its glow. He looks at the backs of Chuck and Knocker's heads. Someone is paying that pair far too much in pensions.

In the corner, a skinny youth takes a swig of his Blue WKD. He's probably underage but his face is hidden beneath the peak of a cap. Maybe that's the intention. Newton watches as he tilts the bottle, a sleeve of tattoos revealing themselves beneath his cuff. He gets up, pulling a pack of cigarettes from his pocket as he shoves open the door.

He could easily be involved in what's been going on in the graveyard. In fact, to Newton, he looks like a prime suspect. Buying, selling, dealing, anything would fit. Ink like that doesn't come cheap. His sort is everywhere, especially after dark. In the precinct and the park, fake

IDs and White Lightning, but to challenge them isn't worth the hassle. They just don't have the resource.

He stops himself there and takes a swig of his pint. Louise always castigates him for doing this. Making assumptions based solely on a person's appearance, giving them a criminal profile whether they've committed a crime or not. He can't help it. As far as he's concerned, you generally can judge a book by its cover.

Take that priest, for instance. Newton has an innate dislike of the clergy, especially Roman Catholics. He knows exactly where this comes from. The army chaplains were harmless enough, *Jesus Loves Me* and *Light of the World*. But he has other Sunday school memories that are more resonant of evil than anything remotely to do with God.

After his visit to the church, he had gone straight home and fired up his laptop. He might have to revise his views on the internet. All the hours spent over the decades, trawling through old newsprint, squinting at microfiche. Now it seems you can do it all from the comfort of your own settee. Or bed, even.

Draining his glass, he goes back to the bar. Nodding at Chuck and Knocker, he faces the optics as he waits to be served. The round he got in on his arrival yielded nothing and he has no intention of standing another. From the corner of his eye, he sees the lacy residue stuck to the sides of their glasses, building to a crusty scum towards the top. They keep the same glass all night round here unless you specify otherwise. There's no law against it but Newton sees this disgusting practice as proof positive. The town is completely entrenched in the past and full of nutters.

The landlord is aware of Newton's preference and

pours him a fresh glass. As he returns to his seat, he thinks of a New Year spent in here. A bloke had fallen through the door, pissed as a newt just after midnight. Nobody knew him from Adam yet he was embraced as a friendly first footer on the strength of his dark hair. In the memory, Louise is wearing the earrings he'd bought her for Christmas. Her cheeks are flushed with wine and what he imagined at the time was happiness.

Things had been different then of course, when he'd still been climbing the ranks. She loved the social side of things, the kudos, as she called it, of being married to a successful police officer. It had never appealed to Newton, which is just as well. He prefers to keep his private and professional lives separate. Some might see their colleagues as an extended family. He isn't one of them. Louise was his family. Still is his family. Yet he can't even remember the last time they had a night out together.

The woman he met in the woods has kept drifting into his thoughts. Newton is an observer, covert when necessary, always discreet. He likes to find out what motivates people, what makes them tick. He tells himself this is the only reason he has given her any thought at all. *What could have brought her here? Why was she walking in the woods that day and how long is she likely to be staying?* She may even have left already. Taking another swig, he is in the process of assuring himself there is little chance she'll ever set foot in a dump like this again, when the door swings open and she strides in.

Newton nearly chokes on his Guinness but he is pretty sure she doesn't notice, so intent is she on shaking the rain from her umbrella. Glancing through the window, he sees the heavens have once again opened.

She orders a glass of red wine and he notes the subtle shift of Chuck and Knocker's heads towards her. She sees it too and rewards them with a smile as she picks up her drink and turns away from them. She catches Newton's eye immediately.

'Fancy seeing you here.' The irony is clear as she walks straight over to his table.

'Hello again. I just called in as I was passing.'

She picks up a mat from a neighbouring table, casts it beside Newton's and places her glass on it. Still standing, she unbuttons her coat from the neck down, slowly. As she slips it off, he sees the curve of her breasts through her blouse. She isn't wearing a bra.

'Sorry, I didn't catch your name.' She hangs her coat over the back of a chair and sits directly opposite, placing her wet umbrella at her feet.

'James or Jim, I don't mind which.' For some reason, he stops short of giving his surname.

'Well, it's good to see you again, James or Jim.' Taking a mouthful of wine, she looks over her glass at him. 'I'll decide later which I think suits you best.'

Newton isn't sure what to make of this remark. As she crosses her legs, he catches a glimpse of thigh at the top of her stocking. She knows exactly what she's doing. Her eyes shift to the window. 'I'd almost forgotten how changeable the weather is around here. One minute the sun's out, the next you're soaking wet.'

'Yes, it can take you by surprise. You didn't tell me your name.'

'Didn't I?' She looks around, then nods towards the empty grate. 'I'm disappointed the fire isn't lit. That's all I really came for.'

'Me, too. I'm hoping he'll light it in a bit.' She is

clearly evading his question, so Newton tries another. 'Where are you staying?'

'Killamarsh Hall. It's gorgeous.'

'Ah yes, I've heard good things about that place. So, what brings you to Black Hollow?'

She doesn't answer straight away, and he gets the impression that like him, she is considering how much to give away. She reaches again for her glass but instead of picking it up, she runs her forefinger slowly up and down the stem. Newton sees a small crescent shaped scar on the back of her hand.

'I've had a recent bereavement.'

'Oh, I'm sorry to hear that.'

'Thank you. I've come to pay my respects and I suppose I just hankered for the old place. There are a couple of friends I thought I'd look up, revisit my childhood haunts. Nostalgia, really.' This time, she picks the glass up and holds it to her lips. Knocker and Chuck have now turned their backs to the bar and are flagrantly watching them.

'You grew up in these parts, then?' Newton keeps his voice light rather than interrogatory.

'I did.' She shivers and pulls his eyes away as her breasts jiggle with the motion. 'It's so cold in here! Could we find somewhere a little warmer?'

Thrown by her directness, Newton scrambles for a response. To his relief, his phone rings in his pocket. Pulling it out, he is thrown even further to see Louise's name on the screen.

'Aren't you going to answer that?'

'It's not important,' says Newton, flipping the phone face down on the table. He wills the ringing to stop which it does, only to be followed by the alert of an incoming text.

'They're quite insistent.' Again, she eyes him over the top of her glass.

Newton picks the phone back up and reads the message. 'I need to talk to you.' Shoving it into his pocket, he drinks what remains of his pint, suddenly aware how it would look if Louise walked in, not that she would ever come in here on her own.

'Actually, it is quite urgent.' Standing up, he holds out his hand, the gesture ridiculously formal even to him. 'I hope you enjoy the rest of your stay.'

She grasps his outstretched fingers and Newton feels the rub of paper on his skin. 'I hope so too,' she whispers.

50

Kate

'I still can't believe it!'

Kate shakes her head, still in shock at what she's heard. 'And I don't think for one minute Anna doesn't know. It's been happening right under her nose.'

Amy nods in agreement, her mouth full of pakora, flakes of pastry dappling her chin. Kate wonders how she stays so sylphlike if this is her usual supper.

'This is gorgeous, by the way.' She takes another forkful of fragrant rice, washing it down with wine. Now the facts are sinking in, her disbelief is fuelling her appetite and the food is gorgeous. 'I'm going to have it out with her. She's been wasting police time.' She sits back, dabbing her lips with a napkin, conscious the wine is making her babble.

'I'll go round there first thing,' she says, placing her knife and fork decisively together on the plate.

'You might be better getting her to come to the station,' suggests Amy.

Kate considers this. Maybe that's where she's been going wrong. 'Do you mind if I pop out for a smoke?'

'Of course not.' Amy gets up and unlocks the back door. 'Just stand here on the step, sarge. Could do with some fresh air in here.'

Lighting up, Kate thinks back to the day she and Anna searched for Archie, the fireside chats. Perhaps things have been a little too cosy. Newton warned her about getting too close. Something else is bothering her, a feeling simmering beneath the surface. One she is reluctant to face.

'Changing the subject,' calls Amy from inside. 'You won't believe what else I found out today.'

Kate pinches her cigarette and pushes it into her pocket. 'Nothing would surprise me anymore.'

'Well, you know I'm not one for gossip but this came direct from Sharpy and he seemed pretty certain.' She pauses to top up her glass. 'Are you sure I can't tempt you to another?'

'No, I'm driving. Spit it out, Amy, the suspense is killing me.'

'Well, he wouldn't say how he knows but apparently Newton's wife has left him.'

Kate is so stunned she almost falls off the doorstep. She re-lights the tab end and turns her back on the open door. Amy is still speaking but the rest of her words hardly register as she plays back events in her head. Suddenly, she needs to get away. Thanking Amy, she makes her excuses, promising to continue their discussion in the morning.

Driving home, she reflects on what the night's revelations mean. Amy is right, as is Newton, any further meetings with Anna must be in a formal setting. Now she is alone, she admits to feeling miffed she could have kept things from her deliberately. She knows she must stamp out any personal feelings, maintain a professional detachment. As for the news about Newton, it explains just about everything.

Pulling onto her drive, she sees it is a quarter past eleven. The sky is clear of fireworks, the moon a swollen globe. Ideal conditions for late night dog walkers. Locking her car, she sets off down the path that runs by the side of her garden.

Standing by the trees, the leaves whisper around her.

As she lights a cigarette, a bat swoops past the moonlit belly of the clouds. At the edge of the fields is a silhouette, the shadow of a dog by its side but there are no bored teenagers, no-one else hanging around. She is about to turn back when there is a sudden change in the stillness and she freezes, every sense alert. A cloud covers the moon and she is suddenly plunged into blackness. Was it the bats she heard, disturbed by her presence? She feels the air move again and this time, the snap of a twig.

'Who's there?' She demands, becoming alarmed now. Torch raised and clutching her keys like a knuckle duster, she holds them in front of her and steps forward, immediately striking something solid but with the softness of a quilted coat. She staggers back as the moon emerges from the clouds.

'Helen! What the hell?'

Huddled under the trees, Helen doesn't respond. Kate hesitates for a moment, uncertain what to do.

'You'd better come inside.' Grabbing her by the arm, she leads her back to the house in silence. Once inside, she slams the door, Luther scuttling past in a black streak.

'What the hell do you think you're doing?'

'I'm sorry. It's not how it looks.'

'It's exactly how it looks!'

'No!' shouts Helen, pulling her hood down. 'I wanted to talk to you, that's all.' She looks pale and plain. Kate has never seen her without makeup.

'Why not pick the phone up like any normal person?'

'I needed to see you and when you weren't in, I waited for you.'

'It's not just tonight though, is it? You've been stalking me!'

'Don't say that! It makes it sound sordid. It's not like that and you know it isn't.'

Kate leans on the worktop, willing herself to calm down.

'I suppose we need to talk.'

'I don't want to talk anymore. I need you to hold me.' Her eyes are almost pleading. Pathetic really. Before Kate can respond, Helen rushes at her. She lifts her arms up to stop her but it's too late. She feels her hair against her cheek, the familiar smell of her. Not knowing what to do with her raised arms, she lowers them gently onto Helen's back. Within seconds, she feels the brush of lips against her neck, the front of her coat being parted.

Kate shoves her across the kitchen, harder than she intends. She clatters into the table, sending chairs flying. Righting herself, Helen faces her, eyes blazing.

'Why bring me here if you don't want this as much as I do?'

'Because I didn't want to leave you out there in the dark!'

'You want to make your mind up,' spits Helen, her face twisted. 'You're just a teasing bitch!'

Kate almost flies across the kitchen. Grabbing Helen's hood, she drags her across the floor. With her free hand she opens the door and pushes her through it, where she lands in a puddle on her backside. She opens her mouth in outrage but Kate slams the door, cutting off anything she was about to say. Leaning against it, her heart pounding, she has second thoughts and opens it back up again.

'You dare come here again and I'll tie you to them trees and call the foxes on you! Now sod off before I call the station and have you for sexual harassment!'

Slamming the door for a second time she sinks behind it, clutching her knees to her chest. As she searches for her cigarettes, Luther pokes his head from around the curtain, jumps down and settles beside her.

51

Newton

It is pouring down as Newton steps outside, soaking him through immediately. Opening his palm, the rain hits the scrap of paper and he closes his fist as the ink begins to run. What on earth was all that about? He hasn't time to think as he races to the car, grateful now he decided to drive.

Wiping his face, he hesitates. Should he text Louise or ring her back? This is the first time she has called since leaving him. She hadn't picked up this morning, which had contributed to his being in the pub in the first place. Now she wants to talk. Surely, this must be a good sign. He presses her number, the phone gripped to his ear.

'James. Thanks for calling back.' Newton strains to hear what's in the background, trying to guess where she is.

'That's OK. How're you doing?'

'I'm fine.' Her next words are lost and he twists in his seat, cursing. Reception in this part of town is always terrible. 'Sorry, I didn't catch that.'

'I said I'm fine. Look, we need to talk.'

He heard that clear enough. 'Yes, we do. I called you this morning.'

'I know, I was busy. Are you free now?'

This sounds promising. Apart from a brief glimpse through the window during his stakeout, Newton hasn't seen Louise for nearly three weeks. 'Of course. I can pick you up if you like.' He's already had two pints but if they grab something to eat, he should be OK.

'It's alright, I'll drive. I'll meet you at the Miners

Arms.'

'No!'

'I thought you liked it in there.'

'I do but there's no privacy.' The thought of walking back in there with his wife, with that other woman still in there is completely out of the question but they aren't exactly spoilt for choice. Why hadn't she given him more notice? He is about to suggest somewhere further afield when she speaks again.

'It'll have to be the Shovel then.'

'Are you joking?'

'I haven't got long and I don't want to go too far. I'll set off now.' The line goes dead, and Newton sits there staring through the windscreen. Louise wouldn't normally be seen dead in that place. Pulling on his seatbelt he starts the car, ignoring the facts it is both totally out of character and completely inexplicable. She wants to see him and that is all he can think about.

Five minutes later, he is peering between the wipers at the Pick and Shovel. It's a shithole, there's no other word for it. He ought to wait for Louise but feels too restless. The wind is rising, the rain blowing sideways again. He gets out of the car and makes a run for it, turning right into the so-called best room.

The place reeks of stale beer and rancid chip fat. The barmaid had been on the search for Archie but her eyes show no recognition as she leans a ropey arm against the pumps. Her fingers are covered in cheap rings, the nails dirty and bitten. Wondering when he last had a tetanus, he orders a pint of shandy and half a lager for Louise. Despite the venue, it feels good to be ordering a brace of drinks again.

Ribald laughter spills from the taproom next-door but

this side, Newton has his pick of the seats. Choosing a table by the window, he is about to sit down when Louise is almost blown through the door. She shakes her umbrella in a strange facsimile of the other woman's entrance half an hour earlier. Newton smiles at her.

'You look well.'

'Don't be ridiculous James, I look like a drowned rat.' She is wearing a new coat and despite her fringe being soaked, he can see her hair is freshly highlighted. The scent of her perfume hangs between them.

'It's good to see you.'

'Likewise,' says Louise but she hasn't even looked at him. Picking up her glass she drinks half of it. Newton's stomach sinks as he takes in her blank expression, her ramrod back. He knows her well enough to realise this is not a reconciliation.

'I'm sorry to drag you here, it just seemed the quickest option. I didn't want to do this over the phone and coming to the house didn't feel right.'

His damp shirt and jeans suddenly feel cold. 'That's OK. Is Georgie with your mother?'

'No.'

'Where is he, then?'

Louise's mouth sets in a grim line. 'He's with a friend. Look, there's no easy way to say this so I'm going to come straight to the point. I want a divorce, James.'

Her words puncture the air. Whatever he thought she might say, he wasn't expecting this. He looks at her. Her skin, her hair, her smell so achingly familiar, suddenly knowing he has lost her.

'I see you aren't wearing your wedding ring.' Pitiful even to his ears.

'Are you not listening to me?' Louise almost hisses

the words, looking over her shoulder as she does so, as though checking they aren't overheard. 'I asked to meet somewhere neutral because I didn't want a scene.' She opens her handbag, pulling out an envelope which she slides across the table towards him. Newton sees a deep flush is blooming through her foundation.

'What's this?'

'You know what it is, James. Don't make this any harder than it needs to be. You know I'll be reasonable where Georgie's concerned.' She snaps her handbag shut and downs what remains of her drink.

Newton opens the envelope. His hands seem to move independently, with a will of their own.

'It can't be that much of a surprise.' Her voice is no more than a whisper even though there is no sign of the barmaid, no-one to overhear.

Newton's mouth is dry, but he doesn't trust himself to pick his glass up. 'It is a surprise actually.' After twenty years of marriage, that's an understatement.

'Things have been finished a long time. I had high hopes for us once but not anymore.' Bending to retrieve her umbrella, she picks up her handbag and stands. She pauses for a second and Newton thinks she might say something more but she turns briskly away and is gone. If not for the envelope and the lipstick on her glass, he would have difficulty believing she had ever been there in the first place.

52

1977

'Bless me father, for I have sinned.' Marie's fingers fly from her forehead to her chest, shoulder to shoulder. She rolls her eyes theatrically. 'My last confession was some time ago.'

Anna can contain herself no longer and they both fall backwards in hysterics.

'Oh, I'm so bored!' Marie sits upright, pulling a fist of grass savagely from the grave beneath them. Anna watches as she plaits the stalks together. Her friend growing tired of her is her very worst fear. The thought of her finding someone else to be friends with fills her with sickening dread. She knows they shouldn't be sitting cross legged on someone's grave but her eyes dart past the stone angel, as though searching for inspiration, anything that will amuse or interest Marie enough to keep her here. As usual, her friend is one step ahead of her.

'We need to do a dare.'

'What's a dare?' Anna thinks she knows but the words are out of her mouth before she has time to stop them.

'Oh Anna, you're so naive!' says Marie, impatiently. Anna turns her head to hide the heat in her cheeks. 'You know, like truth or dare. A kind of challenge. You have to be brave and courageous if it's a dare worth doing.'

Marie squints her eyes in concentration, but Anna is warming to the new game and has an idea already.

'I know! You know the garages at the side of the Co-op?'

'Mmm.'

'I dare you to climb on the roof and jump off!'

'No way!' shouts Marie, her eyes wide. She throws her head back, leaning against the angel and her laughter echoes around the graveyard.

Suddenly, her expression changes. 'I'm serious Anna. I've been thinking about this for a while.' Anna's stomach churns. She knows Marie will want to outdo her and come up with something bad.

'I dare you,' she pauses, pulling the grass plait taut. 'To come back here after dark and sleep on a grave, all night.' She looks up at her, grinning.

'No chance!' shouts Anna and they fall about laughing again.

'Why not?' giggles Marie. 'You'd have Nelly here for company.' She traces the name at the foot of the angel. 'She'd look after you.'

'There's no way I'd get out at night. You know what my parents are like. You could though.'

Marie screws up her forehead, deep in thought. 'I'm not sure. My mum's not been very well lately.'

'Oh? What's wrong with her?'

'She's upset about Elvis. He died, you know.'

The comment is lost on Anna. Probably another saint she's never heard of. Marie has dropped the grass and is now scratching the back of her hand. 'I'll think about it but it would take some planning.' She looks up, her blue eyes deadly serious. 'Do you know what stigmata is?'

Quite accustomed to the sudden jack-knifing of her friend's mind, Anna is relieved to change the subject. She wracks her brain for the answer, she has seen the word before but try as she might, its meaning escapes her.

'Give me your hand,' says Marie.

Without hesitation, Anna does as she asks.

She leans so close, she can smell the sweet earthy

scent of her. Her fingers are cool as she wraps them around hers but then she feels a sharp, hot pain as Marie digs a fingernail into her.

'Ow!' Anna pulls away, rubbing the deep red wheal now blooming on her skin.

'It's OK, look.' Marie holds out her hand and Anna sees a mirror image of the crescent-shaped mark on her own.

'This is stigmata.' She begins scratching again, biting her lip in concentration. 'Like the marks where the nails went into Jesus. You do yours and I'll do mine.'

Happy to have found a common pastime, Anna copies her, scoring the flesh until blood runs down the backs of both their hands. Clearly thrilled, Marie grabs her wrist and holds it tight, pressing her skin into Anna's.

'We are blood sisters now.' At these words, Anna doesn't care how much it hurts. Surely now Marie will never leave her.

53

Kate

'Thank you so much for your time.'

Kate's face hurts as she smiles yet again. She shakes the old man's hand and watches him shuffle away. Glancing at her watch, she lights up, her eyes settling on Helen's empty parking space.

'Penny for the guy, miss?'

Startled, she turns to see a scruffy, urchin-like child sat against the wall, a dummy of sacks and old clothes draped across his knees. The practice has all but died out in Sheffield but apparently not in Black Hollow. Kate is pretty sure he won't thank her if she takes him literally and the crudely drawn grin on the punctured football suggests someone has gone to some effort. Fishing in her pocket, she tosses a pound coin in his direction.

'It'll be dark soon. Don't let me find you here when I come back.'

The boy catches the coin and slides it into his pocket.

'Any chance of a fag?'

'No!'

Shaking her head, she makes a point of grinding the remains of her cigarette beyond any chance at salvage. As she makes her way back to her desk, a feeling of despondency creeps upon her as she mentally crosses off yet another dead end. The librarian had provided a list of names but had steadfastly refused to disclose the private numbers of any of the reading group.

'You do realise this could be construed as wilful obstruction of a murder investigation?' Kate had warned her.

'I'm sorry, that's not my intention,' had been Ms Clark's reply. 'I won't compromise my clients' private data. There's no telling what you people might do with it.' Kate wonders what provoked such a morbid distrust of the police. Tempting though the idea is of turning up at the library with a warrant, she has settled for subtler means and spent the morning trawling through the phonebook and voters' rolls.

Part of her prays Helen won't come in, the other hopes that she will. Maybe then things can return to normal. Last night was nothing short of embarrassing. Unlocking her computer, she pushes the thoughts away.

Anna is due in half an hour. If she was surprised to be asked into the station, she hadn't shown it, her calm acceptance giving nothing away. Kate is sure she won't be so laid back by the time they've finished with her.

She looks back at her list. Every one of them must be tracked down and interviewed but she discounted Ann Brown and Janet Smith immediately. There were dozens of them. The same could be said for Jayne Thompson and Paul Jones. She will cross reference them with the statements already taken but with limited time at her disposal, she has picked the more unusual names to start with.

Jack Gyarmati had stood out straight away. Sure enough, there was only one in the phone book. Answering on the first ring, Kate had been surprised to find Jack was female, with what she guessed to be a strong Hungarian accent, (she sounded like Zsa Zsa Gabor). As the conversation became protracted, she was proved correct. The old lady thought Kate was from the library and grasped her chance to promote the merits of Magyar literature.

Hanging up as soon as politeness allowed, her second call was no more fruitful. This time the accent was Geordie and told Kate nothing she hadn't already known.

'Terrible what's happened and such a pleasant lass. Quite the education on her. There's nothing that girl doesn't know about books but she keeps herself to herself. We go in the Miners after but she's always away home, never joins us.'

Kate doodles down the side of the page. *Maybe Anna considers herself above them, she can imagine that.* Or perhaps as a bona fide intellectual, she is genuinely a fish out of water with the group. Maybe she just isn't the sociable type. It's not as though she doesn't like drinking.

'Your man was here already. I told him, we watched a fillum that night, then Alan took the dog out. Would have been about eleven. I went straight to bed and didn't hear a thing. I sleep like the dead once I'm off.'

The third book club member, Arthur Pine, was the elderly gent she'd just seen off. Insisting on coming to the station, his excitement had been palpable, clearly casting himself in the guise of an amateur sleuth. Eager for detail, Kate's refusal to give him any hadn't stopped him offering his own sage advice. She reads her few scrawled notes.

'The clues will be there, they always are. You don't need me to tell you. Dig, girl and keep digging 'til you find 'em.'

Frustratingly, Mr Pine was a relative newcomer to the town and knew next to nothing of Anna or her father. Kate throws her pen down. Her heart isn't in this. Amy's discoveries have rendered anything the book club can tell them almost irrelevant. Almost but not quite. She knows they can't ignore anything, however trivial it seems.

With five minutes to spare before Anna's arrival, she goes for another smoke, on the fire escape this time to avoid Oliver Twist. She thinks about lighting another but decides against it. On the way back, she stops at the coffee machine, just as Newton emerges from a door with Vardy. He is wearing a new shirt and throws his head back, laughing. Kate considers calling out, telling them of Amy's discovery but it can wait. Today's interview is in the station log if either of them bothers to look.

'He looks remarkably chipper, considering his wife's just left him,' mutters Kate as she slams down the coffees. Amy purses her lips but doesn't comment.

At that moment, Jo from reception puts her head around the door. 'Anna Collins is here. I've put her in room two.'

Kate picks up her notes and folder, annoyed at how nervous she feels. Amy has agreed to lead the interview and the two of them make their way down the corridor.

As she opens the door, Anna turns in her seat. The look she throws at Kate could strike a man dead.

'Thanks for coming in today. This is my colleague, DC Khan.'

'Am I under caution?' says Anna, as she removes a pair of dark woollen gloves. She looks tired but has clearly made an effort with her appearance. Her hair is pulled into a tight chignon and beneath her coat, she is wearing a business-like trouser suit.

'Not at all,' replies Amy, switching on the tape, which they had agreed on earlier. 'But we will be recording our conversation.' As they sit, the scrawls and cigarette burns appear livid on the tabletop, even though Kate has seen them countless times before. Amy presses the record button, declares the date and time and the names of those present in the room.

'What's this?' Anna's expression is now a badly concealed mixture of disbelief and outrage.

'It's nothing to be alarmed at. We just want to make sure we have a proper record of our conversations going forward.' Kate is surprised how much better she feels for saying this.

'Can you confirm your full name please.'

Anna almost spits it out.

'Thank you,' says Amy. 'And your date of birth.'

'Three. One. Sixty-eight.' Kate can almost feel her eyes burning into the top of her bowed head.

'We want to talk to you about a couple things that have come to our attention,' continues Amy. She takes some papers from a folder, each in a clear plastic cover. She spins one round and slides it across the table.

'What is it?' asks Anna, as Kate searches her face for any sign of stress.

'It's one of your father's bank statements,' replies Amy, sliding another towards her. Anna's forehead creases.

'And why are you showing me these?'

'Well, for a start this is a paperless account which appears to have been set up for online trade. We found no details of it amongst your father's things. Were you aware of it?'

Anna blinks before responding. 'I'm not sure.'

'Oh, come on, Anna. You'd know.' The words are out of Kate's mouth before she can stop herself.

'You'll notice some items are highlighted,' continues Amy. 'Does anything occur to you as odd about these transactions?'

Anna glares at her over the top of her glasses. 'I'm

sorry, remind me again who you are. I know DS Fox but there's been so many of you trawling through our business, it's difficult to keep track.'

The muscles in her jaw visibly tighten, her nostrils flaring.

'I'm Detective Constable Amy Khan, as I said for the purposes of the recording, and as DS Fox told you. I'm part of the team investigating your father's murder.' *She really is unflappable*, thinks Kate. 'Now, if you wouldn't mind looking at these statements, you will see we have marked a number of entries. The entries indicate deposits and withdrawals.'

'Well yes, it *is* a bank account.'

Kate remains silent for the moment, happy for Amy to continue. This was her discovery after all.

'The reason these transactions are highlighted is it appears your father was in the habit of making numerous deposits at different branches across the region all on the same day. If you look at the top rows of the first page, you'll see what I mean.'

Anna leans forward. She scrutinises the statement for a few seconds, then looks up, first at Kate, then Amy. 'I don't quite follow what you're getting at. We run a shop. Of course he deposited money. It wouldn't have been much of a business if he hadn't.'

Kate feels it is her turn to interject again. 'This is separate to the joint business account you have at the post office. Only your father had access to this one.'

She waits for her words to make their impact but Anna's expression doesn't falter.

'You told us that despite the till recording everything, your father still wrote every single sale in a ledger.' Opening the evidence folder, she pulls out the one he was using in the weeks preceding his death. Turning to the relevant date, she rotates the book to face Anna. 'Even if the deposits did relate to sales, the figures in here don't match. They're nowhere near the amounts deposited.'

'I assume you've checked the till?'

'We have. Your father was a meticulous bookkeeper. The ledgers match the till exactly. They also match what you deposited at the post office.'

'He obviously wasn't that meticulous. He must have made other sales and put the money straight into this account.'

Amy takes another page from her folder. 'This is from the day before. You will see he withdrew a thousand pounds from this account. Do you have any idea why he would do that?'

'He was a businessman,' replies Anna, her voice remaining calm as she peers at the statement. Behind her glasses, Kate sees her eyes scanning up and down the whole page. She shrugs. 'I presume he was buying stock.'

'Would he pay in cash?'

'Some of our suppliers prefer it. We can't be held responsible if they choose not to declare everything to the taxman.'

'Of course not, but what about the way he was making the deposits? Why would he bank such a large sum in Chesterfield, then drive all the way to Sheffield to deposit more, then all the way back to Meadowhead to pay in yet another large amount? All in cash?'

Anna keeps her eyes down, pushing her glasses up her nose, clearly playing for time. Swallowing as though to compose herself, she juts her chin out and directs her response straight at Kate. 'My father was old school, as I've told you.' Kate wonders if the pause that follows is meant to emphasise the fact she's already told her this in confidence. 'He didn't trust ATMs. It's just an age thing and he would often deliver things himself. He liked to give a personal service. He must have been paid for something in Chesterfield, banked the money, then driven over to Sheffield and done the same. Ditto at Meadowhead. He wouldn't want to carry all that cash around with him.'

'Yet he was quite happy to withdraw a thousand pounds and walk through Sheffield city centre with it.'

Anna's eyes narrow. 'My father has been murdered. What exactly is he accused of?'

'He isn't accused of anything,' says Kate. 'We're just doing our job. There's something else we'd like you to look at.' She pushes another piece of paper across the table. 'These are your father's mobile phone records for the week commencing 3rd of October this year.'

Anna looks at the page but remains silent.

'Most of the calls to both this number and the landline we've been able to corroborate from your father's address book as regular clients, suppliers and the like. The ones highlighted we have not been able to identify.' Kate looks across at Amy to continue.

'Do you recognise the number at the top?'

Anna shakes her head. 'Should I?'

'Not necessarily. What about the one below it? It's a phone box in Grimesthorpe, Sheffield.'

Again Anna looks from Amy to Kate, then back again, her expression blank.

'That's the same day your father made the large withdrawal in Sheffield. Just an hour before, as it happens.' Amy passes another plastic covered sheet across the table. 'This is the previous week. Another call from the same mobile, which is unregistered, by the way. Within forty minutes he was in Sheffield withdrawing a thousand pounds. The day after, he deposited five times that amount.'

Amy waits, giving Anna time to process what's being said. 'OK, have a look at this.' She takes the final bank statement and stabs at the bottom with her finger. 'Can you explain where your father would get nine thousand pounds from?'

The overhead strip lights bounce off Anna's glasses, once again obscuring her eyes. She doesn't respond.

'I'll tell you what I think, shall I?' says Kate, taking a deep breath. She's given this some thought overnight. 'Whatever he's been doing, he's done it for years. Pretty small scale, nice little earner. Let's face it, the shop wasn't making much, he had to do something. He set this account up when your mother died and things ticked along nicely but then a few months ago things changed. Maybe somebody got wind and wanted in. He starts getting calls from unknown numbers, untraceable of course. He's making cash withdrawals same as he's always done except now the stakes are higher. Whatever he was doing, he was good at it. The amounts he deposits the day after are always higher than what he drew out. He thinks splitting it in this way will hide that and it does to a certain extent and he's entitled to pay himself a wage. But he must have hit the jackpot. Bit more than a wage that, isn't it?' Again she stabs at the statement. 'Is this what killed him Anna? Did he bite off more than he could chew?'

Anna stares at her, her face bright red but still she doesn't speak. Something else had occurred to Kate in the middle of the night. 'All these dates, 3rd of October, 19th of September, August the 29th, I'm sure it didn't start this way but they're all Wednesdays Anna, when you're at your book club. What are you not telling us? What was your father doing while you were out?'

Anna takes her glasses off, her eyes burning into Kate's across the table.

'You're the detective, aren't you? You tell me.'

54

Newton

Newton is lying perfectly still, staring up at the ceiling. Well accustomed to the thrum of pain, his whole body reverberates with something very different this evening.

The envelope lies crumpled on the rug where he dropped it. Ironic really. That he should be carrying his divorce papers when for the very first time in his life, he had slept with a woman who wasn't his wife.

That isn't strictly true, he hadn't slept a wink. He stretches, elongating his spine, savouring the feeling of painlessness. His muscles feel like liquid, soft instead of taut. He is sore in tender places, reminding him he is alive and a pleasant heaviness pins him to the bed. He has no desire to move as he drifts in the drowsy hinterlands between wakefulness and sleep.

He thinks of Louise, hard faced and remorseless but the scene in the Shovel seems aeons ago when seen through the lens of what came next. He has no recollection of driving back to the Miners, he doesn't recall what was said. All he remembers is the hotel bedroom, crisp white sheets, warm oil and wine.

He must have told her about his back at some point, which is hard to believe because he never tells anyone. She had insisted on the massage, giggling at first then deadly serious. Straddling him in her stockings, she had warmed the oil in her palms then dripped it onto his skin. What happened next could hardly be termed a massage. Endorphins, that must be it, better than any drug. They're always banging on about them at the pain clinic. Now he knows why.

It won't last but for the moment he intends to enjoy it. Rolling over, he stretches again, amazed at his ease of movement. She must be some sort of professional but in what, he dreads to think.

Reality is beginning to sink in now. Newton has never strayed, never so much as looked at another woman. Never wanted to. The vows he made meant something to him, evidently more than they did to her. The enormity suddenly hits him and two things stand out. The first is that Louise will no longer be his wife. He lets that thought just hang there quietly in his mind, surprised how calm he feels about it. The second is that his belief their marriage was a good one, built on strong foundations and mutual respect was made of sand. The latter disappeared a long time ago. The rest he took for granted. All of it blown out of the water in a single afternoon.

He had never known anything like it in his entire life. *Why had it never been like that with Louise?* As he drifts off into languorous sleep, the last things he is aware of are that he feels no pain and no guilt either.

55

1977

'Will you be alright on your own?'

Anna looks up from the heart-shaped brooch in her palm. She had almost forgotten her mother was there, so lost had she been in her imaginings.

'Of course I will.'

Mother pulls on a cardigan, already halfway across the shop. 'I won't be long,' she calls as the bell jangles and the door clicks shut behind her.

Anna turns back to the jewellery. It's like opening a box of chocolates, she can't decide which is her favourite. Replacing the brooch, she strokes the shining pendants, the marks and embellishments etched on the surfaces. Sliding a ring on her finger, she moves her hand, the light catching the symbols. Hearts, clubs, diamonds, spades. All the rings are too big but she hopes Father will let her choose one when she is older. Perhaps she could take something for Marie, although of course she won't tell him. With nothing but her breath and the silk cloth her mother uses for the most delicate objects, she takes her time, carefully misting and polishing, replacing the items one by one. When she has finished, she slides the box back beneath the counter, locks the hidden clasp beneath the rim and admires her work through the glass.

She feels very grown up being left in charge. Shaking the cloth, she twirls across the floor with her eyes half closed. She could be the proprietress, with a long dress trailing behind her and her name on a plaque above the door. In her mind's eye the shelves are filled with books with a rolling, push along ladder, like the one she's seen at the library. She circles the shop, dusting and adjusting, so lost in her daydreams, she only just hears the shop bell when it rings. Father Vincent stands in the doorway.

'Good morning, Anna and how are you this fine morning? It was your father I was hoping to catch hold of.'

Anna feels her face burn and not only at being caught looking so foolish. Father Vincent has never set foot inside the shop before and why would he? Her family aren't churchgoers and even if they were, it wouldn't be his church they went to. What would a man of God want with playing cards? Surely, there can be one reason only for his presence.

'Whatever's the matter, child?' he says in his Irish lilt, a look of concern softening his features. Instead of the robe he wears in church, he is dressed in a black suit. Apart from the collar at his throat, he doesn't look like a priest at all.

'Nothing, Father. You just missed him. He won't be back until later.'

'What nonsense is this?' Her heart jolts at her father's voice behind her. Turning, she sees him leaning against the curtain at the bottom of the stairs. 'Come on up, Mooney. You'll have to excuse my daughter. She has a very vivid imagination.'

'I keep hearing about this book collection of yours. Thought it high time I saw it for myself.' He smiles at her as he follows her father up the stairs.

Anna lets out a sigh of relief. There are plenty of things the priest could tell him, none of which she would want him to hear. Looking up at the ceiling, she tries to gauge which books they might be looking at but their footsteps appear to have halted. Tiptoeing to the staircase, she places her feet carefully where she knows the boards don't creak. She can hear their voices quite clearly.

'Beautiful dog you've got here, Collins.'

'Left to me he'd get a bob's worth.'

'Your daughter seems fond of him.'

'Well she's on her blasted own. Shoo!' Jack's claws skitter across the floorboards. Cursing, she leans further forward.

'What's your poison, Mooney?' She hears the chink of glass.

'Nothing for me. I've had time to consider and I think I should look at your books and leave it at that.'

'Damn it, man. Don't turn yeller on me now.'

Anna steadies herself against the wall. Her heart is beating so loudly, she misses half of Father Vincent's response.

'— and you know the position I'm in.'

'I do indeed.' The note of triumph in her father's voice is unmistakable.

'Anna!' Her mother's shout rings in tandem with the shop bell. Anna almost falls down the stairs and through the curtain.

'Good grief, girl! What on earth are you doing?'

'Nothing, I just showed our guest up.'

Mother stops in her tracks, her eyes suddenly wary. 'What guest?'

'Father Vincent has dropped by to look at our books.'

'Has he, now?' A flush of pink floods Mother's face as she pushes roughly past her. Anna has never seen her mount the stairs so quickly.

Muffled voices trickle through the ceiling, then the priest emerges from the staircase looking like the hounds of hell are after him. Anna likes this description and tries to remember where she read it. He puts a hand to his collar and smiles weakly.

'Are you alright, Father?'

'Yes Anna. I just remembered there's somewhere I need to be. I'll come by again some other time.' Passing in a flurry of blackness, the bell clangs as he opens the door and is gone.

56

Newton

A gash of gold between the trees is all that is left of the day. Newton emerges from the woods and heads down the hill towards town. The pain had returned with a vengeance, as he knew it would. A walk usually helps but it still feels raw and jagged, the tight brace he is never truly free of no looser than when he set out.

At least the view has proved a welcome distraction. The backbone of England as his geography teacher used to call it. Newton finds the bleakness beautiful, even though these days he can do little more than look. He doubts he'll ever see the highest points again but he will always be drawn here. To the pure air and the peace. He will never stop coming, no matter what state he gets into. The sheer majesty of the peaks always has the capacity to make human problems seem inconsequential.

Lottie is trotting beside him, thrilled to be outdoors but clearly exhausted. There was a time not long ago, she'd be bounding off and back again in zigzags through the fields but her tongue lolls like a scrap of ham and she makes no effort to run ahead. She hasn't been getting enough exercise, which has turned in Newton's favour. Common sense has prevailed and Louise has admitted she hasn't time to walk the dog as often as she should. A shared custody has been agreed. It goes through Newton but it's the best he is going get. The thought of similar arrangements for Georgie don't bear thinking about.

Walking Lottie and easing the pain aren't the only reasons he is out here. He knows it is utterly stupid. There's no need to scour the countryside in the vain hope he'll bump into her, although he can't pretend the idea of encountering her in the woods again doesn't excite him.

And so, he is disappointed as he makes his way home. This is new territory to him, entirely outside his realm of experience. He had felt like a naughty schoolboy flattening out the fragment of paper, hoping the ink was still legible. He hasn't tried her number, stopping short of putting it in his phone. Apart from female colleagues, having another woman's contact details still feels wrong, something other men might do but not Newton.

The whole landscape of his life is unrecognisable. His marriage is over, the stable family unit he envisaged his son growing up in no longer exists. What will that mean for him and Georgie? The prospect of him growing up in a separate house to him is something he isn't ready to contemplate. He knows he'll have to come up with something more imaginative than trips to Playmania and a Happy Meal, which is what they've done twice this week already.

He can't condone his shameful conduct, which seems to be racking up. What kind of man is he? A murderer stalking the town, his personal and professional lives in tatters and all he can think about is her.

To feel tranquil instead of tranquilised, is that really too much to ask? She had finally told him her name as they lay entangled in the bedsheets. The thought pulls him up sharp and he leans against an old post, the rusting remains of a fence jutting from its side but for once, the pain isn't the reason he has stopped. His eyes follow the spine of the hills, his mind seeing something else entirely.

Lottie yaps, pulling him from his reverie. She looks up at him expectantly as he takes the scrap of crumpled paper from his pocket. 'Nothing for you girl,' he says, rubbing the fur between her ears. Pulling out his phone, he taps in the number. Quickly, he ends the call and dials another.

'Good evening, glad I've caught you. I left an ivory dagger with you last week. I don't suppose you've managed to date it yet, have you?'

57

Anna

Time can be a strange thing. It can fly as quick as lightning or it can drag like a sack of stones. Anna has kept herself busy, clearing out her father's things. The battered suitcase proved useful. He won't be needing that again. She'd thrown his clothes into it, his dreadful record collection. All have gone to the charity shop or in some cases, the tip. She has kept a few things. His pocket watch, a pair of silver cufflinks and his favourite deck of cards. She considered having them placed in the coffin but it seemed such a waste. In any case, the cufflinks couldn't be just thrown in, they'd need to be slotted through his sleeves and she couldn't bear the thought of that. But it's been so much easier this time. The idea that this whole place is now hers and hers alone has given her a quickening in her stomach she hasn't felt in years.

If anyone had seen her, they would think her completely insane. Driven by a newfound energy, tipping drawers and boxes into rubbish bags without even looking what was in them. Cleaning with maniacal zeal, she had binned her father's ashtrays with a grim delight. The smell of cigarette smoke will always remind her of him but the stale carcinogenic residue which has clung to this place her whole life, she couldn't wait to get rid of. The surges hadn't lasted. Afterwards she wandered listlessly in the semi-darkness of the shop, stepping around the spot where it happened. Then she lingered for hours, hollowed out and unable to part with anything. She is well versed enough with grief to know it is a kind of madness.

It was only a matter of time before his secrets were discovered but she hadn't expected to be summoned to the station like a common criminal. They could call it what they liked but it was little more than a cell. What her father got up to is something she's always known about, being brainwashed into silence by her mother from an early age. Since it has been just the two of them, things have been harder to ignore but still, she can't help the police. It's not like she has any of their names. Apart from one of course, and he's been here — she knew he wouldn't be able to keep away. Wanting to save his own skin, ever the Christian. She had left him on the doorstep for hours until he finally skulked away.

Time isn't passing as it should be. She considers opening the shop but can't face the goldfish bowl that would be. And so, she just sits here, watching the sunlight move across the walls, one ear trained on the door in case Marie comes back. Her head swims with questions. *Where are you staying? Where have you been?* Then the memories come, dark and malevolent. Time torments her, playing back like a spool of film. Speeding up and slowing down again, lurching and warping. It stalks her from room to room and at its worst, she fears she really is going mad.

Drink is her fast forward button and the day is finally here. She takes a last look in her father's room. The bed is stripped, the wardrobe empty. It feels as cold as the grave.

In the hall she peers in the mirror, blurring the glass with her breath. She has always imagined attending a funeral in a pillbox hat with a veil but she would never have the confidence. She does have a pair of silk gloves though, bought especially for the occasion. Black as the ace of spades, as Father would say of course. She picks them up and smooths them over her wrists, checking her watch as she does so. Time is dragging again.

Standing at the window, she feels nothing as she looks at the people on the pavement. Paying their respects. *Gawping more like.* Susan Barrett is there of course and Olive Stratton. Margaret Wood would be among them if she wasn't herself six foot under.

At last the hearse crawls to the kerb like a giant insect with her father's body in its innards. Sunshine glints off the bonnet, a heap of autumn flowers on the coffin lid. Bronze, copper, gold.

A throb beats at her temples, tightening round her skull like a band. It's usually a sign she hasn't drunk enough but that can't be the case today. She fills a hipflask to the brim, takes a swig for luck then fills it again and slips it into her pocket. *They say alcohol cleans wounds, don't they?* Checking her reflection one last time, she puts one foot in front of the other. Her limbs are stiff as a marionette as she makes her way downstairs. She feels nothing, which makes no sense at all, as this is the worst pain she has ever known.

As she walks, she recites the Lord's Prayer and slowly the car pulls away. Her mind is suddenly scrambled, unable to remember what's expected of her.

Hallowed be Thy name.

She wills herself to stay calm. All the hard work is done and there is nothing left to do except be here. A sea of faces lines the street, staring in judgement. Why don't they bow their heads? Panic simmers but the prayer anchors her, shielding her from within.

Forgive us our trespasses.

Turning away, she stares at the seatback in front of

her. It is a short drive and soon she finds herself emerging onto the church cobbles, blinking in the sunlight that slants across the path. At the edge of her vision, she senses the crowd but keeps her eyes averted. Kate appears, blowing smoke like a fire-breathing dragon but it's the figure to the side of the porch that makes Anna's heart jolt, even though she fully expected her to be here. And of course, she has the confidence to carry it off. The black pillbox hat sits at a jaunty angle on her neat, elfin head. Despite the net obscuring half her face, Marie is instantly recognisable.

Deliver us from evil.

Conscious of eyes on her back, Anna keeps focused on the prayer. Once seated, Kate slides into the pew beside her, her signature scent of tobacco comforting. Dimly aware of the vicar's words, she tries not to look at the coffin where it stands at the end of the nave. That's a word most wouldn't use. Marie would but she won't think of her. She fixes her eyes on the flowers. Did she choose them? She doesn't remember. They look too bright against the wood. Like a harvest festival.

Stumbling, someone puts out a hand to steady her. She nearly falls, triggering a memory of skidding in her father's blood. The grave is like the priest's well, except there's no little boy down there. Just a rotting box with her mother in it, half eaten by the worms.

Removing a glove, she throws a handful of earth onto the coffin. This time the air is still with not a breath of wind. The vicar's words are clear as a bell, but she only hears them in snatches.

Earth to earth.

Across the grave she looks for Marie, strong enough to face her now the worst is over.

Ashes to ashes.

There she is, at the front of course, her veil pushed back revealing her cheekbones and her eyes. She isn't looking this way and is paying no attention to the words of the committal. Anna follows her gaze. Blinking, she looks again but there is no mistake. She is staring at the policeman, the one in charge.

Dust to dust.

Pulling her glove back on she smooths the material and quickly walks away.

58

Kate

Kate rounds the corner just as the hearse pulls up, her cigarette clamped between her lips. She stops dead at the sight of Anna, marooned on her own in the back of the following car. Nobody should have to face this alone.

The press arrived early, jostling for position, swelling the numbers. One of them is halfway up a stepladder, his camera levelled at Anna. How can anyone in their right mind consider that acceptable behaviour? She pinches her cigarette, burning her fingers in the process. Newton and Julie have gone inside already. Standing by the wall, she lowers her head respectfully but keeps her eyes fixed on Anna as she climbs out of the car.

She looks dreadful. Dressed in a black coat, her hair is scraped back, her face has the pallor of a death mask. She is muttering to herself, her mouth jabbering convulsively. The mourners hang back as the coffin is raised but the click of cameras cuts through the air and Kate throws a look of venom in the reporters' direction.

So shocked is she at Anna's appearance, she almost misses the blonde in the pillbox hat. *Who the hell is she? If she's a friend or relative, why hasn't she offered her support before now?*

Once the press and the rest of the mob are inside, almost every seat is full. She would normally sit inconspicuously at the back but something propels her forward. She follows Anna down to the pews at the front.

The service tactfully sidesteps the manner of Charlie's demise. *Taken too soon* and *unexpectedly* are the only references to his brutal end. Sitting so close to Anna takes her back. To her nightshifts in Sheffield, the alco's reek as they were thrown in the cells to sleep the worst off. Amy had noticed, of course she had, and today it is far worse. The sad miasma seeps from her pores, tainting her breath as it wafts over the hymn sheet.

Anna sits straight backed, her black-gloved hands clenched to still the tremor. She stands for the hymns, mouthing the words. Only when it comes to the Lord's Prayer does her voice ring out strong and true.

For Kate, the act of burial is an intensely private matter. She stands back, watching the congregation for any sign, any indication however small, that something might not be as it seems. Julie is at Anna's side by the grave, so she isn't completely alone. Newton shares her contempt for the press and shoos them back before she has chance to. 'Not here, for God's sake!' he growls, almost knocking a microphone out of one of their hands. She turns her attention back to the mourners, in particular the mystery woman, who has watched the near fracas with interest.

The coffin is lowered into the ground. His duties almost discharged, the vicar approaches Anna, his hand on her arm as he murmurs a few final words of comfort. Kate hovers, intending to identify the blonde but to her frustration, she sees her slip through a gap in the hedge that Kate didn't even know was there.

There is no wake of course, a term she has always found ridiculous. There will be no waking up for Charlie Collins.

Driving away, she knows she must put sympathy aside now and focus on the job in hand. After the interview at the station, they had checked the mileage on Charlie's car but apart from confirming he got about a bit, this told them nothing. A phrase Anna used has stuck in Kate's head. *A personal service.* So as well as organised crime there could be any number of merry widows across the region, the grateful recipients of Charlie's ministrations. The investigation is becoming a farce.

As she makes her way up the high street, she sees a van parked outside Margaret Wood's house. That hasn't taken them long. Slowing, she peers over her shoulder but the outline of a man on the tailgate is all that's visible.

Checking her mirror, she waits for a gap in the traffic and pulls in. As she yanks on the handbrake, the now heavily pregnant Alice Ashby appears at the top of the path. The man steps off the tailgate and kisses her on the lips.

If Mrs Wood left the house to her, things have moved very quickly indeed. Talk about jump in her grave. *Could the will have been read, already?* Then she remembers the keys. She still has one herself. Maybe Alice knew the house was promised to her and just couldn't wait. Strange that she never mentioned it.

She wrenches the handbrake off, then stills her foot as a double decker stops right beside her. In the few moments she's been parked here, cars have pulled in front and behind her, effectively blocking her in. Turning in her seat, she sees a cloud of exhaust fumes pouring from the back of the bus.

Kate leans on the horn but her heart sinks as she sees the driver get off, a group of angry passengers streaming after him. This is all she needs. Pulling out her phone, she is about to call Newton when she sees a tiny envelope in the corner of the screen. She recently set up her emails to come to her phone but hadn't noticed any replies yet. She calls Newton but it goes straight to messages. Looking through the back window, she sees the cloud of fumes is getting bigger and a traffic jam has formed. About to throw her phone across the car she stops herself, arm raised. She can't drive anywhere and at least she is legally parked. Tapping her phone she finds her email account and logs in. It must have kicked in today because all her morning's mail is there and she had checked it before heading out. Impressed, she scrolls down and nearly jumps from her seat when she sees a response from HM Land Registry. One of the discreet enquiries she had made after Margaret Wood's death was regarding the ownership of her house.

She flicks past the official blurb. As expected, it was owned by the coal board since it was built in 1902. In 1976 it was purchased by Mr and Mrs Alvin Wood. Good for them, thinks Kate. Just before Thatcher came to power, surely every miner's nemesis. She scrolls further and stops, her blood running cold.

It isn't what she'd expected. It's much, much worse. Surely now Newton will listen to her.

59

Anna

Tearing the dress from her shoulders, the zip almost snaps in her desperation to remove it. Balling it up with her tights, she shoves them into the linen basket. She never wants to see them again. Taking a deep breath, she exhales slowly, tears gathering and dissolving at the back of her throat. The worst is behind her now, she needs to keep telling herself that. Changing into jeans and a sweatshirt, she begins to feel calmer. She takes the flask from her bag, goes to the bathroom and pours the few remaining drops down the plughole.

In the kitchen, the bottles seethe and beckon to her from the pantry. She ignores the tremor in her hands, spooning extra leaves into the pot as she waits for the kettle to boil. Taking her tea into the living room she picks up the book she's been trying to read all week, plumps up the cushions and settles herself in a chair. The clock ticks like a heartbeat but otherwise the room is quiet. How many times has she craved such peace? Now, with no chance of interruption, the words swim out of focus. The smell of ash wafts from the grate but she hasn't the energy to light it.

She sits for a while, absorbing her aloneness, looking at the empty chairs. Suddenly the sound of knocking shatters the silence. With a groan, she throws the book down and makes her way down to the door.

'What the hell do you want?'

'Oh, that's charming,' replies Marie. Is it Anna's imagination, or is there a change in the way she stands, the way she looks at her? Her concern and courtesy appear to have been replaced by the blasé confidence of old.

'Aren't you going to invite me in then?'

Anna steps back as Marie's perfume fills the hallway. As they climb the stairs, something she half suspected is suddenly obvious.

'That wasn't your first trip to the cemetery since you came back, was it? Nice flowers by the way.' Resuming her seat by the unlit fire, she knows she won't try to deny it.

Marie smiles as she unbuttons her coat, her movements unhurried as she takes the seat opposite. 'I wanted to pay my respects.'

'Well you've done that now, so why are you still here?'

'Don't be like that, Anna. I thought we could have our own little wake.'

Anna feels her temper rising. So much for good intentions.

'What do you want? Wine? Vodka? Lager?'

'Ooh, spoilt for choice. Red wine if you've got it.'

In the pantry she reaches for the best bottle, then stills her hand mid-air. What the hell is she doing? Falling into character already, eager to impress. She chooses a shiraz from Aldi.

'This is really good,' remarks Marie moments later, as she stares into the ruby liquid. 'You know, I always saw myself coming back here with a husband in tow, a couple of kids under my belt and here I am on my tod. Shows what I know.' Taking a long drink, she misjudges it slightly, a sliver of red trickling down her chin. As she wipes it away, Anna takes in her scarlet nails, for a second, sees them tipped with blood and the soil on her boot mars the perfection further. She is dying to know what Marie has been doing for the last thirty years but she won't ask. Is she still the same, always looking for adventure? Thrill seeking. She's willing to bet that she is. She thinks of how she looked by the graveside in that hat and suddenly a different question blurts from her lips.

'What's going on between you and that detective?'

'What detective?'

'Newton. He's leading the murder investigation.'

'Is he?' Her eyebrows rise but Anna can't tell if her surprise is feigned or genuine. 'I've been meaning to ask, have you any idea who did it?'

'No.'

Marie tucks her hair behind her ear. 'I hate to say this but I'm just flabbergasted it didn't happen sooner.'

Anna's stomach jolts. She hasn't lost it then. That insatiable desire to shock. She feels her teeth grind but she refuses to be bated.

'So, are you going to tell me what happened then? All those years ago?'

'What happened?'

'Yes. You just disappeared without a word. Even Father Vincent had no idea where you'd gone.' She pauses, watching Marie intently. 'Or so he said. Were the bailiffs after you or something?'

'Not quite,' mutters Marie, knocking back the rest of her wine. Picking up the bottle, she refills her glass. 'Want a top up?'

It hasn't taken her long to take over. *Where did she get such confidence, her with the unmarried mother?* Not that it matters but it had back then. Whereas she with both parents and their own thriving business, she has never had it. *So much for laying off the booze.* Her glass slides across the table as though it has a will of its own.

'Don't try and distract me. What happened?'

Marie leans back in the chair, every inch as though she owns it. Arm outstretched, she rolls the glass in her palm and as she does so, a low rumbling begins, like distant thunder. Only when Anna sees her shoulders shaking does she realise she is laughing.

'You're asking me what happened?' Her expression switches from glee to abject misery in an instant. 'Don't tell me you don't know.'

'I don't!'

'Rubbish!' Marie sits bolt upright. 'You were always the clever one.'

Anna's heart pounds in her ears. *How dare she laugh?* The memory is branded into her. She slops more wine into her glass and walks over to the window. For the first time in weeks the pavement is empty and the police car has gone. She turns back into the room. Suddenly there seems no point pretending.

'I think I know why you had to go but I want you to tell me in your own words. Tell me everything.'

60

Newton

Seeing Marie at the funeral has unnerved him. That's the nearest Newton can get to even remotely describing how he feels right now. Anna Collins was adamant she has no family, nobody at all they could call, so what can possibly be the connection? She's about the right age to be a schoolfriend but surely if they were close, he would have seen them together before today.

Leaving the church, he walks the short distance back to the station, questions bouncing round his head. Thinking the incident room empty, he slams the door with more force than he intends to. Amy Khan jumps up from her screen, her dark eyebrows almost lost in her hairline.

'Sorry Amy, didn't see you there.'

Oh, to have an office of his own. And does the girl never go home? Behind his PC, he shuts his eyes, grateful it's Amy and not Kate. He pulls some papers randomly from a drawer, the image of the woman at the graveside jarring with his memories of last night.

He hadn't been able to help himself. After his walk, he couldn't face going home to an empty house and had told himself it was better than drinking. Now he wonders if another night in the Miners might have been wiser.

She had made no mention of Anna but then again, they'd both kept their secrets. He hadn't disclosed his job, even when she had told him hers.

'Hanging onto pain is like carrying a lead weight around your neck,' she had whispered in his ear, her legs wrapped tightly around him. Surely this wasn't standard physiotherapy. 'But if you go about things in the right way, you can move through it, learn from it, even master it.' He blinks the image away. The idea he could have his own private masseuse is so far-fetched he could weep. He can still smell her, feel her fingers, the caress of her tongue on his skin. She had washed the pain away just like morphine.

'Sir! Have you got a minute?'

'Not now, Amy. I'm busy.'

Whatever she wants, it can wait. He remembers now, the first time he'd met her in the woods. She had told him she once lived locally and later in the pub had spoken of looking up old friends. That must be it. An old acquaintance or ex-neighbour, nothing more. He pumps up the lumbar support on his chair and switches on his PC.

She had seen him, if not in church, then definitely by the graveside. The subject will have to be broached on their next meeting. If there is a next meeting. In the cold light of day the thought of all her other clients puts things into a whole different perspective.

He's never been concerned with this kind of stuff, throughout his entire career, his whole life even. Becoming involved with someone linked to the family of a murder victim, however distant that link might be, is something he would never have believed himself capable of. He has always considered himself above such things and now look at him. The sparse population of Black Hollow alone should have told him it was a bad idea, especially knowing most of its inhabitants' high propensity to gossip. You don't shit on your own doorstep. And clearly, it's interfering with his job. Not for the first time this week his behaviour has been negligent. He almost laughs out loud at the understatement. He should be able to account for everyone at that funeral but instead of watching the mourners, he had spent the whole time watching her. Why had she snook off like that, disappearing through a hole in the hedge before he had chance to apprehend her?

Checking the coast is clear, he opens a drawer. The room is beginning to fill now but everyone is preoccupied, as they should be in the middle of a murder investigation. Popping two capsules from their foil, he swills them down with the cup of cold coffee on his desk. Grimacing, he logs into the Police National Computer and types in Marie's name, or at least the one she has given him. How stupid of him to realise only now that he knows next to nothing about her.

To his relief, the PNC draws a blank. Taking a deep breath, he switches screens and squints at the picture in front of him. *Ivory for God's sake — who has ivory knocking about these days?* The dagger's age has been confirmed as mid-Victorian, which means it is legal and worth a fortune to the right buyer. This doesn't help the investigation but it could give a clue to the kind of contacts Collins had. And something else has occurred to him. The use of his own dagger as the murder weapon suggests the attack was spontaneous, unplanned even. Whatever the case, the killer had come to the Trick Shop unarmed.

Zooming in on the picture, he tries to admire the workmanship, the delicate carving on the hilt. Taking out his notebook, he jots something down on the page.

At that moment, the door flies open, making Newton drop his pen.

'Don't you ever answer your phone?' pants Kate. She

is out of breath and gasping.

'Shit. I must have left it on silent from the funeral.' Pulling it out, he sees numerous missed calls on the screen.

'Never mind that now. I need to talk to you.'

'I need to talk to you too but not here.' Standing up he strides from the room and Kate follows.

'Where are we going sir?'

'We'll go for a drive. I need some air.'

Newton unlocks his car and Kate jumps into the passenger seat beside him.

Pulling her seatbelt across, she is still getting her breath back as Newton swerves out of the car park.

61

Anna

'I knew all along you would know.' Marie sounds almost relieved. She kicks her shoes off and curls her legs beneath her on Father's chair.

'You're not listening! It was only tail ends of conversations, stuff I was too young to understand. I need you to fill in the gaps. That's what you're here for, isn't it?'

The silence stretches for so long, it seems certain she won't answer and Anna isn't sure she wants her to. Marie's reappearance has dragged her back towards things she isn't ready to face — will probably never be ready to face. She gets up and goes off to find another bottle.

'I've been drinking all day, you know,' she says, surprised at her own words as she sways back into the room.

'I know,' replies Marie. 'I can smell it.'

At one time, this comment would have cut her to the quick but Anna no longer cares what she thinks of her. She knows she's already half cut but the awkwardness of her previous visit has gone, their conversation settling into its familiar pattern, even the little put downs. Like they have never been apart.

Opening the wine as though it were hers, Marie refills their glasses, then settles herself back into the chair. She takes a long breath, for all the world as though she is about to embark on a bedtime story.

'It feels like we were friends forever doesn't it, but it wasn't that long at all. I reckon it was only about a year.'

'It was thirteen months.'

'I knew it was about that,' concedes Marie, crossing one leg over the other as she sinks more deeply into the cushions. '*They* must have met long before that. Us being friends wasn't part of the plan.'

'I guess not. My parents never approved of you.'

'And we both know why.'

The clock ticks away a full thirty seconds before Anna speaks again.

'When did you first find out our parents were having an affair?'

Marie frowns. 'I'm not sure. I don't think there was one definitive moment. It grew over time, from something I was vaguely aware of into something I just knew. There are different levels of knowing things, aren't there? Especially when you're a child.'

For years Anna has imagined this conversation taking place. Now it is finally happening, she has no idea what to say. There are things she would rather stay buried.

'I remember that day at your house. When my father came to collect me.'

Marie's eyes seem to glitter at this. 'I had my suspicions by then but now I come to think of it, it must have been the Love Shack that finally confirmed it.'

The dark peaty smell of memory hits the back of Anna's throat. She gulps and swallows it down.

'What happened to *your* father?'

Marie looks up, clearly surprised at the question. 'It's funny you should ask. At one time I thought we might be sisters.'

Anna almost spills her wine. It isn't funny at all. 'Surely, we can't be!'

'Calm down, it was just a silly idea I had. We didn't

even move here until I was eight.'

There's another lull in the conversation and Anna tops up her glass,

'I wonder how long it went on for.'

'I've asked myself the same thing. Many times.'

Anna's anxiety is building, as she knew it would.

'So, who was he?'

'Who was who?'

'Your father.'

'Oh, I don't know. Honestly, I've no idea. It says *father unknown* on my birth certificate and mum would never tell me.'

'It never occurred to me at the time, her being a single parent.' Anna tries to read Marie's expression but it is hidden behind her glass. 'It never crossed my mind, what a huge thing it must've been, her being such a devoted Catholic.'

'Devoted Catholic!' Marie spits out the words. 'Oh yeah, she was devoted alright. Especially when she had her legs spread for your old man!' She gets up abruptly, wine sloshing up the sides of her glass as she heads towards the bookcase. Apprehension creeps across Anna's skin.

'You had a crush on Father Vincent.'

'Ha!' Marie snorts, her eyes on the books. 'Are you joking? It wasn't a crush. I was just in awe of him.'

'In awe? You were obsessed.'

'I really wasn't, Anna. Not with him anyway. I just loved all things Catholic.' She fingers the spines of the books. 'I think I was trying to fill a void.'

'What kind of void?'

'I'm not sure. I was probably overcompensating.'

'For what?' There it is, that feeling. The old familiar

pull. Wanting, needing to hear more.

Marie leans against the bookcase. 'For not having a father I suppose. Before anyone had chance to mention it, I would jump in with some random, fascinating fact. It wasn't just religion, if you remember. I was the font of all knowledge. Art, music, literature. Quotes from famous people I hadn't the first clue about.'

Anna shifts in her chair. 'Of course I remember. You also had a thing for burials.'

'Oh, don't remind me. Although, I never heard you complain.'

'Do you remember that crow?'

'God, yes.'

'That lolly stick cross we made!' Anna is warming to the theme now.

'Snuffed out like a flame,' says Marie, her face becoming wistful, her voice suddenly childlike. Anna feels a thrill that she remembers.

'It's embarrassing how bad I was. A proper little freak.' Marie shakes her head, as she turns back to the books. 'I still love learning, acquiring facts. We had that in common, didn't we? I think it's what drew us together. Oh, look!' Her face lights up as she pulls out a slim, dark volume. Anna's stomach plummets as she opens the cover. *The Picture of Dorian Gray*. Do you know, I've never read this?'

'You ought to. It's really good.' It's been there, untouched for decades. Why hadn't she thrown it away?

'Oscar Wilde,' chuckles Marie. 'I had a thing about him, didn't I? God knows why. I had no idea who he was.' She flicks through the pages, then comes to sit back down with the book in her lap.

'It's funny but whenever I hear his name, I never think

of the writer. I always think of that kitten I had.'

And just like that, the words are spoken, the air polluted. Anna wills her chest to still, the panic crawling up her throat like an invisible hand to stop. It had all been a terrible accident, a childish game gone wrong. Whatever happens, Marie must never find out. It would end their friendship forever.

62

1977

'It's getting dark, girls. You can come back out in the morning.' Her eyes are so tired, Anna hadn't noticed Father Vincent approach across the fields. As he puts his arm around Marie, it's like a dam has burst. She buries her head in his chest, her whole body shaking.

This is the second day now and they have been out here for hours. Surely a tiny kitten can't get far on his own but with no idea which direction he might have gone in, their search has been haphazard to say the least. Maybe if one of the adults had helped, they would have found him by now.

She can't bear to see Marie cry. She is still weeping openly, Father Vincent trying to comfort her. He doesn't seem to mind his sleeves getting wet. As he pats her back, Anna counts the buttons on his cuffs.

'Come along now,' says the priest, taking Marie by the shoulders and bending his head towards her. 'You know the Lord watches over all his creatures, so wherever the little blighter has got to, don't you be worrying.'

By the time they get back to the village, it is pitch dark. Anna says goodnight and Marie and Father Vincent continue down the high street. Knowing how much the kitten means to her friend, she makes the plan there and then. Expecting trouble at being out late for the second night running, she finds her parents too absorbed to notice. Father with his cards, Mother with hers.

After midnight, when she is sure they are both asleep, she takes her father's torch from the sideboard and slips out to resume the search on her own.

Anna isn't scared of the dark. Far from it, she loves the night-time, often meeting up with Marie when the rest of the village are in their beds, creeping through the streets, lurking in the shadows of the graveyard. This time is different, she has a real reason to be out here. Sweeping the torch, she scans the hedge bottoms, calling Oscar's name as loudly as she dares. Just the thought of how happy Marie will be when she finds him fills her with a sense of purpose, driving her on down the pavements, along the paths and back to the fields.

She never meant to go as far as Never Fear, so when she sees the moon's reflection on the water, it stops her in her tracks. She is about to head back when she hears a faint cry. Standing perfectly still she listens, training the torch across the pond but there isn't a sound now except for the wind in the trees. As she edges forward, the old mill looms out of the shadows and she hears the cry again, only louder. She can't turn back now.

Inside the darkness intensifies. The torch flickers and for a moment she thinks the batteries have gone. She shakes it and the beam grows brighter, lighting up the dank stone walls. The crying is very close now and she is certain it is Oscar.

She finds him behind an old oil drum. His ribs are jutting through his fur but Anna has come prepared. She pulls a chicken leg from her pocket, intending to pull off the meat for him but the cat pounces immediately, devouring it in minutes. Stroking his head as he eats, an idea comes to her. What if she brings him food and keeps him here for a while? He'll be safe if she can somehow secure him. By the time she returns him to Marie, she will be so overcome with gratitude, their bond will be sealed forever.

She finds a piece of greasy string coiled in a corner. Expecting it to be rotten, she tugs it and finds it quite strong. A slipknot won't do as it will tighten as he pulls but it's a good length and will allow him to wander about a bit. Getting down on the filthy floor, she coaxes the kitten towards her. He jumps straight into her lap, rubbing his face on her hands. He trusts her and thinks she might have more food hidden. Tickling him under the chin, she puts the torch down and ties the string around his neck, not so tight it will choke him. With the cat in her arms she stands and walks around, shining the torch in front of her. The building is little more than a shell, the floor covered with dead leaves that have blown in but little else. No discarded beer cans or cigarette butts. Nobody comes here. She is about to give up when the beam catches something, a rusty hook sticking out of the wall at just the right height. She winds the end of the string around it, knotting and pulling it taught.

Satisfied he can't escape, she gives him one last pet and walks away. At his outraged yowl, she turns as he throws himself on the floor, bucking and wriggling frantically but no matter how much he squirms, he can't free himself. She leaves him there, his pitiful cries following her into the night.

The next night she comes again, with a Tupperware dish of Jack's dog food. When Oscar sees her, he pulls so hard trying to get to her she thinks the hook will come out of the wall but it doesn't. He strains, his little black paws dancing in the air until she reaches him, wolfing down the food as soon as she takes the lid off. After he has washed himself, he curls up in her lap and she strokes him until he falls asleep. As he purrs contentedly, she wonders if he is safe here after all. She sees the string is frayed where he has tried to chew through it. Careful not to wake him, she unties it and doubles it up, twisting the strands tightly together. He'll never bite through that.

This time he cries so much when she leaves, she covers her ears as she walks away, telling herself it won't be for much longer.

On the third night her pockets are full. She has brought some boiled ham and an inch of cream left over from the apple crumble they had for tea but as she gets closer to the mill, a sense of unease grips her. It feels different somehow. Silent.

She finds the hook on the floor among the dead leaves. Panic rises as she calls his name, over and over again. She searches every corner of the mill, then stumbles out through the trees, right to the water's edge. She scours the ground for his paw prints but it's impossible in the dense grass and the half-light. As the sky begins to brighten, she returns to the mill, exhausted. She leaves the cream and the ham by the oil drum in case he finds his way back. But as she walks away, she knows deep down that he won't.

63

Newton

Newton puts his foot down with no idea where he is headed. He feels like he has been rammed in the back with a rusty shopping trolley but he grips the wheel and focuses on his breathing. They drive in silence through the town and out the other side, past the new housing estates and the abandoned remains of the pit. As the road arcs it climbs steeply, coming full circle into the hills above Black Hollow. He is almost as surprised as Kate looks when he pulls into the rough, stony car park, a sliver of dark water just visible between the trees.

'I'm not sure I know this place,' says Kate, as she peers through the windscreen. 'Where are we?'

'It's called Never Fear, believe it or not.' Newton switches off the engine. 'Shall we get out and walk?'

'What sort of name is that?' asks Kate with a mirthless chuckle. As they fall into step, Newton notes she is distracted by the view and doesn't light a cigarette for a full twenty seconds.

'I'm not sure how it got its name,' he says, his back loosening slightly as they walk. Olive Stratton's account seems inappropriate for the moment. 'There used to be an old mill here but there's not much left of it now. Just a few stones in the undergrowth. I sometimes come up here to think.' *With my dog*, he adds to himself. 'There's a panoramic view of the town, just after these trees.'

The branches thin out onto an open vista. They have driven for only a matter of minutes but the buildings appear distant from here, nestled in a dip between the hills. The streets are neat lines of boxes, plumes of smoke rising from the odd chimney, the spire of one church and the tower of the other like bookends either side. As the land soars upwards, the outline of the pit looms black against the sky. Newton knows this view like the back of his hand. He could point out the disused railway lines, or the old smelting shop but he doubts Kate would be interested.

'Are you alright, sir?'

The question startles him. He turns as she blows a cloud of smoke over her shoulder.

'Why wouldn't I be?'

'No reason.'

'You'd better tell me what it was brought you tearing into the station.'

She takes another drag and seems to gather herself, kicking at a stone before responding. 'OK, so I know you won't want to hear this, but I now have even more reason to think Mrs Wood's death could be suspicious.'

He'd been right to think it wouldn't go away. 'Go on.'

'I drove past just now and there was a van outside. Looks like Alice and her boyfriend are moving in.'

'And?'

'Well sir, I've been making some enquiries.'

'What sort of enquiries?'

'Land Registry enquiries.'

'Right.'

She gulps and he sees her hand is shaking, the cigarette held in front of her like a shield. 'I just heard back from them and to be honest, I haven't fully processed what they said.'

They continue to walk along the path, still wet with puddles. As they reach the water, a bird rises from the dank reeds. Newton waits for Kate to finish her cigarette.

'As I expected, Mrs Wood and her husband bought the house years back from the coal board. With no kids of their own, it got me thinking who the house would go to. That's when I contacted the Land Registry. Before you say anything, I think it was well worth the fee.' She pauses, as though gauging his reaction. Seeing his raised eyebrows, she continues.

'They owned it for less than a year. November 1976 to August 77.'

'What?'

'Do you want to have a guess who owned it afterwards and has done all these years?'

Newton thinks for a second, then it dawns on him.

'Not Collins?'

'Yes, Collins. Like I said, I don't quite know what to make of it.'

Newton comes to a halt. 'Hang on a minute. I thought you said the niece is moving in?'

'She is and that's the bit I'm trying to understand. I know she has a key. So do I, come to think of it. I've been meaning to take it back but I've been avoiding it, after what happened.'

Newton continues walking as he tries to work out if this new information makes things better or worse than before. They are at the far end of the pond now. He remembers following Lottie into the grass when she was a pup, the huge mill stones hidden there.

'As far as I can see, there are two options. Either she thinks her aunt left the house to her, or she's come to some sort of arrangement with Anna. That's if Collins left the place to his daughter, which we have to assume he did. But it's all very quick. I doubt Mrs Wood's affairs have been finalised yet and I know Collins's haven't.

There were no deeds in the flat but his solicitor should have something.'

Kate is staring at the water. It isn't often he sees her without a cigarette. Her features are softened even though she is clearly wrestling with her discovery.

'How does all this fit in with your knitting needle theory?'

She shakes her head. 'I'm not sure anymore, sir. I thought it was suspicious from the off but this puts a whole new complexion on things. They could have killed her in ignorance, believing they'd inherit but now it's got me thinking. They could have killed Collins in the knowledge that they wouldn't.'

Newton hadn't thought of that.

'You said *they*. You don't suspect Alice, do you?'

Kate rubs her brow with her fingertips.

'No, I don't think so. It's just the timing. They'd be glad of the space when the new baby arrives.'

'You can't think they'd murder a defenceless old woman just for a bit of extra space?'

'Maybe it wasn't deliberate. Maybe the boyfriend went round when they found out and she got frightened. I don't know. It's too late now to prove anything. She's been cremated.'

Newton waits for the admonitory glare but it doesn't come.

'Even if we'd swept the place straight away for fingerprints, they'd both have reason for being there as family.' She drops her head, looking utterly dejected. 'I can't believe Alice is involved. She seemed genuinely fond of her aunt. I know you aren't convinced but that cable needle being on the windowsill just couldn't be right.'

Newton bites his lip and lets out a long breath. 'It's a leap of faith, Kate and it was from the start.'

He sees her jaw harden but she remains silent.

'We need to speak to Alice and that boyfriend of hers. I presume they've both been questioned?'

'Of course they have, but I'll revisit the transcript.'

'We need to bring them in formally. Find out if they think they own the house, or whether they're aware who their new landlady is. We can soon verify whether it's Anna. It's a pity we didn't know about this yesterday when you had her at the station. You could have asked her all about it.'

He isn't proud of himself, shifting the focus back onto Kate. Her cheeks redden, which adds to his shame.

'On second thoughts, give me that key. I think it's about time I met up with this Alice and her boyfriend.'

64

Anna

Anna drains her glass, spluttering as she swallows the last grainy dregs.

'Steady on,' says Marie, looking up from the book. 'Are you alright? You don't look well.'

Anna doesn't feel well at all but still she refills their glasses.

'I'm sorry, I'm being a selfish cow,' continues Marie. 'You buried your father today and here's me wittering on. Maybe we should do this another time.'

Anna stares at the bubbles popping in her glass, trying to remember how many she's had. Counting helps to clear her head. 'No, we need to do it now. You can't plan on staying around forever, so whatever you've come to say, just say it.'

Marie closes the book, placing it on the table between them. 'I thought of you, you know. Over the years.'

Anna snorts. 'Yeah, course you did. I've been fine. No need to worry about me.' The room feels suddenly cold and she gets up, reaching for the matches on the mantelpiece.

'Come on Anna, this is me you're talking to. You don't have to pretend.'

'I'm not pretending. I've done alright.' Lighting a spill, she kneels and slides it beneath the coals, willing her hand to stop shaking. *Please don't ask me what I've done with my life*, she thinks, relieved her back is turned.

'I'm glad to hear it,' says Marie. 'And so have I but we both know that's not why I'm here.'

Anna blows on the flames, then returns to her seat.

'I really don't know why you're here. All I've ever known are the bare facts of our parents' affair. Then you left.' She is surprised how steady her voice is.

'Oh, come on! I'm not buying this *I know nothing* shit.'

Anna takes another slug from her glass, the wine sour on her tongue. Squeezing her eyes shut, she thinks of the papers she found. One with its fancy letterhead, the other cheap and thin. She knew burning them would never be enough.

'You're talking about our brother of course. Our half-brother.' There, the words are out. No taking them back.

Marie's eyes light up at her words, as though some divine truth has been revealed to her. Just as quickly they dim and fill with tears. 'I knew, at least I always hoped you did. There were so many times I thought of him and it made me so sad. Knowing he wasn't alone made it somehow bearable. You still being close to him.'

'What?'

'You still being here. Close to his resting place.'

A feeling of dread prickles Anna's neck. 'I think we're at cross purposes.'

'Oh, you know what I mean. Whether we believe in it or not.'

'What are you talking about?' Anna searches her face for understanding. Marie stops mid-swallow and their eyes lock. She lowers her glass onto the table.

'Our brother,' she says, her voice less certain now. 'Our mutual half-brother, as you just referred to him. One half yours, the other half mine.'

Anna knocks back the rest of her wine, an attempt at drunken bravado. 'I hate to break this to you, Marie, but as far as I know, he's alive and well.' She sees the blood run from Marie's face, her skin turning an unnatural, waxen white.

'Say that again.'

Anna's eyes are drawn to a pulse at the base of Marie's throat.

'I said say it again!'

She jumps, the shout jolting her as she scrabbles to pull her thoughts together. Suddenly her head feels heavy and she sinks back, pressing her face into the cushions. She is dimly aware of Marie leaving the room, then of fingers gripping her shoulders, yanking her upright.

'We're not at cross purposes! Drink this and tell me what you know!'

The glass hits her teeth as she thrusts it towards her. Taking a gulp, she wipes her mouth and looks up at Marie.

'I'm really not that clever. I had no idea why you left or where you'd gone to. All I knew was Father Vincent had something to do with it and I hated him.'

'Never mind that evil bastard. What did you mean just now? Tell me.'

'Alright, calm down.' Marie's need of what she knows gives Anna a sliver of satisfaction and her voice becomes steadier. 'I told you, I didn't know anything. Not until my mother died. Then I found a letter among her papers.'

'What kind of letter?'

She has known from the start this is what Marie is here for. Still, her words sound unreal.

'From a convent in Liverpool. Holy Innocents. Is that where you went?'

'Yes but—'

Anna talks over her, unable to stop now she has begun.

'There was a receipt attached to it for eighty pounds. Forty pounds for maternity care, the rest for placement in an orphanage. Forty pounds, Marie! That's how cheaply they sold our brother.'

'No!' Marie jumps up, her hands flying to her temples. 'This can't be right! It can't be!'

'What on earth's the matter?'

'There was no orphanage!'

'But that's where you went, isn't it?' Even as she speaks, Anna knows they are approaching something terrible. Marie is pacing in front of the fire, her whole body shaking. She grips the mantelpiece and Anna's eyes fly to the back of her hand, the scar just visible for a second before she pulls away, her fingers clenched into a fist.

'Listen to me. I don't know what you think you found or what you think you know but I'm going to tell you what happened.' She raises her hands again, raking them through her hair so it stands on end. 'First I need another drink. I take it there's more in the pantry?'

65

Newton

'Christ, Kate. There's more suspects now than when we started!'

'I know, sir. I'm sorry.'

'Don't apologise, it's excellent work. On Amy's part, too.'

Kate lights another cigarette. Newton has never smoked but he can definitely see the attraction. His sense of unease grows with every new discovery.

'Do you remember what I said about things overlapping?'

'Yes, sir. I guess they're bound to in a place like this.'

They have come full circle around the pond again and the light is fading. They shouldn't be having this conversation here but then again, why not? It can't be any worse than the pub. Newton can't believe what he's just heard, his mind even more tangled than when they set out. Would it be right to share his thoughts with Kate? Right now, he is running out of options.

'I'm starting to think all of this must be connected, Kate. Especially with what you just told me.'

She nods, a plume of smoke curling from her lips.

'We don't have a massive drug problem here. A few spliffs in the precinct, teenagers mainly and I know some of the ex-miners have their habits but that lot down the well wasn't small time. I haven't seen that much gear since I worked in Manchester, which makes me think organised crime. Then at the other end of the spectrum I'm pretty sure half the pensioners round here knew what Collins was up to and that's why they're keeping

342

schtum.'

'I agree, sir. I think they're covering their own backs.'

'Exactly,' says Newton. He pauses, then ploughs on. 'Strictly between the two of us, I wouldn't be surprised if that priest is somehow involved.'

Kate's looks genuinely shocked at this. 'What makes you think that?'

'I went to see him,' says Newton, his eyes on the dim outline of the Catholic church below. 'There's something off about him, so I did a bit of digging. On Google.' He smiles, pulling a scrap of paper from his pocket. 'It seems Our Lady of Lourdes has had more than its share of bad luck over the years. Quite a catalogue in fact.' He squints at the list. 'A silver chalice stolen in 1978. Never recovered. Numerous petty thefts of church plate. A pair of candlesticks, an icon of St Dunstan, the list goes on. His insurance must be sky high. Then there was a roof appeal in 2005, abandoned for lack of support. The roof looks in pretty good nick to me, so I'm guessing they got the cash from somewhere. Oh and they've been struck by lightning on three separate occasions. Anyone would think the place was cursed.'

The wind gusts across the water and Kate blows into her hands.

'Come on, let's get back in the car.' They retrace their steps, the pond a rippling mirror in the fading light.

'He's been here since 1976,' continues Newton as he starts the engine. 'So he'll know the whole town inside out and everyone in it.'

'He's certainly a person of interest,' says Kate.

'I think so, yes. Especially as the church's run of bad luck seems to have started when he arrived.' He squints through the windscreen as they bump out of the car park.

343

'It will be nigh on impossible to verify who made those calls Amy discovered, more so to prove it. But I don't believe in coincidences.'

'Me neither.'

'And I'm sorry to have to say this but Anna Collins knows more than she's letting on. I mean, how did she know that well wasn't secure?'

'I'm not sure she did, sir.'

'I'm not convinced Kate. I'll have to bring Vardy up to speed on all this. If we are talking organised crime, we just don't have the manpower but he won't want to pull on the Mets. Not after the week we've had.' At that moment, his mobile rings in his pocket.

'Aren't you going to get that?'

It stops, then immediately starts again.

'They'll ring back if it's important.'

At the next junction he pulls out his phone, glancing at the screen. He thought as much.

'I'll ring them back when we get to the station. The first thing you need to do is fetch your mate back in. Hopefully, the penny's dropped now. She's not your mate, Kate.'

66

Anna

'Do you remember that day at Our Lady's?'

'The church mice.'

'I knew you would.'

Anna holds her glass against her chest, watching the wine's surface pulsate with the beat of her heart. She knows she's incredibly drunk now but she doesn't have to try and second guess, or even think. All she has to do is listen.

'I'm not sure if that's the day she told him but I knew straight away she was pregnant. She had really bad morning sickness. If I hadn't known already, that would have given it away.'

Anna remains silent.

'I was excited. Can you believe it? Even though I knew it was wrong. You know what I was like back then, I loved the idea of sin.' Marie gulps her wine as though she is dying of thirst. 'I remember hoping for a boy! Unbelievable. Wondering what we'd call him. A saint's name, I thought. I had no sense of irony. And I remember her wearing loose clothing.' At this, Anna thinks of the kaftan, the flowing, sea blue layers but still she says nothing. She just watches her.

'And he was there all the time, like a bloody black shadow,' continues Marie. 'Always going upstairs to her, telling me what to do. Nothing was ever said, of course. It wasn't acknowledged. Then one night, I heard her cry out. I knew it was too early, way before her time. I didn't know what to do, so I phoned him. When I think of it now, I should have got an ambulance, anyone but him.

But I had to protect her. I might not have minded the sin but I knew she did.' She takes another mouthful, her knuckles white on the stem of the glass.

'The baby died, Anna, no matter what you think. I should have done something.'

'You were ten years old. You weren't a midwife.'

'No and neither was he.' This time her voice is thick, her hands trembling. Anna watches closely. It has been more than thirty years but she still knows every mannerism. Marie's throat constricts as she juts out her chin. 'She was ill after that. Very ill. I don't know what he'd done to her but she needed more help than either of us could give her. That's why he sent us away.'

Anna's chest judders. She had known, or thought she'd known, had pieced things together. But this, all this suffering. She'd had no idea.

'I'm sorry, I truly am, that I didn't say goodbye but I thought we'd be coming back. We left the cats behind for God's sake! I would never have done that and I know Mum wouldn't if she'd been in her right mind. God knows what he did with them.' She jerks her head, as though shaking the thought away.

'I remember packing things into the back of a black car. I don't know if it was a taxi or someone from the church. It was all very quick, very early in the morning. To make sure no one saw us, I realised afterwards. Next thing I knew, we were there. Holy Innocents.' She snorts as she takes another mouthful of wine. 'Holy Innocents, eh? What a joke. It was full of pregnant women. Girls not much older than us but nobody said a word. It was unspoken, the ultimate sin. I never questioned any of it. All I wanted was for Mum to get better so that we could come back home. If I'm honest, once I knew she was out of danger, I couldn't believe my luck at not having to go to school. I was the only kid over the age of about five, that wasn't pregnant, I mean.' Her lips pucker into a sneer. 'They gave me books to read and spelling tests but there were no proper lessons. Mostly I could do what I liked, which obviously suited me fine.

'God knows how many miles I walked, I had blisters. That's how I found out we were in Liverpool. It made sense, Father Vincent must have come from that direction. I walked and walked, wondering what was happening back here. I never missed school but believe me, I missed you.'

Anna rolls her eyes.

'I did! I wondered if you'd any idea what had happened. I even wondered if your mum had seen it in the cards.'

'I didn't realise you believed in such things.'

'I don't.'

'You still wear your crucifix.'

'It's just a cross, Anna, a piece of metal. Much as I pray your father is burning in hell as we speak, I don't believe in anything anymore.'

Her words are designed to lacerate, Anna knows that but doesn't react. She watches her face fall into shadow as she tops up their glasses again.

'I really did miss you but apart from that, things were OK. And after a while, I had this stupid idea we were going to move somewhere your dad and Father Vincent couldn't get to us.'

'Away from me.'

'I didn't know what to do, Anna. I was just a child. It's OK thinking these things now but I had no control over it. None of us did. When I saw her after, really saw her, standing up with proper clothes on, her stomach was sagging like a pricked balloon and I knew then, knew that it was real. That I hadn't imagined it.'

Anna suddenly sits up straight. She has listened enough. 'Imagined what for God's sake?'

Marie stares at her, her eyes burning.

'He killed the baby, Anna. Father Vincent killed our brother.'

67

1977

The dawn sun is huge, like a fiery disc between the trees. He is easy to follow, like a black marker moving swiftly up the hill. She keeps to the shelter of the branches, as they skirt Hangman's Wood. Gaining on him slightly, Marie is certain the priest is carrying something.

This is no surprise to her, she is used to Father Vincent's ways. His night-time calls and secret hiding places. But as he stumbles on the path, almost losing his footing, she knows this is different. No matter what he has under his cassock, he always walks straight backed. Now in the soft morning light, his outline is smudged but she can see his shoulders are hunched, his movements furtive.

With the ripening wheat as her cover, she follows him through the fields as the sky turns pink. There is only one place he can be heading. Sure enough, as the glassy surface of Never Fear comes into view, he slows his pace. He stops for a moment, head bowed and Marie imagines his lips moving in a silent prayer.

She sees him now in profile, as he slides his hands down his front. There is a bulge which makes him look pregnant as he flattens the black folds. The thought sickens her but she inches closer, knowing the priest can't see her. As he steps nearer the water she holds her breath, waiting for whatever comes next but his hands fumble and he falls to his knees.

It's then that she hears it. A sharp cry, like the mewl of a kitten only stronger. The sun has moved now, so he appears in silhouette, a black hump against the sky. The cries grow louder as he leans, shoulders braced. Then it stops.

Her heart is pounding, blood roaring in her ears. She wants to run but her eyes are held fast by what the priest is doing.

As the sun climbs, it catches the cross on his chest. He stands, the lump silent in his arms now, the edge of the sack hanging down. With a final tug on the drawstring, he lowers it into the water. Blinking, she feels the tears warm on her cheeks and rage burning inside her.

68

Anna

'We settled in a place called Garston,' comes Marie's muffled voice through the wall. Anna grips the pantry shelf. She isn't sure how much more of this she can take. All this time she knew they were to blame but this is the stuff of nightmares. Her whole life is suddenly a lie. Mother had known about the affairs but had she known about this? The dread in the pit of her stomach is beginning to clot. She believes Marie but this isn't the whole story. She knows it can't be.

On autopilot now, she drags another bottle out, her legs like jelly as she staggers back through the kitchen.

'And we lived there ever since.' Marie has continued her narrative all the time she has been absent from the room. 'You've probably noticed my accent.'

Anna flinches at the terrible, laughable coincidence. The only friend she ever had was within touching distance whilst she was studying in the city. It's something she can't even begin to think about for the moment.

'He needs to pay for what he's done. Don't you think so?'

Anna pulls her attention back as Marie takes the bottle from her.

'I think you've had enough for now. I'm trying to talk to you. This is important. I nearly went down there earlier but I couldn't do it. I should go to the police, I know, but what proof do I have? What evidence? Nothing.'

Her words are tinny, as though heard from a distance away. Surely if her story is true, the baby's remains will still be there, at the bottom of Never Fear. The thought is horrifying. Repulsive. It's clear Marie has come here to shock her but why now? Why wait all these years? Suddenly, she feels her father's presence in the room, almost smells his cigarettes. She had thrown down her story like a winning hand, knowing the effect it would have on her but it must be wrong. Surely, all wrong?

'Shut up!'

Marie stops, her mouth half open.

'Just listen to me for once!' At this, at last she is quiet, her diatribe hushed. There is utter silence, except for the ticking of the clock and the spit and crackle of the fire.

'I found two letters. I tried to tell you earlier but you wouldn't listen, you never do. There was one from the convent, like I said. It answered a lot of questions, explained why you had to go away.' Anna pauses, noting the tremor in her hands is at least temporarily gone, as though her whole body is stilled. 'And then a couple of days before my father's death, I found another one.' Again she thinks of the cheap, lined paper, the immature handwriting. 'It was dated some time ago, from someone claiming to be his son.'

Marie's face is ashen. 'But that can't be! The baby died. I saw him do it.'

'I don't know what you saw, or what you think you saw. All I'm saying is I found a letter from someone who said he was my father's son.'

'Show me.'

'I can't. I burnt it. I burnt both letters.'

'Why for God's sake? Why did you do that?' Marie springs from the chair, her hair like devils' horns in the firelight. 'Hang on! This must be some other bastard! Not my mum's baby. Your dad must have knocked someone else up and that I can believe!' Her face contorts as she tosses back the contents of her glass but another possibility has just occurred to Anna.

'Maybe they were twins.'

'What?'

'I said—'

'I heard what you said!' Marie is across the room in a second. She slams her empty glass down and seizes Anna by the shoulders, shaking her.

'You need to sober up!'

'I am sober. Get off me!'

Marie lets go but remains standing so close Anna can feel her breath, can see the rise and fall of her chest. 'What did the letter say? You must remember!'

'Calm down,' says Anna again. Her head feels completely awash but underneath is a far less welcome feeling, one she suspected would happen if it came to this. Marie would love a brother. Of course she would. And where would that leave her?

'Did he sign it? Anna, did he sign the letter?'

'Yes. He wanted to meet. I suspect he wanted money. Something like that.'

'Why? What did it actually say?'

'I can't remember! I burnt it as soon as I read it.'

'What was his name? It must have been on the letter?' Marie's voice is high pitched, demanding, making Anna's head hurt. Why didn't she keep this to herself? Why the hell couldn't she just for once stay sober?

'Jason Brown.' She hears the name before she is conscious of speaking it.

'Jason?' Marie's shoulders slump, her face blank. 'My mother would never have called him that.'

'It's not a saint's name, no. His adoptive parents must

have chosen it. Anyway, it's so common there's no chance of tracing him.'

Marie drags her hands down her face, smudging what remains of her lipstick. 'Do you think they met up? Was there an address? A contact number?'

'No,' lies Anna. 'Although I'm sure the idea of a son would have appealed to my father, so yes I think there's every chance they met.'

'Jesus, Anna. This is our brother we're talking about!'

'Half-brother.'

'So what, half-brother! Aren't you in the least bit curious?'

'No.'

'Well, I am!'

As Anna knew she would be. Pitching forward, she attempts to stoke the fire, the poker clattering in the hearth. She lunges for the bottle before Marie can stop her, spilling wine across the table. Guzzling from the glass, she sees Marie watching her but her features swim in and out of focus.

'I take it you never married. Never had children?'

Anna ignores her tone, the implication clear. She shakes her head.

'Me neither. We can't begin to imagine. Being forced to give up a child like that! Two, if what you're saying is true! Jesus, Anna! Two babies! One dead and one taken away! I can't get my head around this.' She clutches her face in her hands, her fingers raking her skull.

'What are we going to do?' she murmurs after a while.

Anna jerks her head up. 'What do you mean? There's nothing we can do.'

'How can you say that? Knowing he's out there? Our own flesh and blood!' Marie is up again, pacing the carpet, quick, agitated steps.

'That orphanage will be long gone,' Anna hears herself say. 'But I suppose now you've come all this way, you might as well go and ask the man himself all about it.'

Marie lunges across the room towards her.

'You've got no idea, have you?' Her lips peel back, teeth bared. 'At least your precious father's death was quick, not drawn out in agony. She screamed at the end you know, begged to be put out of her misery. Womb cancer it was. Her body was riddled with it and that pair of bastards caused it!'

She collapses into her chair as though exhausted by this outburst. Anna feels herself recoil, as though she has just had her first glimpse of the real Marie since she returned. As she looks across at her sprawled there on the cushions, something crystalises, with absolute clarity. She doesn't want this brother. Any brother. She wants it to be just the two of them. As she always did.

'I can't do this,' mutters Marie, getting up from the chair. 'I can't just ignore his existence!' She pulls her coat from somewhere, the gold lining flaring and Anna sees her expression, full of purpose. Full of intent. Pain erupts within her, almost lifting her from her seat. With a roar, she slams her fist down on the table.

'Ignore his existence? How dare you?' Wine-streaked spittle flies from her mouth, spraying Marie's coat sleeve. 'How dare you come here with this bullshit? Do you think you've got the monopoly on misery? You haven't got a clue!' Clutching her glass in one hand, she stifles a sob with the other as she stumbles out into the kitchen.

Clattering into the table, she collides with the sink. The top of the glass shatters, the neck jagged in her fist.

'You leave me no choice!' shouts Marie from the other room. 'I'll get it out of Mooney, the murdering bastard. I should have gone there in the first place!'

If she doesn't shut up in a minute, God help me, thinks Anna, shocked at her rising fury. And the fear, the old fear growing in her chest. The fear of losing her. She can't lose her again. She looks down at the shard of glass still clutched between her fingers and walks towards the door.

Marie is buttoning her coat. She gasps, her hand stilled, her mouth gaping.

'Put that down, Anna.'

She tilts the glass, light reflecting off the sharp edge like diamonds. Her vision swims.

'Please put it down.'

Panic fills her. She needs to get some air. She staggers past Marie and down the stairs.

69

Kate

Newton is behaving strangely. That was probably his wife on the phone. It pings again and she cranes her neck to see the screen. A text this time, from Amy. He's certainly in demand.

'I'll see you inside,' he mutters as they pull into the station. 'I need to see who this is.'

Lighting up as she crosses the tarmac, Kate pulls out her phone. Passing Helen's empty parking space, she scrolls to Anna's number.

If she's going to do things by the book, she should make the call from the office but she would prefer their conversation not to be overheard. She goes round the back of the building and stops just short of the bins. The only windows this side are the toilets and the stores.

'Kate! Where the hell are you?!'

She almost drops her phone. If he's made a call, it was brief and from the sound of his voice, clearly hasn't improved his mood. She hurries back around the corner. Newton is stood beside his car as though lost. Even from this distance, she can see the shock on his face. She runs towards him.

'What is it sir?'

'Get back in the car!'

Kate throws down her cigarette and pulls open the passenger door. Tugging on her seatbelt, she looks across at Newton. The stubble on his jaw looks black against his milk-white skin.

'What's happened?'

The tyres screech, spitting gravel into the air as the car

shoots backwards then veers towards the road.

'That was Marie. We've got to get to the rectory.'

'Who's Marie?'

Newton's eyes dart towards her. 'Did you see the blonde at the funeral?'

'I did, yes.'

'She's a friend of Anna Collins and she's just pulled a glass on her.'

'Pulled a glass on her?' Kate is struggling to keep up. 'What do you mean?'

'A broken glass. She hasn't harmed her.' Newton turns the wheel sharply. 'She's drunk and incoherent. Marie thinks she could be heading to see the priest.'

Kate grips the edge of her seat as the car careers headlong into traffic. She doesn't ask how or why Newton and this woman are in touch.

Our Lady of Lourdes stands sentinel, its spire stabbing the darkening sky. After the speed of the drive, Newton's steps are tentative as they make their way through the graveyard. Kate has passed here many times but has never seen this side of the wall, the ancient crypts and angels now crouching in the lengthening shadows. She had no idea the rectory was here, hidden as it is behind the church. The door stands open. Newton looks at her then steps inside.

The smell hits her immediately. Incense, overlaid with something thick and coppery. She takes a breath as she follows him in, her stomach tightening.

'Hello! Anyone home?' Her voice echoes up the stairwell but there is no reply. Newton visibly braces himself, then heads towards the door at the end of the hallway. She grips her cigarettes in her pocket.

'Jesus!'

She almost falls on him, as he drops to his knees beside a large oak desk. The blood pools around them like a moat where it has set and congealed on the parquet floor.

'Get an ambulance. There's still a pulse!' shouts Newton, as he leans over the body. He pulls his hands away, slick with red.

70

Anna

The fresh air hits her like a smack in the face, her nails clawing at the bricks. She pulls her fingers away, the knuckles already bruised where she punched the table. Raising her other hand, she sees the glint of glass.

Gasping, she almost drops it. Seeing the fan shaped window, she realises where she is. So, this isn't a dream, then. Not her addled brain playing tricks on her.

She stumbles away, images flashing past the backs of her eyes in slow motion. Crowds on a pavement, kittens in a pram, white, white pages splashed with blood. And Daniel. Beautiful, beloved, lying, cheating Daniel. She swallows back the tears. None of it matters anymore. Closing the gate behind her, she feels calmer than she has in years.

Glancing over her shoulder she checks no one is following her. She walks through the graves, the birds singing like any other day, the names on the stones she knows by heart. She pictures her own grave, soon to be dug somewhere. The thought doesn't bother her, as long as they don't put her in with her parents, that's all she can hope for. She couldn't cope with that for all eternity. In the old days they'd have put her in unconsecrated ground — that would be fine by her. Wherever she ends up, it won't be her decision. Her eyes settle onto the path, walking quite unhurriedly. The fear has gone, the one that's dogged her for God knows how many years. The sweating, gut-wrenching panic that she won't be able to find a drink. She won't need one where she is going.

She had already decided, long before today. There is

no point in living. No point carrying on.

With each step she feels more sober, her life behind her like an open road. All the pain and the lies. The begging to be loved.

It wasn't always like that. For whatever reason, Marie had chosen to be her friend. Even now, a voice in her head tells her it was only because there were so few other girls in the village. At the thought of Marie, she falters. She still couldn't bear her to find out about Oscar, although it pales into insignificance now. She would love to see her reaction to this.

But she won't be alive to see it.

She looks across to where the orchard used to be. Houses sprawl there now, a few trees remaining. A woman stands there with her hood up as though trying to blend into the foliage. Anna keeps her head down and grips the glass tightly, pointing it to the ground. If she drops it here, it could be picked up by a child or an animal. She will keep it safe, make sure no more damage is done.

The footpath is peppered with rabbit droppings. As she steps around them, she wonders if Father Vincent is still alive. She hopes he isn't.

At the bridge, she looks down at where they paddled. She thinks of the last time she was here. If things had been different, maybe Kate could have been her friend.

As she walks by the hedgerow, Marie is by her side, filling her face with blackberries, throwing pips to the birds. The trees whisper as though urging her on, their dark sighs her final companions. And now the sheer green water of memory is coming into view. The stunted trees are just the same, the tall brown grasses. It's right she should come here.

She stumbles down the bank. There are no flies, no bluebottles at the edge of the water. It is the wrong time of year.

The sky is a deep dark swathe of blue, a solitary star right above her. She thinks of her mother and starts to cry. She was her only true friend. She knows that now.

Her cheeks wet with tears, she holds her head up, filling her lungs one last time.

There will be no hangover tomorrow.

She steps forward.

71

Newton

'Are you OK?'

'Shouldn't it be me asking you that question?'

The Miners Arms was the only place Newton could think of to come. Her hotel room seemed wrong in the circumstances. Dark shadows bruise the skin beneath her eyes and her knuckles are white as she grips her wine glass. No matter how calm she is doing her best to appear, her hands haven't rested since they left the mortuary. Being asked to identify the body of a childhood friend, no matter how estranged, can't have been easy. It was a toss-up between her and the book club woman. There was nobody else. Newton can't imagine many things more tragic. He takes a long swig of his Guinness.

'We still haven't found the glass. I'm guessing it went into the water with her.'

Marie stares at the dark red surface of her wine. 'I once had a cat drown up there. In Never Fear.' The comment takes Newton by surprise. *Maybe the place is cursed after all. Maybe the whole town is.*

She looks up, her expression suddenly, falsely brighter. 'What's the latest on Father Vincent?'

Newton checks his watch. 'He'll be going into theatre about now. It's a miracle he was still alive.'

'A miracle,' says Marie. 'He'd love that.'

She looks much smaller than he realised. So delicate. Unable to stop himself, Newton reaches across the table but she pulls away, his fingers brushing the air between them.

'You've had a shock, Marie. Give yourself a break for

now and we can talk about things later.'

'Just promise me you won't believe a word he says, Jimmy.'

Jimmy. She keeps calling him that. His mother's name for him. He takes another swig as the door opens. A couple walk in, looking straight in their direction. Journalists. Newton can spot them a mile off. The place is busy. Knocker and Chuck sneaking glances from either side of the Davy lamp. All this is bloody good for business.

He turns his attention back to Marie. Her eyes are almost feverish, her teeth gnawing the corner of her mouth. He is glad she wasn't there when they dragged the body up. She hadn't been in the water long but her flesh was already marbled and dripping with slime, the lips blue and lolling, like a fish. He had felt a shameful relief at the absence of blood.

'You've known them both longer than most.' He chooses his words carefully. 'Did you ever suspect Anna capable of such violence?'

'Of course not no, I…' Her voice trails off. She reaches for her wine then drops her hand.

'Can I get you something else? A brandy?'

'No. I've had enough.'

'Well I'm having another.'

He nods at Chuck and Knocker at the bar as he waits to be served, willing the beer to speed up in its trajectory into the glass, convinced that when he turns around, she'll be gone.

'You were about to say something, before.' He pulls his chair back up to the table. Marie is still there and has re-applied her lipstick. She leans close and puts her hand on his thigh.

'Was I? I don't know what to think. I expected to ruffle a few feathers but I never imagined this.' Her voice cracks but he hasn't seen her cry. Perhaps she'll wait until she's on her own or until the wine finally gets to her. God knows how much she's had.

'None of this would have happened if I had stayed sober, Jimmy. Going round there straight after the funeral was totally wrong of me. I see that now. It was unforgivable.' She drops her head and moves her fingers upwards, causing a flashback to the hotel, her naked back arched across the bed. He grits his teeth and tries to make sense of the garbled account she just gave him. Was it shock or grief talking? If what she has told him is true, could she really sit on it all these years? Would she come all this way, taking time off work, the expense of a hotel, to turn up on the doorstep of someone she hasn't seen in all this time? He doesn't know. He hasn't a clue what she is capable of because he doesn't know her at all.

'Tell me everything again.'

Marie recounts her tale once more, this time much more calmly. 'So it seems, I'd known about one of our brothers and Anna knew about the other but neither of us ever suspected there could be two. Believe me, I know how bizarre it sounds but my instinct was we had to try and find him. She just seemed to flip at the very suggestion. I would never have brought any of it up if I'd known she'd react like this. I didn't realise how fragile she was.' Her voice is low and querulous, her face close to his shoulder. 'She was steaming drunk, Jimmy. There were bottles all over the place. You'll see when you go over there. I had no idea her life would be like that. I mean, I knew they were bastards and her mother's life must've been grim but what on earth can have happened to her, to get into such a state?'

'Didn't you ask her?'

'Ask her what?'

'Didn't you ask what had happened to her in the thirty something years since you last saw each other?'

She withdraws her hand from his thigh. 'No, I didn't, and now of course I wish that I had. We talked about the past but mainly the distant past. Our childhood.'

Newton straightens his beermat. He thinks of a response but keeps it to himself. Along with a whole host of other things. Marie pulls back her shoulders, as though coming to a decision.

'Please don't be fooled by Father Vincent, Jimmy. He's good at hiding secrets, it's his job, remember. He's a murdering bastard. No doubt he'll say it was a cat he was drowning but I know what I saw. I would never have believed Anna has a violent bone in her body but I wouldn't put anything past him and I've told you their history. Things must've got out of hand, escalated in ways we can't possibly guess at.'

'How do you mean, escalated?'

'I don't know. I've been away far too long.'

'I never asked you this before but why exactly did you come back here?'

Marie's eyes narrow, as though considering. 'I was happy here once. I always wanted to come back and see the place. Face things. When mum died, it seemed the right time and then Charlie being killed straight after seemed like a sign. I couldn't visit while he was still around. It might have been me sticking the knife in his throat.' She gives a hollow laugh. 'As far as I'm concerned, him and Father Vincent were both as bad as each other but Anna's suffered enough. It's not right she

366

should take all the blame.'

'What do you mean, all the blame?'

He sees her swallow before responding. 'She didn't kill her father.'

'So who did then?'

'It must have been Mooney.'

'But that doesn't make any sense. If your theory's true about things escalating, surely Anna would have known and would have said something. Why would she protect him?'

'She wouldn't necessarily have known. They were both secretive bastards. In any case, it would have been her father she was protecting, his reputation as she saw it. There must be things we don't know about. Something Father Vincent's involved in.'

Newton cradles his pint. 'Don't worry. He'll be questioned when he comes round.'

'You're wasting your time, Jimmy. He'll lie through his teeth to protect himself.'

Newton's phone vibrates in his pocket. He pulls it out and reads the few stark words on the screen, then turns it face down on the table.

'I'm afraid he won't get chance. That was the hospital. He died on the operating table ten minutes ago.'

72

Kate

Kate winds the car window down and lights another cigarette, holding onto the smoke for as long as she can. Sometimes she thinks the brief nicotine buzz is the only thing gluing her together. The only thing she can control.

She's been driving around for hours, going nowhere in particular. A thousand times she's been through things, right back to that very first day. In her mind, she walks through Anna's bedroom, feels the blaze of the fire on her cheeks. She can almost reach out and touch her, as she sits there with a book in her lap, reeking of booze.

Despite the time they spent together, she had known next to nothing about her. To Kate that feels like failure. She knows she can't file it away as she is supposed to do, can't see it as just the inevitable end to a sorry existence. Her life had been worth saving. She knows she shouldn't feel this way but she can't help it. Anna's death is down to her.

Newton has told her about the half-brother, who they are now trying to trace. Kate has tried to put herself in Anna's shoes, tried to imagine how she might have felt about him. Her father's death, the long-lost friend's return and then the revelation of a mutual sibling. A lot to take in for anyone.

And what about her father's bank account? It will go to the son if they find him, if it isn't all found to be ill-gotten gains, that is. And where did the priest come into it? Is it all connected as Newton suspects and how much had Anna known? The case has been passed to South Yorkshire Serious Crimes Squad but on and on her mind twists. Questions she can find no answers to.

Newton hasn't mentioned his relationship with Marie Ryan. He hasn't needed to. All Kate's respect for him was restored as she watched him cradle Anna's head in his lap. Wiping weeds and slime from her face as they waited for the mortuary van. As he stilled her trembling hand so she could light her cigarette.

It will all come out in court and it's Newton's business how he chooses to handle it. Whatever he tells Vardy and whatever he keeps to himself, she won't contradict him.

The car in front turns off and the road ahead is clear. Careful to stay within the speed limit, she follows the cats' eyes but even they can't hold her focus. Looking up, she sees the space where the hills should be is shrouded in white, impossible to tell where the clouds end and the mist begins. Like the day they searched for Archie. A day she's trying hard to forget.

Pulling into the car park, she reverses into her space. She doesn't care whether Duffy is here. In fact, some new unfurling part of her hopes that he is. She's about to get out of her car when the station doors open and out strides Helen. Her arms are laden with boxes, coats and carrier bags thrown across her shoulders. *Shit.* Is she leaving? That's what it looks like. Leaving her job, *her career,* seems a bit extreme. Resisting the urge to sink out of sight beneath the steering wheel, Kate sits tight and watches her load what must be the entire contents of her office into her boot. She looks overdressed in her sleek trouser suit and six-inch heels. *Louis Vuitton, by the looks of them.* She considers going over to remonstrate with her but the idea soon passes. With a final slam of the door, Helen is off in a cloud of unnecessary exhaust smoke, tyres screeching as she pulls out into the road.

Kate sits staring through the windscreen, watching as the last brittle leaves fall into the empty parking space. She bends and retrieves an empty coke can and a squashed cigarette packet from the footwell. Getting out, she opens the back door and picks up a handful of tab ends from between the seats, rubbing at a burn on the upholstery. She needs to stop chucking burning fags from the window, especially whilst driving at speed. Locking up, she makes a detour to the bins, the stir of satisfaction detracting from the stink as she tips it all under the lid. Inside the building, she holds her head up as people nod in passing. Everyone knows who she is now. She opens the incident room door.

'Here she is, Pussy Galore!' Duffy grins from the window, his gargoyle's head leering sideways. 'You've missed all the excitement! Miss Moneypenny has left the building!'

Kate slips off her jacket, pulling her face into a smile.

'I didn't miss anything Duffy. I've just seen her. Why don't you make yourself useful and go and get the coffees in?'

The spout closes, the lips pursed in disappointment that she hasn't taken the bait. He gets up from the windowsill.

'Where's the boss?' asks Kate.

'Not sure,' says Duffy. 'Said something about taking some keys back?'

73

Newton

Newton had known as soon as he stepped in there. He knows all about blood. When it is freshly spilt and when it is not. The pool around the priest was already congealed, drying at the edges. Parts of his cassock were stiffening. Newton had knelt in it, his nostrils filled with the stench as he searched the folds for a pulse and looked at his watch. Fifteen minutes had passed between receiving the call and their arrival. Hardly any time at all. Yet the blood was turning brown.

He had watched Marie closely, as he let the facts sink in. As she identified Anna's body and later, when he told her the priest was dead. He had kissed her, he couldn't help himself. Feeling as Judas must have felt.

'I'm leaving tonight,' she said. 'My case is packed.'

'Do you have to go so soon?' He could bluff with the best of them.

'I think it's for the best, Jimmy. Don't you?' And her eyes had fallen onto his wedding ring.

'I'll drive you to the station. Let me just pay a visit.'

In the gents, he had stood at the mirror as he made the call. He didn't recognise whoever that was staring back at him. He had turned on the tap, letting water gush over his hands but still he saw blood all over them. This time when he returned, she was gone. He didn't look through the window. It was too dark to see much anyway. Duffy said there had been no resistance.

Mooney's injury was a deep slash to the stomach. The surgeon who tried to save him had confirmed this. The wound was irregular, with notches and tears, conducive to some sort of blade being thrust into the flesh and twisted before being removed. Newton had already known the wound was all wrong. He had seen it. He had forced himself to look at it and he had lied to Marie. Anna's broken wine stem had been found in the grass at Never Fear. It was far too slender to be the murder weapon.

Newton's conduct has fallen way short of the standards he normally lives by. In the army he would have been court martialled and deservedly so. But he had never told Marie that Charlie Collins was killed with a dagger. He is certain of this. He hadn't told her it was buried in his throat either. These facts were withheld from both the press and the public and the pathologist's words had come back to him, as her hand crept up his thigh. Thrust from below. Not much force.

In the end, they had nothing to hold her on. No evidence at all. Nothing to link her to any of the murders. Things leak out, of course they do. Or Anna could have told her. He sees now that he panicked. Had to distance himself, put an end to the temptation he didn't have the discipline to resist. He can tell himself he made a judgement call but it was cowardice, pure and simple. Something else to add to his roll of honour. He cringes at the thought of facing her again. Undoubtedly, Marie will be called as a witness at some point down the line.

He shoves his hand in his pocket, hoping for the comforting feel of blistered plastic. Instead his fingers brush something cold and sharp. Taking it out, he turns it in his fingers, holds it up to the light.

'I'm popping out for a bit. Something I need to return to its rightful owner.'

Duffy looks up from his computer. 'OK, sir.'

For a moment he thinks about walking, the exercise would do him good but the car park is rimed with frost and there is rain in the air again. He drives the short distance, finding a spot just down from the house. Locking his car, he walks along the pavement, stopping at the wall. A recollection comes to him, not as vague as he'd like it to be. He sees himself sprawled by the lamp post, Kate standing over him. Looking up, he sees a light in the downstairs window and a cardboard box on the sill.

His feet crunch on the gravel as he makes his way up the path. Darkness is falling but the horseshoe glints above the door. He knocks and waits then knocks again. This time the door swings opens. A woman with a stomach like a football stands peering at him through the gloom.

'Can I help you?' she asks. Despite her advanced pregnancy, she holds a heavy looking box against her hip. Newton sees the serpent tattoo, the absence of a wedding ring. From somewhere inside the house comes a loud clatter, followed by a child's wail.

'Looks like you could do with a hand. I came to return this, actually.' He holds up the key but her expression remains impassive. 'It's Alice, isn't it?' From his other pocket, Newton produces his ID. 'I've brought it back on behalf of my colleague, DS Fox. I believe she was here when your aunt passed away.'

'Oh, yes. Sorry, you lost me there for a moment.'

'Please, don't let me keep you on your feet. Can I come in for a minute? Here, let me take that.' Instinctively, Alice steps back as he takes the box from her arms.

The living room looks different from the last time he was here. In the corner is a child's play pen. Within it

373

stands a toddler, his chubby arms outstretched through the bars. Newton is struck by his beauty. His hair falls in coils across his forehead, his dusky cheeks glisten with tears beneath his black, almond shaped eyes.

'It's time for his nap,' says Alice and with one swift movement has him out of the pen and is quickly gone from the room. As her footsteps thud up the stairs, Newton takes in his surroundings. The sofa he remembers sitting on is filled with bags and boxes, the floor around it similarly cluttered. His eyes fall onto the sideboard, where the neat crescent of photos had previously been. Newton never met Margaret Wood but has a feeling she'd turn in her urn if she saw the mess left in its place. A pair of scruffy Nikes stands beside a baby's bottle and a half pack of nappies. Alice really is going to have her hands full, thinks Newton as he carefully places the box down. His mother always said it was bad luck to put shoes on a table. He wonders if sideboards count as he flips one of the trainers and takes in the tread.

The next few seconds come from nowhere. Newton will later curse the inherent sense of enquiry that makes him who he is, the inborn nosiness that means his back is facing the door.

Sensing he is no longer alone in the room, he replaces the trainer and turns. Her eyes wide in terror, Alice stands by the sofa, a broad, muscular arm pressed across her throat but even as he takes in the blade, it is the face of the man behind her that sends a jolt through Newton's heart.

'You just couldn't leave things alone, could you?'

The cleft between nose and mouth is all her, the jut of his chin.

'Think very carefully what you're doing.' The calm of his voice belies his fear. His confusion. 'Whatever's gone off, I know you wouldn't wish any harm on either Alice or the baby.'

'Ha!' The man throws his head back, jerking Alice sideways as he does so, the peak of her stomach lurching with her. Newton imagines the swirl of amniotic fluid, the child's soft, half-formed limbs wrenched within her womb.

'What do you care?' His eyes glitter green beneath thick, dark brows.

'It's Aidan, isn't it?'

'What the hell does my name matter to you?' Spit flies from his mouth, hitting Alice's cheek.

'Aidan, stop. You're hurting me!'

'Shut it!' he shouts, the cords in his arm tautening, his face misshapen as he looks down at her.

'The best thing you can do is let her go so we can talk this through.'

'No!' At first, Newton thinks the roar comes from Aidan but as the two fall across the room, he realises the sound came from Alice. As they stumble towards the sideboard, he sees her arm extend, her fingers strain between the clutter and then a crash as the vase comes smashing down on Aidan's head. He staggers back, his hand flying up as blood begins to pour from his temple. Alice reels towards Newton but he pushes her away.

'Get the young 'un! Get safe!'

Aidan springs forward, his face a mask of blood. Newton makes a grab for him but is shoved sideways, sprawling on the jumble of boxes. Fear clutches his bowels as Aidan heads for the door, then a wash of relief as he heads towards the back of the house. Hauling himself upright, he winces at the new pain bursting in his back. Stumbling into the hall, he hears a door slam. With a glance up the empty stairwell, he opens the front door then stops dead on the step.

In that split second, he sees it over the top of the wall. Aidan must have run from the back of the house, straight into the street. The car hits him with a sickening crack, sending him into the air like a sack of rags. Something flies towards him, landing on the gravel at his feet. As he bends to retrieve it, he hears the car door open. He reaches the end of the path and sees Kate squatting in front of the bonnet. She looks up and shakes her head.

74

Kate

Lights criss-cross the high street like a giant spider's web. Huge pearlescent snowflakes, as far as the eye can see. Kate lifts her foot and crawls a centimetre forward, her gaze following the lamp posts towards the piece de resistance. A vast, inflatable Santa is lassoed, like some festive sumo wrestler, to the war memorial. The council have really gone to town this year. It could be some last-ditch attempt to cover up the damage a triple murder might have caused. Four violent deaths, if you count Anna's, which Kate most definitely does. But the Christmas lights were up long before the blackened ends of the fireworks had blown away, before Jason Brown had made a man-size dent in her newly valeted car.

Kate winds the window down and lights another cigarette. She must try not to be cynical. Traffic might be at a standstill but the pavements are full and the tills will be ringing and that's got to be good for the town.

Things could be a lot worse. He hadn't been dead after all. He'd looked it, sprawled under the bumper, blood pouring from a gash in his head. Newton had almost thanked her, for being in the right place at the right time.

Jason Brown aka Aidan bursting out from nowhere had put things into perspective. As she stared down at what she thought was another corpse, her whole life had flashed before her. It hit her then, with almost as much force as the car had hit him. She can't control these things. It had been a form of arrogance to think she can. And if that hadn't done it, the sight of Alice clutching her little boy, the mound of her stomach in front of her had made her realise. She has to move on to the next case, the next victim. Now, in a secret part of her, she feels she has avenged Anna's death. A kind of atonement. She knows there should be no room for these feelings. At the end of the day, it's just a job.

She had the dream again last night. More vivid than usual but otherwise the same. The eyes, the dark lashes. Pale skin and then down. Down into boundless darkness and an overwhelming feeling of love. Waking too soon, as she always does. She never wants it to end.

Lifting her foot again, she edges forward, the maternity hospital coming into view. On the seat beside her, a tiny Peter Rabbit stares from stitched on eyes, his velveteen jacket resplendent against the newly brushed upholstery. She hopes Alice likes him. *That's if she's even heard of him.*

Suddenly she is laughing. Whether from relief or hysteria she isn't sure but she tilts her head back at the unexpected pleasure, the tension in her shoulders easing as she snaps her spent cig into the ashtray.

Duffy's pathetic pranks are quite comical really. She can handle him. And the other stuff, stuff that really bothered her before, she can handle that too. Let them believe what they want. It's in her best interests really.

She puts her foot down, the road spinning beneath her.

How little do they know.

Epilogue

Morning creeps through the curtains, casting a milky glow across the duvet. Newton stretches his arms, feels the cold sheet beside him, the empty space he's growing used to.

Thank God she never came here. Never visited his home or slept in his bed. Never met his son or his dog.

How he wishes he could put the last few weeks behind him. Turn the clock back, to a time when he could kid himself he still had a marriage.

Newton is by no means a perfectionist but to him, a job isn't finished until all the loose ends are cleared away. Until a case is watertight. Vardy, on the other hand, is a very busy man, the pressure on his shoulders far more than any individual should have to take. Newton can just about see why at first, he'd been quick to accept things at face value. Why when they dragged Anna's body up, he'd started quoting statistics. Newton was aware, wasn't he, of the percentage of victims murdered by one of their own family? Isn't it almost always someone known to the victim?

In the end, he hadn't been far wrong. *The Sins of the Fathers* and all that. He hopes there's no truth in the phrase for Georgie's sake.

It would have satisfied the powers that be, got the press off their backs. All those directly involved in the case would be dead. Doubly, trebly satisfying. No long-drawn-out trial, no further pressure on an ailing justice system. No cost to the taxpayer for their lifelong upkeep in prison.

Kate had been right all along with her knitting needle theory. At least it looks that way. The finer details of

Margaret Wood's death may never be fully known but it will be a long time before he discounts anything Kate has to say again. Not that he is likely to tell her. Not that he's had chance, stuck here staring at the ceiling since his latest back injury, sustained when he was thrown across Margaret Wood's floor. Bed rest had been prescribed, then physiotherapy. Funny really. The ministrations of the six-foot Nigerian therapist were very different to the ones still fresh in his mind. Too fresh for comfort but his back feels better than it has in months. Maybe that jolt as he landed on the playpen has done him some good after all.

Alice had known who her new landlady was — briefly, as it turned out. Her aunt had told her years ago. But she hadn't known the true identity of her boyfriend and no matter what his birth certificate and adoption papers might say, neither had Jason Brown. Newton had known as soon as he saw him. That green stare and those eyebrows, his mouth uncomfortably like Marie's. He was short too, no more than five foot five, which fitted Hastings's comments. The records struck Newton as unusual for the 1970s. Much more likely where a baby was given up, to see *father unknown*. Maybe naming Collins had been an attempt to divert attention. The truth would have ended Mooney's career. *Had he known he was giving up his own son?* Marie's mother may not even have known with any certainty which one of them was the father.

Brown must have come here to seek Collins out, believing him to be his natural father. His presence can't have been a coincidence. Whether he was intent on financial gain or something more personal, he hopes will come out in the trial. The same for Mrs Wood. If he killed her, surely he can't have known the house wasn't hers to bequeath. But what made him flip? Had Collins rejected him, denied his paternity, his whole existence revealed as a lie? And would he really have harmed Alice and their unborn child? Was the whole relationship a cover? Whatever the case, they've got a baby now, linking them forever.

He wonders when Brown first met the priest. The striking resemblance between father and son may not have been obvious at birth but there could be no doubt as soon as the two men clapped eyes on each other, they would see it. Mooney would have been petrified at being exposed. Perhaps he tried blackmail or guessed Brown had killed Collins. He could simply have wanted him gone, in order to protect himself.

Newton winces. Vardy ordered him off sick but not before he'd handed over the secateurs that had landed at his feet in the gravel. The trainers on the sideboard matched nothing but the ones found half burned in the dustbin did. That's what Amy had been trying to tell him. Their print was found on the shop floor.

If Collins had run some sort of gambling den, why hadn't Newton known about it? The drugs haul could point to organised crime but if he was trading online, who knows what connections he made. This is supposed to be his patch, for God's sake. He had known nothing about it and something else has been bothering him. Knocker has never mentioned Collins's gambling, or any resulting change of hands of property. He's definitely had his last pint out of Newton.

The shop and Mrs Wood's house are both boarded up. The lawyers will make a fortune sorting that lot out. Thankfully, not his problem. Knocker never said a word about the priest, either. The bent priest whose church had a habit of losing valuables, not to mention its fundraising collections. *It's like the Bermuda frigging Triangle.* They're all the same round here, he knows that much now. They came out in their numbers when the boy went missing. Salt of the earth, this lot, but when it comes to shopping one of their own, the shutters come down. And that's just it. He might think it's *his patch* but it isn't really. No matter how long he lives here, he will always be an outsider. He bunches the sheet between his fingers, pulling the fibres taut.

He *is* an outsider and that's the way it should be. That's why towns like Black Hollow don't have cosy, local bobbies anymore. He's supposed to be independent, separate from the rest. Not a man who sleeps with strangers.

He arches his spine against the mattress. It's out of his hands now. If there is a link to organised crime, South Yorkshire will find it. The story has been knocked off the headlines by a foiled extremist plot. The papers are full of it. Thank God for terrorists.

The axe Marie came to grind was a different one entirely. He traced the Liverpool convent. The records showed her mother had a stillborn child, giving birth there later to a second. Heaven knows what it must have been like for them. He really hadn't known her at all.

He will tell Vardy everything before the trial. That's if he doesn't know already. He can't risk Marie blabbing to her solicitor, or worse, in the dock. Hopefully, Louise will be too busy with her new life to hear any of it but he knows how slim the chances of that are in this town.

The image keeps coming back to him. Kate's face as they dragged Anna from the water. He failed her on so many levels. That he failed Anna, too, is a thought he can't allow to take hold.

A crash comes from across the landing. Toy bricks clashing together, followed by gurgling laughter. The door opens and Georgie runs in, Lottie not far behind him. They jump on the bed in a blur of giggles and dog hairs. He pulls his son to his chest as Lottie circles then curls herself up, her eyes still wary at her newfound freedom.

Louise never let Lottie in the bedroom. There were a lot of things Louise never did. He strokes Georgie's hair, breathing in the clean, soapy scent of him.

'Just you and me now, kid.'

Lottie lifts her head and gives a short, excited yap. Newton ruffles her ears.

'I'm not forgetting you, girl. Welcome home.'

Acknowledgements

Writing this book has been a journey. I'd like to thank a few people who have helped me along the way.

Thank you to Helen, Maureen and Julie for your early read-throughs and for spurring me on.

Special thanks to Jill. You know what for, except all our memories are good ones.

Thank you to Blossom Spring Publishing, for showing faith in me, especially Pam. I've learned a lot from you.

And to Sarah Ward. Without your inspiration, this book would never have been written.

Most of all, I'd like to thank my sons, Liam and Kieran for always being there for me.

About The Author

Rachael Holyhead was born in the industrial heart of Sheffield. She grew up in South Yorkshire, at the edge of the Peak District.

She attended Carter Lodge Comprehensive School and read History at the University of Liverpool.

A lifelong Sheffield United supporter, she also loves snooker and is an all-round armchair sports fan.

Still passionate about history, she has eclectic reading tastes, enjoying everything from the Brontës and Wilkie Collins to more modern writers of mystery, horror and crime.

As a child, Rachael began writing stories and letters for her Uncle, who was stationed overseas with the army.

She considers Liverpool her second home and loves the city's music, culture and maritime heritage. Her roots remain in Sheffield, where she lives with her sons and her pet cat, Luther.

www.blossomspringpublishing.com

Printed in Great Britain
by Amazon

46329518R00223